The
CABLE DENNING
MYSTERY
SERIES

by
James P. Alsphert

James P. Alsphert
presents

HELDENLEBEN

'A Hero's Life'

A
Cable Denning
Mystery

BOOK
3

Published 2018 by Movies of the Mind

Printed in the United States of America

First printing, 2018

ISBN-13: 978-1-64056-015-4

MOVIES OF THE MIND
www.moviesofthemind.net

CONTENTS

CONTENTS CONTINUED

To Be Continued in Book 4 – The 7 Fates of Kathmandu

PROLOGUE

When I was I kid, I remember hearing the sound of a lonesome trumpet coming from an abandoned house up on Boyle Heights. The haunting and forlorn notes came from a young fellow named Ray Bourne who owned a beat up old trumpet he had inherited from a dead uncle. *Ray Bourne the Horn* we used to call him. He played mostly at night and his sound was always soulful and melancholy, like it was his way of expressing the plight of his poor, isolated life. Like me, he lived with his mother at a time when rent was fifteen bucks a month and people had trouble coming up with that. But his song also spoke of the rise and fall of hope in his world, that place where the birth of a new night was a promise of mystery and romance, adventure and freedom, and release from a life sentence...a result of being born poor. It was all played on magical notes, like those of the snake charmer that would lift the serpent out of the old basket into a bright new life. At least, that's how I perceived the sadness of his heart pouring out through a piece of brass comprised of tubes and valves, cutting into that night as a prince who would be king, or a lost and lonely peasant who aspired to find a wisp of that magic, leaving the ghetto forever, finding his princess waiting on the steps of her castle for him and fly off into the land of happily-ever-after.

Then one day...Ray's music stopped. No one ever knew what happened to him. But I missed his mournful tunes and to this day I can still hear those notes echoing through time into my bedroom window. I guess in a way Ray Bourne's music was my introduction to how powerful music can be, how it can lift you to the heights or pull you down to the depths of emotional despair. The gift of being able to express that spectrum of feeling through a silver-coated brass mouthpiece, made me appreciate the range and power of the human singing voice. I think that's how I became hooked on gorgeous babes in dazzling sequined gowns under the glow of a spotlight in some smoke-filled nightclub, singing the songs of human experience, seeing right through us who were lucky enough to hear her. For me, she became the weathervane of moods for the human condition. She could make us smile, frown, laugh, cry, regret or anticipate what idyllic romance felt like, no matter what the ropes of life taught us. And to think, I owed it all to a young man I never met, a soul traveling through the ethers of eternity long enough to touch the heart of another down and out ghetto rat—a boy like me who grew up to be a man still believing that, like Don Quixote, if you swung your sword long enough at windmills, you'd win the game.

But life didn't work that way. So now when I walk the Boulevard of Broken Dreams late at night, Ray Bourne's music mixes with the streetcars, buses, fire engines, horns and sirens of a city that can't sleep, and can't ever stop its momentum because it was wound around the hourglass of time, and those sands had to be constantly refilled—or else they'd run out and the world would stop spinning. The other thing the city was comprised of was strange, animated creatures called *people*, and they came in many different sizes, shapes and abilities to stand up against the winds of time, survival and fate. Step in front of the wrong bus and you were dead...or step in front of a politician or war-monger and your perception of honesty got altered. Step in front of a hot love affair that was destined to burn out like a meteor across the sky and you might burn out your heart. Lots of us did that. But I had been lucky in life, despite my moral trespasses. I became addicted to three things from an early age: cigarettes, booze and women, probably in that order. I was the poster child for the sins of our ancestors...the pre-suicidal man of the street, thrust upon the world fighting his way into a semblance of identity. So I became a cop. Once I uncovered the filth and corruption that plagued law enforcement, I opted-out, transforming myself into a private dick...a guy who plays the ends against the middle when he has to...the kind of guy who ends up like he started, a latter day Don Quixote, slugging away alone at the injustices humans inflict on one another. But it was always Ray Bourne's trumpet sounds that ripped me back to my simple roots and allowed me a sanity I could find nowhere else.

And after all, things were changing in 1932. It looked like we were going to have a new president to haul us out of the Depression and Happy Days would be here again! I couldn't wait...

Chapter 1

NIGHT BEGINS

I woke up with Zelda Blodgett wrapped around me, and a mocking bird singing outside the window in the avocado tree. Only trouble was, he kept singing the same song over and over until it rattled my brain. But everything else felt fine. A lovely young woman's warm body clinging to my own, the perfume of light rose water in her hair accompanied with the unmistakable smell of lovemaking, those wonderful mixtures of a woman's lubrication and a man's ejaculatory fluids. The sun shone through the greenery like flickering contrasts of light and dark and somewhere behind us an alarm clock ticked away.

I yawned and glanced at the clock. Then I suddenly remembered, that today was the day I was to see my old friend Dr. Jedediah Penn. I kissed Zelda in her hair and she stirred. She looked up at me with those glowing warm eyes and a smile. "Good morning, Cable...God, I'm glad you're really here...I thought I might be dreaming it all." She brought my head down onto her wonderfully sensual and ample breasts. Then she rolled over on her back and pulled me on top of her, immediately spreading her legs and bringing me up to top pitch in short order. I entered her again and we moaned and sighed like honeymooners on our first morning. When she climaxed I could feel a warm, ejaculatory fluid pulse out of her onto my penis. After she gained her breath, she opened her eyes to look at me. "Gees, Cable, I didn't even *know* I could do that!"

"I didn't even know *women* could do that—I mean, I knew they could reach an orgasm, but to squirt their own warm fluids—wow! what a turn-on, babe!" I exclaimed, noting how easily a guy could get addicted to a woman who did that.

"Mr. Denning...you have taken me...to paradise...I am absolutely the happiest girl in the world today—thank you for loving me..."

"Thank *you*, Zelda. You were the surprise woman of the century for me, toots. I had no idea—"

"—by the way, why did you suddenly rush in here last night in a fury wanting me? Did something snap in you or what?"

"It's a long story, lady, let me tell you some other time. One thing I am a bit concerned about, though—we have made love several times throughout the night—without protection, you realize."

She giggled and swung her happy head from side to side. "Didn't you say you'd pump me full of all the babies I ever wanted?" she whispered in a very sexy voice.

"Well, uh, that—that was a manner of speech, Zelda. And said in jest, if you'll remember. Intelligent people usually plan their children."

She put her hand down under the covers and felt where the two of us were enjoined. "I can't tell where I leave off and you begin...and oh, we are *so wet*! My sheets will be stained forever. But I don't care. I've waited all my life for this, Cable. I never in a million years thought you'd want me—and certainly, not like this. I'm sore...I don't even know if I can walk to-day...but I'm happy, Cable, I'm so happy!"

I reveled in her happiness with her, for it was true that this young, lovely woman satisfied me beyond what I could have imagined. "I hate to change the mood, babe, but today I've got to run over to Beverly Hills and see old Doc Penn."

"Oh, yes, I almost forgot." She was still smiling with such a glow that I hated to change her out of the mood. "I'll make us some coffee—and breakfast. What do you like to eat? I haven't got much. Milk, oat meal—that's about it—oh, and some old wheat bread and a little butter."

I rolled off of her and felt my crotch. It was sopping wet and I didn't give a damn. "That'd be swell, hon. Do you have a shower here?"

"No, just an old claw foot bathtub. But it works."

It was eleven o'clock by the time we got ourselves pulled together. Zelda fed me and took a little for herself. "I've got to get back to the office and change clothes. Are you planning to go into the office today?"

She flashed me a smile and then a sheepish grin. "If I can walk. I really am sore. Last night was the greatest night of my life, Cable, and you have been my very first sexual experience. And we did it up great, didn't we?" she laughed.

I laughed with her. "Yeah, babe, we did it up great."

The trolley ride to Beverly Hills was filled with pensive anticipation and afterglow. It was July 6,1932 and it seemed a lot of my life, lately, had been a hurry-by blur. I felt bad about not seeing Dr. Jedediah Penn sooner.

But then again, one never knew where he might be in the world. I would be glad to see him. And thinking about Zelda and still feeling myself inside of her turned me on, to say the least. What strange forces drive our destinies. Just when we think we're going to jog right, we go left. Had I not had that bizarre and otherworldly sexual exchange with Cassiopeia the night before, I wouldn't have suddenly been obsessed with having Zelda. You never know when something clicks in you and what appears to be desperate, erratic thinking at the moment, turns out to be exactly the right thing for both people at the right time! Who'd have known?...I always say, you can't predict life, nor control your own, really.

Penn lived on the bottom floor of a very fancy two-story flat off of Sunset Boulevard. I rang the bell and Polly Parker answered the door.

"Mr. Denning...I'm glad to see you again. Please, come in."

"Hello, Polly," I said, extending my hand. She led me into a comfortable living room where I expected to find Doc Penn sitting in a comfy chair awaiting me. "Where's Jed? I thought the first thing I'd see after your nice face is that old son-of-a-gun with a big grin."

Her face grew drawn. "Mr. Denning..."

"Call me Cable, Polly, I think we've known each other long enough to dispense with those formalities."

"Cable...I must prepare you," she said in her exacting Germanic accent. "You might not recognize Dr. Penn. He has lost considerable veight und is not able to valk anymore. He's actually qvite veak. I advised him against seeing you just now, but he has vaited four veeks und speaks of you every day—so vat can I say?"

"Has he contracted a disease or what?" I asked, very concerned.

"I'll let him tell you."

She led me into a large, sunlit bedroom. There, with longish silver hair, beard and moustache sat a pallid version of the man I once knew to be alert and robust. But I needed to cover the shock of it. "Jed, damn, it's good to see you, you're—you're looking—"

"—cut the bullshit, Cable. I look terrible and my breathing is difficult. So come close and give me an embrace. I have missed you."

He opened his arms for me and I held a little skeleton of a man as my cheek touched his. "It's those cigars and women," I joked. "I told you, they'll do you in every time."

He returned a faint smile. "I notice *you* look good. Brisk walk, healthy complexion, the voice is clear and you seem to be the correct weight for your height and frame. Yet...*you* still smoke, drink and chase women, I presume. It just hasn't caught up with you yet."

He excused Polly and I sat on the edge of the bed. "Damn, Jedediah, what in the hell happened?"

"It's a disease of the stomach—mostly the colon. When I was a young and stupid college boy, it was fashionable to imbibe a bit too much in many things. The fad those days was to take *mineral oil* as a cure all, good for anything from a hangover to constipation. What none of us knew, Cable, was that mineral oil is a made from petroleum, a coal tar product, we are finding out. It cuts off the invisible beta ray from the sunlight's electromagnetic emission, so your body only receives the *alpha* and *gamma* wavelengths of the *infrared, ultra-violet* spectrum. The coal tar product of mineral oil blocks the beta ray—put simply, causing the mutation of healthy cells, especially those of the digestive tract. These irritated cells become vagabond, seeking healthy cells from which to take the proper nutrients. Hence, we have what is known as *cancer*. It's in the stomach and colon, Cable..." He looked at me with those wonderful sympathetic medium-blue eyes. "...it is a death sentence."

I sat there on the bed very saddened. The world could not afford to lose such a brilliant mind, I thought. Let alone, a wonderful man with powerful vision. Also, he has had exposure to those beings who inhabit other dimensions. That was how we originally met in San Francisco in 1927, when I made that journey by train with a very young and sexy Adora Moreno. When I entered the Great Gate in Chinatown, I was also destined to meet one of those other dimensional creatures—a beautiful young woman named Lei-Tao, who every fourteen thousand years emerged from the bottom of a cold lake in China to watch over the now famous *Fen de Fuqin.* What I was never exactly clear about was her birth from within a lotus flower seedpod. It was beyond my comprehension, but Lei-Tao's overseer, a little extra-terrestrial named *Toggth,* assured me it was a very natural and understandable process...Yeah, to *them.*

"Gees, Jed, I'm very sorry to hear that. How much time do you have? And there's no hope?—anything else you can do?"

"If I remain here, it might be about three months, Cable. I'm pretty heavily sedated with morphine at the

10

moment. Now you understand why it was urgent that I see you before...oh—but there is a possible alternative to all this, with one caveat. Our mutual little friend, Toggth, says he can vaporize me and save my consciousness, but I can't take my body—at least not this one."

"And that would preclude dying a painful death?"

"Exactly. I'd forgotten how very intelligent you are."

"I wouldn't go that far, Jed. It's just all the damn aliens I've been exposed to in the past five years or so."

He managed a snicker. "It's remarkable that you're still alive to tell the tale, Cable. Toggth tells me you've encountered some pretty mean demons." He took a deep breath and coughed. "Well now, that said...I have much to share with you. Would you like a drink?"

"Yeah, some of your English gin, if you have it. And I won't smoke—I'm sure it ain't good for your health, doc."

He called to Polly Parker and she served me a generous triple shot. She also provided me with a chair so I could sit closer to Dr. Penn. "Now, all settled in, are we?" he said, checking me out with those intense blue eyes.

"Yep. I'm all ears."

"I've already shared with you the first item on my agenda. So we'll leave it at that for now. The second is far more serious than our piddly little lives, per se. Toggth has visited me a few times. He told me you were in hot water with the head of the *Oculus*, yes?"

"*Cronus-Gor*, one of the would-be gods who came from the Titans originally and gained eternal status as opposed to perpetual. I ran into his wife, a beautiful thing, that alas is no more—her name was *Rhea-*

Saturnalia. I think you know the story of their stormy relationship. Anyway, Gor is after the *Fen de Fuqín* in a big way. But you probably already know all of this. So, please...speak, Jed."

"Yes, I do know most of what you've said. You also got romantically involved with *Cassiopeia*, Rhea's daughter, so Toggth says."

"That tattle-tail," I laughed. "Well, except for one thing. She turned out to be a mannequin-replicant."

"Oh, dear, that could be quite a shock if you become intimately—"

"—it's not important—let's get on with your stuff. I don't want to drain your energies, doc. By the looks of you, we've got about an hour...tops."

"This *Cronus-Gor* character you speak of has been secretly grooming *the Devil's Disciple* for the past few years. He's half-alien and, by proxy, son of this monster you speak of and a simple Aryan Austrian woman, Klara something or other. Your Cronus-Gor supernaturally conceived this super-son, actually born sickly, without Klara ever realizing it and then tricked the father into believing the child was his. But believe me, this demon was carefully picked." Jed's pillow was slipping, so I got up and straightened it out for him. "Thank you. Now...this odd but brilliant evil was appropriately born under the God of War star sign, *Aries*, in 1889. He will be forty-one soon." Then Dr. Penn's voice grew breathy and he sputtered out the words. "This is the most dangerous man the twentieth century shall know. He is what others have called the *Anti-Christ*, in this case, meaning any and all things against love and common humanity."

I was taken aback by the doc's serious tone of voice. "Does this particular evil have a name?" I asked.

"His name? Well, his father was born illegitimate, until his real parentage was confessed, and in his late 30s his records were legitimized and he took his father's name of Hiedler....however, that his father's name was recorded as Georg Hitler may have been how Hiedler became Hitler. And so was born *Adolf Hitler.*

I could've dropped my teeth. Old Cronus-Gor had spoken a name that day he thought he had me by the short hairs—*Hister*—that was the name he called him. Crap, this didn't look good at all!

"In 1923 while you were busy becoming a policeman, Hitler was busy conferring with Cronus-Gor, being promised the gift of gab and the pretext of an energetic righteous indignation against those who opposed his new cause. He needed a country that was down and out, defeated and vulnerable, other than his solvent Austria. What better place to start than a beaten down Germany? So, with the blessing of the *Oculus* and your diabolical Mr. Gor, Hitler proceeds to use his gift of angry oratory. His alien tactics are magnetic and thousands of disgruntled men flock to his side. In 1923 he goes against the existing German government, run by an old has-been soldier, Hindenburg. He's arrested and put into prison. He's treated well there and writes his manifesto, *Mein Kampf* in 1924. Cronus-Gor wants him free now to begin his dirty work, so he mani- pulates the powers that be and Hitler is released from prison, serving barely a year of his five-year sentence. Under the guise of striving to re-build Germany and to make her a strong and powerful nation among nations, he is now free to begin the insidious process for his real plan—to purge all who are inferior to his "pure Aryan race" and the ensuing world domination! In 1925 a radical editor publishes *Mein Kampf* and the world can read Hitler's vitriol. I've read it in its original tongue, Cable, and he spells it all out: the superior blonde-haired, blue-eyed pure-blooded Aryan, the purging of the Jew who, he records, is the cause of the downfall of the West because the Jew is the moneylender of the world and thus evil."

"So who in the hell is really listening to this upstart? Crap, yeah, I've read a couple of news articles on the bloke, but how can one man be so dangerous? And how can little Germany ever be powerful enough to compete with America or France or England?"

"You'd be surprised. Remember, Hitler's magic is his alien god-like parent. This is 1932, Cable, and in November we'll have a new president, Franklin Roosevelt, in our country. Hoover's finished. Everyone blames the Depression on him." He shifted his position on the bed, coughed, spat into a wad of toilet paper and continued. "Anyway, this Hitler is going for the jugular vein of Germany. He aims to unseat the Hindenburg Weimar Republic. Under it all, Cable, is Cronus-Gor's own design of world take-over. Hitler is the patsy of the moment. But with the God of War behind him, I fear for the worst. So, I say to you, my dear friend, beware, keep your eye on the sparrow, as they say."

"Do you really think this guy can overcome millions of other people who either oppose him or don't believe in him? I thought we fought the last war to end war—wasn't that the gist of things?"

"Man is a war-like creature. He fights for principle and real estate, mostly, but a madman fights to destroy for the sake of destroying. Hitler's agenda is to destroy, preserving only the *pure race* he perceives, via Cronus-Gor, as being worthy of populating the world."

"I see. Ten to one he doesn't succeed, Jedediah. Yeah, he might cause a little damage in Europe, but he'll never get here on our soil."

The doc shook his head slowly back and forth as he replied. "They're *already* here, Cable. The German underground is organized and powerful already. It will only grow in the next few years. Adolf Hitler will become Chancellor, then Dictator of Europe, England and then finally, the United States. But Cronus-Gor is smart—he starts whittling away from beneath the streets of men."

"Okay, so you're telling me we're going to be secretly inundated with creeps from Germany, slowly taking over our way of life?"

"Precisely, Cable. If we are not aware and don't act to fight it in every way we know, America will be doomed. We are too isolated, self-assured, and of course, deep in an economic depression—which makes it easy for the eagle to attack the wounded bird."

I thought for a minute. I realized what Doc Penn was saying had validity. He did his homework. "So why doesn't the government send out spies and military to squelch these bastards before they get started?"

"Bureaucracy...politicians act too late. History backs me up on that one."

Suddenly Penn let out a cry of pain. Polly Parker came rushing in. "Polly, it's time for my injection, dear. Please...stay, Cable."

"I told you not to exert yourself by insulting Deutschland again. Hitler is an Austrian. Most Germans are a good und proud people," Polly barked. We must have hit a vulnerable nerve.

"So you've been listening," the doctor said, smiling at Polly Parker.

"Ya...sorry. But I cannot help it. I never know ven you might yell de next cry of pain—like now, doctor."

"Would you prefer I go now?" I asked, concerned for my old friend. "After all, you've been putting out a lot of energy—"

"—ya, Cable...if you don't mind, I think you should go now—"

"—no! Not yet. Ten minutes...ten minutes more with Cable, Polly. Then I promise to let him go. Just give me the damn shot and close the door after you—and this time, I forbid you to listen—because it's about things which you should not know...... okay?"

Polly Parker bent over Jed Penn and injected him with the morphine. He winced slightly but uttered no sound. "Okay...I vill not listen...but I vill count de time...und den you must sleep..."

"Sleep, she says....how can you sleep when your insides keep pulsing like ten men are jack hammering away at your guts?"

Polly Parker looked at me. "So you see vat I put up vith? A stubborn man, dis vun. But I usually vin...Germans usually alvays vin...de German vill is strong, scientific und determined. Ve excel in scholarly pursuits, music, art, philosophy, metaphysics—"

"—don't forget *warfare*, Polly, like the way your people won the last war. They lost a whole generation of young men," I said.

"Dat...vas de stupid Kaiser und his relatives. Zey deserved to be shot. So many beautiful young German boys died..."

"So where's the superiority there, Polly?"

"In de heart und spirit, Cable. Ve vill not lose again...if ve fight another var."

"I wouldn't bet on it. If this Hitler guy takes power, it'll be Germany against the world—not very good odds, wouldn't you say?"

"Time vill tell...time vill tell. Now, you may finish up vith Dr. Penn und I'll busy myself in de kitchen. Fifteen minutes at de most, ya?"

"Yeah, okay." She left the room and Jed Penn summoned me to his side. "You all right for a few minutes more?"

"Yep...I'm duly injected and set to babble on..." he replied, his voice a bit weaker than before.

"Okay, shoot, doc."

"Once there was a stubborn fisherman. He was young and handsome, devoted to boat building and bringing in fresh catches weekly. He had very little experience with the fairer sex, so he was attracted to the prettiest, most artistic and charming young woman in the village. He wooed her and won her. They married, but she got restless. She wanted to leave the fishing village on the Pacific shores of Seattle and live among the bright lights and illusions of New York's glamour life. So she asked her fisherman to come with her. But he told her he was bonded with the sea and the smell of the northwest wind in his nostrils. He said to her that she should go and if she changed her mind, she could always come back."

Jedediah Penn coughed and asked me to pull up his body from sliding further down into the bed. I did so. "So the young woman did discover that show business and the art scene were mostly superficial and decided to return home to her husband. They were happy to be reunited and soon the young but frail Katrina conceived a child. But her body was not designed for childbirth and she died in the process before the child could reach full term. And Larry, her husband, grieved for the prize he had lost. Katrina had been a fine painter and he filled the house with her paintings and mementos that reminded him of their brief life together. She had painted a beautiful surrealistic canvas of a woman emerging from some lovely winged creature and called it 'WOMAN IS A PHANTOM BIRD.'"

"But Larry could not contain his grief, so with one finger at a time, he typed out a note on his shipbuilder's drawing paper, pouring out his sorrow in a letter to Katrina. He then sealed the two pages into a glass bottle and threw it into the sea, hoping it would begin to heal his heart. But fate is a lonely hunter, Cable, and the bottle drifted in the currents to a little town called Carmel, on the California coast. A very attractive young woman, recently divorced and trying to heal her own emotional wounds, found the bottle half-buried in the sand at low tide while she was strolling on the beach by herself one late afternoon. She opened the bottle and read the

18

heart-rending message to Katrina that Larry had written. She read the message in that bottle over and over, took it to bed with her at night, shared it with her lady friends, and lo and behold, Laurie fell in love with the man who had written the note."

Doctor Penn stopped and looked up at me. "Am I boring you, Cable—or being too sentimental for a young, stupid gumshoe?" he laughed.

"No, Jed...I'm a sucker for a good story. Always have been. Please...continue...I love the fantasy it evokes."

"But it isn't a fantasy, young man. It actually happened. You see, Larry Penn was my brother."

"Oh, I'm sorry. Please...continue your story..."

"But how to *find* the phantom man she was now in love with? Upon close examination, she discovered that the stationary Larry had written the message on had a very tiny embossed name at the very bottom of the paper. She talked to local fishermen and found out the local currents came from the northwest and things drifted southeast. Finally, on the bottom of the wine bottle the letter had floated to her in, she found the vintner's name impressed onto the glass: *Glenn Vintners, Seattle.* On a lark, she traveled many hundreds of miles on a trail to find the man she felt already bound to. And one day, she found such a man on the docks cleaning his fishing nets from a day out at sea. She spoke to him, and told him she had found this bottle with his message— that she had read it and shared it with others. Larry was angry and felt it an invasion of his privacy. But Laurie was strong and determined. Larry was stubborn, angry at the world—and the very thought of another woman in his life was unthinkable! Yet Laurie remained in a hotel in town and when he thought about how rude he had been, he sought her out and apologized and offered her a ride in his fishing boat. She accepted and they spoke, but Larry was a man of few words, and Laurie the opposite. But she was so attracted to him that she sat quietly until a natural conversation was able to ensue. Larry liked that and invited her to dinner. Laurie noted that the house was filled with Katrina's things, paints still out, unfinished paintings on their easels, her working shoes still on the floor where she'd left them."

"Finally, Larry began to realize his life was only half-filled without her. But Laurie worked at a job in Monterey and had to return. So after much thought and consternation, Larry took all of Katrina's works and belongings and stowed them in the attic, cleaned up his house and decided to take his boat to California and pick up the young woman he had grown so fond of, if she would have him. In his clumsy way, he typed out one final letter, but this time it was to Laurie. '*If for some reason I don't reach you, I want you to know I'm coming to bring you home to me...because I realized that I had only a house without you in it. Sometimes we don't know that we're only half of a person. If you'll have me, I want to own, to possess, to covet all that you are—and let my heart open, if you'll let me... love, Larry.*'"

"En route to Monterey from Seattle, Larry ran into a terrible storm at sea. Near Cape Mendocino, he noticed a sailboat in distress. It had capsized and a family of three clung to the hull. Larry threw over his white life tire and brought a little boy and the father aboard. But the mother's leg had become injured and stuck under the weight of the mast boom. Larry took off his slicker and dove into the water after the young wife and mother. That was the last time anyone ever saw either of them."

I squinted to avoid the emotions that might be seeping through my own eyes. I took a deep breath. "A hell of story, Jed. So...what's the postscript? There's always a postscript."

"When Laurie hadn't heard from Larry for quite a while, she inquired and found out he had drowned some weeks before. In great sorrow, she went to visit Larry's old father who had known about the budding relationship and liked Laurie. The old man handed her the message Larry had written for her. He had sealed it in a small glass bottle and tucked into his slicker before he embarked on his journey to her. Did he have a premonition of his death? Who knows?"

"So, what's my lesson in all of this, if I may ask?"

"That life has taught me a powerful thing about womankind, Cable. Katrina had it right. Woman *is* a Phantom Bird. She is secretive, elusive, and it is always an illusion that one can possess her. That's what I've learned. I pass this legacy on to you. Love her, honor her, see her as the anchor of the household. But do not attempt to own her. Be her companion, her lover, her friend, but just remember she works best when she's allowed to be who she really is."

I hugged Dr. Jedediah Penn for the last time. "Keep me posted, Jed. If you're gonna do the Toggth thing, let me know. And leave a communication address, will you?" I chuckled.

He offered a vague smile. "If ever I loved a man who lived bigger than life, it's you, Cable Denning. I'm—I'm sorry we didn't…have…more time together…I'll miss that…"

"Aww, hell, we'll meet again, old boy. Count on it."

I walked out and Polly Parker came to greet me. "He really believes dat story. Dumkopf! As if true love vere anything more dan a fairy tale. You surely do not believe in such things, do you?"

"Oh, I don't know, Polly. Life is funny that way. I have trouble getting up some mornings, so who am I to say what is or what isn't?"

She laughed. "Ya! I know vat you mean!"

"So…what are you going to do after…after the doc—"

"—I have been vith him fifteen years now. He has been generous. I shall live comfortably und qvietly. But no more intellectual men."

"Why did you not marry—or was there someone?"

A tear came to Polly Parker's eyes. "I vas like Laurie in de doctor's story. I loved und lost before it could be…und I never loved again. Not dat I couldn't…but now it is so late…I vouldn't know vere to begin, Cable."

"Well, just put one foot in front of the other—and walk. Be good to yourself, Polly. Call me if you need me for anything. And keep me on top of the doc's condition."

Polly Parker hugged me good-bye. "As a young voman, I vonder how I vould have regarded you—lover or threat?"

"Probably both, kid. I'm pretty formidable in a tight clinch."

I got back to the office around 4:30 p.m. Zelda was listening to the radio and dusting the furniture. I softened from the world the minute I saw her, as if all the tension of the day drained away. "Hello, young woman, I'm glad you're still here. There's something I want to do."

She looked at me seriously. "What?"

I came up to her, took her into my arms and kissed her hard. "That's just in case..."

She swooned and then opened her eyes. "In case of what?"

"Well, it's this way. You're a phantom bird, you know."

"A what?"

"A phantom bird—woman, the unobtainable, she who cannot be possessed, that elusive thing man lives and dies for."

"Have you been drinking, Cable?"

"Only a couple of gins at the Doc's."

"For God's sake, we made love all night and I became yours long ago. Only you didn't know it, did you?"

"By the way, how's your ability to walk? Are you still sore down there?"

She blushed. "A little, but that doesn't mean I won't be ready for more later on." She came up to me and grabbed my crotch. "I think if you break me in right, I won't be sore anymore," she said seductively.

I chuckled and put my mouth close to her ear. "So just, uh, when...when do you think I should start breaking you in?"

"Well, I'd say tonight—but how about tomorrow night? I think I need to get a head start."

"Anything you want, babe." I looked at her, took my hands and placed them on her shoulders. "Look, Zelda, I want you to know you came in on the right tide—that you're exactly what the doctor ordered for me. I want to thank you for being you, lady. And you're turning out to be a hell of a woman, and *that* I didn't expect."

"I always told you, if you gave me half a chance, I could be very good for you. Maybe now, you believe me."

I kissed her gently. "Yeah...I do..."

I walked her to the streetcar stop. We stood there in the balmy late afternoon. "I don't think I'd ever want to be without you, Cable," she said, looking up at me like someone who just found home. "I know it sounds stupid and sentimental. But you know me, I'm not demanding or anything—and gees, you're the only man I trust— and for sure the only man I've ever let into my bed. Are you still glad?"

I kissed her nose. "I'm very glad, Zelda Blodgett. You woke me back up, gave me new life—allowed an overworked, underpaid gumshoe a chance to know he's still alive—"

"—can you tell me now—why did you come to me last night in a heated passion?"

"You really want to know?"

"Yes, please...if you don't mind. I have my suspicions."

"Well, there was this Cassiopeia—remember, Saturnalia's daughter? Long story short, she had the hots for me, but turns out she was a mannequin-replica. Not really human, you know. When I found myself stupidly being attracted to her, I became repulsed at myself and all of a sudden something clicked in my brain and I wanted to feel a real live, warm-blooded, breathing human woman—"

"—and I came to mind, is that it?" She looked a little sad. "I knew there was another woman somewhere. I was hoping you just wanted me for *me* and not for some triggering experience forcing you into my arms. In a way it makes a girl feel cheap. Now I know, I was just someone who'd do, wasn't I?"

"Believe me, Zelda, it wasn't like that by the time I got there. And however it happened, you were a beautiful surprise to me, and I've been thinking about you all damn day. Something really good happened. I'd really like to come over tomorrow night. Do you still want me to?"

She looked toward the setting sun and then back to me. "Yes...tomorrow night and every tomorrow night after that. Maybe women like me are stupid, they get desperate and go out of their minds with desire when someone like you comes into their lives. But love is different, Cable, and I'm in love with you. I'm sorry if it disappoints you, but when I give my body, you get the whole package."

"I like the whole package. It's never been any good for me just to get my rocks off. I could feel you last night, and every time we made love I could feel you up the ante of your intensity, your caring for me. I couldn't help but give back to you, doll—I hope you felt some of that."

"I did feel it, Cable...that's why I said a few minutes ago I'd never want you out of my life. I think we've got something here that can grow."

"So do I, babe." I took her in my arms in broad daylight and kissed her long and wet. "That's just a reminder that the wire's still connected to the wall socket—and it's hot."

She took a swooning breath and sighed. "So when does the socket get the plug? I want you, Cable, want you, want you, want you!"

"Tomorrow night...say about eight?"

"Yes, yes, yes....I'm going to wear something you've never seen before. It's naughty, but I think you'll like it."

"I'm sure I'll like it."

Then a look of desperation came over her face, as if a cold wind came out of a hot August night. "Cable. Don't go—come home with me now and make love to me! Stay with me all night so I'll know last night wasn't a dream. I just have this feeling..."

"But I thought you were—"

"—I don't care. When you're inside me it's such a bittersweet pain, even if I am sore, but I couldn't stand to be without it—not now, not tonight. Please?"

"Okay, babe, but I'll have to go back and lock up the office."

She smiled and told me to hurry. I ran up the stairs but when I got to my door, two tall characters came out of the hallway shadows. Odd...they were all wearing black masks. "Mr. Denning?" one of them asked.

"Yeah, office hours are over, gentlemen, and Halloween's not for a few months yet. Tomorrow after ten..."

Before I could do anything else, one of the giants grabbed me while the other one took out a bottle of some clear substance, poured some of the contents onto a handkerchief and swiftly slammed the cloth over my nose and mouth. The floor was falling out from under me. While I still could, I withdrew my handkerchief from my left pocket and let it fall to the floor. At least if Zelda found it, she'd know something was up. The thugs didn't pay any attention to it. I became woozy and I could feel the goons take my arms and drag me down to the end of the hall to the fire exit window. There they opened the window and the last thing I remember was being horizontally fed through the window and Zelda waiting at the curb for me to return so we could go to her little place for an evening of lovemaking.

Chapter 2

BOAK THE MAGNIFICENT

I woke up and it was pitch black. Either I had lost my vision or someone didn't pay the light bill. But there was something else...something that gave me the creeps and raised the hackles on the back of my neck. Like in a dream I'd had when I was banged up and convalescing, I could smell a musty, organic odor. My instincts told me it came from some kind of animal or creature, as if I were a caveman and the goose bumps all over my body were warning lights going on in my nervous system.

I fumbled around in the dark on all fours. I seemed to be in some kind of cell. The floor was concrete and where I assumed the entrance would be, there was a metallic grating that covered what must have been a large door of some kind. But one of the sides also had the same kind of metal grating. I eased my way to that wall and spoke quietly. "Say, there, if you're a neighbor and can talk, can you tell me where we are?"

There was a silence. Then I heard some kind of shifting sound, like the movement of an animal redistributing its weight. Then I heard what sounded so diabolically horrible, that I all but froze. A low hiss-growl of some kind emanated from what I assumed to be the cell next to me. Finally, I got up enough guts to speak again. "Are you human, extra-terrestrial, other dimensional or something else?" I tapped on the metal grating. Again, that low growl and terrible hiss came from something only a few feet from where I sat on the floor.

Just then a light went on outside, where I guessed the door was located. Soon I heard a key turn and in walked a petite young woman in a white uniform, holding a large syringe. I'd seen those goddam things before and knew what they meant. She left the door open and I could see that light came from a single bulb in the ceiling of a hallway of some sort. "Hello, there, are you awake?" She came up to me. She was shapely with blondish hair and chewed gum. "I hope they didn't injure you. What a girl doesn't have to do to make a living these days." She checked me out closer. "You're young and handsome, Mister. It's a pity...a damned pity...I say."

"Whatta ya mean?"

"Oh, how they treat people here. I mean, you know, there are other ways to treat people—nicer, I mean."

I got the feeling the babe wasn't too educated but knew her stuff nonetheless. "How do you mean, treat people?"

"Sorry, I shouldn't have even told you that. The doctor is rather sticky about telling our guests too much."

"I—I heard and smelled something next door that seems alive—"

"—oh, you mean *Boak*? I know he smells bad. When he poops, it really stinks up the place. Daryl can't clean up until Boak's lured into another cell."

"Lured? What in the hell do you have in there—some wild tiger or something?"

"You'll find out, Mr.—Mr.—"

"—Denning, Cable Denning. You can call me Cable."

She chewed her gum faster as she plunged the needle into my arm. I was still too weak and dazed to resist. "Nice name." She withdrew the needle. "Gees, you know

I really hate doing this. You seem to be a really nice guy. What do you do, if I may ask?"

"I'm a private dick..."

"Oh, now I *know* I'm going to like you—uh, Cable. What is that?"

"A private detective, a gumshoe, you know, someone who goes after errant husbands, wives, girlfriends and lovers—and once in a while takes down a bad guy."

"Oh. There are lots of them here."

"What's that?"

"Bad guys. Dr. Voracious specializes in bad guys, I think."

"So what do you do other than shoot people up with drugs and dope and God knows what else?"

"I'm a dancer at a speakeasy four nights a week. That's how I could tell."

"Tell what?"

"That you're a pretty fancy guy, like a cut above most of the men who come into the club. They look at me with half of my clothes off and start panting. And you know—all they want to do is lift up my skimpy and screw me, there, on the spot. No decency."

"Well, guys are guys. Maybe I'd want to do just the same." I knew I had to have an ally if I was ever going to get out of this jam alive. The babe had a cute way about her, and if there was a way I could win her over to my side, I would. "By the way, you do have a name, I suppose?"

"Ziggy—but they call me *Crazy Legs* down at the club."

"Pleased to meet you, Ziggy. Not to be too nosy, but can you tell me where I am?"

30

"That is too nosy, Cable. I'm sorry, but mum is the word. I've already been too friendly with you." Then she stepped back and looked at me. "That's because I like you, I think."

Then I heard a man's voice echoing down the hallway, his footsteps coming toward us. A slight, bent over man entered. He, too, wore a white coat and sported a shock of silver hair, deep-set dark eyes and spoke with a peculiar lisp. "I see you've had your very first treatment, Mr. Denning," he said, his voice was fluid and he spoke with a sort of oddly English accent. His voice was sinister—probably because the mind behind the man was evil and without conscience, the very kind of man someone like Cronus-Gor would hire to do his dirty work. "I'm Dr. Voracious..." He checked out Ziggy. "I see you've met Miss Thompson. She's a pip, isn't she? I don't know how we'd manage without her. It's not easy to find good help nowadays." He came up to me. He had a silver moustache and one of those smiles like the cat who plays a lot with the mouse. "I trust you are feeling—feeling okay, Mr. Denning?"

"I feel shitty. How would you feel? And where in the hell am I, Voracious? And why am I here?"

He smiled an evil smile. Then he looked at Ziggy Thompson. "You may go, Miss Thompson. Two hours— and administer the second shot."

She glanced at me and smiled. "Yes, Doctor..." Then she walked off, leaving the old doc and me alone.

"So what's the scoop? No man likes being locked up like that stinkin' thing you have next to me. How about a few answers?"

31

"Very well, Mr. Denning. You are a lucky man—in a certain manner of speaking, that is. That 'stinking thing' you refer to is *Boak*. I will introduce the two of you later. In the meantime, you are my...my guest...lamentably, though, for a very short while. You see, our guests do not generally stay very long. I sincerely hope it's not the hospitality we offer. Perhaps it's because they seem to acquire a certain....certain *fear* after a while. And then there seems to be an unfortunate disgruntlement and then...they just...just disappear...curious."

"Oh, that's comforting. Suppose you tell me who's next door. Who the hell set you up for this little prank and when's my release date?"

He raised his brow. "Oh...Mr. Denning...there is no release date...I'm afraid this is your last accommodation. Let me explain. Our employer, whom I believe you know, is currently being, shall we say, *attacked* by his daughter and her formidable forces and thus shall be otherwise occupied for an indefinite period of time. However, he wants you to have the honor and privilege of experiencing the world's mightiest *truth serum*—which, I might add, I have perfected in my very own laboratories. But instead of long and tedious hours of miniscule injections, we have modified—perhaps I should say *specialized*—Boak to inject massive amounts of my serum all in one fell swoop—how is that for...for openers? Nothing short...of genius, I'd say."

"Truth serum, eh? And what am I supposed to reveal—the last few pages of *The Count of Monte Cristo* or something?"

He chuckled in a forbidding tone. "Humor is an admirable ingredient, I always say. But I think you know

Mr. Gor is seeking what he describes to me as...as, well......something of great value to him. We'll let it rest at that, don't you think, Mr. Denning? I do hope you'll be....co-operative...it is always a pity when guests let their fear...get the best of them...a pity, when they let it overwhelm them and then lose control of all...earthly functions, shall we say."

All of a sudden I was thinking of poor Zelda standing there on the corner of Franklin and Cahuenga. I wondered what she thought when I didn't come back down. Did she feel I just fled the coop? Or knowing her intuition, I suspected she went back to the office, looked for me, maybe found the handkerchief on the floor outside my office door and called the cops.

I was feeling a little better. Whatever Ziggy Thompson had shot me with began to circulate in my veins. "What are you shooting me with, Voracious? I've dealt with bastards without conscience like you before. You sell your medical knowledge to the highest bidder, and do-in poor slobs like me who will never know the difference. You know, you worm, you won't succeed in the long run. Guys like you seldom do. Genius or not— maybe I don't have what old Gor wants after all— maybe he's just obsessed with something he'll never find, let alone possess. Feature that, you leftover piece of crap!"

"Come now, Mr. Denning. There is no need for such language. Nothing you say—or do—can help you now. Resign yourself...to an early demise. It's not so bad. Look at all the young men who fall in war...do they complain when they perish...for their country? You must look at it that way, I suggest...dying for a cause...you believe in..."

My voice rose to a high pitch and seemed to echo throughout the facility. "It doesn't even matter about your—your smelly Boak creature next to me in that cell. There's a line, you know and people like you, Voracious, cross that line. So you're destined to find out that villainy catches up with the evil doer, and that sooner or later the perpetrator gets caught in his own web and dies the same kind of horrible death he has inflicted on others. And sometimes it's a slow death, maybe mental, emotional—even try a spiritual death—and when his brain rots from the dark poison that has been injected into his own thoughts through the years, by killing countless others in the name of *science,* he screams for mercy from the very thing he caused. But you know what? He doesn't get any mercy, because there is a kind of justice in the universe, one you or I or whatever that poor creature in there didn't create or see coming—and in the end, the books have got to balance and to your fucked up mind, with all its ignorant assumptions, the chickens come home to roost and suddenly you fear for your own mortality—even *you* and all your scientific garble can't figure out the twists and turns of the cosmos. You know why? Because you're part of it, and as rotten as your human self is, everything's inside everything else—and none of us are separated except by thought!" My tirade had exhausted me and I backed away from Dr. Voracious. "I'm a truth guy, Voracious. And that's my truth..."

The doctor stood there in front of me wordless for a minute. Then he resumed that sick smile reserved for the subtly insane. "Indeed, you present a fine argument for the pros and cons of good versus evil. But you see, it is *not* a moral universe, Mr. Denning, and there is no God sitting on a throne with an all-powerful scepter reigning judgment on us hapless humans. No...you see, Mr. Denning, we create...our own...destinies...we make the choices that invariably allow the light or dark side of things we choose to experience. For me, a truly brilliant and devoted scientist, being a pioneer is an exciting thing. For my guinea pigs, of course, it is a different matter. But someone always has to lose in order for someone else to win, a quaint human anomaly. Let me see, the choices are always, 'shall I live or shall I die?' Let's just say, science will increasingly be *selective* regarding those choices."

I was suddenly tired. I took a deep breath. "So, when do I meet your Mr. Boak—whatever or whoever he is."

"Oh, to be certain...within the hour. I shall light up his cage for you, so you two may converse. Despite his appearance...he is...very intelligent...and not only hears every word you speak, but feels the vibration of it on his very tongue." Dr. Voracious backed away, holding the key to my cell in his hand. "I must take my leave for now. Happy visiting hours, Mr. Denning..." The door clicked shut and Voracious locked it. There I stood in the middle of my little cell, apparently lost to the world. What if the doc was right? What if we fool ourselves about justice and comeuppance? What if we live life by bushwhacking our way through the jungle of humanity out there, and in the end, there is no sound at all, just the endlessness of space—or death.

Just then I saw the figure of Ziggy Thompson at my door again. She unlocked it and entered, approaching me with a needle big enough to kill an elephant. But she had tears in her eyes. "I—I overheard you talking to the Doctor. I never heard anyone talk like that, Mister. Something inside me told me I just can't let you die."

"What do you mean?"

"The other serum I injected you with was a slow poison. This...this is anti-venom...I must supply you with it throughout the next few hours. If I get caught, they'll kill me...just so you know..."

"I thank you for that, Ziggy, but why would you do it? Why would you endanger your life for me, just another guy with his head getting closer to the chopping block by the minute?"

"Because you're not just another guy. Believe me, I've known a lot of guys. You're an unusual man, Cable. Maybe you can take me out sometime or something? I work at the *Pink Gables*—near Broadway, downtown. I should say I work in back of it. Just say 'Carmen sent me' and you're in."

She injected me with that large needle and the pain seared through my body. "If it works, I won't forget it, kid."

"Boak has been changed. He's an experiment, too." She pulled the needle out. "I've got to go now. I'll be back in a couple of hours or so." She tipped up and kissed me on my sweaty cheek. "I think you're swell, Cable. I wish I knew you when I was a virgin."

I chuckled to myself. "Why would you say that?"

"Because I'd want someone like you to have me the first time. It was terrible and painful when it did happen. I was fifteen. I know you wouldn't be like that. And I'd trust you. I could hear it in your voice and the way you talked up to Dr. Voracious. I'm sure he didn't know what to say at first."

"Well, thanks, Ziggy. If we get out of this thing alive—you bet I'll take you out for dinner and dancing—would you enjoy that?"

"Would I! I can't remember the last time a real man asked me out on a date that didn't end up in a fucking fest by morning."

"Well, I'm on the level, lady. We'll make it a date."

She quickly exited, locked the door and scampered down the hallway. Then a light went on in the cell next to me and I saw the unimaginable horror Dr. Voracious had planned for me. There coiled in a corner lay the most gigantic *snake* I had ever seen! I shuddered just looking at him. Some primeval instinct went rippling through my body to run. But I knew I couldn't. I spoke lightly, attempting a friendly voice. "I hear you're the pride of the joint, Boak—that is your name, right?" He slithered slowly toward me until only the fine metal grating separated us. Then he rose up like a huge, thick rope until he hovered above me, his wonderful intense golden-brown eyes looking at me. As his neck muscles distended out, I knew he was the king of King Cobras. I looked into his eyes. "I'll be damned. I'd—I'd call you...Boak the Magnificent...because you are that, my dear snake." Then I lowered my voice. He seemed to like that and he was incredibly attentive. "I'm sorry...sorry they altered you, Boak. I'm on your side. Everything man touches turns to shit, guy. Did they hurt you?"

I didn't know if it was a response to the sound of my words or what, but he gave out with a deep hiss-growl that was truly terrifying. It was like being at the edge of a cliff with some cold-blooded thing chasing you and at some point you knew you had to jump. Then he hissed again, never letting go of his eye contact with me. "I get the distinct feeling you're gonna bite me, Boak. You have enough venom to kill twenty of me. Is that what you want to do?" His huge head and neck began to sway as if he was trying to hypnotize me, those intense eyes ever glued to my own. "If you didn't stink so god-awful, I'd pet you. But they really need to clean you up a bit."

Then Boak the Great King Cobra did a strange thing. Almost as if he understood me, he contracted his threatening hood and lowered his eighteen-foot body until those intense, staring eyes were level with my own. Then he opened his mouth as if to yawn and I saw two of the largest snake fangs I'd ever seen. He hissed and growled at me once more. I didn't know what else to do, so I began to sing. As I did so, the hovering specter now at eye-level to me, stuck out his tongue and listened to the vibration of my voice. *What'll I do when you are far away, and I am blue, what'll I do? What'll I do with only dreams of you, that won't come true...what'll I do?* I hummed the rest of the song and amazingly, the snake backed down and came to rest his chin on the cold concrete floor, his eyes now turned away from me, looking out toward the empty corridor beyond his cell. "Didn't you like the music?" I asked him. He became very still and even when I called to him less timidly, he refused to look at me. "Be that way, see if I care." Maybe

38

he found out all he needed to know about me. Yeah, maybe he was intelligent and decided that I was an okay guy and maybe he wouldn't bite me when it came to it. Sure.... wishful thinking, Denning, I said to myself.

Soon Ziggy came back into the cell. She glanced at the huge snake resting on the cell floor. "I see you've met Boak. Isn't he handsome? I used to play with garter snakes when I was a little girl. I always loved the feel of snakes, that cool, almost wet scaly skin." She approached me with her giant needle again. "This is probably going to hurt. The second anti-venom shot is always the most painful." She jammed it into my arm and I winced. "I don't know why it's that way. The last one won't be so bad, I promise." She kissed my cheek again. "You're brave, Cable. And you're tough, like my dad. My dad was tough—a Navy man, you know. He told me one night in the tropics the captain let the crew rest on an uninhabited island. During the night huge man-eating crabs came up onto the shore and dragged away several sailors until their screams woke everyone. It was horrible, my dad said. But he was really strong and rescued a couple of the guys before the giant crabs could drag them under the water to drown and eat them."

I could tell Ziggy was real proud of her father. "Yeah, that's quite a story, Ziggy. So...tell me...what are my chances of getting out of this one alive? You can tell me the truth—I'm really a guy who appreciates truth."

She took out the needle and cleaned it with a cloth from her pocket. "Well, if you want truth, Cable, I really can't say. But I can say what's happened before. First, Dr. Voracious opens that partition separating you and Boak. Then he sends for Daryl with the prodder."

39

"Prodder?"

"Yeah, a big long stick that looks like a cane. Daryl aggravates Boak by hooking his neck, pulling it back and forth and getting him angry. Otherwise he might decide not to bite you—and then Dr. Voracious would be angry. I don't know which is worse. They both can get pretty mad." Ziggy seemed a bit touched in the head to me, but she was all I had. "But if Daryl does his job right, Boak will be left alone with our guest. Now remember he's really pissed, so he'll probably strike at anyone who moves—or doesn't move—just depends on his mood. But he usually does strike, with those huge fangs just dripping with poisonous venom. At this point our guest gets really weird and starts foaming at the mouth and shaking. Then Daryl comes back in and hooks Boak back into his cell and closes it off. By now our guest is trembling on the floor. Dr. Voracious begins to question him or her, usually to extract some kind of information—"

We both heard footsteps coming down the corridor. "You'd better go now," I whispered. "But you didn't tell me the survival rate."

"I think it's zero—but don't take my word for it, because I've never seen all the dead people afterward. Especially now, I won't be able to give you the third shot." She kissed me on my nose. "Bye, Cable, I hope I gave you enough anti-venom stuff so we can go out to that dinner and dancing you promised." She grabbed my arm and looked into my eyes. "Now remember, if my shots *do* work, you'll seem to be dead for a while, the venom will appear to stop your heart."

"So how long will I be dead for?"

"Oh, I don't know...hours, days..."

"And if something goes wrong and I really die?"

"Then we'll just have to cancel our dinner date. But I truly hope you survive, Cable."

"Yeah, me, too, lady. Thanks for giving it your best shot, so to speak," I clumsily joked. She gave me a quick hug and ran out.

Dr. Voracious entered in a jaunty mood. "Ah, I see you have met...our honored Mr. Boak." He went over to Boak's grating and tapped strongly with his fingers. This disturbed the snake and he reared around to raise his body and growl at the doctor. "Indubitably... for whatever reason...he's not fond of me, Mr. Denning. But we make do...as best we can. And he never fails to amuse us...something about a powerful serpent pitted against a mere human stacks the deck, don't you think? But the show is always exciting here at the research laboratories."

"He's the only real thing in here. He doesn't know how to be anything else except himself. I think he's magnificent. I told him so."

"You conversed? How charming."

"I sang to him. I think he liked it."

"Brilliant! That's one area we haven't researched! I'll make a note of it. I've often wondered about the effects of a larger spectrum of harmonic frequencies and all—surely, you've heard of the snake charmers of India—pacifying their reptilian cousins from out of their basket."

Then, just as Ziggy had told me, a weasel-like little man about thirty-five or so entered and pulled up the part of the grating that connected my cell with the

41

snake's. "Here's hoping he'll bite *your* butt someday, you dismal excuse for a human," I declared to Voracious.

"On the contrary, Mr. Denning, I am behaving just *like* humans do... conniving, treacherous, self-important, selfish. Come now, surely you've seen these behavior patterns?"

I didn't reply because Boak began to slither into my cell. Then the doctor exited as Daryl began prodding the snake into a state of excitement. He hissed and struck at the stick until finally Boak was confused enough with anger—and Daryl left. As he locked my door behind him, the little man flashed a sick smile at me and chortled to himself. Then the light went out in Boak's cell and only one small bulb remained in the corridor ceiling. The huge green-black snake, his neck flared out, his eyes now focused once again on me, grew to a great height until he hovered above me. "I didn't make you pissed, Boak," I said, trying to maintain my calm as best I could. "It was those other creatures. They planned it that way. If you must bite me, could you do it on my arm or leg or someplace other than my body—I would ask at least that."

Boak's hissing and angry growl increased in intensity and that guttural sound filled the cell. It was pretty dark and all I could see were those golden eyes reflecting what little light there was and the dead-still trunk of his huge, muscular body. Then, without warning he lunged at me and I could feel a piercing pain in my left shoulder as his deadly fangs sunk into my flesh and knocked me back. He only struck once, then backed away. I stood there frozen from the impact. Then I began trembling as I collapsed to the floor—then every-thing went black.

Mamma Earth

Down a long echoing corridor I could hear voices. Slowly my hearing improved and as my eyes opened, someone was tearing a bunch of boards off the ceiling above me. Soon I could understand the voices. "I tell youse again and again, Mamma Earth, dem dead things is dead things. Youse a goin' by some crazy young whit-ey? Then youse is crazy or mayhaps more crazy den dem folk is!"

"Keep liftin' dem boards, Judah Daggitt, or I is gonna whop your behind with one of these here pinewood stakes!"

"If I wasn't your son and you wasn't my blessed mamma, I'd be using this here spade to cover the dirt back in after that mortal flesh, now passed to putrifica-tion. Sacrilege....I say, mamma, sacrilege to the Lord—to be resurrectin' this here corpse. Goes to show, be times when I'm thinkin' youse is seein' yourself as the one who can raise Lazarus!"

"You shush! That is the consecration of sin, right there—blasphemin' and sinnin' with your mother—Oh, Lord, forgive my ignorant son Judah here...let him know we is a conservin' a life Thou hast made! Let that alone suffice, O Lord!"

Soon blessed sunlight filled the wooden box I found myself crammed into. Two negroes, one a strapping fel-low obviously named Judah and his white-haired moth-

43

er, whose name really did turn out to be *Mamma Earth*. Together they lifted me out of the box and placed me on the ground. I was near a body of water and as the sun warmed my almost-corpse, I realized how weak and helpless I was. I tried to speak, but it was useless, for my mouth had become as dry as cotton and my eyes watered a thick kind of pus. I could barely see my hand, but it was a brownish red, and so was the rest of my body, as I discovered later. Then I passed out again.

The kindly black folks brought me to their humble abode and there, Mamma Earth began to feed me herbs and soups and rub my body each day. I slept on the floor and she covered me at night with a strange woven blanket of buzzard feathers. It stank a little, but it was amazingly warm. Slowly I regained my speech and muscular functions and soon I was walking with Mamma Earth to the little lake nearby. We were somewhere in the mountains above Los Angeles. Why or who transported my body in a makeshift coffin and buried me in an old abandoned church cemetery I'll never know. But Mamma Earth was special. She had the gift of vision, sort of like Crazy Jack but not quite as crazy. Her son Judah worked in an old sawmill during the week, so Mamma Earth and I had a lot of quality time together. "Youse bein' ready to walks youself outta here soon, Denning Man." I told her to call me Cable, but 'Denning Man' was the best she could manage. "Youse sir, you is lucky you ain't deader than dat horseshoe hanging over Judah's night room. I ain't seen nobody come back from the dead as you'in. What kinda viper you said bit youse?"

"A King Cobra," I said, smiling at Mamma Earth's quaint way of speech. "Them's big snakes from India, Malaysia—even places like where your ancestors come from, Muga Muga Boo," I paraphrased her.

She giggled a wonderful giggle, like she always had hidden behind her eyes. It was as if my presence made her feel young again and she lilted when she walked with me, like a young woman feeling reborn. "I never knowed any soul born in that dark continent—Heaven can seal the secret and cross my heart—your poor young man's body was red and black and blue like you was goin' to the Lord, alright, but not yet decayed!"

"Thanks to you." I turned to look into her dark brown smiling eyes. "You saved my life, Mamma Earth. What can I ever do to repay you?"

"Go to church with me this Sunday and sing loud your praise to the Lord, boy. Thank Him for sendin' my heart on His Wings to have me and Judah fetch you outta dat box."

I laughed. Going into a church was as alien to me as walking on Saturnalia's weird landscape outside her firelight cottage. "Alright! Alright! A small price to pay for the keeping of my life."

As soon as I was able, Mamma Earth walked me to a neighbor about a mile away. They were the only local folk with a telephone. I called my office and thankfully reached Zelda. I told her briefly what had happened and she was so relieved that she cried most of the time we spoke on the telephone. I told her I'd be returning to L.A. very soon and I didn't know what to do about maintaining the office since I hadn't been working and was almost out of funds. She said I could come live with her, and I got the distinct feeling that delighted Zelda Blodgett.

That Sunday marked three weeks of absence from Los Angeles. It was August 11, 1932 and I had lost a month of my life somewhere between being apprehended by Gor's goons and tossed in a cell at the mercy of the mad Dr. Voracious—and recuperating under the tender care of Mamma Earth. Many was the time I thought of Zelda and her likely consternation at my disappearance. I wondered what she was doing this minute. Was she thinking of me in loving visions of our incredible erotic nights together, or was she so baffled that she lived each day on the edge, hoping I might return. And my business? I hoped Zelda would maintain it for a little longer before she gave up and a missing person became a dead person to the world. I had given her an expense account to run things at the office for about six weeks. She was probably running out just about now.

"Jesus loves me this I know, for the Bible tells me so..." was only a Baptist appetizer that Sunday as I sat between big Judah and little Mamma Earth. I had noticed a pretty young woman, probably about twenty, eyeing me there on the hard wooden bench. I smiled at her and she looked away, a bit shy. Mamma Earth didn't miss a thing and noticed the innocent flirtation going on between the lovely young thing and myself. She jabbed me gently in the side with her elbow. "Youse ain't suppos'd to be lookin' at that chocolate candy, Denning Man," she whispered. Judah flashed her a disgruntled look.

The real meat of a Baptist Sunday-go-to-meetin', was the hand-clappin', foot-stompin' son-of-a-gun no-holds-barred kind of dancing and singing those folks did. My little chocolate beauty came up out of the audience and did a dance shocking enough to reveal a pair of white panties underneath a fine, white linen skirt. She and a few other women were swaying and singing until finally the music reached a point of frenzy and everyone raised their hands high in the air and started shouting "Hallelujah!" at the top of their lungs. In the meantime, the preacher had been going around yanking everyone out of their seat so they could join the festivities. Mamma Earth pulled me up and out I went to the yelling, screaming, dancing, singing, clapping celebration that a worthy God must have deserved. I thought I had a hoot of a time! And my body was almost back in shape. Hallelujah, brother!

Mamma Earth and Judah got stuck talking to some folks inside the church and so I sat outside among the tall pines that surrounded the little white building with the quaint steeple. Since it was a poor church, all they could afford was a cowbell in the belfry, but it worked. Suddenly I heard a voice behind me. "Lordie, Mister, but you sure are quite a handsome white man, and with a good sense of rhythm, too."

I looked over to this gorgeous young thing with long black curly hair, dark smiling eyes and a body that made you want to bite down hard on a stick to keep from jumping her bones there on the spot. She had a white blouse on and the sweat from all the commotion inside had made her breasts clearly outlined against the wet blouse. They were full, solid young breasts that stood

47

up and out. "Well, you oughta catch my rhythm in other places," I said, teasing her with a suggestive tone.

But to my surprise, she took me up on it. "Well, I'd sure like to know...your other kinds of rhythm, Mr.— Mr. —"

"—Cable...please, just call me Cable."

"Cable? What kind of a name is that? Doesn't that mean some kind of metal wire or somethin'?"

"Yeah, it could. But my name is Irish. So I guess in Ireland it means something else. What's your name?"

"I am Floradine Louisa Carpenter, bred and born in Los Angeles, California. What about you?"

"I'm pleased to meet you, Floradine—yeah, me, too—Boyle Heights, the last place on earth to be born..."

"Well, you try the black ghetto, Cable. It doesn't get any filthier or harder than that. Young men without job possibilities or educatin' sell dope or do nothin', while young girls are sold on the streets to earn enough to feed the family. That's what I saw...and it sure ain't changed much."

Just then Judah came out to tell me that he and Mamma Earth were invited to have supper with some of their church friends and I was welcome to come along. I declined and said I'd mosey on home. I glanced at that lovely young negro woman all dressed in white. "Would you like to walk me home? Do you know where I live?"

"Everyone knows where Mamma Earth lives. She's a legend 'round these parts. A genuine, bona fide healer."

Retrograde in a Minor Key

We walked on for a while and she instinctively took my hand. I glanced down. It was the first time in my life I saw a black woman's hand meshed in my own. I don't know why, but it felt good, like somehow I was proud to know her and her people. "Do you always take the hand of a strange white man?"

"No," she answered, still looking straight ahead. "Just yours. Most honkies are just honkies to me. But you're different. Mamma Earth told me something about you." She stopped. "I never did make love with a white man before. But when I look at your mouth, your hair, the way you smile and talk—I think I might like you." And then she frowned. "And, you know, black men can be very cruel and thoughtless."

"So can white men, lady," I said, remembering a few I'd known.

"But not you, Cable." She studied my face. "It's almost like you're from a different star or something." She laughed. "My, my, my, don't I sound romantic, carryin' on so! Are you afraid of romance? It's a funny color to paint. I find many men not afraid of sex, but scared to death of romance. Or maybe it's just me."

"You've got that right, Floradine—and it ain't you...you're lovely and vibrant—and *intelligent*, a pretty good combination, I'd say."

"—Hey, mystery man, just call me Flo...I always told my Mamma, it flows better, get it?" she laughed.

We stopped again and I turned to face her. I let go of her hand. What was I getting myself into now? "People try to define things, like love, romance—but there's nothing wrong with great sex, either. Sometimes a guy's desire drives him to pure sex and nothing else matters, including 'romance' *or* love. Something decent and usually controlled in him gets overcome in the moment and love or sympathetic emotions get tossed out the window."

She laughed a happy laugh. "Is there someone in your life you can do both with? You know, boy, the girl loves you...yet once in a while you both just want great sex, as you call it."

The lady was smart and articulate. I avoided answering her question directly. "How old are you—and you seem educated beyond the normal ghetto orphan."

"I'm right-on, right-on, right-on twenty-five, honey...five-feet six, 37-23-36, no kids, not a virgin anymore, studied zoology for two years, switched to the biological sciences and possess a bachelor's degree in that field. I need to go for a doctorate soon."

"I'm impressed. So how did you get to be here in the boondocks far from the maddening crowd?"

"Well, baby boy, I might just as well ask you the same question. I don't even know what you do, honey chil', as my folks would say."

"In a nutshell I was a cop who became a private eye who had the hero's dream, the guy who could make a difference. But so far, I've lost three people I loved very much, two of them to gang violence, one to leukemia. This last escapade is part of an ongoing vendetta a weird creep has against me. Somewhere in L.A. there's a lab that houses a genetically altered King Cobra making it the world's most gigantic and most deadly of creatures. He's being used to inject a massive amount of truth serum into his victims, of which I was one, with his huge fangs. He bit me. Then I died and someone took my body way up here and buried it. Dear Mamma Earth and Judah dug me up because they happened to notice a fresh grave that didn't belong in the abandoned church graveyard. Mamma Earth nursed me back to health and here I am, almost ready to go back to my work as a private dick."

"Private who, honey?"

"It means private investigator, or short for private detective."

She giggled. "Oh, sure—for a minute, I thought you was one of *those* men servicing other men. But somehow it ain't you, Cable, is it? So how come you didn't die of the snake bite?"

"Because, like Mamma Earth, I owe a hell of a lot to a petite little nurse who doubles as a stripper at night—she injected me with anti-venom serum before Boak the Magnificent bit me."

She took my hand and put it to her chest and closed her eyes. "You owe her a lot. Your life is star-crossed with women—they are drawn to you, private eye, like ducks to the water, ain't that so? Why am I here? I've got folk here. My father died several years ago. My mother's sister, Letisha, lives up here, does the maid thing for a rich couple over on Bowden Hill. So I come to visit now and then." She looked at me and started swaying. It scared me for a minute because it reminded me of Boak and his mesmerizing act. "But you...you're like a poem to me, Cable. '*Let me see what glowing star is sparked, as this lonely hunter enters my longing heart—should I let him in too late, or is his love for me his fate?*'

51

We reached Mamma Earth's front porch. "That's nice—who wrote it?"

"A French writer from New Orleans about 1839. Her name was Nanene Emily Foray, that rare educated woman of color."

I was getting restless as we approached Mamma Earth's humble little shack. "I think I probably need to go in to rest now, Flo."

She checked out my eyes. "What you're really meanin', white boy, is that you're bored with a pretty black woman who won't fuck you on the spot. Ain't that sort of how it goes?"

"No, you're wrong, Missy. Hell, woman, I find you sensual and appealing, uninhibited like a lot of black gals, but I'm on a different mission here. I've enjoyed the walk and your company. That's it."

"That's it?" She seemed a little put off. How can you figure a dame? "I was hopin' you'd want to know me better. It gets awful boring up here with dull days with nothin' to do and lots of church functions. I told you Mamma Earth told me something about you. You've seen *them*, been with *them* and probably even did some whoopee with at least one of 'em, huh? It was Mamma Earth's second sight and she told me about you—said she had a vision about you one day while washing your head, very eerie and all, mysterious—I mean, way out there, up there," she said, looking up to the sky. She stood on the porch looking so damn attractive I was feeling uneasy and wanted to kiss her. "Now, let's make the connection, honey chil'. You see, my advanced curiosity has led me to believe that in the world of organic chemistry, humans are not what once they were. Some-

52

thin' is missin'. Now...what and just where could that missin' somethin' be?"

"How would I know? Yeah, so I've had a little exposure to some strange dimensions and alien beings—but they're them and we're us. My intuition tells me we're kind of slow on the evolving scale—"

"—land sakes! It's sure enough *devolvin'*, Denning Man," Mamma Earth said, coming around the corner. "We is less now than we was then! And that ain't no God consecratin' mistake. The Lord had a perfect plan for his own under Heaven. Someone's messed with the Divine Plan."

"I thought you were off to a nice afternoon supper, Mamma Earth," I said. "Flo here is an intelligent and perceptive lady, so we were discussing the possibility that the human race is in *retrograde*—going backward like you said—*devolving*."

"A little thumpin' was goin' on inside my innards— that I shouldn't be leavin' black and white to mix their blood together. Floradine Louisa Carpenter, I was seein' your hot panties fly up for this here whitey in the sight of the Lord *and* Reverend Bartholomew. *'As a woman thinketh in her heart, so is she...'* I says..."

Flo tittered and smiled at Mamma Earth. "Mamma Earth—you are right, I cannot lie to *you* of all the souls meanderin' on this earth. But truth is, though I might have been winkin' an eye or two at Cable here, we have been in earnest conversation."

"That'd *better* be the case, chil'—especially seein' as the twos of youse is on different good ships passin' through the night, and never the blood should meet."

I was curious about Mamma Earth's early statement. I knew her visions and intuitions were highly tuned, so I thought I'd tune in myself and reap some of the benefits of that gift. "You were saying 'devolving' when I said *evolving*...what did you mean?"

"I already said, Denning Man. We is less than we were 'cause bad folk have been tamperin' with the intent of the Lord. Hell and damnation comes on a venomous tongue these days. Amen and Hallelujah!"

"You mean like Boak the snake, we've been modified from our original state?"

"Modified, codified—everythin' 'cept satisfied...them demons done it bad to us'n of God's chillin." Then she looked at Flo. "Floradine Louisa Carpenter, you'd better be goin' soon 'cause Denning Man needs his rest—he's still a recuperatin' man." Then she glanced at me. "I whopped her behind *and* her Mamma's, and they is both naughty women, not knowin' when to keep their panties up or down."

I flushed a little as I cracked a smile to myself. But Flo seemed indignant. "Mamma Earth! You haven't been seein' my way with men since—well, since I first came back here to visit five summers ago."

"Well, just 'cause you was born in L.A., it don't mean you have to behave like one of those dirt-street hussies sellin' their snatches for bread money." Then she turned back to me. "You be takin' some rest now, Denning Man. I came back for some maple syrup for them flapjacks the Johnson's are servin' up for Judah and me."

"Okay, Mamma Earth..." I said. The old woman gathered up what she came for and departed, not saying another word. I looked at Flo and she at me. We laughed heartily. "She still thinks you're sixteen, I think."

The afternoon was starting to cool off and I could feel a chill setting into my bones. I knew the healing process wouldn't be an overnight miracle, despite Mamma Earth's marvelous caretaking. "Cable...will I ever see you again?" Flo asked.

"I don't know, will you? Life is a guessing game any way you slice it, Flo. Do you want to meet again? I'd be happy to share with you some of what I've learned from—from other dimensions...if you're interested. Maybe together we could link up the chemistry that caused humans to lose their lofty rank in the hierarchy of Creation."

She looked at me with a very sexy expression. "There's another chemistry I'd like to link together—with *you*, Cable. I'm thinkin' Mamma Earth is goin' to be gone quite a spell...and Judah has to travel down to the lumber mill tonight."

"So what are you saying?" I asked, as if I didn't know.

She took my hand and led me into the cool of the forest until she found a hidden, private spot. The floor of the forest was a carpet of pine needles. She unbuttoned her blouse, unzipped her skirt, pulled it down and took off her panties quicker than I could blink! "As I said, I've never had a white man, Cable, have you ever had a black woman?" she purred in a most seductive tone in the shade and shadows of the late afternoon forest.

I felt awkward. "Uh...no...and as Mamma Earth said, I'm not healed up yet—and besides, I might get a little embarrassed. Black men are said to be more mightily endowed—"

"—it's never the quantity, but the *quality*, Mr. Private Eye Man." She came up to me with that perfect naked body of hers, undid my britches, knelt down in the pine needles and began to arouse my family member. I must've been really healing well because I had no trouble coming to full attention. Flo was a wonderful lover and pulled me down on top of her, using our clothes as a blanket from the sharpness of the pine needles. She took my head and placed it between her marvelously large and tight breasts, those dark nipples coming to grand attention as she opened her legs and let me fall between them. Then she wrapped those wonderful slim, long legs around me. "I'm—I'm feelin' a might scared, Cable, but I want you...I do...I do..."

"What are you scared about? Besides the fact that we're two grown adults having unprotected sex, I'm pretty safe."

"It's not that, remember, I'm a chemistry major—I'm not fertile just now. It's something else...it's that I'm fallin' for you, Denning Man. It's so damn quick like, and once I have you, I know me—I won't be wantin' to let go anytime soon."

I thought for a second. "Well, maybe we oughtn't to be doing this."

"Are you kidding? I'm hotter than a pistol full of gun powder for you right now and I don't know how to be puttin' the brakes on...." She sighed and breathed heavily. "Take it, Cable...I'm giving it to you..."

And the lady wasn't kidding. I sank into her beautiful, abundant womanhood like a hot knife through creamy butter. I hadn't had a release in a long time, not since that last morning with Zelda. So when I came, it was like a flood of thick, white jelly injected into Flo and I knew she could feel the warmth of it penetrate her body.

Afterward, we lay together in the quiet of the on-coming evening. We were both spent and complete. As my essence leaked out of her, Flo dipped her finger into it and tasted it with her tongue. "Ah, Cable...you lubricated an already very lubricated lady..."

"Thanks, babe. I had a wonderful climax—were you able to come?"

"No, but it's not unusual for me. Good lover men have been pretty scarce in my life, contrary to Mamma Earth's sayin' so, that I've been havin' to take care of myself a lot of the time. I'm seein' it'd take a while to retrain some of my vaginal response nerves—and we can have a lot of pleasure and funnin' in the mean-time...while I'm getting used to a man again." She smiled up at me as she took my hand. Are you willin'?"

I laughed. "Oh, yeah, willing, lady—but I'm not sure if I'm able. Pretty soon I've got to get back to *my* reality, and I assume you to yours."

"But after all, we *both* live in Los Angeles. How about it, Cable?"

"I don't think so, Flo. You see, it's this way. Since 1927, when I was a cop for the Los Angeles Police De-partment, I got mixed up with other dimensional be-ings, almost married a hybrid half-alien, have a friend who is kind of like an other-worldly counselor to me, and have a diabolical organization after my ass because I know too much. What I'm trying to say is that it's hard

57

for me to see my way past that *right now*, if you know what I mean. And there is a little gal I've just started seeing...I wouldn't want to hurt her by starting up with some other beautiful babe." I was dressing while we talked and I noticed my trousers had a pretty large wet place just about where my knees were.

She looked down at the ground and started shifting pine needles around with her foot. "I knew you was a mysterious man. What I didn't know was that you keep livin' on the edge...the tie that binds us to the grave. On the other hand, I could say it's because I'm black and you're white that I'm takin' a back seat to some Caucasian female. You saw me like some hot little number dancin' my little ass off, up in front of everybody in church this morning, didn't you?—and I'll bet you thought 'she'd be a nice little piece of ass'—but don't take anything seriously with these folks, after all, they are inferior and pretty low on the priority list of Cable Denning's life." Her eyes were misting. "But I'm not going to think that, Cable. I feel you're a fine man and you take me as you find me. I like that best. Of course I'm disappointed, but that's just like life, ain't it? I find someone who feels good in my arms and between my legs—and zip! He's not available. The story of my life."

I reached for Flo but she backed away. She grabbed her clothes from off the ground and began to dress. "None of that negative shit is true, Flo. We came up the hard way—both of us—you know what it took to make either of us rise above the stench and dismal hopelessness of being born in the ghetto and pulling ourselves up by the bootstraps to be somebody, *anybody*, someone with self-worth, someone who rose up to be better

58

than the sum total of our parts, being able to plug our talents in so the world wouldn't notice we came from a dung heap on the back lot of some cesspool called ignorance and poverty. Like me, you used what wits and talents you had, to get you where you are today. Growing up isn't holding hands with someone nice who lives down the lane, or someone other than ourselves we can count on. The 'School of Hard Knocks' has taught us *that*—yeah, no free lunches, no handouts, not even that extra kind word from the preacher or butcher or the guy or gal who seems friendly—but in truth, everyone wants something—just like you and me today—I would be lying if I told you I wasn't thinking of that warm, wet pussy of yours when you were dancing your little heart out up there in church and your panties were on parade flashing by me, or that you didn't want something from me, a cunning woman with desire or curiosity to have a white cock inside of her because it might feel different. Isn't that the kind of truth we're used to? Isn't that the thing we have to face every week of our lives—the confession to self that life stinks and it's a hell of a lot harder when we're not born with a silver spoon in our mouths, but instead we were raised on moldy oatmeal and a roof that leaked when it rained, and wore hand-me-down clothes that never quite fit? That's where we came from, Flo...so forgive me if I seem a little hard boiled and see life from a different hilltop than most people."

She was flabbergasted with my rhetoric. But now she was crying openly. "God...now I *know* I'm fallin' in love with you! I'm so confused, Cable...I want to give *me* to someone, and I want him—do you hear me? I said I want to give me to someone...just as I would want us to feel a genuine belongin' that's not likely to be goin' away any time soon." She wiped her tears with her naked arm. "But I'm tellin' you, Mister, I never heard no human man ever talk like you just did. How do you think up them words so fast?"

I chuckled. "Forget it, Flo, it's just a gift of gab I have. I get on a roll now and then, and words just come tumbling out in some kind of flow or rhythm, I don't know—it just happens."

"I'll say..." She finished dressing. Then she shrugged her shoulders. "Well, even if we never do it again, it was wonderful, Cable. And yes sir! You are one intense lover man. Now I'm going to smell you until I get home and wash. Which reminds me, I gotta avoid Mamma Earth— she's got a nose on her, she does. She'd be smellin' you on me and would probably tar and feather the both of us."

We laughed. "Yeah, Flo, thank you, too...and maybe Mamma Earth is right, maybe you don't know when to take your panties off, or leave them on..."

"Oh, yes I do, Mr. Smarty. It was right takin' 'em off for you. I'm just thinkin' of how I'm gonna suffer the consequences of withdrawal...in case...in case I get to hankerin' in the middle of the night when that place between my legs aches and my chest starts breathin' fast and hard and heavin' like a hussy in heat."

I had no answer for her. We walked back out into the clearing that led to Mamma Earth's little shack. We embraced but said nothing. I watched as she pulled away and walked down the little lane back toward the village.

It was hard saying good-bye to Mamma Earth. She had not only saved my life, but became my guide and teacher of those simple wisdoms that make up fundamental answers to life—the ones we all complicate with our egos and endless striving to mess up what is already perfect. We treat each other like strangers and often neglect or mistreat those closest to us. But I was reminded by Mamma Earth, that in the nest where we all come from, we're joined at the hip of creation, like it or not. Sure I'm a loner, but I still seek out that dark, smoky den in the middle of the night when the sound of music pulls me in like a pied piper and some babe with a warm, sexy singing voice draws me to her, becomes the director of love, tears, joy and regret that haunts every human heart. Then we drink and laugh and cry with each other, joining in that timeless ritual of camaraderie until the sun comes up and it reminds us life is a strange discord of contrasts, and that we are *both*, the isolated loner and the seeker of mirth and life and love with others.

And Floradine Louisa Carpenter? I never saw her again. Mamma Earth was spot on. We were the right ships crossing on the wrong night, bound for different destinations. But I would always remember my days in the foothills of the San Gabriel Mountains.

Chapter 3

THE EVIL THAT MEN DO

I hitched a ride in a poultry truck bound for Pasadena, full of cackling chickens. Big Judah had given me a few bucks with the promise I would send it back to him via the mails when I got back to L.A. I took a bus and finally the trolley to Franklin Avenue. I couldn't find a phone anywhere on my journey, so I was arriving unexpected. I had been buried in my clothes and Mamma Earth had washed them as best she could. She also washed any paper money I might have had. So all that was useful in my pockets were my keys and a pocket comb.

I climbed the stairs to my office on the second floor. The door was open so I walked in. Zelda was leaning against my desk talking to a very pale-skinned man about my height, but thinner. He had very blonde hair and piercing blue eyes. He got up to greet me. Zelda ran to me with no regard that there was someone else in the room. "Cable!" she cried as she embraced me. "Are you okay—why didn't you call?"

"Sorry, babe, I came in on a chicken truck to Pasadena, then took the bus and streetcar to get here. I tried, but couldn't find a public phone." Zelda backed away as I faced the man in my office. "And you might be?" I asked, checking the guy out pretty good.

He decidedly enunciated with a heavy German accent and his voice was clear and low. He clicked his heels together, bowed and spoke very crisply. "I am

Helmut Becker, Mr. Denning. I am delighted I foundt you." Then he looked at my disheveled clothing and sun-tanned face. "But I see your last adfenture must have tousled you somevat. Vill you be afailable tomorrow? I am fery...dessirous...to speak vis you."

"Yeah, I guess so, but not until mid-afternoon. I have a lot of catch-up work to do. I've—I've been gone...quite a while," I said, looking over at Zelda who couldn't wait for the man to leave.

"Very vell, zen. Say sree o'clock? I shall be prompt. I make it a point to be precise about tzings. I hope you practice ze same disciplines, Mr. Denning?"

"Well, I don't know about that. But three is fine."

He reached into his pocket, walked over to my desk where Zelda stood and counted out five one-hundred dollar bills and plunked them on the desktop. "Zis...iss a retainer...it iss yours to keep...vezer ve do business—or not. For ze pleassure of meeting ze famous private infestigator, Cable Denning."

"That's awful generous of you, Becker, but I don't know if I'm *that* famous. What if I disappoint you?"

He laughed. "Ya...das iss goodt—to haff humor! Und you vill not disappoint. I haff confidence in zat. I am hopeful ve may vork togezer." He glanced over to Zelda and bowed. "Miss Blodgett, delighted to haff met you." Then he exited and quietly closed the door behind him.

Zelda and I looked at each other in silence. Then she walked over to me and held me. She was quietly crying. I stood there holding her like a parent holding a child who had fallen down and scraped her knees. Finally she spoke, whimpering. "Weeks, Cable...weeks of not knowing. The last thing I remember is waiting for you at the curb as you went back to lock up the office. I waited fifteen, maybe twenty minutes. I went back upstairs and found the handkerchief. I just *knew* something terrible had happened." She looked up into my face. "I called the police—and you were right—they were absolutely no help. I don't know if I can live like this. What other women have you put through the ringer until everything except the love is squeezed out?"

"Probably most of them, Zelda. I promised you nothing—getting involved with me intimately. In fact, if you'll remember, I fought it for months. I didn't want you to go through what you just went through."

She ignored my statement and studied me. "You've lost a lot of weight. You're pants are barely hanging on you. I've got to fatten you up a little."

"You mean you still want to see me after—after all that?"

She stepped back to look at me. "Maybe when a girl's freshly in love she'll suffer through a lot more long absences and an emaciated lover. How often do things like this happen? In fact, I still don't know what happened."

"In a nutshell, I got chloroformed, kidnapped, injected with poison in a secret laboratory, bitten by the largest snake you ever saw, died and got buried in an abandoned church cemetery, got resurrected by a kindly old black woman and her strapping son and she happened to be a healer in the best sense of the word. And here I am..."

"Gees...that's terrible—ghastly! And you're really telling the truth, aren't you?" Zelda's eyes were suddenly very wide-open and her words measured.

64

I decided to leave out the part about Flo and our little escapade in the forest. "Yep, you know me, kid, I'm the truth guy, remember?"

"I don't know how you survived the nightmares you just described, Cable, but to tell you *my* truth, I really don't want to know. What you just described was like going to some kind of horror movie—and if it's a reality, then it's outside my ken, mister. And I think I prefer to look the other way. Is it possible for us to resume where we left off?"

"I don't know, is it? There's one good aspect about this whole thing: to some people I'm officially dead and they won't be looking for me for a while." I didn't like the serious look on Zelda's face. I knew something had changed in her. Maybe spending all those days and nights in a turmoil of uncertainty—not to mention my own predicament—made her withdraw her feelings in order to protect herself. Sometimes love hurts. "I wouldn't blame you if you dumped me," I said, feeling that it might be best for both of us in the long run.

She looked at me even more surprised. "I hope you're joking, Mister Denning. In case you've forgotten, on the morning of the night you disappeared—and the night before—I was deflowered by you in the most ardent of ways. I gave myself to you. I bonded with you and somewhere along the way I fell in love with you. Now you're suggesting that I dump you just because you've been gone for several weeks without explanation, leaving me with a thousand questions and the office to run alone? That would make me want to dump you? Naw...not me, Mr. Private Detective. I don't know exactly what it is, but becoming a woman with you seems to have matured something in me, like overnight. Notice I'm not so condescending all of a sudden. I thank you for that, Cable. Maybe for the first time in my life I'm really thinking and acting on my feet. So the answer is *no*—I don't want to dump you and I want you to take me home right now and make love to me."

She was right, I had never heard Zelda Blodgett talk like that. "That sounds swell, Zelda—but you can't go around making demands on people who may or may not be in the same mood you're in," I said, raising my voice a bit.

"Oh, are we having our first argument, Cable? Because if we are, then let's not shout or yell at each other, okay? Maybe a couple of pairs of boxing gloves would be better."

We both laughed. "Come here, babe," I said. She ran back into my arms and I kissed her hard. "Yeah...I could probably get in that mood you're talking about with a little coaxing from my friend here. Let's go home and tomorrow you can fill me in on all the office crap."

"Okay, but your mother called several times while you were gone. I didn't know exactly what to say. I just told her you were away on an assignment."

"Thanks, Zelda...that was the right thing to do. I've gotta go see her. Ever meet my Mom? She's a wonderful woman—a lady."

"I'd like to meet her," Zelda said. I always got that feeling when someone you're currently bedding wants to meet your mother, she's interested in getting on the approved "check-list" of prospective wives. But that's just my take on it. I know Adora and my mother got on great as two women who simply liked each other a lot. Who knows?

During the night after Zelda and I made love, a song kept rattling through my brain, haunting me. The voice sounded like Misty Sheridan singing '*I Cried for You*' but it really wasn't true. I didn't think Misty was crying over me. She had proved to be a frightened little girl inside, and at best, a fair-weather friend. And I was never sure of her sexual orientation. '*I cried for you, now it's your turn to cry over me...*' the lyrics went. Sometimes your brain tortures you like someone putting a pillow over your face and socking you from the other side of it. You go through those places of fear and falling down that endless rabbit hole, your brain sputtering out all the doubts and fears you have inside, and then your fears come true, because you attracted them and so you cross the street only to have a Mack truck hit you at eighty miles-an-hour--and suddenly you're splattered all over town and the pieces of flesh that once were you, suddenly come to life and become living duplicates. Hundreds of them, hundreds of you, walk up and down the busy thoroughfares, dodging into a nightclub, walking into a haberdashery, standing on a corner watching a sexy skirt walk by, or sitting alone in some rotten bar nursing a gin tonic and smoking a Lucky Strike there in the dark. Maybe in the end, we cry for ourselves. '*Every road has a turning,*' the lyrics said, '*and that's one thing you're learning...*' But who knows when that moment is? Who knows when the deck gets shuffled and you find yourself on Easy Street sucking on Manhattans from the 30th floor penthouse? Life's funny that way. Everything you thought wasn't relevant somehow *becomes* relevant and those Eddie Cantor movies aren't really that funny, they're just *life*, the pratfalls and happenstances that make the mosaic called human existence. For the most part, we think ourselves into what we become. We cry foul when the wind turns against our sails and the sea gets too choppy to navigate anymore. And a lot of people give up then, sitting it out on the sidelines, coasting through this unbearable existence without contributing even one piece of yesterday's toast crumbs to the world, supplying no legacy— and in the end, leaving behind no trace of their having been at all.

After she got me kick-started and caught up in the morning, I gave Zelda a couple of days' off. Punctually at 3:00 p.m. in walked Helmut Becker, spotlessly dressed in a light-brown suit with reddish tie, a wide-brimmed European dark-brown hat and brown shoes so shiny you could use them to comb your hair. I noticed an emblem on his tie that reminded me of some ancient symbol I had seen before in a book I was reading on the meaning of symbols. Carl Jung had done some research on what he called the '*collective unconscious*' and symbols were an important part of what humans drag up from many thousands of years of symbolisms and their meanings. Now I remembered where I had seen the black bent-cross inside a red border. The *swastika* had been featured in the Los Angeles Times as the emblem for a new National Socialistic party in Germany, if I recalled right. But I knew it was many thousands of years old—having its origin in antiquity somewhere, from the Indus Valley, Mesopotamia, to swastika geometry on woven baskets 600 years before Christ. I got up as my most recent benefactor walked into the room, approached my desk, extending his hand. "Herr Denning—*guten tag!*...und I hope I am on time for our *verabredung*."

I took his hand. It was tight and solid with not a lot of flesh attached to it. "Yes, you're just as punctual as you said you'd be, Becker...if you mean our meeting."

He looked around the room. Then he spied Zelda's plants. "Vun can alvays appreciate...a voman's touch, eh? Ze spider plant iss particularly appealing to me. No doubt ze industry off your comely little secretary, Miss Blodgett. Her fahzer iss a German-American scientist, most able. He had cross-coded different fruits of ze vorldt—most notably ze berry family—und fame rode into hiss stable, so to say, viz ze giant strawberry."

"Yeah, I know about that. But how would *you* know? Zelda has told me about his formidable accomplishments. It's hard to beat the old German brain—I mean, when you think of Goethe, Beethoven, Schubert, Schiller, Herschel, Wagner—even Gustav Mahler, whose fourth symphony I happen to be fond of. Especially that slow movement...it kind of transports me."

Becker scowled. "Ze first vuns you mentioned, are genuine German championss of genius, but Mahler iss a Jew, und his vorks are considered...vell, let us just say...*inferior*."

"I see," I said, knowing the score behind the rising anti-Semitic movement in parts of Europe. "So I guess Mozart, Karl Marx, Mendelssohn and Einstein don't count then."

"Not ven compared to ze superiority of ze German mind und ze unadulterated pure blood off ze true German people. Ze Jews know how to 'market' zemselves to seem more zan zey are, Herr Denning."

I didn't want to go any further with *that* prejudice. "So...you laid five-hundred smackers across my desk yesterday. What can I do for you?"

He fiddled with his dark-brown tie. "Ve know...many tzings...about you, und Miss Blodgett...but vat brings me here? Vell, ve have information zat leads us to believe zat you haff—in your possession—certain knowledge haffing to do viz ze high science of *electromagnetic repulsers,* vich are usually used in conjunction viz *capacitated light absorbers*, Herr Denning. You may haff heard ze term, *anti-gravity*?"

"I can't say that I have, Becker. But it sounds interesting." I wanted to change the subject. "I notice the ancient bent cross emblem on your tie. Old women wove baskets using that symbol long before Christ. Whoever designed the white background with the red border has adopted it most attractively. What does it represent in today's modern setting?"

"*Danke.* It is ze emblem of ze National Socialistic Party in Deutschland. Just as you here in America vill soon haff a new leader, so vill ve. A champion off a new vorldt for a pure peoples, *Ze Sird Reich* iss about to be born, Herr Denning, und vill last a sousand years, putting to shame ze inferior races who *detract* from ze purity off our *ubermensch*, a people destined to rule..." His eyes widened and he seemed to take a bus to some other disturbed place within him.

Yeah, I know about him. He's gonna come out with guns smokin' and take out anybody who doesn't agree with him, right?

"Vell, I vouldn't say zat...but you haff a point...how—uh, how, vould *you* know about our future *Führer?*"

"Let's just say I got it from the horse's mouth. The one who personally picked your so-called 'Führer'. A creature-who-would-be-God and groomed him since his conception."

"Vas iss zis you say, Herr Denning?" Becker inquired with rapt attention.

"I shouldn't have told you that much. But it doesn't really matter, because causes like yours are hell-bent until you destroy yourselves in the end. Your *Hitler*, isn't even all human. He's a plant, Becker, bred and born through a human female, but just as alien as Louis Pasteur's virulent microbes killing off people with warm milk. You're following a creature bent on his *own* brand of world domination. And guess what? In the end he'll play you Krauts for the sucker, win or lose. And you know why? Because it doesn't matter to him if a whole nation of people follow this Pied Piper Hitler, right to their own destruction. There's always another chump waiting around the corner. He picked you guys because just now he happens to be pre-occupied with a warrior-like daughter who's waged a war on him, and he could be gone quite a while." I took out a cigarette and offered one to Becker. He declined, so I lit up and sat back in my comfy chair. He was intensely studying my face. "So, you can understand why I saw you coming. I was fore-warned by the old sly one himself as he was trying to find ways to split my head open and reveal the kernel

71

under the walnut shell. So don't bullshit *me* about your superior race crap, because from where I sit on top of the hill, I can see you're being led down the garden path of total annihilation if you fail—and servitude to a nutso alien if you succeed in killing off half the world's population."

Helmut Becker just sat there shaking his head. "I cannot belieff vun man could know so much as you do Herr Denning. Maybe you know...*too* much. And ze vay you orate—you could easily come to vork...for us...und be handsomely paidt, viz ze best of liffing conditions, beautiful vomen surrounding you—und ze opportunity to excel in ze vorld beyond your vildest dreamss. I could offer you zat."

"Thanks, but no thanks, Becker. You see, I'm an Irish immigrant's son, white skinned and pure all right, but not your kind of pure. I grew up in a slum with foul air from nearby factories and foul, emotionally damaged and underprivileged kids who fought daily for a place in the sun—one tiny scoopful of real estate someone else didn't want to take from them. You Huns have a different mindset, the kind that can't quite get it, that it's not a race of people that counts, but the *individual*, and you'll never know when you pull the trigger to kill someone, whether you might've liked them."

He mused quietly for a moment. "Privately, I share your view...but you see, in my official capacity, ze mechanism of vorld domination ofer a stupid race of people takes, shall ve say, a most enjoyable *priority* over vat you might consider an equitable treatment off individual human beings. So vun Pollock is as dead as ze next Pollock, und so fors..."

I took Becker's five-hundred bucks out of desk drawer and tossed it across the desktop toward him. "In that case, I don't see how we can do business, Becker. Here's your dough. I'm a busy man."

He looked surprised. "But I *vant* you to keep it. Zat vas my pledge to you yesterday. Und incidentally, I don't belieff you are quite as ignorant regarding ze *antigravity* knowledge as you say. My sources indicate, Herr Denning, you know a great deal more...zan you are currently villing...to *share*, shall ve say?"

"I'm going to say it for the last time, Becker—I know nothing about the mechanisms of space ships or flying saucers or whatever the hell you're talking about. I've got nothing to hide. You already know other things about me, and inasmuch as I've been exposed to other dimensional creatures, there is no testimony to the existence of extra-terrestrial spacecraft with operational systems as you describe. The beings I've been exposed to don't need three-dimensional travel vehicles to get around—they've overcome gravity in a different way— simply by teleporting *themselves*."

His face lit up. "Exactly! Oh, please, do keep ze money, Herr Denning. You see, *zat is exactly* vy ve vant you to vork for us. You haff obserffed ze process by vich zese ozzer dimensional beings, as you say, effortlessly move about in ze unifferse. Such a discovery vould revolutionize everysing—because it can be appliedt to terrestrial spacecraft used in varfare. Ve haff already almost perfected a peerless veapon zat vill shoot concentrated light beams at tze enemy, searing ze flesh und carrying on—vell, right srough ze body. Uncover *zat* knowledge for uss und ve vill make you ze richest man in America!"

I thought for a second. "Or the deadest...what makes you think I'd trust you guys any further than I could throw you, Becker? I may be younger than a lot of your scientists and a lot more stupid—but I ain't *that* stupid!"

"I like ze vay you talk, Herr Denning—somevere between a man of knowledge und a cowboy. You could easily be a spokesman for ze *cause* here in America. How about it?"

"You know, Becker, it's never been just about money for me. Yeah, sure, I gotta eat and keep a roof over my head or end up in skid row and all, like the next guy, but if you don't do what you love in this world, you end up dead on arrival at the local morgue without a legacy, or at least the knowledge that you did what you wanted to do with your life. Ever feel that way?"

"Yes...as a matter of fact...all ze time. I am *enchanted* viz vat I do. And ze benefits are many. By ze vay, it comes to me by vay of checking up on you, zat you frequent musical bars und enjoy ze Jewish composers like Berlin, Gershwin, Kern, Hammerstein, Rodgers? Secretly, I adore zeir music, but I am not allowed to say so publicly. Anyvay, I have recently enjoyed an evening out at a new nightspot called *Ze Trocadéro*. Zere is a beautiful young voman who sings viz a varm, sensual voice—and va-va-voom! Her feminine attributes are equally stimulating. I highly recommend you, uh, how iss it you say? 'Catch her act.' Her name iss Julie Halliday, her signature gown iss light lemon sequins viz almost see-srough breast design. Appealing, to say ze least, especially to a young und virile man such as yourself."

"Thanks for the tip. I've heard of the club opening, just never been. I'll go check it out."

"Zo…vere do ve stand, Herr Denning?

"Where *do* we stand?"

"Vell, I am hopeful zat you retain my five-hundred dollar gift. All I vould ask in return is zat you *obserff* zose ozzer dimensional creatures you speak off. You might effen ask zem how zey do vat zey do, eh?" Then his expression became squint-eyed and sinister. "As it iss, Herr Denning, you already know too much. You see, I am, shall ve say, *assignedt to you*. Yet you are valuable to us—so vat to do? It also occurs to me zat I sink I might like you—as a man und person. You have vat ze French call, a certain *panache*. So, how about it? You vork secretly for me, I vork secretly to keep you aliffe—does zat not sound equitable? Vizout me, I do suspect your life span vill be quite limited."

I squirmed in my comfy chair. "That's sounds to me like an offer I can't refuse, Becker. I don't know what it is about you guys, but you seem to trade in human life as if it were a commodity."

"Zat's vat ve do…zere is no more to it." He reached across the table to take my hand. For whatever reasons, I extended mine. "Zo…I vill be checking in on you periodically. Until ve secure an experimental laboratory und headquarters in America, I vill be back and forth to Deutschland." He took a printed card out of his pocket. "Zo…if anysing of significance should occur, telegram me at zat address in Germany."

He got up to go, straightened his tie and donned his handsome brown hat. "Thanks for the dough, Becker. It just so happens you came along at precisely the right time, talking about you Krauts and your precision."

"I am glad for zat, Herr Denning." He bowed and clicked his heels together. "From our Prussian ancestors ve haff learned zat often ze enemy is vizin...so do not betray us, I beseech you. Only ill tidings can come of such singss, I'm sure you know." Then he remembered something. "I almost forgot. Ve haff an assignment already for you. Ze most likely candidate for president off your country, Franklin Roosevelt...German by extraction, and of course not Jewish...anyvay, he iss scheduled to meet viz a very high und influential figure in ze German hierarchy. Zere iss a secret meeting room—und an equally secret double vall srough vich you can hear conversation on ze ozzer side. I vould like you to attend. You vill gain entrance to ze building as a regular looking Irish-American, zus raising no suspicion. You vill be guided vonce you are inside, by a Günter Zoringer. He vill know you. You vill travel by train to Vashington, D.C. in sree veeks time, arriving in Vashington on September the 8th."

I was a bit miffed that Becker was already making demands of me. "Are you asking me or telling me I've gotta do this thing?"

"It doesn't matter. Ve need ze job done und you need ze money. Not only vill all your expenses by paid for, but upon your return ve vill giff you a healthy bonus of two-sousand fife-hundred American dollars, vonce you haff giffen us a full report."

"Doesn't that mean I'm kind of spying on my own country?"

"Call it vat you like. I vould call it eaffesdropping for a fee."

I walked him to the door. "Yeah, I think I kind of know that, Becker. It's kind of on the edge of betraying my country—I'll do it because they're also crooks, those guys who tell secrets behind closed doors and fraternize with a potential enemy—and still have the guts to call themselves *Americans*. But you know, I've lived on the edge between life and death most of my life, first as a ghetto rat fighting off the ethnic gangs, then as a cop and now people like you who want to rule the world."

"Vell, vat can I say, in your slang-filled language, ve might say, 'zat's ze vay it goess,' eh?"

He walked out and the phone rang. "Yeah, Cable Denning here."

"Cable, this is your mother. I was so concerned. Are you alright, my son? Your nice secretary told me you've been away on an assignment, but I detected worry in her voice...as if—"

"—hi, Mom, I'm fine. Just a few unexpected turns, that's all. I'm on top of it now."

"Good...you don't know how relieved I am to know you're okay. By the way, your Aunt Lily died during your absence and willed me her home on Vine Street, you know, the one up on top of the hill?"

"Wow! That's great, Ma! Now you can live in a decent neighborhood and have plenty of space. I'd like to come see you—how about this weekend—are you gonna be home?"

"Where do *I* go, Cable? The neighborhood is even less safe than when you were a child. There are increasing numbers of black people moving in from the other side of Boyle Heights. They're forming gangs and fighting the Italians and Mexicans, always for territory. Oh, dear, it never changes, does it?"

"It seems that way, Mom. So what about Saturday? And I'd like to bring Zelda—the secretary you've been talking to on the phone."

There was a pause. "Is she your new flame, Cable? I know it's been hard for you after Adora...I miss her terribly. She fit you so well." She took a deep breath. "But life moves on, and I will be happy to meet your young sounding secretary."

"Say....Saturday around noon?"

"That would be fine. See you then. I love you, son— and I'm happy you're back safe and sound. We'll talk about the Vine Street house—remember—it was 2166 on the corner?"

"Yeah, I do. Your sister was kind of a recluse, wasn't she? I mean, we were only there three or four times since I was a kid, right?"

"Lily was odd. When your Uncle George died, she seemed to float, sort of like I did when your father passed on. It's hard, you know...."

"Yeah, I know, Mom....see you Saturday with Zelda, okay?" We hung up and I was looking forward to visiting her.

I called Zelda but she wasn't in, so I sat back in my comfy chair, trying to figure out how in the hell I get embroiled in so damn many intrigues. Now I had a secret agency of the frickin' German government after me. I had the sense I'd better walk the straight and narrow with these guys. I had the feeling they meant what they said. As I was in deep thought the phone rang. "Yeah, Cable Denning here."

"Well, don't sound so removed, Mister," Zelda's happy voice announced. "I was out in the garden when the phone rang and I thought it might have been you. Did you call? I don't know why, but since you came back, all of a sudden I feel domestic."

That gave me a slight shiver. "Yeah, I did try to call. Them's pretty dangerous words you're sputterin' there, lady. Does that mean you're scheming to entrap me with your plants—or your love?"

"Maybe both...Gees, Cable, I miss you so much. You know we're still making love unprotected. But I love it. Maybe I can't have babies. All I know is that it feels so good having you in me and smelling you after you've left for the office, like today."

I smiled to myself. Dames are odd, I thought. "You like that, huh?" I queried her.

"Yep...I don't know how I'd live without it. In such a short time, you made me part of you, Cable. I mean I know independent Zelda still exists, but there's another part of me that's just as happy belonging to someone. Sounds stupid, doesn't it?"

"Naw, I think it's just human nature—and a lot of women are wired like a radio to be receptive to a man, and she tunes her station in to him. I think it's kind of special, to tell you the truth."

"Do you, really?"

"Yep. Say, my Mom called and said she just inherited a real nice house from my Aunt Lily, who died during my absence. It's at the end of Vine Street, not too far from the Hollywood Dam and just a hop, skip and jump from my office. Anyway, she wants to meet you—how's Saturday about noon?"

"You mean it, Cable? You really want me to meet her? What do you think she'll think of me?"

"Hmmm....scandalous, sensual, gold digger type, definitely a hussy out after my bedroom manners and of course my millions..."

"Really? She won't think that...will she?"

"Oh, I'm just joshin' ya, doll. Of course Mom will see you as intelligent, safe, dependable, punctual—"

"—sounds like a good pocket watch. I don't want to be a pocket watch to your mother. How will she see I'm good for you?"

"By how much sex we have during the week? I don't know. Women sense women, Zelda. I'll leave that up to you two."

"Oh...well—anyway, yes...I'll be happy to meet her. Are you coming over tonight? You'll notice I haven't been sore anymore when we make love. I'm getting broken in, I guess."

I laughed. "Yeah—you sure are, sweetheart."

"You just called me *sweetheart*. That's the first time you've called me that."

"Eh....don't let it get to you...I call everybody sweetheart. One of those innocent colloquialisms."

"Do you think we could have a getaway sometime soon? Maybe spend a weekend by the ocean or something? Would you enjoy that? If I don't mention it, you'd probably never think of it..."

"Yeah, you're probably right. Sure, that sounds fine. By the way, I have to travel to Washington, D.C. in a couple of weeks or so. How about that getaway after I get back? I'll be a couple of grand richer, too!"

"Cable! That's great! So Helmut Becker turned out to be a good client then, huh?"

"I don't know if I'd say that—but he's generous with someone else's money—so why not?"

"So you didn't answer—are you coming over tonight?"

Yeah, sure...I've got a few things to finish up here—what if I call before I come?"

She got a naughty tone in her voice. "You'd better come first—and then call out my name in the dark, Mister. I love it when you come in me and get so excited you keep calling out my name."

"I do that? Hell, it happens with all my babes, babe."

"Oh, you! You always make light of something that is very precious and meaningful to me."

"It is to me, too, Zelda. I'm sorry...I'm just a big mouth. See you soon."

"Yes...but never soon enough, Cable...good-bye..."

We hung up and I lit up another Lucky Strike, poured a small shot of cheap gin and sat back thinking of my workload.

Things were coming down on top of me like the San Francisco earthquake and I was pinned under the debris that humans conjure up for each other because nobody's contented with who they are or where they fit or don't fit. People are born in the middle of things that are already in the middle of things, and in that confusion they do unto others for a myriad of reasons that define the parameters of their misery and dissatisfaction with the human condition. But they hide it and conform because fear motivates the everyday psyche and governments cash in on it, because nothing controls others like fear. There's a kind of moral *norm* that people define themselves by, an illusion where they feel it's safe to be part of the moral majority of their tribe, go to church on Sunday, walk in the park, shop at the same places, vote for the same idiot that pulled the wool over their eyes last election, keep a stagnant regimen of everydayism and make sure their children grow up just like them. Thus the status quo becomes a quagmire of sameness and stagnation. And what happens to those who dwell on the fringes of the accepted norm? They become the outcasts, the loners, the mentally and emotionally unbalanced, the rejects of society, judged because they *don't* fit into the conformity of an homogenized experiment called the United States of America, a dream of ideals glued together by a constitution that had already been amended more times than Carter had pills. Anyway, it all ended up by the rich getting richer and the poor supporting the rich so they get even richer while the poor got washed down the drain to oblivion.

Speaking of which, I had a hunch I should consult my old friend Crazy Jack, so I hitched a streetcar down to Los Angeles Street where the leftovers of society hung out as the last stop before ending up wrapped in a cardboard box headed for the local morgue. The nameless invisibles, I called them. There they existed, in the world but not a noticeable part of it, cast onto the sea of desperation and insanity.

Jack lived on the top floor of the four-story Panama Hotel near 5th and San Julian streets, a rundown heap of a place where you could eat well if you caught a rat crossing your dinner table. It had been some time since I had seen Crazy Jack. He was born psychic and was nuttier than a fruitcake. Or was he? I knocked on his door. "Hey, Crazy Jack, it's me—Cable Denning—your old buddy!" There was no answer. Jack had warned me about keeping Honey out of the *Bella Notte*, a nightclub on Wilshire that was owned by the big time players of the local Mafia, run by a guy named Jack Dragna. But a jealous, unbalanced killer by the name of Frank Laggore killed Honey with his .38 because he couldn't have her—and because I beat the shit out of him and threw him off a moving train some months before. "I got some Lucky Strikes for you, Jack...are you hangin' around in there?"

I heard a rustling. "I don't know! I don't know!" Then the door opened and there stood Crazy Jack. "Cigarette! Cigarette! Cable...see you! Cigarette!"

"So how've you been?" As was our ritual, I took out a Lucky Strike, gave him one, lit it up for him and tucked the rest of the pack into his shirt pocket.

"I don't know! I don't know! Jack sick! Sleep lots..."

"I always seemed to catch you when I'm squeezed like a sandwich between a rock and a hard place, eh? I've got some new barnacles about to attach themselves to me—what can you tell me about them?"

"Good cigarette," he said, puffing away as if his life depended on it. "World change...bad men! They want Cable Denning—but I don't know! I don't know!"

"What do they want me for, Jack?"

"I don't know! I don't know! Jack sees...*gold... knowledge*...poor people...country...war...war caused by people with slant-eye! But I don't know! I don't know! Think Jack sick, Cable. Now...breathe...hard..." His hair was mussed and tousled on the top of his head as if he'd had a thousand mornings without ever washing or combing it.

I was wondering where in the hell the "slant eyed" thing came from. But I never knew Jack to be wrong—about *anything* he ever prophesied. If war was coming....hell, I thought it would be the Germans, under such subtle manipulators like Helmut Becker. "I'm sorry you've been sick, Jack." I took a twenty out of my pocket and gave it to him. "Here...buy yourself a good couple of bottles of gin. Cures it all for me, chum. So what else do you see?"

"Ladies...lots of ladies—ha! ha!...Cable ladies...one green...happy to be with lots of green and pretty flowers...plants...she good...good heart for Cable—but I don't know! I don't know! She to give Cable little plant...that grow inside her...but she go away—oh!" Then he grimaced in pain. "Go 'way, Cable Denning— head hurt Jack too much—you dangerous—but I don't know! I don't know! Cigarette good!"

I knew the babe he was talking about was Zelda, but I couldn't make sense out of most of the rest of it. I thanked Crazy Jack and left. Late afternoon was turning into evening as I turned the corner at Los Angeles and

Main to catch the streetcar to Zelda's place. I thought I'd stop in a little speakeasy I used to frequent when I was a cop and have a quick drink. *Paddy's* was one of those places you step down into and find a world of the unknown familiar. Speakeasies were noisy concoctions of successful business people and mostly middle class men and women escaping from the humdrum of their everyday lives. A lively little combo played as a few couples danced among the crowded tables and chairs. Just then some babe in a shiny black outfit came up to me as I stood at the bar sipping a gin that came right out of someone's bathtub with the taste of their feet still in it. "Will you come with me, please?" the young woman in black requested of me.

"Why, lady? I'm pretty happy right here..."

"Please...I have been asked to bring you to someone. Come with me and I won't have to break your groin or your legs," she said in a matter of fact voice that made me think she meant it.

"Well, if you put it that way, I guess we'll take a walk." I felt for my .38 inside my breast pocket as we walked out the back door to an awaiting car. Once inside, the dark-haired little beauty with the tough look on her face blindfolded me—I knew the routine. I didn't fight it because somehow I didn't really feel threatened. Those fear-hackles weren't showing up on the back of my neck around my hairline. And I was right. We drove a few blocks into an alley, it seemed. I was ushered out of the car and into a building. We got into an elevator and descended. Then the blindfold was removed and the lady in black disappeared. Another woman, but this one in a very strange outfit—that of a female Viking warrior or the like. "Mr. Denning," she addressed me in a stern but polite voice. "You don't remember me, but I was in your office not too long ago."

I didn't remember the babe, and even though she had a nice figure, she wasn't anyone to write home about, either. I was led into the very same room where I had heard the terrible voice of Cronus-Gor some weeks before—not to mention being shocked by his demented prank...putting Jane Slaughter's sliced-off hands into a covered silver server on the table and having me lift the lid.

"Cable...Cable...I am glad to see you...sorry about the way we had to get you here."

Suddenly I was looking at Hestia—better known as *Vesta*, Cassiopeia's vengeful and martial sister who now waged war on her evil father, Cronus-Gor. "Well, well, well...it goes to show...you never know who you meet when you walk the streets of Skid Row, now, do you?"

She laughed. "You always find a way to make people laugh. Cassiopeia told me that before she—she—"

"—yeah, say it, go ahead. Before she started to malfunction as my midnight lover—and got her rocks off, only to suddenly turn into a dime store mannequin and have no real flesh and blood in her—she sure seemed real to me."

"I know...that must have been terrible for you. But it was our mother's only way of mortalizing Cassiopeia before my father could get a hold of her and destroy her. Now she's back home and has a real body. At least her heart and spirit were here on the earth with you— and I know she was very fond of you, Cable." Vesta opened her cover vestments and exposed to me a pair of large, half-bared breasts. "I assure you, *my* body's real flesh and blood. I insisted on it after seeing what mother did to my sister. So...anytime you feel like fooling around with a half-Saturnian lady, let me know." Then she winked at me. "Only kidding."

I chuckled to myself. "So, how's the war with Dad going? His parting gift to me was a gigantic, deadly poisonous snake, modified to inject me with the world's most potent truth serum."

"Oh, dear, that's terrible. But he can sure think them up, can't he? Well, look around...you'll notice *I'm* in the old *Oculus* headquarters—*and he isn't*. My girls and I managed to force him off the planet in order to engage us in combat. So, I guess, I've summoned you to say good-bye, Cable. You were very good to my mother and sister. None of us will ever forget you."

"Well, you're a strange bunch of women, I'll say that," I said, still gazing at her bulging breasts. "And I hope you wipe your Dad's butt all over the universe. I don't see how lovely and intelligent females like you and your sister came out of an asshole like that. Goes to prove, it ain't necessarily *like father like daughter*, is it?"

"No, I suppose not. He's been a mean, selfish, greedy, lusting creature. I'm personally ashamed of him." Just then an alarmed young woman came racing in and informed Vesta that she was needed immediately. She ran up to me and kissed me squarely on the mouth. "I wanted to do that the first day I invaded your office. Thanks, Cable, for being the good guy to us—and good-bye. Have a good earth-life—maybe we'll meet again. If you ever have a son, send him our way—I mean, if he turns out to be anything like you."

She dashed off and I was led back to the elevator blindfolded. Soon I was out on the street again, still on my way to the streetcar stop, when I realized I wasn't very far from "Crazy Legs" Ziggy Thompson's *Pink Gables*. After all, she was the gal who saved my life from the deadly poisons of Boak the Magnificent. I walked down Broadway and saw the pink neon lights flashing on and off. I took a deep breath and walked around to the side of the joint as Ziggy had instructed me. I rapped on the door. The peek-window opened and an ugly mug checked me out. "Yeah?" he growled.

"Carmen sent me," I answered.

He opened the door and I entered a noisy room of colored lights and thick smoke, laughter, shouting and the usual drunks teetering at the bar. Up on the small stage three babes with very little on did their hoochy-koochy dance to the tune of some sexy blues number played by a combo of three. I spotted Ziggy Thompson and moved away from where the rest of the lecherous men stood trying to get a good view of a loose breast or an incidental crotch exposure. As the number finished, I waved to Ziggy and when she spotted me her eyes went wide and she clamored down the side stairs and came running to me. There in the middle of the room she jumped into my arms and kissed me deeply. "Oh, Cable! I thought I'd failed and guessed when they buried you—you were *really* dead!"

"Hiya, Ziggy. I'm here to keep my word—first to thank you for saving my life—and second, to honor my promise by taking you out to the best dinner and dancing date in town!"

She teetered back and forth. "I'm so glad to see you! Yes—I'd love to go out with you. You're still a damn handsome man, Cable Denning. See, I *do* remember your full name." She took my hand and led me through some backroom curtains and out into the alley. "Phew! Now we can talk. So...when can we have our evening together? I'm still with the laboratory and all. They killed Boak, because his natural venom kinda got all mixed up with the truth serum—and no one could control him, not even Daryl. Poor Boak kept hissing and growling and writhing and striking at the air until the Doc had him shot in his cage."

"Sorry to hear that. You know, for a minute I could swear he could really hear me and understand me...and if it weren't for your stupid Daryl agitating him, he may not have bitten me."

"You know, I can believe that. I could talk to Boak, too. I'd stand and talk to him at the front of his cage and he'd come over and listen to me."

I took out a couple of Lucky Strikes and offered one to Ziggy. She took it and I lit us both up. "I'm glad that's over, Ziggy. That was some kind of nightmare. Never want a repeat performance of that or anything like it!

"I don't blame you." She took my hand and put it on her face. "I'm so sorry I was part of bringing you so much—"

"—forget it, kid. We're here...now...and that's all that counts."

"So how did you get unburied and who saved you?"

"A wonderful old black woman who lived somewhere way the hell up in the hills—maybe fifty or sixty miles from town. She nursed me back to health—and here I am."

She quickly leaned up to kiss me. "Just checking to see if you're still warm and alive," she cracked. "So when can we go out and celebrate that you're still alive—and thank me for helping you?"

"Maybe a day next week? What days are you off work here or for Voracious?"

"Sunday or Monday...that's it."

"Well, how about next Monday night? We can go to a new place someone told me about—it used to be the Café La Boheme, but that was closed after it was raided," I chuckled. "Now it's called *The Trocadéro* and is *the* place to go—ever been?"

"No, but I know the singer there—Julie Halliday used to work here at the *Pink Gables.* She's a real good singer, too."

"So do you want me to pick you up Monday about seven or so?" I asked, not having a clue where this young woman lived. "By the way, I don't know how you do it, night after night, I mean flaunt your things out there in front of those dirty, lusting guys?"

"It's always about tits and pussy with guys, you know...so you show 'em a tempting bit of what they came for, they buy lots of cheap liquor and I keep my job."

"I see...so—shall I pick you up?"

"Nope...it's okay...I'll meet you there...how about eight?"

"You got it." She hugged me tight and told me again how glad she was to see me, but I was getting a little leery about just how *much* she missed me and she seemed a little...too...friendly with the Saturday night kisses she was tossing my way.

It was getting on to nine by the time I dragged myself into Zelda's little place. I knocked on the door. She answered. "I thought you were going to call before you came." She stood there in her slip. "And it's already after nine, Cable..."

I took a big breath. It was for these very reasons that I preferred a life alone. Sooner or later women make demands on you, want to haul in the rope they think they've got around your waist. "I thought *you* said you wanted me to come first, then call out your name in the dark. So, that's exactly what I'm gonna do." I took her hand and led her to her bedroom and pushed her onto the bed. I started peeling my clothes off and before she could do much more, I got onto the bed, and pulled her slip off, undid her bra and slipped her panties down her legs and threw them to the floor. Without a word I took my tongue and wiped it slowly up Zelda's leg. She trembled and moaned as I got closer to that magic palace between her legs. As my tongue licked the already thick, wet outsides and darted in and out of her most private sanctuary, she spread her legs more and more until she pulled me up into her and we made that kind of crazy, desperate love that teenagers do when everything is so clumsy and new.

When it was all over and she lay there sighing and breathing in the moment, I rolled off of her and whispered into her ear. "Zelda...Zelda...I'm calling Zelda...can she hear me?"

She pushed my head away with a big grin on her face. "Oh, you! Next time, gees, don't take me so literally. Now I'm all full of you again."

I smiled down at her. "I thought you liked that."

"I love it, Cable...I want to be saturated with you, like when I water my thirsty plants and the residual water rests in the bottom dish...I was thirsty for you."

I had never heard anything quite so quaint and lovely. "That's really a wonderful thing to say, Zelda. Thanks for that—thanks for wanting me that much. You might not think that I think about these things, but I do."

She got up and lit a candle by the bed. Then she looked at me with a lot of feeling in her eyes. "I'm happy that you do, Cable. Do it again sometime soon...water me, tend me, trim me—and I'm going to risk saying this—please *love* me."

I wanted to say it back to her.... say that I loved her. But it was always so damned trite, speaking those perfunctory words in a temporary state of sexual bliss. "Keep tuned, babe...and don't be too far away...and by the way, don't forget, we're visiting my Mom this Saturday—that still okay with you?"

We sat naked at the edge of the bed. "Yes, I'm looking forward to meeting her, but I'm worried about you going to Washington, D.C. I just have this feeling. I'm having second thoughts about this guy Helmut Becker. You know we talked before you got there that day. Now that I'm reflecting on it, I got the distinct feeling he was like two people. He decided to show me one of his faces.....and maybe you the other?"

"I don't know. Right now he's not breaking any laws or particular principles of mine that put up my red flags.

A little eavesdropping for pay here and there—hell, Zelda, it's what I do when I chase down some wife who's screwing her husband's best friend, isn't it?"

"I guess so, but just be careful. I mean, keep the eyes in the back of your head open, okay?"

"Yeah, okay..." We slipped under the covers and held each other as we drifted off into a peaceful sleep. Damn, I thought, the world was just about perfect right now— what else could a simple gumshoe raised in the dumps of East L.A. want?

Look Into The Sun

They say you should never look directly into the sun. It'll blind you. I think it's the same way with truth. A lot of people can't look into its center because it's too incredibly bright for them, so they avoid it. But something in me turned like the proverbial worm and I *had* to make truth my priority. Sure, sometimes little white lies slip in and out of human experience and we discount them as not having particular significance. But the big things, the glaring sunlight of fundamental bottom-line shit—now *that* revelation you can't avoid if you're a truth guy. Yeah, I'd like to take down guys like Herr Helmut Becker, Dr. Voracious, Cronus-Gor and all the mean sons-of-bitches who hammer truth into a convenient piece of hot metal they can bend with the anvil of ulterior motivation. But I'm not God—at least not today—and I can only do so much with each circumstance of truth I'm confronted with. So I do my best—and sometimes my best is good enough—and sometimes it isn't.

The other end of my truth was my thing with women. I loved women. Yet if I got too close and enmeshed in their Venus fly-traps, the pull of that siren moon would ensnare me into slavery and habit—and sooner or later, they'd start putting their clamps on me. Women seem to want to make the men in their lives part of their *The Project of the Month Club*. Maybe they don't mean it, but women are nesters and when the kids come, the guy seems to take a back seat, sentenced to mow the lawn on Saturday morning or putter in his garage to busy himself with hobbies that make him forget he's been relegated to second citizen status. Yep, avoid the temptress moon. Even my relationship with Zelda was heading toward some kind of unconscious regularity and I had to admit some kind of sexual addiction continuously attracted me to her bed. And that was the power of the Venus fly-trap that hooked you into her world, even though she needed you to make it work right. I don't know, maybe there was a balance somewhere. If one looked for flaws, I suppose one could find them. Honey was too independent, Adora too pliant, Zelda—too what? Time would tell.

Zelda met my mother with her usual tact and kindness. I could tell that her memory was beginning to fade when she incorrectly related certain memories and brought up unpleasant things of my childhood that were better off left alone. But I let it slide under the table. "So, Mom, when do you want me to help you move into the Vine Street house?"

"Oh, anytime next month. A lot of legal things have to clear before I can receive ownership. But I put it in your name, so when I die, it will already be yours, without any of the fuss these inheritance things tend to involve."

"Well, thanks, Mom. So...I'll get a couple of guys, myself—and maybe even the plant lady here to help us move you in. It's got a lot more space than there is here....will you be able to fill up the rooms so it'll look lived in?"

"I've decided to keep some of your aunt's furniture—and then give away some of what I have accumulated here. You know how it is. We scrape and save and then we have too much junk. You should see the garage, just full of things I'll never use again." Then she looked at Zelda. "What about you, dear? Are you and Cable planning to—to share a house? I've a lot of things you might want."

Zelda looked at me. "Well, Mrs. Denning, we have no plans that I know of. You do know I work for Cable."

Then my mother surprised me. "Yes, but I also know you sleep with him. I can see it in your eyes, young woman. It's okay. Cable will tell you I'm no prude. It's just that there have been so many women in his life—perhaps he's just a fickle man, not like his father—"

"—Mom!" I said, a little annoyed. "I don't think Zelda's private life is really your concern..."

"It would be if she comes through my door carrying your baby." She looked at an astonished Zelda. "Miss Blodgett, I've always wanted Cable to settle in with one woman and give me a grandchild. Do you know how lonely it is cleaning the house day after day, listening to the radio, or looking out the kitchen window washing the same dishes over and over—just to keep busy?"

Suddenly Zelda was crying and she got up, came around the table and draped herself over my mother, holding her. "I understand, Mrs. Denning. I know Cable's gone a lot—and it *is* lonely not having anyone to really talk to. Would you enjoy coming over to my little place and staying with me for a couple of days or so?"

My mother turned in her chair to face Zelda. "You...you would want an old lady for company? No one has ever asked me that—I don't know what to say."

"Just say yes and I'll come pick you up someday soon. How about when he's gone to Washington DC next week?"

I checked out both of their faces. I knew Zelda really meant it and I could see my mother was responding to her kindness. "Sounds good to me," I said. "I'll come over with Zelda and we'll both take you back to her place. I know you'll love all the different kinds of plants she has."

"Oh, do you have plants? I have a few, but it's so hard to keep them alive anymore —maybe like me, huh?" she laughed.

"Yes, my father was a botanist and invented a few cross-breeds, he became famous for a huge strawberry."

"You don't say? I'd be delighted to come stay with you—may I call you Zelda?"

"Please...do..."

Chapter 4

ALL THE GOLD IN THE WORLD

It was Monday, August 23, 1932. I found my way to *The Trocadéro*. By the time I entered and made a reservation it was 8:30 p.m. and there was still no sign of Ziggy Thompson. I went to the bar and ordered a lime drink and immediately poured half of my gin flask into it. By 9:00 p.m. the band was in place, the lights went down and on the stage walked a doll who nearly took my breath away. She was a dazzling light-yellow blonde with a maroon silk gown that fit around her like a second layer of skin. She wore nothing around her neck because it didn't need anything and her shoes were cordovan heels that shone in the spotlight. Her large blue eyes sparkled under the lights as well, and an attractive mouth with medium lips melted you where you stood when she smiled. Her voice was warm and had that kind of self-assurance that said, 'Hey, Mister, you want me? Well, let me taunt you a little bit more and *then* tell me how you feel?' She was singing a very classy version of *I've Got My Love to Keep Me Warm*—and for a minute I wished it was me who would be keeping her warm tonight.

There was a refined, well-dressed gentleman standing next to me at the bar. He was tall with blonde hair, blue eyes and when he spoke, he had an obvious Germanic accent. It seemed the whole land was being filled with Krauts. "Now...zat's a lady who can sing!" he remarked.

"I'll say," I answered, turning to check him out. There was no doubt, Julie Halliday gave Misty Sheridan a run for her money. Halliday's style was enigmatic, as if the voice didn't match the body somehow, yet they all came together up there on the stage. She wasn't unusually large busted, but what she had was pushed up and bulging healthfully out of the top of her gown. I estimated her to be about thirty because the voice and demeanor of the woman had a maturity about it I liked, as if she'd been around the block a few times but always in a classy setting.

When she finished, the tall blonde man sitting next to me spoke. "By ze vay, I'm Fritz." He reached into his pocket and drew out a fifty-cent piece. "Heads she comes to me...und I flirt viz her...tails she comes to you und *you* flirt viz her."

"What if she chooses some other bloke? I don't like the odds, Fritz. By the way, my name is Cable...Cable Denning..." We shook hands. Fritz flipped the coin and it came out heads. Hell, the babe was his.

Sure enough, after Julie Halliday finished her singing set, she came off the stage and made a beeline for the bar. "Harry," she addressed the bartender. "Did Herman call?" The bartender shook his head and she turned to look at Fritz and me. She smiled, but contrary to Fritz's predictions, she approached me—but not before pausing an instant to look at Fritz and I could have sworn there was some familiar eye contact between the two of them. But I was thinking too much like a damn private dick. "Good evening, sir," she said. "Are you having a good time at *The Trocadéro*?"

98

"You bet, Miss Halliday. I enjoy your singing very much. This is my first time here."

She looked me over. "Such a handsome man to be alone on such a lovely evening in Los Angeles," she said in a rather husky, warm voice.

"Well, truth be known, I was actually supposed to meet someone here around eight. But she didn't show. Maybe we got our wires crossed." But that wasn't the truth. I had this niggling feeling in my gut that something went wrong with Ziggy's schedule today because I had pegged her for a dependable doll with a lot of hidden talent and intelligence. I didn't think she'd be working for that son-of-a-bitch Voracious if she didn't have quite a bit upstairs.

"That's too bad, Mr.—Mr.—"

"—Denning, Cable Denning," I said, extending my hand. She took my hand. It was warm and comfortable.

"I'm Julie Halliday, Mr. Denning. I am very pleased you chose *The Trocadéro* tonight. You...should take the time to eat here one evening...the food is prepared perfectly by Herr Gustav Zetterling, an international German chef,." I don't know why but I got the chills the way she pronounced the chef's German name. It was if she said it letter perfect and the vowels and consonants were native to her own tongue.

"Your—your German is very good, Miss Halliday. Did you study it in school? I have a good ear for those things."

She looked a little restless as she glanced over to Fritz at the bar. Now I knew there was a connection between the two of them. But what? "I love languages," she replied, with her old smile and charm. "But I feel so badly that you are alone...will you come sit with me for a few minutes? After all, it's a slow Monday night. Let me buy you a drink of lime seltzer."

I told her I would gratefully accept her invitation and we sat at a table reserved for her near the stage, just as the management had done for Honey way back when. The band played a nice soft, danceable version of *After You've Gone* and the light from a candle on the table glowed on her beautiful, flawless skin in the semi-dark of the room. "You're a lovely woman, Julie Halliday," I said. "Your skin is strong yet delicate. There's a difference between dolls and broads, you know."

She laughed and wrinkled her brow. "Thank you for the flattery. Now *that* distinction I've not heard before, Mr. Denning."

"Call me Cable. Well, you see, a doll is a classy dame, one with style, intelligence, personality—the kind of babe a guy like me doesn't go home with unless it's under very special circumstances—and never the first time I see her. Now a broad is a kind of loose gal....you know, the one who comes for fun and a good time with some bloke she just met and is willing to hop into his bed for a night."

She studied my face. "I would say you pick your ladies quite selectively. And you don't have to take any of them home, because you're not a desperate kind of man, are you? Women come to you. Why do you think this is so, if it is?"

"I don't know about that, Miss Halliday. I just know what I want and what I don't want. Yeah, sure, once in a while I slip and end up in the sack with some good looker who's just as drunk as I am. But that's a rare night." I had been holding back any information regarding Ziggy Thompson, hoping the babe sitting directly across the table from me would speak up.

"Please...call me Julie. I'm—I'm very interested in you, Cable. I hope you don't think me forward. Don't worry, I'm not going to ask you to take me home with you. But out of curiosity, could you tell me what lucky young woman was going to meet you here tonight?"

"That's the funny part about it, Julie. She said she knew you—her name is Ziggy Thompson. Says you worked together or something at one time?"

Her face paled. "I—I have only met Miss Thompson a few times. She worked in a house of ill repute, the speakeasy in back of the Pink something or other—"

"—*Pink Gables.*" I smelled a rat but I couldn't put my finger on it. "It's, uh, rather strange, I'd say. I definitely got the impression from Ziggy that the two of you were friends, or the like...at least at one time."

She was listening to the music and swaying to and fro. "I would ask you to dance with me, Cable, but it's against house rules here. Then everyone would want to dance with me and I'd never get any singing done—"

"—let alone light up the stage with that sexy dress of yours."

"Thank you. I think you're a special man. Would you—would you consider meeting me for an after hours drink tonight? I promise I won't bite you or—what is it women say about men?"

"You won't 'come on' to me, I think that's it."

"Yes...I won't come on to you. But you are handsome, Cable, rugged with a certain abandon in your make-up—an irresistible combination, I'd suggest."

101

"Thanks for the compliment, Julie." I was thinking about Zelda and that nice warm and wet specialness between her legs. Yeah, I'd like to get home to that, I thought. "Thanks all the same, Julie, but maybe some other time."

She seemed surprised. "You know, I believe you're the first man who's refused me—in *any* department. No wonder women want you...you're the unavailable man, aren't you? That always draws a female. I guess it's being mysteriously aloof or something." She got up. "I hope some other time then, Cable." I took her extended hand and she walked away toward the bandstand. I glanced to see if Fritz was still at the bar checking us out, but he had left.

On the way home I quickly checked in to see if Ziggy Thompson had come into the *Pink Gables* that night. No one had seen her. Puzzled, I boarded the streetcar out to Zelda's place. When I got in and was taking a nice hot bath, suddenly the bathroom door opened and I had company. "Would you like a bath-mate? I got a little lonely out there."

I chuckled and smiled up at Zelda. "Sure, babe, come on in, the water's fine." She joined me and I watched as the fine, young body with everything in the right places sat between my legs.

"I've been thinking, Cable...about your mother. Wouldn't you like to give her a grand child? It almost killed me the other afternoon when we were there. She has nothing much to do anymore, and no one for company. Who wants to live if you feel you're of no value to anyone anymore? I know how that feels. When I first met you, I was a student bookworm, a nerd whose only real company was my plants. I couldn't even get a guy to *look* at me, let alone date me. Can you imagine yourself in that position?"

"Frankly, no, Zelda. But what would you have me do? Maybe up on Vine Street I'll see her more often...she'll be close by."

"I doubt it. Sons are more independent once they leave the nest. Especially with Moms, and if the father's dead, what do you really have in common with your mother? Have you thought about it—really thought about it, Cable? What if she dies and there's no heir to take over the Denning name? I know...you're only thirty-one today, but pretty soon you'll be forty and the years go on—"

"—Zelda," I said, trying to keep as gentle a tone as possible. "We are who we are—you'd want me to marry some babe just to satisfy my mother's feeling of *empty nest*?"

She was quiet for a moment. Then she spoke softly, almost under her breath. "Cable, I would have your baby. And I would go over and visit your mother and see the happiness on her face every time she held his tiny little hand in hers."

"Zelda, you're talking nonsense. Even if all things were perfect with a partner, I haven't got a pot to piss in...I'm so broke. Yeah, we've got a few bucks from Becker to hold us over for a while—but in my business and with the Depression and all—well, you just can't count on things."

She made a big sigh. "I guess you're right. Gees...I just hate to see your Mom suffer day in and day out..."

I reached around and put both of my hands between her legs. She sighed. "You know what I was thinking about all the way home?"

"No, you naughty, sexy man, what?" she tittered.

"Licking on that beautiful pussy of yours and then taking you around the world with my cock," I said in a low, sensual voice.

"God, Cable, you're going to make me faint. How did we get to be so sexy together? Ever since that night when you came back from that mannequin lady or whoever—you've really wanted me, haven't you?"

"Yep, and that's just the first verse. As I said, I'm going to take you away for a couple of days, after I get back and we move Mom."

She turned in the tub and brought her full breasts into my chest, kissing me so hard it wedged the back of my head up against the wall of the tub. "That's for you, Mr. Denning. Let's dry off and go to bed. I'm starting to get wet for you in the bathtub!"

Oh, Captain, My Captain!

Washington D.C. was a dirty town. I remember reading Walt Whitman when I was a kid. *Leaves of Grass* was a classic by the sensitive, feminine man who looked like an Adonis male yet was probably homosexual. But who in the fuck cares? He was real flesh and blood with guts and a heart that wouldn't be stopped—simply because he was judged by lesser men. I recall an essay of his when he spoke of watching President Abraham Lincoln, passing beneath his hotel window, driving his own buggy, while making his way to the White House on the filthy, muddy streets during the Civil War. And how painfully bittersweet it must have been for Whitman to walk among the beds of the wounded, the dying and the dead, lying there in makeshift hospitals. He sat with a seventeen year-old, held his hand as he read to him— and then felt the limp nothingness when life left the pain-ridden amputee.

I had no sooner cashed in to my hotel when I was visited by a Günter Zoringer, the contact Becker had promised I'd meet up with. He was a dark-haired middle-aged man with a quick step and spoke excellent English. There was no discernible German accent. I guess they could train these spies pretty damn well. "Tomorrow evening, Mr. Denning," he was instructing me, "we will convene at eight o'clock here at this address: 1718 Jefferson. Please memorize it. You will see a walk-down entrance to your left. When you get to the green and white door, knock only *once*. If you forget and knock more than that, you will be shot."

I was taken aback. "You fellows really do play for keeps—what's the matter—can't you guys stay on your toes without a little target practice now and then—just for fun, no doubt?"

"You will find no humor in this mission. I urge you to follow instructions to the letter. Now...I will greet you at that green and white door. Have your own revolver out and cocked. If it is not me who greets you at that door, shoot whoever answers it. Is that clear?"

"I don't kill people I don't know and may even like, Zoringer. That wasn't part of the deal. I'm your eaves-dropper, and that's it, remember?"

"Then I will have to have Herr Richter accompany you down the stairs at 1718 Jefferson. And he will do the knocking with a drawn weapon. You Americans have conscience about some things, and no concern whatsoever about others."

"That's the way I like it, Zoringer. That way it'll keep you guessing. You do know your pay-rate isn't all that great, especially when you realize I'm putting my life on the line here—and if for any reason we were caught, I'd be tried for high-treason and bumped off by a firing squad."

"Human life in itself has no value, Mr. Denning. Forget all your moral fantasies. Leave them behind with your menial work world and the women who share your bed."

"So tomorrow then, eight in the evening—1718 Jefferson."

"Yes. Take a taxi. Arrive early, surveillance is essential. When you see all is clear—nothing that does not belong or any untoward behaviors—proceed. I will see you then." He clicked his heels together and left.

True to his word, a guy named Hans Richter showed up just as I descended the steps to the green and white door. He drew his luger and knocked once. The door opened and there stood Günter Zoringer. Richter disappeared. I was led through a maze of hallways and doors until we came to a little room that must have served as a cloakroom. There, Zoringer pressed a place on the floor with his foot and a small panel opened, just large enough for two medium-sized men to enter single-file. Soon we ascended until we were in a very narrow corridor, apparently sandwiched between two walls. At this point I was instructed to remove my shoes and we walked another twenty or thirty feet and then turned left into a small indentation. I was also told earlier that if I spoke even one word my throat would be slit then and there. So I didn't talk, but put my ear to the wall as he indicated. Then strangely—Zoringer left, and there I was alone in the stuffy, cramped space.

Soon a heavy accented German voice greeted another person who obviously had entered the conference room. "Mr. President," the German voice spoke clearly, "I am delighted to meet you."

The very distinct voice of Franklin Delano Roosevelt responded. "I'm afraid I'm not Mr. Hoover's replacement quite yet, Minister Schock." The two men must have shaken hands and taken seats. "Thank you for coming here. I know it is a long journey for you. I hope our American hospitality has greeted you with respect and comfortable lodgings."

"Ya...ze best, Mr. Roosefelt. I am grateful."

"So...onto the agenda at hand, I suggest."

"Ya...ve must address vat iss openly on our mindts."

"As you know, Minister Schock, my country is in dire financial circumstances. May I be blunt?"

"By all meanss, Mr. Roosefelt..."

"Thank you...the mismanagement of money and illegitimate distribution of funds has caused our initial collapse economically. The American economy is based on industrial manufacturing of goods. Add to that, the petroleum industry, coal mining and a few other miscellaneous enterprises. We have vast reserves. We make the best steel, lead, gold, silver, other ores of course—and from those basics we create a myriad of product, as does your country. But the problem is, with the consumer unable to retain viable purchasing power, the economy has stagnated. Frankly, we need a large shot in the arm to stimulate things. My plans to initiate internal work programs, such as something called the *WPA,* that I've conceived, can only serve a limited number of low-wage compensational labor-intense jobs. And we are a growing nation, with hundreds of thousands of immigrants arriving monthly. Therefore, I am obliged to suggest to you, Minister Shock, we need a major stimulant from *outside forces.*"

There was a silence. "As I haff indicated to you prior, Mr. Roosefelt, ze German government iss at your service ze minute Adolf Hitler becomss Chancellor. At zat time he shall implement a plan to regain German territory zat vas stolen from us during ze last var und off course, ze cursed Treaty of Fersailles."

"Does Mr. Hitler have a time plan for that project?"

"Ya...*vun year* from ze time off hiss election to ze *Reichstag.*"

"I am amazed! You must have already implemented much pre-planning, no?"

"Oh, ya, Mr. Roosefelt. Soon-to-be Chancellor Hitler hass guaranteed us *perfect timing.* As you are elected President of ze United States, our leader vill become Chancellor. Ze folloving year, 1933, he shall become *Führer und Reichskanzler,* zerefore leafing all major decisions in ze handts off ze *National Socialist German Vorkers Party.* Ve are blessed vis Von Bismarck's assistance, essentially surrounding us vis ze mightiest industrial power off all ze landt: *Krupp, Faben, Siemens,*

Flick und military fehicles manufactured by *Folksvagen*." Then the German's voice rose. "Ve vill be *infincible*, Mr. Roosefelt!"

There was another pause. "I am impressed, Minister Schock. But I am still, if I may be so bold, pressing for an answer from you. May I offer you my true concern?"

"By all meanss, ve are here at a great time for great decisionss."

"Frankly, Mr. Minister, the United States *needs a war* in order to accelerate the full implementation of our industrial capacity."

"Zere *vill* be a var. May I put to rest any concernss you may haff, Mr. Roosefelt. Vis our combinedt technology, ze United States may secretly prepare for var und be mighty und infincible, as ve Germans—vizin fife yearss. Unbeatable...betveen us, ve vill control vorldt commerce. Our *Führer* vill dominate Europe. Ve vill help you ofercome Canada, Mexico, Central und Souss America."

Another silence. "But what will trigger such a war for us—and who will be the enemy? Presently, we are at peace....with either alliances in place or simple diplomatic understandings of non-aggression."

"Your closest competitor for territory iss in ze Pacific, Mr. Roosefelt. For exsample, Japan iss resentful off American possession off many Souss Pacific islandts. It vould not take much to profoke zem to var. Und off course, zey are small und unprepared for ze might of ze United States und Germany combined. Zo...it stands to reason, you haff a perfect situation to stimulate your economy by engaging ze Japanese in ze Pacific corridorss. Does zis not sound plausible to you?"

"To be sure, Minister Schock, I am quite impressed with the homework you and your government have done."

"Ve are nossing...if ve are not *sorough*, Mr. Roosefelt. Ve vill be ze most efficient machine in ze European tseatre."

"Somehow I believe that, Minister. Then I shall meet with my Cabinet and outline these plans, keeping, of course, certain information absolutely top secret."

"Ya...*top secret*." There was a rustling of papers and a couple of chairs slid back on what sounded like cement flooring. "Zen, may I report to Herr Hitler zat ve are in accordt."

"You may, Minister Schock. I find you very discreet and diplomatic. And again, I thank you for taking that long journey to come and see me. You will be hearing from us in the near future through our diplomatic couriers. You will also have a direct telephone line to me once I am installed in the White House."

"Very vell, Mr. Roosefelt. I bidt you a most pleasant goodt efening."

My ear had become numb glued to the wall. Günter Zoringer suddenly re-appeared and tugged at me and we exited the building, back up to street level. "Whatever you heard, Mr. Denning, is knowledge that cannot be divulged to the outside world, you understand."

"And why didn't *you* eavesdrop with me, Zoringer— seems to me two witnesses to history are better than one."

"Oh, but didn't you know?" he said slyly. "A famous Chinese saying, '*Monkey who does not hear does not know,*' and only *you* know. Thus I am exempt from the responsibility of carrying the burden of your new knowledge."

Suddenly I realized they'd trapped me. I had no idea what I heard behind those closed doors was going to be as earth shaking as it had been. Now I would forever be the man who knew too much. It dawned on me in that moment that they had set me up. I would be the patsy and the fall guy if ever things got out of hand and the Germans needed to bail. Nothing like a good ol' American spy dying at dawn for German espionage, in front of a firing squad! "Yeah, Zoringer, now I get it. Let's just hope this blows over smoothly and I can get on with a normal life."

"You have never had a normal life, Mr. Denning—and you shall never have a normal life until the day you die."

That didn't sit too well with me. "Well, then, here's to a short life. You know, you Krauts are clever, really. I didn't see this one coming. So what's next?"

"Before you return to Los Angeles, tomorrow you are to meet with Dr. Becker. He will arrive here later tonight. The two of you will take a little trip together. Even *I* do not know where you will be taken. But I assure you, Dr. Becker has an unusual experience in mind for you. He likes to reward his loyal assistants. Expect a pleasant journey, Mr. Denning." With that, Günter Zoringer disappeared down the street into the dark. I hailed a taxi back to my hotel room.

I got into my room exhausted. Roosevelt's words were still echoing in my brain, "*the United States needs a war in order to accelerate the full implementation of our industrial capacity.*" That alone gave me the willies. But I didn't have a lot of time to reflect on it. Suddenly there was a movement in a dark corner of my room. I drew my .38. "Hold your fire, Cable," a familiar voice spoke.

Out of the shadows stepped a little creature with a warm smile on his face. "Toggth! You son-of-a-gun—you're always surprising me! You coulda got shot!"

"No, Cable...my magnetic thought concentrations froze your gun mechanism. Go ahead, point the revolver at me and squeeze the trigger."

"Crap, Toggth, I don't wanna hurt you...don't tempt me..."

"Pull it!" he exclaimed. And so I did. But the trigger on my .38 wouldn't budge. "Those are the first steps of *trust*, Cable."

"So, hello to you, too," I said rather sarcastically.

"Hello!...Quite a conversation we overheard tonight, wasn't it? You know I am still puzzled why humans are constantly thinking about money and possessions and destruction. Doesn't that puzzle you?"

"Hmmm...so you heard, too, eh? Yeah it does...but I think it's the nature of the beast."

"Perhaps the *present* nature of the beast. I know it was not always so—and hopefully great transformations will happen in the future." Then he hopped on my bed and asked me to sit next to him. "Now...I have one more thing for you to do tonight before you sleep."

"Oh, I can't wait for this one, Toggth. You always come up with wall-bangers alright. What is it this time?"

"Well, do you recall how Lei-Tao transported you to the Cave of the Seven Truths?"

"Yeah, she had me drink some kind of mixture—or potion...it was red and gold and tasted kind of sweet, if I remember."

"Yes, exactly. So guess what? You will now have a second opportunity to drink such a liquid refreshment."

"I will?"

"Yes. If you please." Just at that exact moment a golden chalice appeared on my nightstand. "Drink it all down at once and then let its influence guide you to me. I will greet you at the other end. Trust me?"

I half-smiled at this little creature I'd grown so fond of. "Trust you, little guy..." I went to the nightstand and gulped down the whole thing. Again it tasted sweet and almost instantly I got dizzy and found myself floundering all over in my head. Then I collapsed on the bed and all went blank. What seemed like seconds later I could hear Toggth's voice call my name. I opened my eyes and I felt great. Everything about me was younger and clearer and brighter!

"Now, follow me." It looked to me like we were still somewhere on the earth plane. I could see a few trees in the distance, a clear night sky and half a moon lit up the earth enough for us to see our way. Toggth led me to an embankment. There were some bushes up against it. He poked his head inside one of the bushes. "I know it's here somewhere..." he said, sounding a bit confounded.

"What's where?" I asked, completely in the dark.

"The lever."

"Oh."

"Ah!" He pulled his head out and came back to where I stood. "Now, just so you understand, normally to arrive at this location, we would have to fly a plane,

113

take an automobile, get aboard a yacht, travel by water for an hour, get off, take another airplane, get off again and ride another auto to this destination."

"For what?" I asked, increasingly perplexed.

"You'll see..." We walked around the embankment to its other side. Suddenly we came upon four men dressed in military helmets, uniforms and imposing rifles. Immediately Toggth raised a hand and the four soldiers dropped to the ground, fast asleep. A huge metal door with electronic buttons stood before us, obviously leading inside the mountain embankment. Toggth brushed his fingers across the black buttons and the door silently swung open. He walked ahead and I followed. I couldn't figure for the life of me, what in the hell he could possibly be wanting to show me in the middle of the night in some unknown, remote location? Then all of my wondering turned into wonderment. My little host opened a final door and there before us lay endless rows of gold bullion lit by dim light bulbs as far as the eye could see! I thought I had lost my senses and the potion Toggth had given me was playing tricks on my mind.

"Oh, my God, *all the gold in the world!*" I croaked.

"Not quite, there is more in England with the Rothschild Empire and other countries. This...is what humans live, fight and die for, Cable...the very thing that could give them abundance on the physical plane, they hoard by many thousands of tons—ten city blocks of pure golden bars, piled sixteen feet high. This is how they keep money valuable, nations suppressed and war the inevitable battle of the have-nots versus the secret *haves.*"

I stood there stunned. Suddenly a patrol of a dozen or so soldiers came marching down the main ramp. Toggth grabbed me and we ducked behind a huge pallet of gold bullion. They passed and the little elfin-like creature smiled at me. "Damn, Toggth...you sure in hell get me into a lot of shit, you know that?"

"Not really. But had you not seen this, Cable, there would always be a piece missing in your earth-puzzle. Now you know gold is controlled to the tune of the political machine out there spinning everyone's brains dizzy. The United States government has only three men who know about this—and they are members of the *Oculus*. But they do not own it. There exists an International Money Fund that secretly controls your country and the rest of the planet's teetering little nations. It is fiercely protected by the *Oculus*—and, I might add, Cronus-Gor's now-endangered organization. It appears the rising German plague is about to erupt and take over the domination of the earth."

"Will they succeed?" I asked, having my doubts. I was recalling Cronus-Gor's prediction that in grooming Hitler, he would change the world and maintain dominance.

"Maybe for a short while. Especially, as you heard this evening, in Europe, perhaps parts of Africa and southeast Asia. But there are always alien enemies vying for first-place among the stars. Even the so-called *superior German mind* cannot overcome them."

I looked down the ramp where the soldiers had gone. "What about those poor blokes, working and believing they're protecting U.S. property?"

"Like all military strategies in the world, Cable, a few self-serving men send millions to their deaths under the pretext of protecting one's home, family and country. It has always been a lie. It is so today." He took my hand and we started toward the entrance. "The military guard is assigned here with no knowledge of how they got here—nor will they have any memory of ever having been here. They are exterminated after a three-year tour of duty. Just as the three men who know how to get here and access the cache of imponderable wealth sitting inside these mountains. On their seventieth birthday they are terminated, if they live a natural life that long. They are never to live a normal life. Sound familiar? Just like you-know-who told you this evening. When I heard FDR speak, I knew you would realize all world leaders are in cahoots, but in truth, they do not run the world. But you already know all of that. Cronus-Gor may not return any time soon, but to be sure, other alien despots will try to swagger their ways into world dominion—and until a *true vibrational uplifting* takes place, the pitiful state of human kind shall continue."

"So you heard *everything* tonight?"

"I was 'breathing down your neck,' so to speak."

"Oh. So what now?"

"You go home and go to sleep. I must return to the *Cave of the Seven Truths*. I hope this experience teaches you, Cable, the terrible deception governments impose upon their subjects."

"Oh, yeah, I got a good eye *and* ear-full. Nope...I won't forget this one anytime soon, Toggth. Thanks for the education."

The next thing I knew I was turning in my bed and woke myself up snoring.

The Grand House of Pleasure

That night I slept surprisingly well and when I awakened, it was after nine a.m. and I felt great. I was in the bathroom when the phone rang. I got to it. "Yeah, whoever this is, I'm barely awake yet..."

"Mr. Denning?" the very sexy, soft feminine voice then announced, "This is Sylvia—I am to escort you to a place of rendezvous...in order to meet with Dr. Becker. May I come up and dress you?"

I thought I was still dreaming. "You wanna what?"

"I am your escort and assigned to you for this day. Will you please allow me to wash and dress you? Oh....and please do not ready your own clothing, as I am bringing special clothes for the occasion."

"Occasion? What the hell are you talking about, lady?"

"I will be at your door, #327, Mr. Denning." She hung up.

What the crap was Becker up to, I wondered? I sat on the bed and lit up a Lucky Strike. Soon there was a timid knock at my door. I wrapped a towel around me and answered. There stood a gorgeous dish in her early twenties looking up at me with warm blue eyes and a smile. She carried a large shopping bag. Her hair was red and she stood about five-four with a healthy bust filling up the tight-fitting green-silk dress she wore. "Mr. Denning? I'm Sylvia," she said, in that same soft, sexy tone—as if with the intent that I would need to bend closer to hear her. I let her in. "Please allow me to do my job, or else I will get into trouble with—with my employers."

"Hello, Sylvia. No, we wouldn't want that, now, would we?"

"If you will step into the shower, I will accompany you." I did as the babe said. The warm water poured over me and soon Sylvia joined me in the shower naked as a newborn birdie. Then she soaped me down from head to toe with an expertise that made my body begin to tingle. She took a washrag and scrubbed me down ever so gently. When she got to my genitals, she took my balls and penis in hand and carefully massaged them to semi-life so that my cock rose to half-mast and my balls tightened in the sack. "You are most generously endowed, Mr. Denning." I assumed she was a courtesan of some sort, but she was obviously instructed to give stimulation and relaxation—and not sex. Soon she turned off the water, dried me and herself off, then led me into the main room, reached into the bag and got out a fancy suit, shirt, shoes and tie made of an expensive gabardine, dyed in a handsome dark-brown. A fancy felt fedora came with the ensemble. As she dressed me, everything fit to a tee.

"Who knew my measurements?" I asked.

"I only know what I was handed this morning, Mr. Denning."

"Well, they're right on the money." I looked at her marvelous nude body. "Talking about measurements, I'm pretty good at sizing up dolls. Shall I take a guess?"

"If you wish," she said, undisturbed from her task at hand.

"Hmmm...I'd say you were about 36-24-36...how am I doing?"

She rose up from putting my pants on and kissed me gently on the lips. "I don't do this with all my clients, but that's for being so co-operative—and at ease with me."

"I wouldn't say that, lady—I mean it is early and all—but your naked person doesn't exactly relax me."

But she kept to her business and finished dressing me. When we looked into the mirror together, I looked like a million bucks! "You are a very handsome—and now debonair—man, Mr. Denning. May I ask where you are from?" She had no accent so I assumed she was no Kraut sent to spy on me.

"California—born and raised. I'm a private dick in L.A."

"A private dick?" She looked confused.

I laughed, because I always knew I got the babes with that line. "A private dick—*detective*—you know, the kind of guy who goes around probing into the secret lives of others, unraveling mysteries and such."

She giggled a sexy little giggle. "Oh."

"Do you put out?" I asked boldly. "Or are you a—uh, well—"

"—do you mean do I make love to my clients? No, Mr. Denning. When we are hired, we are trained in certain specialties. I'm a *greeter* and not comfortable, honestly, with the thought of men penetrating me all day and me having to pretend I like it."

"Yeah, I don't blame you there." I checked myself out again in the mirror. "Not bad, eh? I could've been a male clothes model—what do you think?"

"Definitely," she laughed. "But we'd better go now."

"I'm getting hungry. Can we stop off for a bite?" Then I thought for a minute. "Crap, I don't even know where we're going or who you are or anything—including the fact that this could be my last day on earth and you're that angel sent to make it easier to cross over."

"I like the way you talk, Mr. Denning. No, you will be treated to a highly pleasurable day before you return to Los Angeles. I am instructed to make certain you rendezvous with Dr. Becker at 12 noon sharp. Yes, we can do anything you wish—even stop off briefly at a coffee shop first."

"Then let's do it."

We got out onto the street and we walked over to a place called *Arnie's Coffee Emporium* and found a booth. She seemed to brighten up as we sat opposite one another. "I haven't done anything like this in ages. It's always supposed to be very prestigious—we serve lots of millionaires and the like."

"Well, you're talking to Mr. Simple here, lady. I was born in a tough East L.A. ghetto and came up the hard way. Simple was a way of life, and still is for me."

"I like that, Mr. Denning...I wish I had—"

"—call me Cable. Are you—are you happy with what you do?"

"In case you haven't noticed, there's a Depression on—and for a girl to find *any* kind of job is fortunate. I was a starving college girl when I was discovered by a female recruiter for the organization I work for." Then she checked herself. "Oh—I'm not supposed to even tell you that much. I'm sorry, but I have to keep shut about anything pertaining to the organization. I'm sure you understand."

We chit-chatted for a while and got along swell. It was getting on to about eleven-thirty and I felt comfortable with Sylvia. "I don't want to get you in trouble, kid, so I guess we'd better get that taxi and get us where we're going."

"There's no taxi, Cable, I'm driving. Also, I must ask you to wear a blindfold for a few minutes while we travel. No one is supposed to know where we're going—ever."

She drove along for a while and I could tell when we crossed a bridge because I could hear the tires clickety-clack across the sections. "So, do you have a boyfriend—or husband?" I asked.

"We're not allowed—at least officially. Some of the girls do. But do you want to hear something strange?"

"Yeah, I like strange.... strange is my second name these days..."

"Well, when I was washing you down this morning in your shower? For just a flash I felt quite *domestic*....you know, like I had a glimpse of what it could be like having a full-time man and all. But it was *you*, Cable—I think you bring that out in a girl. You disarm a lady by just being yourself....without pretense."

"I do? That's nice to know, Sylvia. Thanks...I'll make a note of that when I strategize to seduce my next female."

She giggled. "If you were going to be here long enough—I could be that female, Cable. I'm twenty-two and have never been in love."

"It's not all it's cracked up to be, Sylvia. It's like a roller coaster ride. You get pulled up to the highest peak, then it lets go and down you fall, then you wake up one day with a broken heart and you're back where you started. I know, I tried— and I crashed a couple of times before I learned you can't own anyone and you can't give your heart away. Why? Because you're still you and you gotta live with that someone who you call your 'self'. And everyone's on a different journey. And never...never take up with a dangerous man, or a bloke like me who's got death written all over his forehead. He'll bring you the worst heartache of all because it always hurts worse when someone you love leaves you too young. It's hard to burn that memory out of your craw. You always limp a little after those experiences."

She took my hand. "Do you hurt a lot inside, Cable?"

"Yeah... every day and twice on Sundays. And sometimes you can numb for a while with another babe, but it always jumps back out at you from the dark, when you're not looking. And some days...are worse...than others...memory is a terrible thing when it comes with regret..."

She squeezed my hand tighter but said nothing more as we rode on for a few minutes in silence. Finally the car stopped and she removed my blindfold. We were in some dark garage. We got out and took an elevator up to the top floor of some huge building. We walked to a golden door and she pushed a button. Another voluptuous thing answered the door and we were let in. Standing at a counter wrapped in a huge towel stood Helmut Becker. He smiled and approached me. "Herr Denning! Glad to see you...again," he said, shaking my hand. I glanced at Sylvia, as Becker nodded to dismiss her. "Didt you not findt Sylvia a vonderful vay to start off...ze day's festifities? Are you hungry...sirsty?"

I didn't want to get Sylvia into trouble, so I skipped the part about *Arnie's Coffee Emporium*. "Not hungry, Becker, but I could go for a good quality English gin and tonic."

He led me to a wet bar and I was served a generous gin. Becker then motioned to me and we entered a private room. "Zis room iss *sound-proofed*, Herr Denning." He had me sit on a comfortable sofa opposite him. "Velcome, by ze vay, to *Ze Grandt House off Pleasure*. Your effry fantasy may be expressed here. It iss my vay off extending my gratitude for your most excellent accomplishment." Then his voice grew serious. "Now...you must tell me effry detail off vat zat excellent memory off yourss retained."

"Well, it's pretty easy to figure, Becker. Your new soon-to-be *Führer* and our soon-to-be President, wanna bring on a *war* to soothe their indigestion and ailing economies. Your *Deutschland* cronies such as Krupp, Faben, Siemens, Flick and even the wheels of Volkswagen—all manipulated by Von Bismarck—think they can own Europe, Africa and parts of Southeast Asia within a very short time. And the price for this takeover? Franklin Delano Roosevelt will look the other way while Germany sacks Europe as long as Germany promises to stimulate a war for us as soon as it can. Your emissary, one Minister Schock, indicates it will be a Pacific war—maybe sparked by provoking the Empire of Japan as America takes over the South Pacific islands, one by one."

Helmut Becker's attention was wrapped around my every word. "Excellent! Most excellent, Herr Denning! You haff provided uss here in ze United States vis vital, indispensable information. You see, Herr Hitler und Minister Schock keep many secrets from us—ve off ze German undergroundt here in America. You haff brought us 'up to snuff,' as you might say."

I was thinking of Zoringer's abandonment of me during the eavesdropping session. "So now I'm dispensable, right?"

Becker looked at me with a fatherly smile. "Vell, you *vould* be—merely becauss off vat you know—und you do know by now you vere set up to spy-und-tell—und zen be eliminatedt becauss, simply put, you vould know too much to remain alife. Such a liability ve cannot permit. You see, vat you know hass now become a negotiable commodity. But...ve haff vun *fly in ze ointment*, Herr Denning...you see, even zough ve know you are not privy to ze anti-graffity knowledge ve originally vere misguidedt to belieff, you *vere* correct about our future *Führer* being half-alien. Und frankly, zis bozers us. As you zen suggestedt, perhaps he iss using my beloffed Deutschlandt as fodder for his var machine—und in ze endt, he may vatch it go down in flamss if ze tides off var should change against my Fazerlandt. After all, he is Austrian on his mozer's side—"

"—yeah, and alien on his father's side."

"Und so...zat predicament leads uss to haff discovered vun ozer sing about you, Herr Denning. Herr Hitler's fazer vas pursuing you for a knowledge you alone possess. He vas seeking a golden capsule entitled *Gott*

Unserer Väter. Somehow you came into contact viz it, learned its secrets—und now guess vat? *Ve* vant it!"

"It looks like old Cronus-Gor and his sick hoodlum criminals get around after all. Here I thought he was just the hidden head of *Oculus Pyramis Mandatum* hoarding all the gold in the world to control just how long he deems the human race should dwell in poverty and hardship."

Becker's eyes widened. "You haff *seen* him?"

"Nobody's seen him, Becker. He keeps himself conveniently invisible. Oh, but you can hear his threatening tone of voice, alright."

"Und you'ffe *spoken* viz him?" he said in amazement.

"Yep. He even presented me with a pair of severed hands under the lid of the dinner server. Some poor young woman who played the piano and never hurt a soul, and lived quietly until she met me."

"Yes...I've heardt he can be *findictive* und *revengeful.*"

"And that's only the first verse of that horror story..."

He brightened up and laughed. "Vat a joyous occasion, Herr Denning—to sink I am sitting across from ze one man who knowss not only ze *how* off Creation—but ze *vhy* off it all!" Then he drew serious and leaned forward. "Zo...zat iss vhy ve cannot...dispense viz you...qvite yet." Then he brightened again. "Und now I offer you a day off unparalleled pleasure. You may frolic to your heart's content viz any or all off ze beauties engaged to delight all off your sensess! Zo, ven you get back to Los Angeles, you vill be bubbling viz satiation. Vat do you say to zat?"

"Well, it's a mixed bag, Becker. Sure, I'll enjoy myself today—but I still know I've got you hanging over my shoulder panting for the *God of Our Fathers*. Frankly, I wish I'd never heard of it."

We parted and a lovely young woman led me into a steam room. Only thing was, once I got stripped and looked through the fog of the damn place, I discovered I was the only male in a room with ten drop-dead gorgeous females! Boy, was this gonna be a day!!

A rather tall, buxom woman came up to me. "Hi, my name is Ginger. Just to let you know, there are three phases to your Pleasure Dome journey today. First is the steam room here. The girls will give you any kind of pleasure you desire. Usually this is the 'warm up' area where you relax, steam up and allow yourself to be massaged by as many young ladies as you can tolerate," she said, smiling. "The second phase is the Altered State Paradise. That's where you may have the drug of your choice and take a specified journey with up to three of our young women. They will be taking the same opiate you will be, so all of you will share similar erotic fantasies together. The third phase is the All Night Ecstasy phase, where you will choose but one girl to spend the remainder of the night with. She is especially trained to delight you in every possible way, including simultaneous multi-orgasms. Check out time is twelve o'clock noon. Do you have any questions, Mr. Denning?"

Hell, I was still reeling from the delights of the *first phase*! "No, Ginger," I said, "I guess I'll just go through the ropes one at a time and select my solo babe when it's bedtime..."

126

"Very well, then...please enjoy yourself—and don't be afraid to ask for what you want. Remember—anything goes!" She walked away and I drifted into the midst of six or seven young women awaiting my presence. This phase was more of a rubdown, wash and scrub session. A couple of hours later when I emerged, I felt pretty good. Some minor fondling went on as part of the natural course, but that was it. I decided to skip the "Altered State Paradise" because it promised to be more 'altered' than I was willing to go—plus I wasn't into drugs, except my smokes and booze. So, by five in the afternoon I was ready for beddy-bye. There was only one gal who seemed appealing enough to me who I felt I could spend the night with. I was also thinking about Zelda and how much more enjoyable it is when you start with a virgin like she was and break her in as her one and only stud-lover. Yeah, Zelda had become *made to order* for me.

Her name was Michelle. She stood about five-ten barefoot with raven-black hair clear down to her bottom. She had a nice face and a body to match. I didn't think I could go wrong with Michelle. When I came up to her and told her I was ready for bed now, she seemed relieved. She told me what "Love Chamber" to go to and that she would join me shortly. I walked down a long hall with probably fifty such "Love Chamber" rooms until I came to #38. The door was open and I entered a light-pink room with a sunken Cleopatra tub in the middle of the floor and a humongous triple-sized bed with silk sheets just a few feet from the tub. A refrigerator contained all the English gin I could drink in a week, phallic looking candles sat on every available surface and a large bathroom with a walk-in shower was just off the bedroom. Since I was already naked, I plopped on the bed and closed my eyes. In just a few minutes I heard the door click open, and then lock. I lifted my head to take a gander at the dark-haired beauty only to feast my eyes on a voluptuous redhead "Sylvia! What in the hell are you doing here?" I asked, puzzled.

She put her finger over her lips and ran to me quickly. "Cable! I traded with Michelle and told her to take the night off. I *will* sleep with you if you want me to, but that isn't really why I came."

I studied her face, trying to figure the dame. "Well, then, suppose you share with me exactly what you *did* come for. After all, all those other babes have been building me up hotter than a pepper all day—and I was kind of expecting some adequate release for a thirty-one year old bull who's gotten a little horny here..."

"I know, and I'm sorry. But please hear me out. This is a horrible place. So many of the young women come here only to be groomed as a commodity, to be sold in other parts of the world. You know, like drugged up, made sex slaves and sold to some Chinese emperor or Arab sheik or South American drug lord or the like.? I've avoided it only because I'm very good as a greeter and the more intelligent women who are attractive get first crack at that. Do you follow me?"

Oh, yeah, I was right up there with her on the White Slavery thing in this country. White-skinned and vulnerable young women were carefully watched, and when they 'qualified', they were kidnapped, drugged and eventually sold to some mogul whose lust used up young babes like a box of tissue on a bad cold. "Okay,

128

Sylvia. So what can I do about it? I'm only one guy here, you know—they've got goons protecting this place like the Maharaja's palace. And some of those women I saw in the steam room probably double as wrestlers!"

"Take me with you! I'll die if I stay here, Cable! Greeters only last so long, and before they get too old, they'll do the same with us, as with all the rest of the girls—dope them, gag them and put them on a midnight boat to the Orient—or wherever."

"Now how in the hell could I get you out of here? As I said, this pleasure house is locked up as tight as the vault at the Rockefeller bank. Remember, I'm a private eye, and before that I was a cop. I see the details. They don't want you girls to even *think* in that direction."

She snuggled her flawless white body into mine and put her head against my chest. "I'm begging you, Cable. I'll do anything for you...anything except *not* have a life of my own."

I thought for a minute. "I don't know, kid...it's dangerous shit dealing with these people. You know the guy who invited me here?"

"Your Dr. Becker?"

"Yeah, my Dr. Becker. He's one of the snakes who lives underground and schemes daily how to do in our country. I'm a kind of double-spy, you might say. So..." I felt sorry for Sylvia. I knew how short the fuse was burning in her life, as it was for hundreds of these young women who came here innocently enough, only to discover in horror, that places like this were fronts for something far more nefarious, thoughtless—cruel. I thought for a minute. "What floor are we on here?"

"The fourth. All the Love Chambers are on the fourth floor."

I got up and went over to the only window in the room. It was large but sealed. "How good are you at scaling walls backward, descending—on a bunch of linen tied together?"

"Good, I think," she said, trying to gel my idea in her brain.

"If you can get me a sharp-wedged screwdriver with a stout putty knife without triggering a new world war out there, we might be able to escape together. But it would have to be very late when the patrols don't suspect and think everyone's in some kind of sexual ecstasy or wild trip."

"Yes! I know where the tool room is—and the maintenance man goes home after six or so." She hugged me real tight. "You'd do that for me? What if we don't make it, Cable?"

"Then we're dead, Sylvia. There's nothing more to it."

She pulled away looking at my face in agony. "Oh, God, I couldn't live with myself knowing I was responsible for your getting—"

"—I just said *we'd* be dead—that's you too....so it wouldn't make much difference now, would it?" I thought fast. "You drove us out here today—where's here—where are we?"

"In a suburb of D.C. It's kind of out in the country, though."

"Good. Once we're out, do you have access to a car?"

"Yes, I have the keys to the one I drove you out here in."

"That's good. So, if we can get outta here, you can drive us to a train station—going the opposite direction they think we might go?"

"Yes!" She ran over to me and kissed me all over my upper body. "I'd go anywhere with you! Thank you!"

"Now, careful, lady, I'm still kinda trigger happy between my legs. Junior there has got his pistol cocked, so to speak—and I'd say it's a bit dangerous playing with that fire down below just now."

"So...? I owe you at least that. I would be glad to take care of—"

"—naw, you don't owe me anything. I think I hate what these people are doing more than I hate losing my life. I know it's stupid, ain't it? It's been going on for centuries—yet I care about it *now*." I sat back down on the bed. "Who am I kidding? One guy trying to stop a corrupt, horrible system of sex slavery that's funded with big bucks and enough momentum behind it to launch us to the moon. Ha!"

Sylvia joined me on the bed. "Every little bit helps, Cable." She took my chin in her fingers. "Well, at least there'll be one less young woman sold to the highest bidder..."

"Well, tell you what. I need to sleep on it for a couple of hours. I'm tired from being massaged, washed and scrubbed all day—starting with *you* at eight o'clock this morning."

"It was nine."

"Whatever you say..."

"May I sleep with you? I promise I'll keep to my side of the bed—you can see how big it is—and when we're refreshed, maybe you'll have reached a decision."

"Yeah. Okay..." I said, peeling back the covers and climbing in. Sylvia did the same on her side of the bed.

Escape From Harm's Way

I dozed restlessly for a while. I could feel Sylvia's body shaking clear across the bed. I knew she was filled with the kind of fear that people get when they have to face up to the possibility they might not be around anymore in a few hours. I could also hear her whimpering quietly. I was always a sucker for a crying dame. I mean, a guy just doesn't know how to handle it when some babe goes off with those salty droplets and he feels helpless. So I did the only thing I knew how to do. "Hey, kid, over here...come on over..."

Immediately she slid over to me and I opened my arm and tucked her head under it. "I'm sorry, Cable, I'm such a baby, huh?"

"Shhhh....! I'm still thinking." Sylvia cuddled closer to me and her large warm breasts felt good against my ribs. I guess I knew it would happen, but as soon as that dish touched me, my male response system turned on and Mr. No brains-between-my-legs began to come to attention. I always knew he had a mind of his own. She must have sensed it, because her ear was against my chest and she could feel my heart rate speed up. Women are great at things like that.

Without any further words, she reached down to touch my now-swollen member. "Oh, Cable...is that your private *dick* responding to me?" she whispered into my ear.

132

"Well, it ain't Captain Ahab," I kidded her. Then she slid down my body until her mouth was encompassing that naughty part of my manhood that so often misbehaved. Before long we were both breathing hard and moaning and Sylvia moved that gorgeous red mound of hers over on top of Cable Denning, Jr. In short order we both exploded together and though I knew it wasn't even the fourth of July, there were fireworks going on all around us. We were both probably so filled with tension that our coupling was a good idea after all, a kind of *therapeutic release*. Sylvia was an affectionate young woman and I could tell she would make a wonderful companion for the right guy someday. *If there was a someday*. Right now, I would've bet odds against it.

Around midnight we stirred from our cocoon and Sylvia dressed and went to fetch the tools. I showered and quickly dressed. By the time she got back I was ready to go. She came up to me, took my hand and put it up into her crotch. She sighed a big sigh. "I love smelling us, Cable. I wanted you to feel...before I wash up."

"Yeah, babe, we were wet—and wonderful—together."

"I'll second that, Mr. Private 'dick.'"

She had selected the right tools and I cut and scraped my way around the putty that sealed the parameters of the window. I had asked Sylvia to put a light on in the bathroom so I could at least work with some visual aid. It was hard going, but in a couple of hours, I had loosened the window and began easing the glass edges inward to our room. Finally I grabbed the top and carefully lifted the rest up and out. In the meantime, intelligent Sylvia had tied together all the bedding we had, plus she had found some rope in the tool room. Well—at least, I thought, we were going to make it down to street level. I cinched the rope to the large spout in the step-down tub and insured that by tying a few turns around the nearest legs of the huge bed and secured them.

I told her we were ready and I'd go first just in case she needed me to support her pretty bottom if her hands got tired on the way down. She laughed. "You are so naughty...can you see under my dress?"

"Yep."

"Damn, Cable, don't look then."

"Why not? I've seen it before, haven't I?"

She didn't respond as we descended. We had to be extremely quiet as we passed by the other three windows on our way down. Fortunately the drapes were closed and we made it to the ground. Immediately, she grabbed my hand and we ran for the garage quite a ways around, toward the front part of the building. We hurried in, found the little Ford coupe and she got in. I cranked the engine, jumped in next to Sylvia and off we went. There was a gate about a quarter of a mile from the *Grand House of Pleasure*. Sylvia wasn't sure whether or not there was a 24-hour guard posted there. "Let's assume there is," I said. "You drive up and stop as if we were checking in before we exit."

"And what are you going to do, Cable?"

"You leave that up to me." Then I told her to pull over. "Okay...change of plan—you get in the passenger's seat, pretend you're really sick, okay? Just do it...don't ask any questions."

I drove the car up to the gate. As suspected, a nice enough guy in a uniform with a gun and holster greeted us. "Good evening, folks." Then he glanced at the fine acting job Sylvia was doing as she trembled and moaned in her seat. To me, it sounded more like a recap of our love making scene earlier, but it seemed to convince the guard.

"I'm Dr. Denning...the young lady is ill—I must get her to a hospital immediately. Will you be kind enough to inform one of your guests, Dr. Becker, that I'll have breakfast with him in the morning?"

"I'll do my best, sir." Then he took his cap off and scratched his head. "I'm sorry, but I must check your credentials—I have no recollection of a Dr. Denning on staff." The dummy excused himself to go look at the registry and I gunned the motor and off we went, fleeing from the hapless guard. We laughed together like school children who had run away from school and were truant. Sylvia directed me to the train station. "Shit!" I said. "I don't have enough dough to pay either of our ways. We can go back to my hotel room and get my stuff."

"No! They'll look there first once they've found us missing. I've got about three hundred dollars I've saved. Where shall we go?"

I thought for a minute. I knew I had to get back to work in L.A. in a few days at most. "Maybe we'll just keep low profile as Mr. and Mrs.—find a sleeper car and go to Chicago. There we'll check out the northern route that goes through Denver and on to Montana, I think. I'll make my way back to California via Washington or Oregon—wherever the Southern Pacific goes."

"*You* are going back to California. Where am I going? I'm as good as dead in D.C. just about now, so I can't come back here. I know how to wait tables—and once I was a fish feeder in a zoo. I'm really good at it, too," she laughed.

"Well, you can come with me if you want and then we can sort you out when we get situated. I'll even show you my Private Dick's office on Franklin."

She looked at me funny. "Do you have a girl in L.A.? I can't imagine you not having several..."

"Yeah, as a matter of fact there's Zelda who's probably missing me a bunch just about now."

"Zelda?"

"She's my secretary—and we kind of got involved— you know how it is. Anyway, I've had some pretty staggering losses beginning around 1929—and I don't mean the stock market. I lost my fiancée to an insanely jealous gangster's bullet, and another lady who nursed me back to health—and I went for her in a big way—got cancer of the blood and died two years after Honey. So, it's been slim pickings ever since, I guess you'd say."

"Except for Zelda. Is she pretty? Intelligent—and no doubt—good in bed, right?"

"Right on all counts, Lady Godiva," I said.

"Lady who?"

"You know, the babe who went around on her horse naked—an historical figure. I just figured you've been naked so much in the past eighteen hours or so, the name would fit—it's hard to recognize you with your clothes on."

She giggled heartily. "Oh, you! You make me laugh, Cable. I love to laugh. But you know, I don't even know

136

her and I'm already jealous of Zelda, or at the very least, envious. Why couldn't *I* have found you first. I think we'd make a swell couple, don't you?"

"Well, it's a bit early to tell, Sylvia—but from all indications, I've seen worse matches..."

We ditched the car and took a taxi to the train station. We booked an overnighter to Chicago for that evening. We played sightseers for the rest of the day and I was most impressed with the Lincoln Memorial. It kind of felt like I was looking at the foundations of what our country might have been intended to become. Instead, even during Lincoln's time, self-serving corporate-minded bankers, stock brokers, speculators, politicians and other criminals collapsed the South during that civil war, took its gold, stripped it to a second-class loser while the North prospered.

But Sylvia looked nervous. "I have this feeling we should have left on the first train to Chicago, Cable. I don't know—it's—it's like I can feel eyes watching us."

"We would have, but they didn't have any sleepers. The less we're seen, the better, as I see it."

"I guess you're right. I suppose I'm just running scared. Hell, I don't even know what I'm running to."

"One step at a time, little lady—it'll work out..."

That night we boarded the train and were glad to have our own little room. It had two bunk beds, like the time Adora and I went to San Francisco—what now seemed ages ago. Once we were inside, Sylvia came up to me and kissed me softly on the lips. "Do you want me to get undressed? Or have you already had too much of me that way?"

"Ha! Are you kidding?—you just wet my appetite in the pleasure palace." I took her into my arms and kissed her hard. "And you sure gave me a lot of pleasure. You'd have made a good courtesan."

She slapped my arm. "Damn it, Cable! Always making light of my affections for you. They are real, you know."

I felt bad. "Yeah, I know, doll...I'm sorry, I do have a big mouth that runs overtime. It's all so damned crazy, but I'm really comfortable around you."

"Me, too," she said, holding onto my arm.

"Are you hungry? I could eat the conductor—if he was tasty. Tell you what...I'll go and check out the dining room and come back for you in a few minutes, okay? Stay put until I get back."

Chapter 5

THE DEATH SPIRE

She nodded and I left. The train was crowded because there was a big Methodist celebration in Chicago, one of the black porters told me. I checked things out and made reservations for about a half hour later. I started walking the eight or nine cars, back to ours. I knocked on the door but there was no answer. "Hey, kid, it's me," I said. I tried the latch. It opened. Instantly I smelled a rat and drew my .38. But it was too late. Sylvia lay on the day bed, her eyes wide open with that blank stare you could find any day at the city morgue. I checked out her pulse. There was none. I spotted a little blood at the sides of her mouth. She had been doped up enough to stop her heart. I was filled with anger and trepidation at the same time.

"You chust can't save zem all, Herr Denning...after all, she betrayed us—und vorst off all, she betrayed us viz *you* as an accomplice." Becker surprised me by walking out of the bathroom where he'd been hiding.

I wanted to kill the son-of-a-bitch then and there, but he had his gun trained on me. I had to hold pattern. "You know, Becker, I was just on the edge of saying, gee, maybe I might like this guy even *if* our ideologies and politics differ. But now, you lower yourself to this!" I said, looking down at Sylvia's body. "You know, I didn't even know her last name..." I glowered at him. "How in the shit did you find us? We were like needles in a haystack in this city!"

"You undterestimate us, Herr Denning. Zere iss *nefer* a time ven you are not being vatched. You needn't be sentimental nor remorseful, Herr Denning. You need to brighten up." He looked down at Sylvia's gorgeous body lying there in her white slip. I guessed she was changing clothes when Becker did her in. "Maybe ve should have a slight pity for your *geliebte*, she vas goodt looking..."

"So, how'd you do it, Becker? You damn Krauts keep coming up with the latest ways to kill—the newest potions of death."

"Oh...it's so simple, really. A derivative of iodine und hemlock herb...a pinch of zat and a dash of zis, as ze old alchemists used to say. Ze deadly combination requires only vun little tiny forced svallow. Your lady zere fought brafely to stay alife, Denning...but in ze endt, treachery—it—it—vell, you know vat I mean—zere's alvays a comeuppance for it. Often ze offenders pay...viz zeir liffes." Then he looked at me. "But—forget *her*—zere are millionss more chust like her—und chust like *Ze Grandt House off Pleasure*, each exotic female holdts her treasures."

I was bending beside Sylvia's body, stroking her arm. "Until you decide to sell some of them off as sex slaves to the highest bidder, you son-of-a-bitch."

"*I* don't sell ze girlss. I abhor zat vorld, for your information. I frequent ze house off pleasure becauss for me zere iss nossing more intoxicating zan ze perfect bouquet of vomanhood *au naturel*."

I was trying to keep my tears back, because I knew I was close to attacking Becker in a rage of revenge for killing my little female friend and lover. I felt very sad. "Why?...why did you have to *kill*, Becker? Why didn't you send her to Siberia or something? Did she have less of a right to live than you do?"

"A goodt qvestion, Herr Denning. But it iss, as I saidt, zere are many beautiful und intelligent vomen in ze vorld, all viz breasts, lips und zat marvelous somezing betveen zeir legss, ya?" Then he cleared his throat. "Vich remindss me. I realize zis might be a bit awkvardt und difficult for you zis effning, but life doess go on. Here's ze plan—und vhy ze young voman vas expendable." He cleared his throat again. "I haff a very important under-groundt guest directly from Hitler's side. I surmise our Führer-to-be exercised all manner off sretts to sendt Herr Stanshousen to us. It appearss our new leader hass a yen for ze *Gott off Our Fazers* as vell."

"You guys never stop, do you? So what do you want me to do about it? I don't want anything to do with you, that damned golden walnut or any part of this ugly Fas-cist movement. In fact, if it'd do any good, I'd blast you right now with my .38. But you know what?—guys like you are like weeds—as soon as you cut a bunch of 'em down, new ones pop right back up. Your kind are hard to keep dead, Becker."

"Is zere a lesson for me somevere in your state-ment? I do bore razzer quickly...so let me finish. I am going to exit at our next stop und take an airplane to Chicago vile you are enjoying ze sleep luxury viz your girlfriendt here. But off course, I cannot trust you vanting to 'stick aroundt,' as you Americans say. Zere-fore, I am going to escort you to ze dining car. Zere I vill make sure you are seated. You vill be joinedt by a trustvorthy—und I might add—*deadly*-trainedt assas-sin. Please...don't zink too much...everysing vill become crystal clear ven ve meet again in Chicago." He started out the door and took one more look at the corpse of Sylvia. "By ze vay, her name vas Sylvia Alexander—nice name, don't you zink? I'll see you in Chicago...oh, und don't you vorry a smidgeon—Miss Alexander's body vill be remooft by ze time you return from dinner." He left and I felt my whole world collapse. It was not only in turmoil, but I had been responsible once again for the death of a beautiful young woman. That weighed heavily on me.

I picked myself up, washed my face, combed my hair and made my way to the dining car. I tried looking out the window, but it was dark and all I could see was me looking back at myself. I looked old, worn out, beaten. How could an almost thirty-three year-old have lived through so many experiences, pushing the envelope of his life? And now this. I supposed some ape of a goon was going to be my bodyguard until we reached the Windy City by the lake. I took out and lit up a cigarette, when a luscious babe dressed in a very sexy white outfit started walking down the dining car aisle. Somehow from a distance she did look familiar, but as she approached me and started cracking a generous smile, the cigarette almost dropped out of my mouth. It was Julie Halliday, the babe at the nightclub where I was supposed to meet Ziggy Thompson that night! I stood up as she approached me. "Mr. Cable Denning...we meet again...may I join you?"

I didn't say a word. I sat back down and let her seat herself. Fuck being a gentleman with vipers like these! She placed a small white purse on the table and hailed

142

down a waiter. She ordered a drink and looked at me again. "What is it—cat got your tongue, as you Americans say?"

Shit, the babe wasn't a local after all! She sure fooled me that night when we met and she pitched me her line. "I knew I smelled a rat when your face turned every shade of pale when I mentioned Ziggy Thompson, the other night. What did ya do, bump her off, too?"

Julie Halliday's smile disappeared. "She knew too much about our scientific work under Dr. Voracious. And she was getting a little—how do you say it—*pushy* with her laboratory associates?"

"So now she's just plain old nurturing the soil six-feet under, is that it? Why do you bump off so many of the people I happen to like?"

"I'm sure, Cable—it's purely coincidental."

"I should've known when you pronounced the chef's name that night in perfect German—your vowels and consonants were too pure. So, you're one of them, eh? A plant, a spy-assassin with one too many slip-ups for my taste, lady."

"Yes...I am. It's who I am and what I do. Singing is a marvelous cover for me because I dearly love all kinds of music. But I miss the old German folk songs I grew up with. Your American songs are too *Jewish* for me, idyllic romantic love served on a sentimental platter. No wonder your bourgeois American life styles are so hopeless. Life is never that way. Romantic love is a fabricated illusion, fed to you by the commercial vendors to keep you dumber that you were the generation before."

"Well, that's your opinion. I happen to *like* the dream-thought of romantic love—and Jewish or not—

those great songs of Berlin, Kern, Gershwin, Porter are mini-works of art. Plus they reflect how people really feel. People like you probably don't have a heart or sympathetic feelings that tell you when somebody cares enough about you to love you—and then turns around and has the courage to tell you so—now that's *life*. And some people can't help loving others, or being in love with someone, or even falling in love with someone who's really unattainable. But you know—something like that makes you pull yourself up by the bootstraps and find the guts to stand up and declare yourself, even if you fall along the way...because someday you'll get up again and dust yourself off and live to love another day. But at least when your life is over and the fat lady laughs, you can say you loved...and maybe, just maybe, lived a little along the way."

Julie Halliday seemed out of her element. She didn't know how to respond to what I had just said. "What a brilliant thinker you are, Cable. I had no idea. I knew you were intelligent—a cut above the average—but your mind is razor sharp and analytical. I like that."

"Well, shove it, lady—I don't like *you* and I didn't say that for your benefit. I said it because that's my stance in this life—that music can and does transform people, heal us from the rage of the world and also the unsettled conflicts raging in us."

"Too bad brilliance like yours is wasted. How sad...to think we could use you in the wonderment and unfolding of *The Third Reich*, the new age of common sense and reason, because our Führer's genius will build a world to last a thousand years or more. And once the impure have been eliminated, there will be peace and sanity."

"Yeah, and isn't it funny, I'm one of the impure. Now who's being ideal?" I said, putting out my cigarette. We ordered and I couldn't wait to be out of this woman's sight. Isn't it funny, I thought, a gorgeous dish like her...on the outside you'd never suspect how twisted and sick her mind was. She even seemed normal when she talked. But she's loonier than a bedbug on catnip. "Your Führer will shine and glow for a while, and then your so-called thousand-year 'Third Reich' will tarnish from all the murder and the mayhem, the senseless horrors, the empty promises and something else will rise out of its ashes."

"An opinion, duly registered, Cable. The weaker ones see us as having no emotion, sympathy, empathy or compassion for the human dilemma. But it's quite the opposite. By eliminating those whose lives are a blight upon the world, we will bring about a pure-bred race of beings who will demonstrate the deepest emotion of all: love for the beneficent iron hand that rules, and with impartial decision, returns the earth to balance and wellbeing."

"So who's gonna call the shots on just who gets to stay and who gets to leave on the 'elimination train'?" I put the question to Julie Halliday. When I was a rookie in the police force, I remember once arresting a disorderly drunk and hauling him down to the station. All he did was break a chair and punch out an obnoxious bartender. But I still had to bring him in on an assault and battery. After he was half-sober he begged and pleaded with me to let him go. After all, he had a wife and kids at home, he would lose his job, he was sorry—but most important of all, I recall standing across the interrogation table from him and he said to me, "Officer Denning, you have no heart, no emotions, no sympathy for the human condition. You seem to respond or care, but you don't, really."

Believe it or not I pondered that man's words for years. I still do. But...*what if through many prior lifetimes we are given the opportunity to purge away the weaker aspects of human emotion?* And what if the next stage, after all the wailing and tears, anger, purging, violence and passionate falling in love with love, comes an advanced evolution—a refinement—a freedom from being ruled by emotion? What if caring is the *action* of love helping someone to help themselves? I agreed with the Krauts on one important point: why knock yourself out trying to save or rehabilitate the unwell—whether they're nuts, poorly bred or inter-bred, a drug addict with a burned out brain, the very old and infirm who wish to leave anyhow, the psychopathic individual who could be anyone from a serial killer to a politician or dictator of a country? I think it was *Nietzsche* who said get rid of those who do not contribute to their own daily lives, to the lives of their families, their local environs or leave a creative mark upon the world.

"It is always the survival of the fittest. The weakness is always indicated and we simply accelerate the removal process. Dr. Becker is very big on that one. Most thinking men and women tend to feel that sooner rather than later is *much* better."

"Ah...so...we have irreconcilable differences of opinion. Perhaps you've forgotten one important thing. The goons in charge of implementing these elimination processes can very easily become diseased by the power they're suddenly delegated to wield. You know, the chain being as strong as its weakest link and all?"

"Everyone checks on everyone—that's the joy of the program and why it will work. It's kind of like Karl Marx Communism without Karl Marx. Adulate the beauty of the highest thought, and you have begun to climb the mountain."

"Good luck, lady. But don't come whining back to me if your Führer's plan backfires at some point." I studied the large blue eyes and the yellow-blonde hair that fell to the nape of her neck. She had nice skin. "So now...what evil and subversive thing have you got planned for me, Miss Assassin?"

She put her finger to her lips to shush me... after all, there were a few tables up in front of us but most everyone was blabbing so much no one could hear us anyhow. She let a smile fill her face. "You astonish me...here you are facing possible death and you make light of it? Perhaps you are never truly aware of the danger you are exposed to?"

"I don't know and I don't care. Why not just spell it out...what's the scoop?"

"Well, as Dr. Becker probably told you, we are entertaining a very prestigious minister from Hitler's secret entourage. It seems you have something our leader wants. Therefore, we wish to stage an impressive torture—enough to frighten even the hardiest personage, and therefore, impress that minister as to our methods, regardless of whether or not we get anything out of you."

That gave me the shivers. "I see...and I'm the after dinner mint or the main course?"

She laughed. "Oh, Cable, you simply disarm me. How can anyone be serious when you're dissecting everything I say? But it *is* bizarre...what they have planned. Frankly, I'm a little concerned for you. I hope your heart is strong. By the way, how old are you?"

"You oughta know, you've read all the files on me, I'm sure—everything from my age and toothpowder, to the women in my life and my penis size."

She laughed again. "You're a laugh a minute, Cable! I mean it—you could be one of those dry comedians, a little sardonic—you know..."

"Well, I might make more dough at that than I'm making now chasing down errant husbands and wives."

"Anyway, I happen to know you're thirty-one. I'm thirty. You're an older man. Should we date, you think? Dr. Becker says he definitely does not wish to kill you at this time. That would be rather counter-productive, he says."

"Well, yeah...that would be my take on the subject. So what now?"

"You'll go to your compartment with me and wait until we're picked up in Chicago in the morning. If you so much as try to touch me, seduce me or attempt an escape, I am authorized to exercise any and all measures to subdue you."

"Short of killing me, of course."

"Yes." She looked me over and took a sip from her soft drink. I paid the bill and we got up to go. I noticed an unfriendly face checking us out over by a small bar.

148

She picked up on it. "Oh, don't pay any attention to Wally—he's here to insure your delivery in case—"

"—in case I do happen to seduce you or somehow get the upper hand...?"

We got back to the sleeper car. Sylvia's body was gone. There wasn't a trace that she had ever existed. "It is a shame in a way. Under different circumstances we could've been friends," Julie Halliday said, her lovely blonde hair hanging partly on her face.

"Oh, I doubt that, lady. You see, I have this aversion to rotten women who present themselves as decent babes and who moonlight as singers on warm Los Angeles evenings."

She drew her gun on me. "I hope you have no aversion to heights, Cable."

"Heights? Well, as a matter of fact, I do. When I was a kid—"

"—hand over your weapon to me, please," she threatened. I knew the doll was well trained, so I didn't try any tricks and handed her my .38. She immediately unloaded it, tossed the bullets on the floor and put the empty gun in her purse. "I'd just hate spending the night having to hold you at gunpoint," she said.

"Well, you could spend the night just *holding* me. If we were naked, just think, we wouldn't have to worry about guns and things."

"I thought you didn't like me."

"I don't. But sometimes necessity calls for extraordinary measures."

She thought it over. "I really don't think that's a good idea, Cable—as tempting as it may sound. The Party wouldn't approve."

149

"Oh, it's the Party, is it? Seems it's either the *Order* or the *Party*—who thought up all this cloak-and-dagger crap?"

She snickered. "Oh, you do have a great sense of humor, Cable. But for now, let's just say the *National Socialist German Workers Party* is in control. And since I have the gun, I have decided to utilize part of your idea. Please take off your shirt."

"Wha—?" I stammered. "What the hell for?"

"Do as I say," she said firmly. "Including your undershirt—what is it you Americans say?—*strip*?"

I looked at her strangely. "Uh...yeah, something like that." I did as the lady with the luger said. I tossed my shirts on the floor.

"Now your shoes and pants, if you don't mind."

I sat on the day bed and obeyed the lady. "If you don't mind my repeating myself, this sure would be more fun with the two of us. It's a bit chilly in this car."

She thought it over. "You know, I wasn't always this harsh, Cable. Life's hardness toughens us up—and in Germany after the war, one either did that—or perished. Secretly, I must admit to you I enjoy much of your American Popular Songbook. And I'm also a woman, believe it or not, even though I've not had a lot of men in my life—"

"—oh, I believe it alright," I said, looking at that pretty face and knock-out figure of hers. "And when I first met you, I saw you as a believable singer up there with your tits pushed up and that gown hugging all the right places—not to mention you could actually sing."

"Why are you so irresistible, Cable? Are you this way with all women? Do you chip away at them until they finally succumb to your—your sexual charms?"

"Yep—you're a killer—I'm a *woman* killer," I laughed. "Nothing could be further from the truth in reality, though. You see, I smoke, drink and chase skirts to help blank out the numbness life wants to leave me with every morning when I wake up to face another phone call or some dame who wants her husband watched so she can take him to the cleaners for all he's worth. Or some politician, like a Roosevelt or a Hitler—demagogues set up to serve even more powerful factions working secretly behind the scenes. So you see, I'm not all that secure being human."

It was the first time I saw a look of sympathy in her pretty blue eyes. "I sure do like the way you talk, Mr. Detective. So why are you this way and why should I take my clothes off to join you?"

"Because I'm a fun guy to be with—and it kind of evens the score."

Without another word, she undressed silently. She seemed a bit embarrassed, but she had the prettiest pink nipples I think I'd ever seen. She dropped her clothes to the floor and sidled over to me still with her gun-in-hand. "So you think this is the best way to subdue this guy without killing him?" I asked.

"Maybe," she said in a soft, breathy voice. She put her arms around my waist. "When I hold you...like this...it makes me feel restless...and want to do...this..." She tip-toed up and kissed me softly. Her gun hand was shaking and I knew some part of her was softening up and she was responding to the woman inside of her, the

151

one who was steaming deep down there in the magma of her personal volcano.

"What about what you said in the dining car—you know, the one about touching or trying to seduce you?" I said, testing her.

"I've still got the gun," she whispered into my ear.

"Yeah, but I've got a gun, too. Only mine's attached and it could even be more dangerous than the one you've got in your hand."

"Really?" She took the barrel of her gun and came up slowly between my legs, the cold steel shriveling my balls. "You keep your gun cocked and I'll keep mine loaded," she said, taking the barrel away.

I chuckled. "You see, you're a regular comedian, too."

"Do you think so?" She backed me up to the day bed and gently pushed me down onto it. Then she sat on my lap, facing me. "It's even cold in here with the two of us touching. Will you get a couple of blankets out of the box over there?"

I eased her off my lap and did as the lady asked. I came back with two large, grey blankets. "I hope you know what to do with these," I kidded her. "I can tell you are cold." I said, looking obviously at her nipples.

She glanced at those hooters sticking out from her chest. "Yes...you're right. So if I lie down with you and we cover each other with the blankets, can I trust you?"

"To do what?"

"Not to escape."

"Is that all?"

"No."

"What then?"

"Can you hold me without my gun in between us?"

152

"What about *my* gun in between us?"

"That's different. I might enjoy it if I can trust you."

"I'll make a deal with you. Tie my hands so I can't do anything much, and I'll just lie here and take your punishment."

"Oh, but Cable, I really want your arms around me ...." she breathed it out, taking out the bullets and letting her gun drop to the floor. "Now we're even..." She threw herself around me and we tucked under those warm blankets while Julie Halliday did her version of *Makin' Whoopee* on me.

A couple of hours later we woke up inside those blankets, wet from the perspiration of love making and close quarters, not to mention the fluids that emanated from certain parts of Julie's anatomy. I got up to pee as she awakened and reached for her gun. Then she remembered she had tossed the bullets. "A lot of good that's going to do me," she said.

I came back in and kissed her on the nose. "That was great, kid—where did you learn to, uh, to make love like that?"

"From you...I just followed your lead, Cable. And you were wonderful, by the way. I wish we weren't on opposite ends of world intrigue and politics."

"Yeah, so do I. Somehow love making makes it easier, doesn't it?"

"Yes...especially with you."

I needed to probe deeper about my fate this day. I had already softened her up a bit, so next I had to get some information about what it was that Becker had planned for me as a demonstration model for the *Amer-*

ican Reich. "Thanks for that, babe. I was wondering, however, if you could share a little bit more about what the German Fates have in store for me today."

She smiled and then drew serious. "It's terrible, Cable. The German underground refer to it as the *Punkt des Todes* or the *Spire of Death* in your language. Several 'suicides' recently have ended their lives on the sidewalk five-hundred and sixty-eight feet below the spire. You will be suspended on a thin rope from the spire and asked to confess all you know about you-know-what—or the rope will be cut and down you go! And all of this takes place at night, which is very frightening when one cannot see—"

"—you diabolical sons of bitches! Who thought that one up? And just where is this located, if I may be so bold?"

"It's the tallest building in Chicago—appropriately, the meeting place for the bourgeois Christians in the community—Chicago Temple Building. So you see, you will have traveled 660 miles from Washington D.C. only to meet an untimely death."

"And this is all for real?" I asked, knowing my fear of heights.

She got up with a towel she had gotten from the bathroom and wiped herself, for as she stood there, the product of our love making experience began to leak out. "Yes, I'm sorry, Cable...it's a terrible way to instill fear into people. But we cannot have sympathy for such things when the *cause* is all that matters."

"Is that how you see it—that only your hair-brained 'cause' matters? What..... individuals are suddenly now

154

relegated into a group of sheep to obey the underground master?"

"Something like that. Espionage is a tough game. You ought to know. Even without your trying—I've read your transcripts—you've become embroiled in terrible things and caused the deaths of several so-called 'innocent' people. Do you want me to name them?"

I cringed. "No...but you're right. I feel like shit about that."

"I need to wash up and dress before we arrive in Chicago. I want you sitting on the toilet seat without *your* clothes, looking at me. I'm taking my luger. Please don't make me shoot you." And that was the hardcore insides of Julie Halliday. But now I wasn't sure I believed all of it. Her sexual passions had reached a peak and for a minute I could feel a living, breathing normal woman underneath all the cloak and dagger shit.

We finally both dressed and got ready to detrain.

Before we disembarked the train, Julie pulled me aside. "I'm sorry, Cable. But no matter what happens, I want you to know—"

"—save it lady. To me, you represent all women and no woman, just another twat in the dark—so don't rank yourself too high."

She looked surprised and widened those already big blue eyes. "I see," she said, checking out my own brown orbs. "It's that way, huh?"

"Yeah, of course it's that way. I soft-soaped you to pump whatever information I could get out of you. Isn't that what spies do?"

"Yes...it's what spies do. But you don't have to be so bitter. It's been a long time for me between men and I—"

"—don't pat yourself on the back, lady—put yourself in my shoes, Cinderella. Don't start regretting what you've already become. Do your job and get on with it." I turned and walked away, and found my way to the metal stairs as the black porter smiled and asked us all to watch our steps as we detrained.

Becker and the creep who was watching Julie and me aboard, comprised our greeting party. "Safe und soundt...I see Miss Halliday delivered on her end of ze arrangement."

"To be sure, Becker, your cohort should be complimented. She did her job to the letter—and then some."

"Oh? You mean abuff und beyond ze call to duty?"

"You might say that," I said as Julie joined Becker and the goon. I knew she had heard me and I hoped it hurt a little.

"Herr Denning says you are to be congratulated, Miss Halliday. You are fast becoming vun off our best...field personnel."

"Thank you, Dr. Becker. I do my best..." she said.

They held me at gunpoint in some grungy hotel until about 10:00 p.m. Then we boarded a shiny black limousine awaiting us outside. We drove to what appeared to be somewhere downtown. I didn't know Chicago, but the buildings were getting bigger and taller as we proceeded. Finally we were at The Temple Building, which turned out to be a skyscraper church, The First Methodist of Chicago. We entered and took a freight elevator to

156

the top floor. There we met another goon who carried a large suitcase. But standing in the shadows with two other men stood a tall, lanky guy with a nice fedora. Becker brought me up to the man. "Minister, I vould like you to meet Cable Denning, Private Detective."

The guy looked me over and spoke with a higher voice and...yeah...you guessed it...a German accent. "Vell, ve meet at last, Herr Denning. I hadt almost given up zat you vould be foundt..."

With me in tow they walked up a long flight of stairs into what must have been the tower of the building, which culminated in a very pointed spire. About forty feet from the very top, they tied a rope around me, careful to thread it through my belt loops. Julie stood back with the other hit man we had encountered on the train. "Don't forget to send my love to everyone back home," I quipped.

"It iss refreshing to hear humor from a man about to die—perhaps, Herr Denning," the Minister said.

"I kind of like it that way, Minister whatever-your-name-is."

"Oh, I apologisse, my name iss Heinrich Stanshousen, at your service."

"Well, Stanshousen, forgive me if I don't click my heels, but we've got a saying here in America, *tell me who you go with and I'll tell you who you are*. And right now I think your choice of accomplices could be improved on. When was the last time you checked the want ads for better personnel."

"Your vit iss also refreshing, I must say." Then he looked at Becker. "Vell, Dr. Becker, I suggest ve get on viz it. I vill simply…vitness…ze procedure, if you don't mindt."

"Of course, Minster." Becker turned to the guy who had secured me with the rope. I glanced at Julie. She seemed fidgety and was finding it hard to look at me. "Franz…secure ze rope." The strong little guy tied an end to a steel pillar that served as reinforcement for this part of the base of the spire. From this point going up, it had to have been an engineering challenge. "Now…Herr Denning…for ze last time before ve suspendt you ofer ze building—und hope ze tezer doess not prematurely break—I vill giff you one last time to tell us *vun*, vere *Gott Unserer Väter* iss located und *two*, vat iss encoded onto it—und vat doess it say, to ze precise detail…off its content und priceless knowledge."

I glanced around at everyone. Inside I was shaking. I dared not look over the precipice. I would instantly get those butterflies that gave one the idea that his number might be up and falling from great heights was my least favorite way to go. "My answer's still the same, Becker…suck a lemon." I glanced over again at Julie, who cringed when I insulted Becker. He was her boss and you just didn't do things like that! But *I* just did. So what else could they do to me? Torture would obtain even less results, so I thought. And even though Becker had indicated he didn't intend to kill me just quite yet, and this was a show for Hitler's representative from the good ol' Fatherland, what if that thin rope did break and down I went, hurdling with increasing speed about ninety-miles an hour to my death? *That* was the scariest part of it, not to mention my basic fear of heights.

"Very vell, zen—Franz, suspendt ze stubborn man ofer ze edge off night. It iss fife-hundred und seventy feet to ze very hardt cement below...just ze sought of it makes my own heart...uh...*flutter*..."

Franz grabbed my mid-body and slowly lowered me over the edge. From an adjacent building a spotlight shone on the golden spire of the Temple just above us. It was an eerie feeling, looking up at this thing representing church and God while murder was being planned under its holy roof. So there I was dangling in mid-air. I dared not look down but kept my eyes closed or when I did open them, I looked across and over the rooftops of other buildings not quite as high as the Temple.

But soon the Minister grew tired of getting no results. He leaned over to look at me. Then he turned to Becker. "Dr. Becker, I sink ve vould obtain better results iff ve changed sings by suspending ze prisoner *upside down*, viz ze rope tiedt only to hiss ankles."

"But, Minister," Becker protested, "ve could much more easily lose him zat vay. At least ze belt loops—"

"—am I or am I not superior to your rank und station, doctor?

"Ya, mein Minister. It shall be done," Becker answered.

I was hauled up, the rope was ripped out of my belt loops and re-tied around my ankles. It seemed that Franz liked me a little, because he wrapped my ankles several times around with that thin rope. Of course, he may also have thought if the rope was thin, it might cut into my flesh and they'd lose me that way. I got a quick glance at Julie, who stood nervously smoking a ciga-

159

rette. The minister checked both of us out and put two and-two together quickly. "Miss Halliday, I belieff? Perhaps...perhaps a voman's touch...vould serff to accelerate sings. Let's perform a little play off our own...let's say...a *drama*...und Herr Denning vill play ze victim— und you—ze interrogator. How does zat soundt?" She mumbled something to the Minister, but I could tell she dreaded it. "Goodt! Now, let's play...curtain...going up!"

Becker told Franz to lower me head first into the abyss. This time I was sweating and trembling all over. As the blood rushed to my head, I found I couldn't close my eyes without getting a terrible headache. So I was swung out there in the middle of the night, ever gently two and fro, watching tiny lights from automobiles traveling the streets of downtown Chicago.

"Now...like a pendulum...Franz...sving Herr Denning back und forth in effer videning arcs." He laughed a diabolical laugh. "Oh, how I like zis! Dr. Becker, zis vas a brilliant suggestion. Perhaps now ve may obtain vat ve came for, eh?"

I was sick with nausea and my headache was pounding, coupled with my rising fear. How much later I can't recall, but Stanshousen had Franz halt the swinging and hauled me up to eye level with Julie. Then it was her turn to act. "Herr Denning...I will ask you only once...where is the *Gott Unserer Väter*?"

Barely conscious, I looked into Julie's eyes, then spat at her. "Go...go fuck yourself, bitch!" I croaked. Immediately she took out her luger and hit me hard on the head and everything went black.

Chapter 6

THE DAY AFTER YESTERDAY

I woke up in a gutter, my head pounding. It was still nighttime. I tried to get up, but best I could do was roll on my side and look at my feet. I was bare-footed and my ankles were bloody as hell. I must have thrown up, because my shirt was stained and smelled of vomit. After about an hour of struggling to get my bearings, I realized I was in a gutter by an alley. At first my eyes couldn't focus and I could see no land-marks that might've given me a clue as to where I was. Then all of a sudden I saw a neon sign across the street—*Alberti's*—and I realized I was on Franklin Avenue in Hollywood within a hundred feet or so of my office! Whoever had dumped me here knew where I lived.

I eventually got up and staggered my way toward my office building. It must've been pretty close to dawn because the sky to the east was beginning to lighten up a little. I climbed the stairs to the landing and barely made it to the door. But the door was locked and I had nothing in my pockets, let alone the key to my own office. My pants were ripped, my shirt dirty and torn open, my ankles bleeding and my skull still hurt like Hitler's army had started marching inside my head. I slid down in front of my office door and passed out once again into oblivion.

I lost all track of time and I was fighting off a huge, long dragon with Toggth and Jedediah Penn wielding swords next to me. The fiery beast lunged and spit flames at us, but we kept advancing. Pretty soon a beautiful dark-haired lady appeared on top of the dragons head, and whispered something into its ear. It stopped battling us and settled down, much like a good dog when the master talks it down. The lady had no clothes on as she approached us. Then suddenly Toggth and Jed Penn were gone and I could hear the lady call out my name. "Cable...Cable...my God...can you hear me? It's me, Zelda!" She seemed to be looking up at someone. It was Andy Kurfess, the mailman. I opened my eyes from the dream. The dark-haired woman was Zelda! "I don't know what to do," she was explaining to Andy the mailman. "If he's hurt badly I shouldn't move him. But I can't let him stay out here and continue to attract attention. Someone's going to call the police if he stays out here!"

"Shucks, Zelda, I can help you in with him. Maybe it can be we drag him for a spell without injurin' him up much more, don't you suppose?"

"I—I guess you're right. Okay, let's do it." I could feel my sore and aching body better now as the two people grabbed my legs and dragged me into my office. "Gees...blood all over the place, ripped out britches, bleeding ankles, a large bump on his head, torn shirt, nothing in his pockets. I don't understand what's happened here—I'm so confused, Andy."

"Sure wish I could help more, Miss Zelda. But I've got to get on with my route. I sure hope he mends up okay."

"Sure...thanks for helping, Andy. See you tomorrow." I could hear Zelda running hot water in the bathroom and soon she came and got her arms inside my own and continued to drag me until we were in the bathroom and I could feel the steam from the tub in my nostrils. "Gees, Cable, how you get yourself in such messes I'll never understand. I hope you're mostly alive and you can hear me. I don't know what to do! I mean, should I call the police or what?"

I tried to open my mouth and speak but nothing came. It was as if those bastards in Chicago had tightened that hanging rope around my neck all night. So I pointed my finger back and forth to Zelda in the "no" sign. She got it. She finished undressing me and together we struggled for fifteen minutes until finally I plopped into the water, dyeing the water a pale red from all the blood that must've been on my body. Zelda washed me, drained out the water and refilled it. Finally in a couple of hours I began to come around. "Zelda…!" I finally wheezed. "Zelda…glad…glad to see you…"

Her face filled with tenderness at the sound of her name. "Oh, God, Cable! I almost died worrying about you! Can you tell me if you're hurt badly any place?"

I smiled weakly. "Nope…head aches…feet…really sore…no clothes…money…keys…" And then I reached for her hand. She clasped mine tightly. "…no girl …either…"

"Not true, Mister. You do have a girl, *me!* That's if there's anything left of you when you heal back up." She looked hard at me and shook her head. "I don't know how long I can do this, patching you up every time you go away on a perilous and mysterious assignment. You're worse than taking care of a plant—at least all they need is good soil, some fertilizer, sunlight and water. Sure, I've looked after the office and all, but we're supposed to be running a business here—and if you're off gallivanting every month or so...well, it makes it tough for your business—not to mention us."

"—you're right, Zelda," I squeezed out a loud whisper. "I'm sorry...never meant...to bring this...on...top of you..."

"Well, the important thing is that you heal now." She let me soak for another hour or so. She fed me some chicken noodle soup and eventually I was able to get out of the tub with her help. She helped me flop into my bed. I missed my raggedy old bed with the moth-eaten top blanket. The phone had rung on and off all day and Zelda did her best to field the calls. Near evening she came back into my room and sat quietly on the edge of the bed. She helped me prop my head up. "I want you to get well fast, Cable...I have a surprise for your birthday. Do you even know what day this is?"

I thought through the fog in my brain. "It's—it's the *day after yesterday*...whatever that is..."

"I'll be nice and give you another chance."

"That's swell, babe. What day is this?"

"It's September 7, 1932, big boy. There are only six more days until your special day. Wait 'til you see what I've got planned."

I reached out my sore arms for her and she gently floated into them. "Thank you, Zelda Blodgett, I...I owe you...."

"Owe me what?"

"Just...just a saying...of app—appreciation...."

"Oh. Well, you really don't owe me anything—if you owe anybody anything, it's that you owe yourself some good rest. Also, we've got to move your mother some-

164

time in September. Too late now before we—we celebrate your birthday. You'd forgotten, hadn't you? Boy,
are you lucky you've got me to remind you whether or
not your head's on straight..."

Zelda's voice started fading into the background as
her nervous patter went on and on. Soon I was out
again into the land of dreams.

Candles in a Row

By September 12th, I was up and around. Zelda's
surprise happened to be a three-day trip together to
Santa Monica and the surrounding beaches. She had
rented a cheap motel and wanted to ride all of the hand-
carved horses on the famous Looff Hippodrome carousel and take me to the highest point on the Ferris wheel
and kiss the hell out of me. That sounded like a good
deal to me—and a generous gesture from that little
woman who tended to me after the world had eaten me
up and spat me out. I'd been out of commission for quite
a while and we hadn't made love since before I left on
that ill-fated trip to Washington D.C. It would be nice
leaving the world behind with Zelda by my side.

We arrived in Santa Monica feeling pretty good. One
wonderful attribute about Zelda was that she was never
demanding, but gave me my own time and my opinions,
even if she didn't happen to agree with them. We stayed
at a dump called *The Harmony Shell*, run by a couple of
gin-drinking retirees whose names just happened to be
Harmony. Mr. and Mrs. Harmony took an immediate lik-
ing to Zelda and me. So of course, we told them we were

on our honeymoon and we intended to spend every waking or sleeping moment together. That took care of the evening's entertainment of playing cards, the Santa Monica old time guided tour and a fishing trip out to Catalina to reel in some big ones.

Instead, we meandered up the coast on Roosevelt Highway, walked along beaches and ventured up to Point Mugu where there was a dangerous curve that in 1930 was planned to be bypassed by blowing a hole right through the middle of the Mugu 'Rock'. A monumental undertaking that hadn't, as yet, been accomplished.

It was our second night and I noticed Zelda was really frisky and feeling her oats. I saw glimpses of the child-woman who lived within her and practical adult woman whose first name was Responsibility. We were tired after a long day of hiking, walking, laughing, hugging, kissing, eating, drinking and peeing.

For some reason or other, I remember that night. We sat up in bed talking. "Days like these never come again, do they?" she said.

I lit up a Lucky Strike and puffed the smoke up to the ceiling. "Oh, I don't know, why not?"

"Because they're like photographs. They get stilled in time, Cable, and someday all you have left is the memory. It's like everything in life reaches its zenith, you know—like my plants—I've grown the most beautiful flowers you've ever seen. But when they reach their prettiest day, it only lasts for a day or two and then petals begin to fade already. Sometimes I feel like that. Like I've reached my zenith with you and I don't know how long my bloom is going to stay."

"That's a rather depressing attitude to toss at your birthday boy here. Hell, take each day as you find it, Zelda—live it the best way you know how, breathe it in and take the bitter with the sweet, throw your lucky coin high up into the air and hope it comes down heads for you. The human condition is a guessing game at best. Our bodies will grow old and wrinkle with time, our brains take that long journey through memories and regrets, and then to senility, and...maybe—our hearts will look long and hard to find love. But if two people have something—I mean, something *really* special together, they'll still feel like raising their feet and dancing to whatever is left of life's music. What else can we do?"

She smiled at me and took my hand. I put out my cigarette and tucked her under my arm. "I've been in love with you so long now, and for a while I thought I could be that one special person in your life, you talk about. But I don't know anymore. Maybe I'm just going through a change of some kind inside myself." Then she got this devilish grin on her face. "But I do know one thing I'm feeling tonight for sure, mister." She took my hand and put it up between her legs. She was sopping wet and her lubrication was thick and viscous. "I am horny for you, Cable Denning. Do you know how long it's been since we've made love? I held out while you were recuperating, but now you've got no excuses, buster, and you can feel how much I want you..." She clicked the lamp off on her bed stand and began bringing me to attention. Soon I began to realize how built up I was for her and before long we had plunged into a wild night of ecstatic love-making never before equaled

167

by us as a couple. Over and over she reached an orgasm, whether I did or not. We had no other people in rooms directly adjacent, so we let out with our whoops and yells of sexual, passionate delight until morning found us collapsed on one another.

When she got back from the bathroom that morning, I remember she sat on the edge of the bed rocking back and forth like a child with a teddy bear in her arms, humming some little children's rhyme. "Cable, are you awake,?" she asked, still humming to herself.

"I am now..." I yawned. "What time is it?"

"Who cares? I have something I want to tell you, though."

"Yeah? What is it?"

"I feel special this morning. Like last night I became a real woman—I don't mean just because of the wonderful sex—but something else happened. I can't explain it." She took my hand and placed the flat of it against her stomach. "Here...I feel this special feeling...like thousands of tiny bright little lights are lighting up my tummy from deep inside, swirling and twirling in there...happy."

"It's probably thousands of my happy little sperm swimming their way around inside your vagina," I quipped.

She tittered like a little girl. "Maybe...but I just wanted you to know...how complete I feel...how happy I am..."

"Me, too, Zelda. This is probably one of the best birthdays I can ever remember."

"You mean even better than the one Honey threw for you before--"

"—a lot different, lady...you and I are natural together, *organic*, unplanned, spontaneous. I think that's one of the wonderful things about you, Zelda."

She fell back onto me, looking up at the ceiling. "I will love you forever and ever and ever, Cable Denning. I just can't imagine how someone could find greater happiness than I'm feeling this minute. I guess this is that photograph I was talking about. We're living it right now, here...in this quaint little motel room in Santa Monica, California."

"Not to put a damper on anything, kid, but weren't you the one that brought up how challenging it is being with a guy like me—forever coming home beat up?"

"As long as he doesn't come home dead. Yeah...I think I'm alright...except for losing you *that* way. Your drinking, smoking, looking at other women, going out to listen to the music you like, the sexy cocktail singers—maybe even another woman now and then who happens to fancy you—but I would always want you to know where *home* was, Cable. Can you understand what I'm saying?"

"Yeah, I think so, doll. I've never been too domestic, so it's not in my nature to picture you and me and baby make three in some bungalow where the faucet leaks and I have to mow the lawn on Saturday mornings."

She laughed. "No, I guess not—domestic you aren't, Mr. Thirty-two year old man." Then she turned to face me. "But that can't stop me from loving you all the rest of my life now, can it?"

I drew her to me and kissed her long and quietly. "No, babe, it can't."

When we got back to L.A., I told Zelda I wanted to visit Adora's grave. She had looked at me rather queerly, but nevertheless asked if I wanted her to come with me. I said yes, because it would be the first time since Adora's death that I would have the guts to stand over the grave of perhaps the only woman I ever truly loved completely.

On September 21st, we helped my mother move out of the ghetto in East L.A., where I was born, and into 2166 North Vine Street in the Hollywood Hills. By the 30th I was back to work full time and getting a lot accomplished and business was good considering the Great Depression was at its peak. I hadn't heard from any of that treacherous gang of German spies and thugs who had all but done me in at the top of the Temple Building in Chicago. Had Becker satisfied his calculating boss, Minister Stanshousen? Why had they chosen to dump me in the gutter near my own place? And whatever happened to that deceiving, attractive wench, Julie Halliday, one-time torch singer down at *The Trocadéro*? Huh......sometimes it's not a good thing to speak too soon.

It was a Friday afternoon and I was looking forward to spending time with Zelda walking in Griffith Park when the phone rang. "Yeah, Cable Denning here..."

"Cable? Thank goodness you're still alive! Uh...this is Julie Halliday..."

I hung up. There are some people you just don't care if you ever see again as long as you live! She was one of

170

them. The phone rang again. I picked it up. It was Julie again. "Yeah?"

"Please—before you hang up again—I ask you to hear me out for just a minute. You knew that night Dr. Becker had to satisfy Minister Stanshousen, and that he had already tried everything else to force the information out of you. Stanshousen wanted to frighten you within an inch of your life. I saw how you were suffering that night—so when it was my turn to interrogate you, I told them I lost my temper and clonked you on the head with my luger and knocked you out. That stopped the fun and games they were having by suspending you over the edge of that terrible building. I couldn't take anymore, Cable! I was suddenly cursed with caring what happens to you—I don't know— maybe it was the love-making we did the night before, the way you kiss, how you talk and touch me. I also knew where you did business on Franklin Avenue. So I urged them to dump you on the sidewalk near your place. Stanshousen wanted to drug you and kidnap you back to Germany with him. Dr. Becker, for his own reasons—and I, for mine, convinced Stanshousen that we'd be more successful at extracting the information from you here in the United States. After all, we had an original contact with the Chinese woman for whom you originally procured it—after you found it hidden in that knight's armor in the hallway at Hearst Castle."

"You know about that, too, eh?" I queried her, astonished she would have privy to that information.

"Yes, Cable, I know so much about you. That's another reason why I felt myself wanting to be—well, wanting to be closer to you."

"So I guess I owe you for at least that—you stopped them from exporting me to *Deutschland über alles*, huh?"

"Yes. I know all the rest, and I wouldn't blame you if you never wanted to see me again. Fair's fair. But I wanted you to know that—and also to know that Stanshousen has given Dr. Becker a deadline to have both the *God of Our Fathers* capsule *and* the entire content of your brain concerning that item, on his desk not a minute later than December 31, 1932. They mean it, too, Cable. They're dealing with some pretty bad aliens who claim they have the scientific know-how to extract specific information from specific brain cells. You need to become anonymous, Mr. Detective."

"How in the hell can I do that, Julie? And why? If I show fear, that'll feed right into those bastard's hands—that kind of shit is what they live for. And speaking of which, you sound like you're on the outside looking in—what happened, did you lose status for slugging me with your gun?"

"I've been temporarily suspended. That's a kind of discipline Stanshousen revels in. He is a child in men's clothes. Anyway, will you ever forgive me, Cable? I know how badly you were treated. I fell down on the job and now I hurt both of us. Can we be friends?"

"I don't know...I'm a funny guy that way. You know that old saying, 'Fool me once, shame on you—fool me twice, shame on me!' I ain't playing the sucker game with you anymore, Julie."

"But I'm also a woman, Cable, and enjoyed every second of our intimacy on the train. Doesn't that count? I gave myself freely to you."

"That's *your* problem now, Julie. But I'll make a deal with you. You stay out of my life and I'll stay out of yours. Oh, and as for Ziggy Thompson, I hope there's an assassin's Hell somewhere for people like you. She didn't deserve to die. Even if you killed her out of 'duty' to the oncoming freight train called 'The Third Reich,' little gals like Ziggy were out of bounds. You've got a choice, when it comes down to it, you know. It's kind of like the young man who joins the army and suddenly finds himself with a rifle shoved into his hands. He has the choice *ahead of time* to say he's not gonna kill someone he might've *liked. You* had that choice, lady."

Her voice was remorseful, soft. "You're right, I liked Ziggy. So now what, Cable? Dr. Becker will be back for you, as I said. Hang on or disappear from the world. December 31st is just around the corner. Will you come see me sing?"

"That's a definite negative, Miss Halliday. I gave you my reasons. You see, once trust has been breached, for me there's no other way except down...whether it's with a babe like you or anybody. Good-bye, Julie, next time don't take the train." I said and hung up.

My gut told me this was the day for housecleaning. I had this yen to catch Misty Sheridan in her musical lair. I called Zelda and told her to get decked out in her best. She was excited when I told her we were going out for dinner and dancing. What I didn't tell her was that I was using her as a buffer between Misty and myself. I don't know, maybe I didn't have the guts to face Misty alone, maybe I was afraid to pick up something that never got started, even though I knew it was finished.

The *La Monica* was busy and Zelda and I made our way to a booth I had reserved earlier. Zelda looked like a million, radiant, her skin alive and flushed with love and life, those marvelous large breasts of hers bulging tastefully out of her low-cut black dress that clung to her body like wax paper on a wet surface. She had her hair up in a swirl that I liked and her lovely white neck looked just right for kissing and biting, I thought. The minute we sat down in the booth she took my hand and held it tight. Something had changed about Zelda Blodgett. Maybe it was that being a sexually active woman had matured her in some magical way. She seemed more certain of herself, articulate and knew how to say what she was feeling at the moment.

"Gees, Cable, the first time you took me here I felt so inferior to all your good-looking women—not to mention that singer you had the hots for—but now, I feel I can hold my own with any of them." She kissed me lightly on the cheek. "Thanks to you." A waiter came and we ordered the usual soft lime sodas and as soon as he'd gone, I took out my flask and spiked our drinks with some good English gin. Zelda lifted her glass to me. "I love you, Mr. Denning, and always will..."

I looked at her as I raised my glass, looking at the lovely creature she had become. "I guess I can say it, too, Zelda...I love *you*...and that's that, kid. Don't ask me again."

She beamed and took in a big breath. "God, Cable, that's the first time...you ever told me you loved me. Do you really? Or are you just echoing my feelings?"

"Naw," I joked, "I'm only kidding. How could anyone love a bookworm nerd stuck away in a hideaway bungalow who wears thick glasses and surrounds herself with plants?"

She slapped my shoulder. "Damn...oh, you...how do you do it? You have a way of disarming a girl, making her fall in love with you—and then dismissing the whole thing as if it were just another one of your dangerous adventures."

"Well? Maybe you *are* just another adventure to me—*definitely* dangerous—ever think of that? Maybe we were ships passing in the night that just happened to meet, hang out together—and something stuck—so here we are."

"Stuck...yeah, that's a good word. It stuck...we stuck...like glue...or like when we make love and you don't come out of me for a long time. We get stuck together and I never want you to leave that place between my legs. Do you think the two ships might make port together?"

I laughed. "I don't know, lady. Who does? All I know is that I'm here—*now*—with you and that's all we've got."

Just then Misty Sheridan walked onto the stage. She was wearing that red-sequined gown that drove men crazy. Her red hair shone in the spotlight, that white skin of hers off-setting those blue eyes that exuded sex and wonder at the same time. The bar was lined up with guys gawking at the beautiful woman, poised like a pro, ready to deliver her song as the band struck up a nifty version of Gershwin's *I've Got Plenty Of Nothin'* and people started tapping and moving their bodies to her music. Yeah, maybe that was the way it was, she had ended up with nothing—but maybe it was plenty for her, maybe souls are destined to be with other souls. Could it have been her destiny to be with Edie Clason after all was said and done? But then there's the male view, all that fantastic woman going to waste not being fucked by him in the darkness of a passionate night when two naked people enjoin the way nature intended. I don't know. Life has a funny way of twisting things around.

When Zelda first saw Misty, I could tell she reacted with a little "Aha!" in her head, that I had come to see Misty, and she was the protective baggage. But I felt it coming, so I decided to head it off at the pass. I bent over to Zelda and kissed her long in that dark booth, sending her the message, "*It's you I'm here with, Zelda...*" I think she got the message, because when our lips drew apart she looked at me and smiled. Then she took my hand. "Gees, you feel good tonight, Cable."

The place was busy and our waiter seemed to have forgotten us and we were out of drinks. So I told Zelda I was going up to the bar to get us some refills. "Say goodbye to her for me, too, Cable," Zelda declared from her seat. I did a double take. How could she have known? I smiled sheepishly, nodded and made my way to the crowded bar. Misty spotted me after her song and left the stage. She walked over, trying to get to me through the lusty men wanting to paw at her.

"Hello, Cable...thank you for coming to see me."

"Hiya, Misty. Yeah, I kind of wanted to see you one more time."

She glanced over to the booth where Zelda sat in the semi-dark, the candlelight making her face seem aglow.

"Only one more time? I see you have your nice little caretaker with you," she said a bit sarcastically.

"Zelda and I both enjoy your music. How've you been?"

"Okay, I guess. How have *you* been?"

"Oh, pretty busy. I've—I've had a few interesting adventures out-of-state in the past month or so. Some were pretty hairy—let's just say I'm glad to be alive."

"And I'm glad you came, Cable." Then she looked into my eyes. "Regrets, Cable? I mean do you have any concerning us?"

"Nope. Sometimes I wonder what might have been. But we all make decisions—right or wrong, good or bad—and most of the time we're obligated to stick to them."

She took my hand and led me to a dark place on the side of the bandstand. "*I* have some regrets, Cable." I was looking back and forth between her lovely and eyes and those gorgeous white breasts of hers, trying to figure out which I liked best. "I regret not giving us a fair chance. I still wonder about fulfilling all those feelings I had for you that night when—when you and I began our overtures."

"Well, life is kind of stingy about giving away fair chances—"

"—please let me finish. I had a wall, Cable...couldn't get to my womanly feelings...too hurt to know I could fall in love with you. Instead, I ran back to Edie—where I could feel safe. Now I wonder if I didn't make a big mistake. I still think about you in my bed—but even more than that, listening to you talk, touching you, our intelligent conversations. I really wanted to be your

177

friend, too. So, you see, I failed all my own tests. How's that for truth, Mr. Truth Guy?"

"Thanks, Misty. I appreciate it. But when the water passed under the bridge, it took the boat with those two people—it's too late even for regrets, lady. Regrets hang you up in the past. Stay with today, it's your best bet." I started to move away from her. She grabbed my arm. "Some night, after work—would you consider coming home with me?"

"Thanks.....but no thanks, Misty. As I said, water under the bridge. I've moved on, doll. I suggest you do the same."

I walked away and came back with the drinks to the booth where Zelda sat, her eyes checking out my own. "Thank you, Cable. I know you finished it." I slid in next to her and toasted her. She took a sip. "I also know you really wanted her at one time—I mean, even more than you wanted me. Has all that changed now?"

"Yeah, babe, it changed big time when I found out that you were better in bed than any ten Misty Sheridans," I chuckled.

"There you go again, making light of it. What will I do with you?"

"You're doing it, Zelda, you're doing it...just don't stop..."

We walked out just as Misty began to sing what must surely have been her swan song to me. I have to admit I was touched by the pathos in her voice as she put her undefined feelings into a song entitled, *There Goes My Heart.* Zelda paused with me at the doorway long enough to look at me to make sure the decision I had made was the right one for me. *'There goes my heart, there goes the one I love, there goes the boy, I wasn't worthy of,"* the lyrics went. Sometimes in life the right things happen at the wrong time and the round peg doesn't fit into the square hole. That's the way it was with Misty Sheridan. There in the semi-dark of the club I took Zelda's hand and squeezed it. Then she knew I was leaving the beautiful singer in the red-sequined gown and would not look back again. The last lyrics I ever heard from Misty Sheridan were the poignant words of the song. *"I never thought that he, would pass me by...there goes my heart, and here am I...."*

Everyone falls down at some point. What makes the difference is the ability to grit your teeth and get up again. It was Saturday and I was on my way to Adora's gravesite with Zelda sitting beside me on the streetcar. Catholic cemeteries have a different feel to them. *Sacred Heart* was small, a few acres behind a gleaming white old wooden church. We made our way across the spongy lawns to a few graves sprinkled under a large elm tree near the end of the property. We found Adora's tombstone and suddenly I found myself wanting to feel something standing over it. But it had been too long. It was like I was visiting the grave of a faraway memory, someone I used to know, but now she was all but a stranger to me. Memory fades, love goes away somewhere and the sweetness of her tender touch and kisses went away with her.

I took Zelda's hand and clasped it tight. "Zelda...I was expecting some—some outpouring of emotion, some kind of feeling of loss. But I feel so little. Like a faded flower pressed in a book I mislaid."

Zelda unclasped her hand and leaned her head on my arm. "I don't know what to say, Cable. You've probably been beaten and battered up so much that your emotions are on strike. Sometimes *I* feel that when you make love to me. You're with me...but not..."

I felt frustrated. "But I really *loved* her, Zelda—she was a tender branch on my tree—the kind of babe men kill for—you know, beauty, brains, a great body that gave great sex—a woman who wrapped herself around her man and bent with his every move."

"You forgot something, Cable..."

"I did?"

"*Love*...she loved you—really loved you—and from what you say, she was completely yours—but she didn't die for you. She would have wanted to live...knowing you are hers...that's how a woman is...her nest is not really complete without the man she loves."

"But I was gone so much—and it was hard to break old habits, even when we got a little cottage together. When I was with her, I was happy. But on my own back at the office, I still liked to go out to one of those joints with some hot dame singing her heart out, a place where I could be released, set free from the hum-drum of the everyday world. Smoking, drinking, chasing skirts...like I was addicted to a life style I would never want to change."

"See...? Now you're remembering. I know sometimes you want to stuff painful memories back in the box. But maybe it's best to let them air out, so you can start to heal them inside yourself."

The time was up. There was no longer a reason to stand over Adora's grave. The afternoon was balmy. A slight breeze from the ocean that blew Zelda's dark auburn hair and the strands lit up with the sunlight like a golden-bronze nest of colors. I turned to look at Zelda. "I have you now, Zelda. I swear I never saw you coming, and after Honey and Adora, I thought that part of my life was finished, it hurt so damn much. You don't know how happy I am you're with me." I took her hand and we walked away. I would never visit Adora Moreno's gravesite again. What was over was over and we all fall down into that deep six place sooner or later. I just hoped I wouldn't bury any more beautiful women who walked into my life.....and died because they did.

Chapter 7

WORLDS WITHOUT END

The Flower Shop

It felt funny having only until December 31st to live on this crazy mixed-up planet with so many wonders. The great mountains, expansive prairies, tall forests, exotic jungles, hidden lakes and water falls and beautiful, endless blue seas. It was October 30, 1932 and I was feeling really good about Zelda and me. We had found a rhythm in our lives of togetherness. She helped out at the office during the day and we made intense, passionate love at night. She fitted around me like a sleeve on my old sweatshirt and her intelligence, wittiness and even disposition worked out just fine for both of us. Yeah, things were going swell for a young private eye plying his trade in the septic tank of the Los Angeles underbelly.

So this one afternoon while chasing down some errant housewife who was having an affair with her milkman, I stopped in a new flower shop on Sunset Boulevard near Gower. It was called *Bouquet Land Florist* and stood street level about mid-block. Tomorrow was Halloween and I decided to buy Zelda some flowers and take her out for a nice dinner, and later we'd come home and play our own version of 'trick-or-treat', but I had the feeling there'd be more treat than trick once we had our clothes off.

I was wandering around the array of marvelous flowers when I came upon a bucket of roses. But one rose particularly stood out. It looked like a perfect rose to me, balanced petals in pink, yellow and white blended colors. I took a sniff and suddenly felt transported. I had never smelled such an incredible flower in my life! "That...is *The Breath of God*," a voice said behind me. I turned to find a little creature of a man with bright yellow eyes and a kindly smile. "There is no other essence like it in the world. When you have absorbed that scent into your olfactory glands, the world will change for you—"

"—why do you have only one?" I asked. "I'd like to have a dozen or so of these."

"Oh, no, sir. That would be overwhelming for the human body. One such rose mixed with these, the *Talisman*, are all you need. The lady in question will be most pleased with that bouquet, I am quite sure. The *Talisman* rose has just recently been hybridized...1929, I believe."

"How do you know it's for a lady? What if it's for a sick male friend in the hospital or something—or my mother?"

He looked at me and smiled a broad grin. "Look at your face, sir. It is flushed with youth and the fruits of lovemaking. I am certain it is intended for some lucky female who is pollinated by a virile male such as yourself. Am I wrong?"

"No, but you sure as hell are personal, Mister. Do you expose all your customers with that kind of detailed analysis?"

"Oh, no, only those whom I see are sporting enough and possessing sufficient wit to withstand the irony of life. Shall you take a dozen *Talisman*?"

"Yeah, that sounds swell. Can you fix it so they'll last until I get home?"

He nodded and took the bucket from the counter, shook off the excess water from the dozen *Talisman* roses and wrapped them in newspaper. I noticed he had carefully removed the single *Breath of God* rose from the bouquet.....I asked him about it.

"Oh, I'm sorry, but I cannot let the *Breath of God* leave the premises. You see, it serves as an attractor so people like you will purchase my other roses."

I mused. "I see...so how much does just one cost?"

"I told you, sir, the *Breath of God* must never leave our presence. They are not available in numbers. There is only this one—and it is *never for sale.*"

"May I smell it again?" I asked, anxious to again experience the *exquisite* essence from that single beauty.

"I must ask you to be moderate, sir. The *Breath of God* is a *transmogrifier*, and you run the risk of experiencing withdrawals and addictive behavior."

I laughed and looked at the little man whose bright yellow eyes were staring up at my own. "Well, whatever—but what the hell is a transmoger—or whatever you called it?"

"It has the power to transmute consciousness, alter the way your brain thinks, intoxicate you until you...you want no other...thing in your life, except...the *Breath of God.* Nothing else will do..."

I raised my eyebrows. "You're kidding, right? It's a plant, for God's sake, Mister! It's just a rose with a great scent—and that's it!"

"No, sir, I assure you...that is not 'it' as you say—and I ask you to refrain from inhaling..."

Just then his phone rang and he went to a wall behind the counter to answer it. While he had his back turned to me I quickly picked up the gorgeous multi-colored beauty sitting on the counter and took a deep whiff. Suddenly my head began to spin and I felt light-weight as if I were about to float to the ceiling. I began to see swirling colors and my body began to twitch. I walked away toward the exit, trying to shake the effects of the damn flower. By the time the little man was off the phone I was in a slightly altered state. "Whoa! That damn thing is potent, alright—you weren't kidding, buddy!"

He looked alarmed. "Sir! I positively instructed you to take no other benefit of the rose's essence—but I see you did. And I'm afraid, you will suffer the consequences.," he warned me.

I smiled sheepishly, still feeling a bit dizzy. "So what will happen, Mr. Florist—will I float to the Land of Oz or something?" I laughed.

But he was deadly in earnest. I'd been a cop and a P.I. long enough to see now he wasn't joking. "You must come at midnight—tonight. Not a minute later. I will administer an antidote for you. Else-wise you shall experience great discomfort and transformation."

"Yeah, right, buddy. How much do I owe you?"

I paid two bucks for the dozen roses and left the joint. I was still stepping lightly on my feet and my vision was a tad blurry. I had never heard of toxic roses before, but I think I had just experienced one. Dinner with Zelda was exceptionally quiet and she seemed to be pre-occupied with things other than me. At least that's what I sensed. So finally I had to see if I could dig it out of her. "So what's the Halloween scoop, babe—black cat got your tongue tonight?"

She smiled at me across the table. We were at an Indian restaurant called the *Khuśa Rāstā* (the happy way)over on Highland Avenue near Wilshire. Some good-looking little belly dancer was doing her thing out in the middle of the floor. She was half-dressed in gold macramé and a rather sheer skirt with little panties underneath. "It's not you, Cable, if that's what you mean. I'm sorry, I guess I'm not too much of a Halloween girl."

I studied my lover's face. "I know you better than that, toots, and something's eating at you. I'm here to listen, you know. I hope you realize I can keep secrets pretty well by now."

"It's—it's nothing...just stuff going through my head." She reached across the table for my hand. "I think I just need you to take me home and make love to me—make me forget all the thinking crap..."

"Well, that was sort of my intent." But I had 'thinking crap' in the back of my own head as well and I was still feeling a bit strange and woozy from inhaling one whiff too much of *The Breath of God* rose at the *Bouquet Land Florist*. I withdrew my hand and picked up the check to glance at it. "Man, $4.79 for two people for a little Indian food—outrageous," I said.

"Speaking of which, you haven't paid me a penny in wages for six weeks. I'm—I'm saving...I could sure use the money, Cable."

Her tone was strange, a little distant. "Yeah, of course—I just thought you would take out whatever you needed to pay yourself from our slush fund."

"You need to sign the checks, Mr. Private Investigator."

"Oh, yeah...." I said, not even recalling when last I signed a check for Zelda.

We got to Zelda's place and she immediately went into the bathroom and told me she was going to take a bath. She seemed a little pale and listless by the time we got home and I could swear I could hear her vomiting while she ran the bath water. I didn't say anything. Matter of fact, I wasn't feeling all that great, either. When she came out she was even more washed out than before she bathed. "Are you feeling okay—I mean really, now—don't bullshit me if you're not."

She took off the towel wrapped around her body and slipped into bed. "Just some female stuff. In fact, I don't think I'm able to make love tonight, Cable. Hope you don't mind. Could you just hold me?"

That kind of saved my ass as well, because I had swung out of the romantic mood several hours ago when I first took a whiff of that stupid, potent rose at the flower shop. "Sure, doll, my pleasure." I slipped into bed beside her and realized my body was clammy, an unhealthy warm wet.

Zelda noticed and put her hand on my forehead. "You're hot, Cable—and really steaming...are you not feeling well?"

I thought for a minute. Should I or should I not tell her? But being a truth guy, I decided to take the chance. "When I bought your flowers today from a new florist on Sunset, I took a whiff of some exotic rose that was among the Talisman I bought for you. The essence of

187

the damn thing knocked me for a loop and it made me feel pretty dizzy. What's your wise assessment, O Zelda Blodgett, Plant Lady Extraordinaire?"

"What was the name of the rose—and where is it now?"

"*The Breath of God*, the proprietor called it. He took it out of the bouquet of Talisman the minute I purchased it."

"I've not heard of that one. But they keep coming out with new crosses all the time—you know, hybrids that look like several different kinds of roses in lots of colors—except blue—no one has ever been able to produce a blue rose."

"So, anyway, even though the owner of the joint told me not to take another smell of the thing, when the phone rang and he turned his back, I did. This time it was like I was gonna blast out of my body and I got *real* dizzy. When he got off the phone and looked at me, he knew I had cheated and taken another whiff. He got a bit miffed. Then he told me to come back at midnight and he'd give me an anti-dote, because things would only get worse."

Zelda's eyes widened. "Gees, Cable, some flowers are toxic to us. Just as some leaves, roots and/or seeds are deadly poisonous. But why would he not administer an anti-dote right on the spot when you fell under the spell of the rose? Don't you think it rather odd that he would have you come over to his florist shop at midnight?"

"Yeah, and he said not a second later. Like he's into some kind of ritualistic mumbo-jumbo or something."

She frowned. "I don't know how you do it, but you get yourself into the most bizarre circumstances. So are you going to go at midnight?"

"Yeah, I was thinking I might. I didn't tell you because I didn't want to spoil your evening going out and all—but I've been feeling rather weird all day, right up to now. The guy at the florist told me it would get worse and I'd really need to go see him to get rid of the rose's effect on me."

"Then I'd go."

"You wanna come?"

"I would.....but God, Cable, I've been around plants all my life. Plus I'm feeling light-headed and crampy tonight. I'd better stay home and get some sleep."

"Sure, babe..." I said, thinking it was now 10:30 p.m. and I had to be at *Bouquet Land* in an hour and a half.

The Blue Rose of Noda

At three minutes to midnight I was at the entrance to *Bouquet Land Florist*. I was feeling pretty rotten. The streets around me were spinning and I had to lean against the building to remain upright. I tried the door. It was locked. At precisely midnight the door opened all by itself and I entered. But it wasn't a florist shop anymore! The minute I got in, the door closed and locked behind me and I could hear some strange hum all around me. Then the little man who had sold me the roses stepped out from behind another door. It sounds crazy but in the semi-dark of the humming room, his eyes glowed neon yellow, sort of like an owl's when the headlights of a car hit them at a certain angle.

As I stood there teetering back and forth, my vision blurring on and off, I began to see the baldheaded creature as something not quite human—and the yellow eyes came forth. "I am sorry you have to be mixed up in this, sir. But I warned you about the rose, did I not?"

"You shouldn't have had the damn thing hanging around here in the first place!" I exclaimed to him, having a hard time focusing my eyes. He said nothing but motioned for me to follow him. We went through the doorway from which he had entered. We were in what looked like some kind of spacecraft control room, definitely science fiction. In the middle of the room was a short pole of some sort, on top of which stood a deep-dish tray with blue, glowing rims. In the center of the tray sat a large blue rose the size of a large cauliflower! "What's going on here—where in the hell are we? And what happened to your flower shop?"

"Please do not be alarmed," he spoke in a gentler voice than earlier in the day. It was almost as if he was trying on voices and attitudes to accommodate me. "I have prepared the proper antidote to restore your state of being."

"My state of being is just fine, whoever you are. That hum...this room...it's a flying craft of some sort, isn't it?"

"My name is *Firt*, by the way. *Eli Firt*. This is not exactly a moving craft of the type you are used to. This is the control room of a dimensional travel apparatus. It does not go anywhere, nor does it move by propulsion of any kind. It is an *ultra-dimensional portal instrumenter*—and appears from another vibrational plane of existence, which we call a *syndrome*. That is a state not normally present in your time."

"Oh...uh-huh..." I said that, looking around the interior of the room. Hologram-like buttons and small colored lights filled an entire wall and there were no seats. "So, let's get on with it...not only am I feeling lousy and disoriented, Mr. Firt, but my girlfriend is expecting me to return momentarily."

"I'm afraid that isn't possible, Mr.—Mr. —"

"—Denning—Cable Denning..." Things were getting crazier by the minute. Maybe I was dreaming and didn't know it.

"Mr. Denning...I must apologize, because I was mistaken about being able to administer the antidote in your planet's atmosphere—"

"—whoa, there, buster. What do you mean by 'my planet's atmosphere?'" It was then that I realized that feeling I got up the back of my neck was not my imagination. This little guy was an alien!

"Okay...so now I know...you're a visitor from another planet or star system, right? I mean, not native to the earth." I was thinking of all the ones I had encountered since that fateful first day at the Los Angeles morgue, when I saw that the corpse's throat had housed that golden capsule that everyone was so bent on possessing. Hell, the planet must be crawling with aliens from all parts of the galactic neighborhood! "But why the phony front with the flower shop and all?"

"Oh, that. Well, we try to fit in where we can. But as in your case, we are sometimes remiss in 'pulling it all together', as you might say."

"Yeah, something like that. So you're one of the *good* aliens?"

"Very good, I assure you, Mr. Denning.

"So what now?"

"We must journey with the Blue Rose of Noda to restore your wellbeing. You will be absent a few of your earth days."

"Then I've got to give Zelda a call. She'll worry. You know how women are."

"We cannot do that, Mr. Denning, I apologize in advance."

"And just why not?"

"Because we are already in a *trans-dimension*, not in the same frequency domain as your planet."

"Oh, that's swell, Eli Firt!"

"Just call me Eli, if you don't mind. May I call you Cable?"

"Look, buster, kindly alien or not—you just kidnapped me—and I don't take kindly to things happening against my will. None of this would have happened if I hadn't smelled that damn rose of yours—and speaking of which—why in the hell did you have it out there in the first place?

"She...wanted to draw you in..."

"*She?*"

"*Noda*—she is the blue rose you see over there in the center of the room. She provides the blue light that allows the Great Golden Scroll of Noda to be read clearly."

"So now it's about the scroll again? Who else in this cock-eyed universe wants it?"

"There was no other way for her to attract you into my floral shop. I knew once you took one inhalation, you would take another when my back was turned—such is her irresistible power."

"You mean you go around talking to a rose all the time?"

"That is her maiden form. Noda is one of the seven goddesses of protection. I believe you encountered an oriental lady on your planet—*Lei-Tao* of the *Fen de Fuqín*?"

It was all so surreal. I was expecting to wake up from this weird dream any minute and find Zelda sleeping peacefully beside me. Sometimes life hits you between the eyes like a thug with a baseball bat hitting five-hundred, and you know you're gonna be hit and you might not make it out of the coma because no one cares if you live or die when you're in the middle of a life that is in the middle of itself. People have a tendency to look away out of their own fear, when someone's in trouble or lying there on the sidewalk with a couple of slugs in their chest, or a woman's screaming down a dark alley because she's being accosted by some worthless vermin that roams the night-streets of the city. Yeah, I'd seen it all—and realized in the here and now, that nobody knew where I was—or where I was about to be kidnapped to. "So you even know about that, too, eh? What are you—some kind of fraternity of overseers?"

"You might say that." He looked up at me with those glowing yellow eyes. In a way the diminutive creature reminded me of Toggth, my little alien pal from The Cave of the Seven Truths. "Now I must prepare you." He pointed to the large blue rose in the middle of the control room. We walked to it and he had me place my left hand gently over the flower.

"Do you...do you happen to know a little creature, sort of like you, named Toggth? He's kind of Lei-Tao's overseer."

"He's my brother, as you would say it. Many thousands of your years ago we came from a race of *tzaz gemnii*, a genus of beings created to do *good* or to generate a positive, as compared to those who would violate the *Sacred Law of Personal Sovereignty*." I liked more and more the way this little guy talked. And who in the hell would guess in a million years that he and my little buddy Toggth were brothers? But they did look alike, sort of. Huh...small world...or more like...small universe.

"All that sounds great—these laws of the cosmos and all—but what good are they if they're violated all the time by vicious idiots who don't give a rat's ass about goodness or positive and all the other attributes humans are supposed to be evolving toward?"

Eli ignored my question. "Now...it is time to *be there*...those golden bars over there," he said, pointing to what seemed to be railings like ballerinas use when they practice at the barre. I went over and put both hands around the railing. "Please close your eyes and hold on, Cable." Then there was a whirring and humming that seemed to penetrate my entire body, yet it didn't rattle my nervous system.

Soon the control room turned into an orange-blue paradise, with a pink sky above and incredibly large trees with light-green moss hanging from their branch-

194

es. Eli still stood beside me. "Wow…" I marveled, "this is pretty close to my vision of Heaven, Eli. I sure as hell hope I don't blink and it all disappears!"

He snickered. "No, Cable, *this* is more real than your synthesized earth plane dimension. It is perpetual. Nothing dies here but has to be energized by magnetic radiation from that pink sky you see up there."

"You don't say. When will marvels never cease?" Then I began to feel nauseated. "Say, pal, I think we need to get me that antidote real quick like—I'm not exactly feeling like Tarzan at the moment."

"Oh, yes, of course," Eli said as he took my hand and led me to an exceptionally large tree with a blue door at its base. He knocked. The door opened and suddenly we were in a space twenty times the size of the tree! Eli smiled at me. "Another…perpetual effect denoting the potential of dimensional mastery. Nothing is as it seems, so we learn."

"I'll say," I muttered, looking around in the vast interior of the tree.

Then a very feminine voice spoke from seemingly nowhere. *"It is all frequency vision, earth dweller. That is why you are pursued by others who seek the Fen de Fuqín. Once having viewed the golden capsule, your vibrational memory banks recorded all of it. Those who pursue you know this. They are able to trace that frequency vision you have within your mind."* I could see no one. But the voice was friendly and spoke slowly and distinctly. *"Welcome to Gwiw Faun. I am Noda, Guardian of the Blue Light. That light is what enables the Fen de Fuqín to be decoded easily. Some have stolen its secrets. But none have perfected it."*

"Dearest Princess of the Blue, Cable here is in immediate need of the antidote—please?" Eli requested.

There was a slight pause. *"Oh, dear, yes! I am sorry you have suffered the ill effects of inhaling me."*

"Inhaling *you*? Can we cut out the crap here and just administer the stuff so I can get back to Zelda—*please*?" I said, a little impatient with the formal shit.

"You inhaled some of my essence. Humans are blustery, aren't they? Either looking to the past in remorse or anxious about the future—but seldom able to live in the moment." Then a little pedestal appeared in front of us. On it stood a stark-white chalice. *"Please drink it. It will restore you."*

I went over to the drinking vessel, picked it up and drank down the contents. It tasted marvelous, a mix between mango, guava, pineapple and cocoanut, I thought. "Wow! This is pretty good stuff!" Immediately I could feel my veins fill with vitality as my head cleared and began to feel like my old self—only better. "Thanks— mind if I call you Noda?—it's pretty quick-acting, whatever it is."

"Yes, please do. I am gladdened you are responding to the Odeo nectar. In your earth legends, this is known as the Nectar of the Gods."

"Well, it sure in hell is potent, I'll say that. I suppose it's life perpetuating and all that?"

"Yes...what is your name?"

"Cable—Cable Denning. You can call me Cable, if you like."

"Yes, Cable...what does that mean?"

"I haven't got a clue—it's an Irish name, northern Europe on the earth. You know how things get stolen from other things and evolve into something else...so there you have it...now can I go home?"

"I wish it were that easy, Cable. The effects of the Odeo nectar can be worn off only in this dimension. In your three-dimensional existence, they would melt your organs and turn you into a—how would you say it?—a mush of some kind. And you would be formless. Form is originated by the magnetic flux of specific frequencies from a created matrix. The Odeo nectar maintains that matrix here on Gwiw Faun, but would destroy it on your planetary dimension."

"Oh, that bad, eh? So what are we gonna do? You know, I do have a life down there—up there—in there—or wherever in the hell my dimension is."

"I realize you do not know it, Cable, but at the moment from your head down you are pure spirit-body, and only your head is man-body. The Odeo nectar will equalize those very different vibrations. What is it like to be a human being?"

"To tell you the truth, Noda, I'm not sure. I think I know how it was originally *supposed* to be, I mean, that people had hard work and good will as their credo. Back then they were more connected to both the earth and their religious or spiritual feelings about things. Now, its fear and greed and money and lust for dominance or power—and division by ethnic eyesight, breeding like a bunch of jack rabbits—people judging other people because their skin is a different color and their cultural habits different. I always say you should stick to looking at the *individual*—ask the question—'do I or do I not like this individual person?'. Now, when can you get me the hell out of here?"

197

There was a pause. Then the room filled with this iridescent blue light that glowed all around me and inside me, making me breathe it in. And out of nowhere appeared this fabulous dish with blue hair, blue breastplates and a very sheer blue gown descending to her ankles. She wore sparkling blue slippers. Her face was perfect, nice nose with small nostrils, deep blue eyes and a slightly pouty warm mouth with lips to match. She seemed tall to me, maybe five-seven or so. *"I have formed for you out of your imagination—using the frequency vision I spoke of earlier. Do I look like you imagined I might look if I were a human woman?"*

The babe was a dish! "Yeah—that and then some!" I said approvingly. "And to think you're still really a blue rose?"

"Yes. The Blue Rose of Noda has no age or aging. I have always been who I have always been. But I am curious...is it true that human being females mate for other reasons than procreation? And if so, why?"

I glanced at Eli who shrugged his shoulders. "Well, you got me there, Noda. Maybe sex is a therapy, you know, a way to unwind your body from the tensions of the human condition. And of course there's the exchange of warm emotions, touch, caring , loving someone. Or, what the hell—it could simply be nature's way of getting the two sexes together, which, from my point of view, may not happen as naturally as one might think, considering the different way dames think. So it's probably really just about sex and perpetuation of the species, you know..."

"Sex? That is an exercise?"

198

"Well, yes and no. Not in the ordinary sense like working out with barbells or climbing mountains. But yes inasmuch as it takes a lot of energy to make love— err...have sex—and one thereby receives the physical benefit of exercising the body and advancing the heart rate, and all that good stuff the medical world is beginning to remind us of now."

"*If I remain in this strange form, will you teach me about human female sex?*"

I was staring at those wonderful tight breasts tucked away in that blue armor. Her light-blue translucent skin glowed with a delicacy. Frankly, I was a bit embarrassed about teaching this babe about the birds and the bees, plus I was thinking about what Zelda might be thinking about now and why I wasn't in bed with her fast asleep. "Uh, I'm not sure it goes quite like that, Noda. Remember what I said about emotions? Well, it takes a thing called *desire* to trigger the emotions, and I'm just not sure that a being who goes around in the form of a flower most of the time can learn to have those kinds of responses."

"*All living things are sentient, Cable. A rose, a rock, a tree, the air, a golden capsule also has a life of its own. Just because it is in a different form from yours does not mean it does not feel.*"

"That's probably so, but I don't know it for a fact. Besides, I've really got to get home. I'm feeling restored enough now, so how about sending me back down that ol' dimensional portal?"

She stood a few feet away. She was studying something about me. "*You are still about three-quarters in the altered breath-body.*" There was disappointment in her voice. *"You'll have to wait here in Gwiw Faun for a while longer."*

"And how long might that be? I've learned that *your* dimensional timetable doesn't always jibe with mine."

"Perhaps two or three of your planet's revolutions."

I was feeling pretty chipper but thinking what an irony life can be when all you do is step out to buy a pretty girl some flowers and end up in another dimension with a little creature-man and a blue flower that becomes a babe when she gets a little horny! "That's three days!" I complained, thinking again about Zelda and my P.I. business.

She started to approach me, then she backed away. *"I—I must return to my flower state—I'm feeling strangely."* That said, she began to disassemble in front of me and soon she was once again only a voice in the large space inside the blue tree! *"There...I'm myself again. I apologize, but I obviously cannot remain in your kind of form very long. Besides, there are so many disadvantages to your physical form, the presence of intestines, surely being one of them. Vulgar, messy, ugh!"*

"Well, animals are animals—gods, gods...and goddesses."

"Yes. Cable, I have brought you here for two very significant reasons, in addition to administering the antidote."

"Why didn't you say so before? I was wondering why you tricked me in the first place, having me end up here—wherever here is..."

She addressed the small man-like being standing a few feet from me. He had been silent as we spoke, his hands folded in front of him. *"Eli, I had better tell him*

200

now. Either he will not comprehend it, or he will and be able to utilize the result for good."

"He *is* human, Her Blueness, and quite ignorant, as is the entire species of humans."

"Hey, wait a minute here! You shouldn't go around knocking my species, even if it's true and I may resemble your remark, Eli."

Eli seemed to ignore my statement. "I defer to you, O Princess of the Blue Light. I shall stand at the sidelines while you enlighten Mr. Denning, if you don't mind."

"Thank you, Eli." Then it seemed her voice turned to address me. *"Cable, please be seated."*

"I would, but there's no chair in this huge room."

Suddenly a very comfortable blue-upholstered chair appeared out of nowhere! *"There is now...please...sit..."*

The chair was extremely comfortable and I felt like lounging in the damn thing all day and maybe even taking a nap in it. But it was clear that Noda had other plans for me. *"Now..."* she said, her voice very matter-of-fact. *"The first thing I wish you to know..."* All of a sudden the room went dark and the beams of a blue light shone upon my body. I couldn't tell where the source of light came from, but the light felt very good on my body. Then all of a sudden I felt a pull on the front of my head and what I saw next I'm still not sure of to this day! It seemed streams of golden lettering or symbols pulled out of my head into the blue light beams. Perhaps thousands of them.

"What's going on, lady? Hey, Noda—are you there? I feel a bit light-headed with your pulling at my head and all—"

"—it is the entire content of the Fen de Fuqín. We must start from the beginning, Cable. First know that Creator Gods, Photonos and Audianos, the gods of light and sound, respectively, fashioned the Fen de Fuqín to assist all beings who held in question the origin of the cosmos. It was a mighty task to place into symbolic form not only how the universes were formed, but why. It was kept safely for countless millennia in The Cave of the Seven Truths and guarded over by gifted maidens fashioned from the Lotus pod and endowed with the ability to transform their shapes, if need be. That is how you met Lei-Tao—who, most unfortunately, sampled your male earth ways and was disgraced. Toggth, Eli and his brethren serve as overseers to the great golden capsule. When an evil species called the Beldens penetrated the Cave of the Seven Truths and confiscated the priceless capsule, they brought it to your earth plane. But knowledge of its existence seeped out into the world of men and all at once so many desired, perhaps you would say, 'lusted' for, the priceless precious. Greedy to possess it at any cost, believing it would give them unlimited power and eternal existence, the selfish, the wealthy, individuals, organizations, governments and other alien transplants to your planet, waged a battle over owning the Great Invincible. But of course, Cable, it cannot be owned, nor will it grant unlimited power, and certainly it will not render a mortal human a timeless existence—the physical form is too dense and of lower vibration."

"I could've told you that," I said, listening intently to the lovely musical voice. But inside I was dying for a Lucky Strike. But I thought it best not to smoke here in

Noda land. You never know if the whole damn place would go up in flames or something.

She continued, ignoring my words. *"When it was stolen, Toggth and Lei-Tao were on duty for about six hundred of your years already. They were heart-broken and disturbed by the loss, as you can well imagine. By your Great War, a terrible conflict where so many perished needlessly, the Fen de Fuqín was kept by a scientist then working on the formative steps of understanding the atom, one of the larger building blocks of cosmic structure. Many humans had already perished in pursuit of the golden capsule. This scientist's name was Gregorio Sandor, and he had a son, Boris Sandor, who became a medical doctor. But the current possessor of the Fen de Fuqín, one Mr. Charles Lowry, a very wealthy individual working for an organization called the Oculus Pyramis Mandatum, was suddenly eliminated and the great precious disappeared."*

"You mean you guys knew about Cronus-Gor and the whole *Oculus* thing and did nothing about their stranglehold on the earth?"

"It is not for us to do, Cable, but to be. We are all conceived to serve specialized roles in our respective dimensions. Our role is doing by being...and that is sufficient to fulfill the whole conscious self, for in the act of being there is a silent action that moves energy through purpose and intent to manifest that purpose."

I got up from my chair and the blue light disappeared. I paced up and down with my hands folded behind my back. It was all so crazy—in fact everything about my life right now was nuts. A lot of what Noda said was above my head, but I got the gist. The human race was fucked. "Okay, so finish your story and bring me up to date, if you don't mind."

"Yes. Somewhere along the way very imposing criminal elements that secretly dominated the city of Los Angeles, allied themselves with the Oculus. When they eliminated Gregorio Sandor, they also stole the capsule. But Cronus was not aware of this since the 'mob', as you might call them, had other motivations for the Fen de Fuqín, and that was to sell it to the highest bidder without Cronus knowing about it."

"So they set up a patsy known as Blinthe—and when Dragna came to claim it for his own resale intentions, he killed both Ardizzone and Blinthe, but not before carving out a space in back of Blinthe's tongue to house the precious golden capsule in order to hide it from anyone who might be after it other than Jack Dragna himself. Then they got rid of any traces of identification on the corpse, such as fingerprints—or even a belly button. Now, quite by accident, Dr. Boris Sandor, who just happened to work at the Los Angeles County Morgue as chief pathologist...discovers, while dissecting Blinthe, the very same precious item his father had been protecting and overseeing for many years. But now Sandor wants it for himself, maybe for money, maybe simply for the possession of the thing. But the new crime boss Dragna knows Sandor's got the capsule, so he has to eliminate him. He contacts Chicago and calls in the heavy guns, a guy named Matrangas and his little imp, Jinx. They save my life after Sandor conked me on the head in his sealed vault while he was showing me your golden precious, but then proceeded to tell me I knew too much. So guess what? Suddenly I'm expendable, too.

Except for one thing. I saw the *God of Our Fathers* up close and in person—"

"*—and what is even more dangerous, under the blue light of Noda, which Dr. Sandor had discovered from his father's earlier research, you were able to absorb the entire content of the capsule...as was Dr. Sandor.*"

"You should have been a detective, Noda," I laughed. "So Dragna fetches Matrangas from Chicago to dispatch Sandor to get the capsule into his hot and greedy hands. Only when I bargain with them for my life—that I can save them a lot of time by telling them where the capsule is hidden in the vault, did they agree to take me to the hospital. I was pretty banged up from Sandor's bludgeoning me. It was an even trade, my life for the directions to the *Fen de Fuqín*. Only when Matrangas and Jinx get back to the vault, someone had beaten them to it, and bam! suddenly those two get dead."

Noda's voice was terse, almost fearful. "*And the knowledge of the Fen de Fuqín is magnetically inscrolled within your very cells. All any enemy needs is my blue light penetrating your head and as you saw, the coded information will spill out into the light beam.*"

"But what the hell good is it if they can't decipher it?"

"*There are those who think they can, Cable. Your species is quite inter-mixed with aliens from many quadrants of the nearby star systems, Cronus being one of them.*"

"Yeah, I know. I've—I've encountered a few along the way. So now what?"

"*It shall all be revealed soon. But you must persevere. Now you see, Cable, why you are in such great danger?*

But there are two other things you should know, perhaps some of this knowledge will help to protect you.

"I can't wait for this one," I said, with my tongue-in-my-cheek.

*"All star systems, all life forces, all consciousness is forever experiencing what your prophecies called the **End Times**. All things are perpetually in their end times, as occurrences, advents, events and free will decisions transform the elemental experience of both individual and collective societies. Your next 'end times' experience is about to descend upon the earth. An alien force is preparing to plunge the world you know into chaos with a war so large in scale, it's magnitude never yet having been experienced by those on your planet—that is, within recorded history. Of course it has happened again and again— thousands upon thousands of your years ago."*

"Yeah, I think I know about this war thing. I was privy to a secret council meeting between the United States President-elect and a German emissary. They're planning it as we speak."

"It will be terrible, Cable. Millions of your kind will perish in the maelstrom. Your country will not know warfare on its soil, in this or the next century of your time, but you will be surrounded with conflict."

"Thanks for the heads-up, Noda." I was kind of falling in love with her soft and very feminine voice. "I wish I could see you again. I wouldn't mind exploring with you in that male-female sex thing, but I don't think it'd work so well, especially now that you tell me you can't stay in my kind of human form too long. I mean, we'd barely get started and you'd have to became a damn blue flower again!"

She giggled. "*I do like you, Cable. I wish things were otherwise, but they're not. So we must remain contented with the privilege of knowing one another in this manner.*"

"Yeah...I guess you're right...too bad, though..."

The Anointed

"*One more thing that might help you during the remainder of your earth life. Some of your histories, like the story of Enoch, for instance, speak of individuals becoming **anointed** and taking on super-human capabilities. There is a light-infusing oil made from the core of your earth sun. It is difficult to explain it to you, but I shall try. In its essence form, it is how I can maintain my wonderful blue aura and everything around me. When you become anointed, you are preserved within the radiance of that light-infusing energy. I know one in your dimensional plane who can anoint you. Are you willing to seek him out? He is timeless, ageless and lives in a tiny hut on the top of a Himalayan mountain. To the outside world he is known in your dimension as 'Holy Man,' but if the truth be known, he has a mischievous twinkle in his eye.*"

I chuckled. "Sounds like Santa Clause, except it ain't in the North Pole. I'd—I'd, uh, be very interested in getting 'anointed' by this guy." How do I get there and how long would it take to get there and back? After all, I've got a babe on the string and a business to run."

"*I don't know. I travel instantly. But I know you cannot. Weeks, of your time, I'd guess. He is rather remote by your standards.*"

"That makes it rather challenging, Noda. As much as I'd like that anointing blessing and all—I don't know—being human in the twentieth century earth, especially America, ain't no easy task. We still have to work our butts off to earn our daily bread, if you know what I mean."

"We don't eat—food—as you do. I sip only from the Odeo nectar flower. One drop sustains me for an indefinite period of your time. Speaking of which, I am in need of solitude just now, Cable. Will you forgive me if I leave your presence? I am sorry for the inconvenience I caused in your life. But it was necessary that you know these things. I hope the knowing will counter-balance the frustration. But beware of the Moirai, Goddesses of Fate, for some may attempt to prevent your accomplishment in this quest for Anointment. Beware...be-warned...and be-brave..."

"So how do I avoid these so-called goddesses?"

"You cannot...if you have entertained them in your mind and approved of their presence, consciously or subconsciously. Have you?"

"Well, I was just curious as to whether they were babes or not—"

"—then you have let them in. They heard your silent call and now, one by one, they will amplify many times over the lessons of your life."

"Maybe I didn't accept them. I would not enjoy being told what to do by a bunch of dames minding everyone else's business." I was disappointed to hear the babe had to leave. I was getting pretty enamored with that voice and manner. "Well, I guess it's just me against that world down there, eh? Sometimes I feel like the lone hero in Byron's poem, Manfred, climbing to his destiny only to perish in the end. I read his poetic drama when I was about eighteen. The proud, defiant ghetto rat, tormented by his upbringing tilted his sword against the world. And maybe unconsciously I summoned the Seven Spirits to forgive me for killing the only things I ever truly loved, my Astartes—the women who died because of me. I can still quote Byron: "*My injuries came down on those who love me—on those on whom I best loved—and I never quelled an enemy save in my just defense...but to her, my embrace was fatal...*" So he climbs the mountain, resisting religion, spurning the Devil, embracing only lost love until he dies on the mountain top."

I heard a sniffling. "*Oh, Cable, you made me cry. Is this how you earth dwellers exist—in pity, sacrifice, regret?*"

"That's about it, Noda—toss in a little lust, greed, money-love and a few wild nights with a babe—and you've got it...end of the story."

"*I must leave now...I send the warm winds of my sisters with you. May you fulfill your highest purpose, for I know the journey in your present life is not a light one. But do not be saddened by the earth life, after all, it is but the dream you dream, the hologram you wish for yourself unconsciously. Take it as an adventure. But as I said, beware of the Moirai, they hover near the Great Ones. Live fully—die peaceably...*"

At that moment I knew she was gone. I could sense her presence dissipate until hardly a trace remained in the room. I looked over at Eli. "So that's it? She leaves me with this impossible puzzle to work out? When do I go back home?"

He walked forward toward me. "That's it, as you say, Cable. We'll see how you feel in your tomorrow. Now you should sleep."

"You know, life is self-defeating, Eli. Just when you get out of the bathtub and you're shiny bright and clean, you have to take a shit! Now tell me that isn't perverse."

"I don't have to do those dirty things—all we eliminate is air, you know..." the little guy said, displaying some one-upmanship.

"Lucky you. By the way, this Himalayan fella, what is his name and what province of the mountains do I look for him in?"

"His name is *Lama Daíshi* and you must seek him near *Kathmandu, Nepal*. He lives at the base of *Mount Shivapuri*, among the green and verdant forests and he walks the valleys below. He is a great and wonderful being. He may not like you, though. His olfactory glands are highly tuned—he may smell the corruption of death and violence around you."

"Now, that's a hell of a thing to say, Eli. I wouldn't say that about you—even if I felt it might be true."

"Well, it isn't—and I'm just cautioning you in case you decide to visit *Lama Daishi*. My brother has told me some things about you. He *likes* you and feels you are a unique being."

"Well, I like Toggth as well. So there, hot shot—being judgmental isn't all that good for your breathairian health, little man."

"I'm truly not that fond of humans, Cable."

"Neither am I, but I still have to live with 'em, for now at least." I asked Eli where I could bed down for a while. Suddenly I was drained from the conversation

210

with Noda of the Blue Light. He led me to a most lovely room where light blue everything seemed to envelope one. I thanked him, plunked on the floor and wrapped myself in a blue comforter and fell into a deep sleep.

Chapter 8

THE TRUTH ABOUT GOOD-BYES

How long I slept I didn't know. But I could feel I was somewhere in home territory because Ray Bourne's haunting trumpet was wafting through my brain like a longing I couldn't reach. I woke up with tears running down my cheeks and memories flooding my guarded heart like a dam had just burst and the water was hitting me head-on like a fist of grief on a June night when the girl you were dancing with just collapsed in your arms, dead. And maybe that part of me *was* dead, I don't know. What does it take to revive something you've been burying for a long time?

The other end of my life was the malice that I faced in the eyes of those who pursued me. I was beginning to see my living out this life as *the man who knew too much.* Thugs and murderers, secret organizations, criminals and gang bosses running the city I loved to hate and hated to love—yet did.

And what about Zelda? How would I explain to her I simply disappeared into a flower shop that turned out to be a dimensional control chamber three nights ago? Oh, yeah, that'll be good.

I could smell the aroma of flowers and cuttings all around me on the floor. I shook my head awake, sat up and looked around. I was in the back room of the *Bouquet Land Florist.* My first impulse was to call Zelda and try to explain. But where would I start? I thought it best to face the music head on and talk to her in person. I got up, still a bit wobbly. Just as I was heading for the bathroom, Eli entered and looked me over. "My, my...you do look a lot worse for the wear, Cable. How are you feeling?"

"Lousy. How would you feel if you just had your teeth kicked out of your mouth and you knew your days were numbered?"

"It need not be as bad as all that. I really think *Lama Daishi* can help. But I wouldn't hesitate too long. You will be a bit unsteady for a few days until the *Ódeo nectar* wears off. Your chemistry isn't used to its particular molecular constituents."

"Yeah, well, my chemistry isn't used to getting it in the shorts for doing nothing but minding my own business either, Eli. I'm still pissed at you and your blue princess for kidnapping me and screwing up my life for three days."

"I don't know what else she could have done, frankly. Noda did what she did with a lot of consideration and caring for you, Cable. You know, 'forewarned is forearmed,' they say. She saw your pathway as pretty rough, even in earth terms. But they say the gods do not give you more than you can handle at any given time. Be brave, my boy, you have it in you to vanquish your enemies and win new friends—always...for every negative thing, there is a positive counterpart. Besides, remember—as Noda reminded you, the earth life is but an illusion, a short stay in a hologram of experience and learning for your higher self."

"It all sounds good as a Sunday sermon, Eli, but you're not out there in the trenches facing off with those bastards who can't help but be cruel and deliberate about how they decide to kill you. Nothing is safe here, nothing sacred—"

"—*you*—you are sacred, Cable. Please, don't reduce yourself. Stay aloft and fly. If indeed you've chosen this life to be the true hero of the hour, then stay on top of it. Wield your sword with authority and you will be helped by those in the invisible world as well as those who will come to your aid on the earth side of things."

"What about you? Can I count on you to help?"

"Unfortunately, I must be about other things in other dimensions. But Toggth will help. He is pledged to assist you however he can. And he will—he's most capable, you know."

"Yeah, I know...I like your brother. I sure in hell hope he's there when I need him in the days to come."

"He will be." Eli extended his hand. "I will be off soon. This little shop has served its purpose and I have 'sold' it to a nice Italian man. Please patronize him when you can...flowers...for weddings, funerals, parties—or maybe you should take a bouquet home to the lady who is confused about your whereabouts?" He went over to a table, grabbed a bunch of lovely roses and handed them to me. "Here...maybe it will take away some of the discord between the two of you. Hurt can be mended in many ways, perhaps this is one of them."

I shook Eli's hand and bade him good-bye. I had a feeling I would never see him again. I got out onto the sidewalk, lit up a cigarette and left.

The Truth About Truth

It was late afternoon by the time I got out of the flower shop with my roses. I took the yellow car over to Zelda's place after checking in at the office. She left a note that she had gone home early. I was dirty and needed to clean up. I knocked at the door. She answered. "Oh...it's you...you look terrible." she said, her voice soft and disconsolate.

I stood there with the roses, feeling rather sheepish and inarticulate. "Hiya, babe...may I come in?"

She looked at my unshaven face, disheveled hair and wrinkled clothes. "We've been out drinking for a few days, have we?" She opened the door and let me in. I looked around. Suitcases and clothes were strewn about, and pots and pans stood stacked on the little kitchen table in boxes. "I'm—I'm right in the middle of things here, Cable..." Then she stopped what she was doing and looked up at me. "I'm leaving you, Cable..."

I felt the bottom just drop out from under me. I was helpless, wallowing in confusion. Clumsily I handed her the roses but she refused them. So I quietly fetched the vase off the kitchen windowsill, filled it with water and put the new roses in it.

"You're what?"

"I'm leaving you...I can't take it anymore. I realize you tried to warn me that the danger would get to me. Well, you're right—it did!"

"At least let me explain, Zelda—I don't know if I can tell you all that happened—or even if you'll believe it, but I gotta try...will you hear me out?"

She took a deep breath. "I suppose so. Want a cup of coffee?"

"Not really, I could go for a good stiff drink just about now."

"You mean you haven't been—"

"—no!" I said firmly. "I've been somewhere else. So first off, know we're not talking about other babes here, local gangsters or jail time for rowdy behavior in a bar, okay?"

She kept her voice low. "Okay, Cable. Let's hear it."

I explained the whole story the best way I knew how. But I could see something in Zelda's eyes had changed. And it wasn't even that she didn't love me. I knew she did. But something else had altered her thinking or brought new decisions to her heart and mind. "So...Eli brought me back to the flower shop—and here I am, a little worse for the wear, but still kickin' and I missed you like hell, babe—I really wanted to get back to you that night, as I said—ask Eli—but I was getting sicker and sicker from that shit in the rose and they had to cure me in *their* dimension. There was no other way."

"May I ask this Eli character then—for verification of these events?"

I made a face. "Shit, I forgot!—I'm afraid that's not possible. He had to get back to Noda's dimension—which is also his—and take care of what he really does, whatever that is. He sold the flower shop to an Italian guy, who I haven't met."

"I see..." she said that with a lot of hesitancy, as if she didn't believe a word of it. Then she took a big breath and exhaled. "I'm still leaving you, Cable. I love you too much to take this anymore—this insecure, undependable, crazy existence you're entrenched in with both feet. I was going to leave a note, but you beat me to it. But I'm glad I could tell you in person. I called a cab and I'm leaving for Arizona on the train tonight. I'll be staying with an aunt outside of Phoenix."

"But why? I need you, kid. I told you how much I missed you—and fought to get back home to you. Doesn't that count for something?"

"Not anymore, Cable. As you tell your clients, everyone has a story. I have mine, too. Only I can't tell you all of my story just now. Maybe sometime when I've gathered it all together."

I felt stunned, abandoned. "You mean I'm losing my secretary, too? What in the hell am I gonna do, Zelda? I come back to find myself back at square one when all I wanted was to come back to you and take you in my arms and kiss you and smell your hair, the nape of your neck—"

"—Cable! Please! Don't try to make me change my mind. I can't. It's too late for that." She wiped the tears with her sleeve. "Just let it be what it is. Let me finish packing."

She went about putting her things in suitcases and boxes. She told me she was shipping some of her kitchenware to Arizona and someone would come and call for them and would I try and be here when the moving company arrived. Finally she was through. She looked different, somehow. Her face had changed a bit and she was pale and drawn. I offered her a drink and she took it. I poured one for myself and stood opposite her and toasted the lovely young women I had come to know and love. "I guess all I can say is 'the best to you', Zelda.

Forgive me for not understanding. But I don't. And that's my truth."

"I don't know the truth about your truth anymore, Cable."

"I understand, babe. May I tell you a story?"

"If you want to, but you just got through telling me a doozy. Besides, the taxi will be here any minute."

I gulped down the rest of my drink and put the glass down on the kitchen table with a clunk. "Zelda, once upon a time I knew a young policeman who believed in magic. He was lonely, and somewhere deep inside himself, he was searching for someone. He was hurting pretty bad inside from a youth that had damaged some part of him, the part that allows love to pour freely in and out, like breathing. But he didn't give up on that belief in magic...that somewhere, some day, some night, in some smoky, noisy nightclub, on a street of dreams, the park across the way, a lonely carousel at an amusement park—*somewhere*...he'd find her. And she would find him, because deep inside of her in the lonely nights, she heard that same music the policeman heard wafting through his head and heart, and one of them would walk into a room and there the other would be.....and they would find each other.

Then one night, it happened. From his past experience, though, he knew it couldn't be, that at the very moment he was looking for her she would suddenly appear—nor could she be seeking him on that same night. But there they would stand, facing each other...and suddenly both of their worlds changed. It would be a world they both were born for, a silent recognition that one love could meld two hearts, and there they were.

What to do? How would they respond as they each beheld the beloved?"

"God, Cable, that's exactly how I felt the day I met you when you came over early, looking for Honey."

"Then at some unrehearsed moment, there is an unspoken agreement, a promise to yourself that this is a right person for you. So the two of you work at sharing one love, one life, one ideal expression of passion and belonging. And it seems to work fine, seems to fill that emptiness, the one place in both of you that needed filling, while every other waking hour of the day or night, was spent doing what you did—working at making a difference in the world because you were young and believed in better causes, believed in *truth* as the sharpest knife in your box.

They say that proof of love is that it grows a little or a lot every day. And that life becomes the fulfillment of that dream you privately harbored all those years. And when you're in full bloom with that other person, there is nothing you can't be or do in this or any other world. Suddenly the small and pithy things humans are and do around you have no meaning, because you have ascended to loftier places. Now you have arrived....perfection radiating from that love like new rays from the sun each day, and the night bringing those intimate touches there in the darkness, that awaken all those other senses that slept through those haunted, agonizing years."

I stopped and turned to look at her. She was crying, standing there shaking, her jaw trembling. "You are telling life stories, Cable, you are telling me my own dream, my own story—and the story of almost every single person on this...this planet. It's true, when I found you, I was a lonely bookworm, a young woman escaping into her books, her work, her education—but also running away from the woman in her, denying to herself that someone like you could exist in this world. But you did...and *do*. It was never about sex for itself, in the end, but sex was the vehicle, the medium that drove me through the rutty road into your heart. And your heart sparked mine. Down deep it was about holding and being held, someone to bring me through the night so I wouldn't start crying myself to sleep from the loneliness."

I was moved by her words. She had grown so much, matured into the genuine article. I was proud of her. I continued. "But the policeman left something out, Zelda—something just as important as all the rest put together. What he didn't know then was the simple fact—*that's not all he was*. No one person could fill all the holes inside of him. So he tried out many others as well, seeking balance, seeking comfort. Sure, at first it's the excitement and the booze and cigarettes, the music and dancing, the late night rendezvous, the nervous patter, the sensual high when you slip your hand under her dress or unbutton her blouse. So the policeman began to realize life was an irony, a dirty trick played by nature urging him to reproduce, breed his brand into existence by giving him a pair of rose-colored glasses so he'd see only the unblemished perfection of sex and desire. But then the policeman looked around, talked to others, attended the murders and beatings and suicides of those who had believed as he had—that romantic bliss would heal all the garbage you carried inside since the day you took your first breath on the earth."

"God, Cable, that's so black and white. So...what's the answer, then? Carry the ideal around with you for the rest of your life? Or to get on with it and accept that no human couple will ever be perfect, but there's enough love there to get you through with a little left over, or maybe that your lover became your friend as well."

I lit up a cigarette and looked out the window. "The true answer is that you were always looking for *yourself* and didn't know it, Zelda, you were seeking that complete part of you that sings in the night where all is well and doesn't wail through the veil of tears in self-pity. *He* learned how to be happy being with himself. And you know, somehow he was never alone when he didn't want to be. He found a dimension that had lived in him the whole time, beyond time. And this dimension was filled with other beings, wiser and stronger and more evolved than he was. It was a place that had a direct connection to the whole universe. No one had ever left *home*. God and good and perfection...and *love* is there...the one thing none of us can live without had always lived there. But the policeman learned that *he* had to love himself completely before he could love anyone *else* completely. And if the one he loved thought any less of *her* self, then it would never work, for the love would limp along until it finally self-destructed. And one day it would be over..."

"Is that what happened to us, Cable? Did you love yourself less than my capacity to love you?"

"I don't know. Either someone is right for you or they're not. Or maybe they're right for the time you are supposed to be together. But what I mean is, people come into relationships bringing all their flaws, shortcomings, their own pathos...again...an irony, a strange harmony of contrasts that make it impossible to completely fulfill the other person. Why? Because that's not the other person's job—it's *your* job, as I said, to fulfill yourself first. Then, if we're lucky, we can love another who equally loves themselves."

She stood there looking helpless. I went over to the dresser and got her a tissue. "So now I found *me*, I guess. I keep telling myself that's enough, to fulfill myself, as you say. Maybe it is. I told you once I would always be in love with you. And that's how it will be. I can't stay for all the reasons I've already told you, but the main one is that I'm not strong enough to lose you and still survive it. Please don't try to find me. I'll be fine. I'll still be needed. My aunt needs someone to look after her in Arizona."

The horn of a taxi was beeping outside. I grabbed her two large suitcases and brought them out to the waiting yellow cab. The driver opened the door for her. I grabbed her and took her aside. "It can't end like this for me, Zelda. You gotta know—I want you to live with me, here, inside somewhere," I said pointing at my heart. How empty and forlorn and trite my words must have seemed to her. "Are you sure you're okay? I know you've been complaining about your appetite lately and your stomach problems. And you've lost a little weight."

"I'm fine, Cable. I'm not okay, but I'm fine. Go back inside, the meter's ticking." I reached out to hold her once more, but she backed away. "No...Cable...if I hug you—or kiss you—I'll never be able to say good-bye. I think you know that. I'm just not as strong as some people. So...the young policeman became a private investigator who loved one of his secretaries for a while. Leave it at that...please, Cable..." Then she turned and got into the taxi. I watched as the taillights disappeared. It felt like a baseball bat had just clobbered me in the gut. It ached and my heart felt sore. But the creature inside somehow goes on. It doesn't have any emotions, doesn't miss anyone. It's kind of like the appetite, it just needs to be fed and it doesn't particularly care who feeds it, what it's fed or what happens to the nutrition after it's used up.

I went back into Zelda's little cottage. It was November 3, 1932, on the eve of the presidential election. FDR was a shoe-in, most everyone was sure. Things come crashing down when you're not looking, just like when lives end unexpectedly. I looked around and said goodbye. I turned the latch on the front porch door and locked it, then turned away from the shambles that represented Zelda Blodgett and me. Cable Denning, Private Eye, the man who never knew the truth about good-bye, walked off into the night, listening to Roy Bourne's trumpet as it haunted his head and heart. Yeah, maybe tomorrow everything would feel different, maybe I'd smoke and drink until I was numb and get on with the bothersome phone calls made from desperate housewives, husbands, lovers and miscellaneous lost souls looking for a way out of their current dilemmas. And maybe—who knows?—I'd even hire a new secretary. But I did wonder about one thing. How in the hell would I get to Kathmandu half way around the world? And where would I get the dough to take that long boat ride into the next unknown adventure waiting in the wings for one Cable Denning, the private dick who knew too much? If, after all, I was to believe Julie Halliday and Helmut Becker and his Deutschland gangsters, I had but a couple of months left to live on this planet, and I had better light a fire under an action plan!

Chapter 9

THAT'S MY DESIRE

It was November 15, 1932. Franklin Delano Roosevelt was our new President, German Chancellor Adolph Hitler was rising like a meteor to power—but the depression was getting worse as people's homes were being foreclosed, jobless rates continued soaring and the secret money-makers were getting richer by the day. I was also getting antsy about getting out of town before Becker's hordes descended on me, or any others seeking the *Fen de Fuqín* that might come storming into my office with a death warrant.

Just as I was muddling around in my thoughts, the phone rang. "Yeah, Cable Denning here..."

A very fresh, young voice came on the line. "Mr. Denning, my name is Verona Farina and you were recommended to me by Ziggy Thompson some time ago."

"Yeah, lady, it must've been some time ago because Ziggy Thompson's been *dead* for a while now."

There was a silence at the other end. "Dead? Are we talking about the same young woman—who worked at night—"

"—as a hoochy-coochy dancer at *The Pink Gables* downtown."

"Oh, my...I had no idea...I am so sorry. I really liked her. I didn't know her well, but the one night we did meet, she spoke very highly of you and said you were dating her. She needed someone—"

"—well, yeah, that's all well and good, Miss Farina, but Ziggy never got to her first date appointment with me. So let's not talk about it, okay? So what can I do for you?"

Her voice got very quiet. "I believe my fiancé is seeing someone. I would like to hire you to discover the truth."

"The truth, eh? Yeah, I've got a pretty good record with truth—even though I've been known to slip up now and again."

"Well, who hasn't....wouldn't you say? How much do you charge, is it—Mr.—Mr. —"

"—Denning, Cable Denning."

"Mr. Denning."

"I get twenty smackers a day plus expenses, which includes carfare, photographic film and traveling expenses if the job takes me out of town further than the public transportation."

"Well, that's very clear and precise. I think I can afford you."

"Then I suggest you make an appointment with me and come on up to my office, so you can give me the whole scoop."

"Yes. Are you available today?"

"Depends on the time." Truth was, business was sagging and I needed the dough but quick. "It's 11:30 now. How about around one o'clock this afternoon?"

"I can't. I work at that new Broadway department store in customer service until six. Are you available evenings? I could be there by about seven, if it's not too far from the Broadway on Hollywood Boulevard."

"Nope, just around the corner, sort of, on Franklin. Yeah, for a working girl, I guess I can make it work for us. Seven it is, then."

I told the dame where my office was located and we hung up. I chucked down a couple more gin tonics, lit up a Lucky Strike from that green pack I liked so well and sat back in my chair. Maybe this case would last more than a week, I was hoping. Funds were low, but a working girl probably didn't have much dough and I almost felt guilty taking it from those who did an honest day's worth of labor out there in the salt mines of customer service, listening to both the legitimate and the scammers complain about one thing or the other. I was beginning to drift back to the immediacy of getting the hell out of Dodge City when the phone rang again. "Yeah, Cable Denning here..."

"Cable..." a very soft but familiar voice reached my ear and I felt my stomach go weak and my heart race. "It's Zelda, Cable. I've been thinking about you a lot. Are you okay?"

At first, I didn't know what to say. "Yeah, kid...I'm fine...how about you? Did you reach your destination in Arizona alright?"

"Yes. But I miss you so. I'm back to crying myself to sleep every night—like before we got together..."

"I'm sorry, Zelda...I wish you hadn't left so damn quick. Hell, I think we could've worked it out. I'm really not a bad guy, once you get to know me. I'm kind of like one of your plants, I grow on you after a while—and all I need is some good soil, some water and sunlight. Isn't that what someone told me a long time ago?"

227

She attempted a chuckle, but it didn't come. "...and some fertilizer. You fed me, Cable, gave me life inside myself—my heart, made me smile, and now—"

"—let's not go there, Zelda. It's kind of painful hearing your voice from so far away. I still care about you, kid."

"I told you I would always be in love with you—and I still am..."

"So why aren't you in my bed? Life's short, in case you haven't noticed, babe."

"I—I can't. I told you—I could never take losing you while we were close. Like my plants, I was growing around you with my leaves and vines, rooting inside you with my heart. If you died, then I'd die—and that's how close it got..." She began to whimper.

"So what's the matter with that?" I joked, trying to make light of an awkward situation. "Hell, in the Orient, wives, lovers and concubines get burned on the pyre right along with good ol' hubby."

Now she snickered. "You've got me smiling again, Cable." Then she broke down. "I don't know what to do! I can't live without you—and I can't live with you, just now."

"What's this 'just now' crap? I'm here now, doll, and you're not."

"I've promised to take care of my aunt Hermie."

"Aunt Hermie? How old is she?"

"She's infirm because she has a palsy of some kind. I have to wheelchair her around. She has a son who comes and goes—mostly goes. I've committed myself to be here—at least for now."

"Well, how long?"

"Ten or twelve months. Then I'll make other plans, maybe."

"Maybe? Jesus, Zelda, you're so damn vague."

"I'm sorry. I just can't say anymore now. Please try to understand and give me this time."

"I might be dead by December—or on my way to Kathmandu in Nepal, traveling to some dude who's going to anoint me."

There was a silence. "One of your stories again—please don't tell me these things, Cable, it only makes things impossible between us. I really believe so many of your tales to be preposterous."

"I guess you've forgotten guys like Helmut Becker, or Cronus-Gor or all those other clubs, orders, gangs and organizations who are after me because of something they think I know."

"No, I haven't forgotten." Then I could hear her sniffling again. "Cable...you were my only love...you made a girl into a woman. And this woman needs you. But I can't come to you."

I pondered this for a minute. "Do you want me to come to you?"

There was another long pause. "No...if you did, I would pack up everything I own, go away with you and follow you around like a little slave girl."

"Well, what's wrong with that?" I said, again trying to lighten the moment.

"I've got to go now. Please know I'll never stop loving you...and be well. I'm holding my own. So don't worry, okay?"

"Easy for you to say. You're the mysterious one here. But please call me now and then, will you? And Zelda...if you change your mind..."

"Yes, Cable, I know...good-bye..."

She hung up and I was left there holding the phone. I put it on the receiver hooks and got out my bottle of gin, poured a big one and took a drink. Sometimes it just felt good to numb up and forget the bullshit of the world, whether it was coming from men, women or aliens!

By the time seven o'clock rolled around I was a bit drunker than I thought I would be. I guess I was still thinking about Zelda's phone call when there was a knock at the door. I got up to open it. I was a bit dizzy. Maybe a residual of the *Blue Rose of Noda*, I thought. A petite little blonde stood in front of me. She was about five-four with big blue eyes that revealed a pertness. Her lips were glossed with a light pink lipstick, a nice little nose and a figure to match. "Mr. Denning? I'm Verona Farina...I believe you are expecting me?"

It must've seemed to her that I was staring. But it was the gin and my responses had slowed down a bit. "Yep...you came to the right place, lady." I opened the door wide and swept my arm down in a welcoming gesture. "Please come into my parlor—the spider said that to the fly, you know. There's a chair over by my desk."

She smelled the cigarette smoke, the gin-tinged air and probably the stale sheets of my bachelor's bedroom. "Do you mind if we keep the door open? Just to be on the cautious side. I mean, I don't know you or anything—and if you'll pardon my saying so, you appear to be a little inebriated. Is this so?"

I came around my desk and sat in my comfy chair. "You got it right on the money, honey. I'm nursing the remnants of a phone call, you see. An old flame called me just before you came. You know how old flames can be, don't you?"

"Yes. I think my current boyfriend, who's supposed to be my fiancé might be one of those soon." She looked around the room uncomfortably. "So that's why I'm here."

"Okay..." I said, trying to gather my brain cogs together. "So tell me your story, Miss Farina. Everyone has a story. That's what I do...listen to stories a lot of the time."

"Where shall I start?"

"At the beginning. Oh, and what number boyfriend is this we're talking about? How old are you? I learn a lot by cutting out the bullshit and getting right to it, if you don't mind."

She seemed offended at first, but then took a deep breath and faced me. "Do you always use bad swear words around your clients?"

"Not normally, lady, but you see my mouth is a little loose from the gin tonics. Would you like a gin tonic?"

"Absolutely not. Don't you know alcohol is illegal?"

"No...you don't say...where did you learn that?" I teased her.

She gave me a dirty look. "Well, I'm exactly twenty-five—on Election Day. I'm so glad we have a new president, aren't you?"

"I don't know, he hasn't proved himself yet. All politicians are grafters and the real deals are made behind closed doors, lady."

She frowned. "You're not very positive about things, are you. So, anyway, I've only had two serious boyfriends in my life. Todd is the second and the only one I've even considered marrying."

"Bad move," I said, not even knowing why I said it. "Pert and lovely young things like you should play the field until you've stacked up at least a dozen guys to choose from. Two ain't enough, doll."

"I don't think you're in a position to judge that, Mr. Denning, thank you," she said rather indignantly.

"Okay, okay...so continue..."

"Todd and I got together right after I broke up with Jimmy—I was really miserable and Todd comforted me. He was very sensitive for a man. Most guys seem rough around the edges, maybe like you."

"Another bad move, Miss Farina. You see, you don't take the rebound relationship too seriously. Like our new president, he has to prove himself...with time...were you intimate with the young man?"

She looked at me wide-eyed and got up. "Well! I've never heard such offensive conversation from someone who's supposed to be a private investigator with outstanding scruples and all—"

"—cut it, lady. If you wanna run out that door and find some other bloke who will talk dandy words to you and smell of expensive after shave lotion, then go now, just walk out. But if you want someone who cares enough to get the job done right, I'm you're guy!" I checked out her eyes. They were impatient with anger. "Why in the hell do you think you came to *me*?"

"You tell me—I'm beginning to wonder why!"

"Because you limp emotionally, because you're twenty-five years old and you can't kick-start a romantic relationship long enough to go the distance—let alone love someone. Do you love this Todd guy?"

"Yes, I think so..."

"*Think* so? That's the trouble with you dames—you wanna marry a guy you're not even sure you love. And tell me, while we're at it, what *is* love to you? Is it some legal way to shack up with someone, tell society now it's okay to have kids, pay taxes and live happily ever after in a little house you can't afford? And then it's kids and school and cars and work and fights over money and suddenly you realize even if you did love the guy, somehow the love sneaked out under the door and all you're left with is bills and old age. Is that what you want, Miss Farina?"

She stalked toward the open door, mad as a wet hornet. "You're terrible! You're a disgrace to your business!" Then she began to cry. "Awful men like you shouldn't be allowed to have a license to practice!"

I got up and went over to her and took out my handkerchief. She took it and dabbed her eyes. "I'm sorry if I come on a bit harsh, Miss Farina, but I'm trying to save us some time here by getting to the quick of it. Can you understand that? And, yeah, my style isn't for everyone, especially the faint of heart who hide behind the apron skirts of well brought up mid-western America where apple pie and church on Sunday are part of the ritual of a stagnant nowhere life. Boyfriends, lovers, fiancés and gigolos can come and go, lady, but you're stuck with yourself for life. And you know...I personally think you're a pretty nice self, someone a guy who took the

233

time to know you would respect, admire—yeah, maybe even learn to love in a genuine, lasting way."

She handed my handkerchief back to me. "Oh....I could be so mad at you. But I have to admit your indignant pounding away at me has a true ring to it—even if you are a bit drunk. But if it was really your ex-girlfriend that called and upset you—then I understand, I guess. So...."

"Do you wanna stay or walk out that door, Miss Farina? The choice is yours—you won't owe me a penny for the benefits of my expert opinions and experience tonight."

She hesitated. "Well...I don't know why, but somehow I think you know your business—you certainly seem to know human nature. So, if it's okay with you, I'll sit back down and tell you my story."

I held out my hand. She took it. "It's a deal...and I'll try to be a little more considerate of my language and a bit more diplomatic with you."

"Thank you," she murmured as she walked back to the client's chair in front of my desk. She took in a big, deep breath and exhaled. "I don't know...somehow I feel lighter just venting all the stuff we already discussed."

I took out a pack of cigarettes. "Smoke?" I asked.

"Yes...as a matter of fact...yes...I don't normally smoke, but right now I think I would like a cigarette." I handed her a Lucky Strike and lit it for her. She took a deep drag, coughed a little and then sat back in her chair. "Now, Mr. Denning—I think I'd like some of that gin you were talking about. Otherwise, you'll think me a prude when I speak and start judging me again. My father always told me that drinking buddies get along better than one who does and one who doesn't."

I smiled. "That's the spirit, doll! You're a woman after me own heart, you are." I poured the babe a drink and was surprised to discover that when I asked her if she wanted the tonic in it, she refused. "Like it straight across and down the gullet, eh?"

"Well, as I said, I'm here and I don't want to dislike you. Especially if you're going to work for me."

I handed Verona Farina the drink, we toasted and I sat back in my comfy chair once again. "Okay, sister, shoot. I'm all ears..."

She took a couple of awkward puffs on her cigarette and put it out in the ashtray. "As I said, I met Todd just after I broke up with Jimmy. Jimmy was pushy and all he wanted to do was have sex without anything else...you know the type."

"Yeah, in other words, a normal red-blooded American male."

"You can call it that. I thought it was animal, though. Oh, we'd walk in the park now and then. But I wanted to be romanced, taken to a nice place for dinner, hold hands on the pier in Santa Monica." She then took a sizeable gulp from her glass of booze. "But Todd was very different. In fact, it was quite the opposite with him. He took me out, wined and dined me, we took long walks and even hiked up to Griffith Park Observatory from the bottom of the hill. By the time my wounds over Jimmy had healed and I was feeling things for Todd, I realized he had hardly touched me at all. He even got down on his knees to propose to me. When I said I needed to think about it, I also asked him why he hadn't made any serious passes at me, or even kissed me goodnight, but just gave the best hugs. He said he needed to save that for the marriage night—or a honeymoon. In this day and age I thought it rather curious, but by then I was falling for him and I accepted it."

"Another big mistake. May I interrupt you here and get to the core of the matter?"

She drank down the rest of the gin. "Yes, I guess, if you must."

"You need to check out Todd's sexual identity. Here's how I see it. He's using you as a cover for his either latent or active homosexuality. It's an old ploy such men use. How old is Todd?"

She seemed shocked and her big blue eyes opened even wider. "Mr. Denning!" she exclaimed, the gin beginning to affect her speech a little. "What you're implying—"

"—I'm saving you some time and grief, lady—and call me Cable."

"Alright, *Cable*...I just don't think I like you. I'm trying...but I'm not doing so well...you are an obnoxious man, pushy in your own way like Jimmy—and certainly would not make a model husband for *any* woman!"

I chuckled. "You got that right, toots. Yeah, I love smoking, drinking, chasing hot skirts, stepping down for some fresh air in a smoke-filled nightclub in the middle of the night, listening to some sexy babe in a low-cut red sequined dress sing her little heart out and turn on half the men in the audience. I love the thrill of the chase, the minute you know she wants you and you put your hand up under her dress for the first time and she likes it—"

"—please! Mr. Denning—uh, Cable! That is vulgar, immoral and thoughtless! How can such men like you exist and not live in some sewer somewhere!" She stood up and looked at me indignantly. "Do you have another drink? Then I'll go...I really don't think we can do business together. Especially when I know what an un-Christian attitude you carry in your heart."

I was floored. What kind of audacity did this babe have? "Oh, so suddenly you're pure and full of scruples. Well, how was it in the dark there with Jimmy with your legs spread and his manhood thrusting into you? How 'Christian' was that? Isn't there something about fornication in the Bible?"

She suddenly quieted and sat back down, looking cute as hell with a pout on her lips. I poured her another gin and placed it in front of her on my desk. She took the glass and gulped the whole damn thing down! "That's different. I thought Jimmy would ask me to marry him, and—"

"—so you wanted some free samples first, is that it? Be a lot of things, Miss Farina—but don't be a hypocrite to *yourself*—you can lie to the world out there but keep the honest stuff for your own true confessions. It's easy to lie to yourself. All it takes is a quick rationalization that the world outside of your judgment is lousy and you're okay with bending the commandments or laws, rules or regulations that exist ideally for everyone. I see it every day—the corruption in the politics of power and control—that covert bending of the law done by your local judge or senator or president. It's the same for guys and dames."

She looked up at me from out of her glass. "Call me Verona. So now that you've judged and condemned me, and called my boyfriend a fag, and insulted my Christian upbringing—why should I stay?"

I pointed to my office entrance. "The doors still open, Verona. Either walk through it, or go over, close it, come back and let's get down to the business at hand."

She got up, a bit tipsy from that big slug of gin and walked over to the front door and closed it. Then she came around to my side of the desk. "I'm not afraid of you, you know, Cable Denning. I might be small, but I'm feisty. Ziggy told me you'd probably be pretty good in bed—if she got you that far. But I guess you were thanking her for something—"

"—yeah, like saving my life. But the scum I was talking about earlier...got to her...and now poor Ziggy's down there with the rest of the worms, making her way to the land of the hereafter."

"That's a terrible thought! Are you always so gruesome? How did she save your life? She never said."

"It's a long story, toots. Sit down and let's get Todd's story told instead, so you can go home."

Then she surprised the hell out of me. "What if I don't want to go home, Cable? What if I want to stay here with you and smoke your cigarettes, drink your illegal liquor and sleep in your bed?"

I didn't have an immediate come back. "Did I hear you right? Are you the same babe who only minutes ago was pouring out vitriol and insults at me like a bad batter swinging away at curve balls?"

"I know...it's strange what cigarettes and alcohol can do, isn't it?" Her voice slurred somewhat and she put

238

her foot up on my knee and lifted her skirt to show me a leg. "I may not have the hottest pair of legs in the city, buster, but they're pretty, and they can be warm and sensuous—plus I like the tone of your voice and the way you talk and how you don't give a damn about anything. I wish I could be like that." She burped. "But I can't. So I thought maybe you could teach me something. How old are you?"

I took her foot off my leg. "Too old for your kind of dame, Verona. I'll be thirty-three next year. And it's not true about me not giving a damn about things. *Some* things I care about a lot."

"Name one..."

"Well, there's truth...that's a big one for me...I don't mean little white lies—but the big stuff, the real zingers that make the difference in life. But it doesn't come under the banner of some church, religion, sect, tribe or particular cultural belief system—but outta me—the guy who has to live with himself and hope to hell there *is* a tomorrow and some of the bad guys you've put down will stay that way. So that's the second thing...mopping up the streets and alleys, taking down a hoodlum who either belongs in jail—or dead. Seeing justice done by weeding out the vermin that haunt the underbelly of this fair city of ours. It's kinda like life, it ain't perfect, but it's all we've got...and this metropolis is all I've got. We kind of live and breathe together, I've gotten used to her rhythms and she mine, so we have a pact. I help clean up the vermin, garbage and shit disguised as humans and she allows me the privilege of stepping down into a classy nightspot to hear some great music...or gaze upon a beautiful babe who's all sex and sequins. And meeting the kind of people who go there, the wounded, lost and lonely of the world, those that hurt so bad they can't take it up on top anymore without a shot of whiskey, a few smokes and a good time pouring out their troubles on the disenfranchised of this world. So what's your excuse for living?" I asked her, watching those big blues of hers get bigger as she listened and she swayed a little, standing above me.

She took a big breath. "You're such a great talker, Cable. May I kiss you? Just once, if you don't mind."

"What happened to Jimmy and Todd—and your story?"

"Screw Todd—and I already screwed Jimmy—I...I just met...just met a real man tonight, Mr. Big Shot."

"And who might that be?" I laughed.

"*You*...you, Mister. You changed my mind. So you lost...lost some business, but gained a free whore for the night, if you want. Except I don't charge, so I'm even cheaper, aren't I?"

It was hard to believe all this was coming out of the mouth of the seemingly prudish Verona Farina, who seemed to have done an about face in less than a half hour! It goes to show, you never know dames—how they think, what they're really like underneath the protective cover called social protocol and morality. But I was nevertheless surprised to hear this young twenty-five year old spew out all that boldness. "I'm—I'm not that easy, Verona. I may be a little drunk, but I have my own set of commandments, the first of which concerning gals, is don't go to bed with a babe you don't desire—or who doesn't desire you naturally. The second commandment is don't mess with an undecided chick who's engaged—and third, do not hit on a married woman who's hitched to some bloke she seems to be in love with."

"I'd still like to kiss you," she persisted. "Like I said, just once." She leaned over and put her lips very close to mine. "May I?"

"It'll cost you twenty-five bucks—my first day's fee working for you tracing out your possibly misbehaving boyfriend."

She went over to her purse on top of my desk, took out the money and slapped it on the desk in front of me. "Here...never say you never got paid for it, Mr. Private Detective." She bent her head down and slowly put those warm lips of hers onto mine. Actually, it felt pretty good, as if every bit of the outside of Verona was a big sham and her kiss told me of a warm, sensual, loving woman locked inside there somewhere. She began to breathe harder as she put her arms around my neck, still clinging to my lips. Then she pulled back. "It's been a long time for me, Cable...it seems we're both hurting...maybe we could comfort each other a little tonight? I promise I won't make a pest of myself and get right down to making you happy in your bed. I'm not too much of a talker in the bedroom...what do you say?" she whispered.

It was true, I was a little drunk and running from the memory of Zelda and my feelings for her that lingered in my gut like an old song whose melody keeps haunting your life because somehow something was left unfinished. "Just so you know it ain't *love*, Miss Priss."

"No...I would never expect that from a man like you, Cable. That's what makes it fun—and safe. And talking about safe, I think we will need some protection. I'm feeling very wet and fertile tonight."

Again, I was amazed at the babe's frankness. "Well, that isn't the usual line I hear from a gal who wants me."

"So...what is the usual line?"

"Please, Cable, just fuck me—I don't care—I want you! Or something like that, I believe."

"Okay, then, 'please, Cable, take me to bed, fuck me—I don't care—I just want you!" she intoned in a teasing voice.

"Okay, you asked for it." I got up and picked her up into my arms and carried Verona Farina into my mussed up bedroom, you know, the one with the stale smelling sheets and filled ashtrays. I threw her onto the bed and she quickly pulled me on top of her. She took my hand and put it up her pretty pink dress until it clutched around her wet mound. "You weren't kidding, lady," I whispered in the dark of my room.

"I told you. But I am worried about getting pregnant. Will you please use one of those terrible rubber things?"

"Yeah, sure..." I got up to check in my desk drawer where I thought there might be one of those dreaded things. I took my clothes off, and she disrobed entirely and slid into my dirty sheets. But I was having difficulty staying erect and trying to slip the damn thing on at the same time. "I—I think I have a confession to make here, Verona. I've never used one of these before—honest. I think the mechanical thought of having to put some shitty insulation between us doesn't agree with my mister-between-the-legs here."

She got out of bed and kneeled beside me and carefully took my responsive manhood into her mouth. It didn't take long for my erection to fill her whole oral cavity, but I wished it were filling another one of her cavities. She stopped and looked back at my very erect member. "Wow! Oh, boy, mister! Will you give all of that to me?—here!" She handed me the condom again, but I had the same problem. As soon as I tried to slip on that damn balloon, down to Droop City he went!

"I don't think this is gonna work, lady," I finally said in total frustration. But she was too hot to handle and she pulled me down onto the bed and spread her legs and helped me roll over between them. The second I felt the hot, wet warmth of her pussy, I started to grow again like the magic bean in Jack and the Beanstalk. And the more my magic bean swelled and extended itself to the doorway of her womanhood, the more she panted and moaned until she grabbed my butt and shoved all of me into her. Almost instantly she came off with a wild orgasm and rocked me wildly until I felt I was going to penetrate her vagina so deep that I'd come out somewhere on the other end of her body! She begged me to come into her and I wanted to, but at the very last second, with all the will power I possessed, I pulled out and came all over her belly. She screamed a primitive response of ecstasy. Finally after about fifteen minutes of cooling our engines down, I rolled off of her, our bodies sopping wet with sweat. Then she took whatever liquid was left from her belly and wiped it on both of her nipples. "I've never...I mean I've *never* felt it like that, Cable...God, you're good! I really know what you mean about that stupid rubber sleeve and all—but what's a girl to do?"

243

"You did the right thing, lady," I said, proud of myself for having withdrawn at the last possible minute. "I wouldn't want you to get—"

"—now that wouldn't be appropriate now would it, Cable?

" No....that's a little like Russian roulette, isn't it?"

"It's exciting pulling that trigger with you...may I stay the night—and maybe we can do it again a little later?

"Well, I have a rule about that, Verona. One-night shack-ups don't get to stay. One of us has to go before dawn—so, since this is my shack—guess who gets to ride the streetcar home?"

She looked at me strangely. "You wouldn't do that...sending a poor, defenseless girl out into the cold night—I mean anything might happen to me. It's not safe these days, Cable."

I thought it over. Yeah, in a way times were changing. It wasn't as safe as in previous years to send a babe home on public transportation in the middle of the night. "Well, I guess I could—"

"—If you let me stay a little longer, I can wash up and go directly to work from your office."

"Alright, alright...so let's try and get some shut-eye. You kind of wore me out —especially for a self-righteous Christian broad who yelled foul when I told her my truth and said I was a disgrace to my business."

She traced her fingers around the hair on my chest. "That was then...I think...I've formed a different opinion..." She kissed my lips gently. "I really enjoyed you, Cable. Thank you."

I cuddled her into my arms and we drifted off into that kind of sleep when you're always aware someone else is beside you you're not used to. She fondled my private parts a few times during the night and got quite a rise out of me, but I wasn't about to risk entering into that warm and wet Venus flytrap of hers again this night!

Morning came with a fog bank from the sea covering the city. Verona Farina got up early, washed and dressed. I was just putting on my pants when she came in from the bathroom, looking very different than the naked young woman who had spent the night in my bed. "Now, Cable, we must pretend none of this ever happened, okay? You keep the twenty-five dollars I gave you for your expert advice—and my favors were free of charge. May I call you if I want to get a little tipsy again and make love with you? It sure helped me forget Todd for a while."

"I'm not a for-hire sex machine, ya know. So, what about your Todd?"

"You're a good teacher. I think I'll call it off. A real man tastes so much better—and you're a real man, mister."

"Well, thanks for that, Verona." I stood up to face her. "But somehow I don't think we should have a second go at this thing. I was a little drunk last night and mooning over Zelda—and acted quite unprofessionally, I might add. Also, I apologize for probably punching at you with some pretty harsh words. I'm good at that."

She seemed surprised. "Not see me again? I thought we could be secret lovers—you know, the magic kind—

those who nobody ever suspects are seeing each other?"

"I'm sorry, Verona. Part of me is all burned out wanting to do that kind of crap anymore. Besides, I've known a few beautiful dames who really loved me, and kind of spoiled me from having casual sex in the middle of the night with a brand new almost-client."

"Is that what you think of me? Well, maybe you are a two-faced man like most men. I thought you were different."

"Hey, lady, it's too early to argue...and I'm not awake yet. Come on, I'll see you to the trolley."

"Don't bother, buster, I get the message." She grabbed her purse from off the desk and stalked out of my office. And there I was, half-dressed looking at a closed door in a quiet room. How does one figure those strange detours we all take in life—the ones that don't make any sense—and desire of the moment takes us over like a mesmeric demon, forcing two bodies together in the dark of a bizarre night? I never heard from Verona Farina again. C'est la vie!

Pearls Get Lonely, Too

It was November 26, 1932 and I planned to spend a quiet Thanksgiving Day with my mother in her new place. For some reason I still had an odd taste in my mouth when I thought about the last time I got laid. Verona Farina seemed a cheap way to get your rocks off—even for me, I thought. It's funny how some things just don't quite sit right. Two people meet, rub each other's hair in the wrong direction and end up in bed together.

But I suppose it's like the rest of life...most of it doesn't make much sense when you really think about it. My mother's new dwelling was a quiet place, considering it was situated up at the end of Vine Street directly above the now booming Hollywood. The house, at 2166, sat on the SE corner of Vine and Ivarene streets. It still had a large lot even after three portions of the original near quarter acre had been sold to help pay off the purchase of the house. The property was dotted with trees, most of them encircling the front of the property. A promising young Avocado tree on the back lot, and a very large Eucalyptus at the top of the Ivarene side....then moving down there was a magnificent Jacaranda tree that, dropping its flowers, created a carpet of lavender on the natural pathway below. Almost right on the corner was a young Ponderosa Pine tree. Moving along the Vine side, a huge old Pepper Tree, with a particularly fragrant Cup o' Gold Vine that intertwined in its branches, then finally a Kadota Fig tree. Pepper trees were prolific all over the Hollywood area. Inside this fortress of trees, gracing the middle of a small lawn bordered by flower beds, there was a wonderful Catalpa tree that the neighborhood kids loved to climb and just sit in the crux of the trunk and talk about their dreams and plan their lives. The Hollywood hills ascended steeply from there, and a few homes were beginning to sprout out of the hillsides, some precariously. Nestled in the hills above was a reservoir. I remember it's official opening and dedication in 1924. An exciting day for the Hollywood and Los Angeles area. The builder, William Mulholland and several local dignitaries were gathered for the event. Since then, my office being close by, I've enjoyed many a stroll around the perimeter—hoping to walk and think myself into some kind of solution to matters stranger than fiction that manage to find me around every corner.

My mother seemed happier in her new home. I greeted her with my usual son's love, with embraces and kisses. She had been a beautiful and stately woman in her prime. Now she sagged a bit, but still had those marvelous high cheekbones and twinkle in her blue eyes. We were glad to spend the time together. We sat at a large dark oak table still in the house from my eccentric Aunt who had died and left the house to mother. She served a wonderful ham, pineapple and sweet potatoes with fresh crisp string beans on the side.

After dinner I lit up a Lucky Strike and leaned back in my chair. "That was marvelous, Mom—you still have it, kid. You were always the best cook on the block."

She smiled. "You're just remembering the best dishes, son. I've had some real disasters in my time as well." She studied my face. "Have you heard from Zelda—just curious, that's all...."

"Yeah, about two or three weeks ago she called and told me she had arrived safely in Arizona. That was a strange one. I never quite figured it—I mean, why she just took off. Yeah, sure, I'm not the easiest bloke to be around, I guess, but I thought we had—"

"—she's completely in love with you, Cable," my mother interrupted, looking sternly into my face. "Did you ever understand that? I'm not even sure you comprehended how Adora—or even Honey loved you. But each woman loved you deeply in her own way. Where have you been, son? Your father once told me you were

248

a lot like his brother, an adventurer who never quite took life seriously."

"Brother? I didn't even know Dad had a brother."

My mother got a strange expression on her face and for a second, I could swear her eyes misted. "Yes, he ran off and disappeared and went abroad after your father returned home from being sick." Her face seemed to draw sad. "He came back for a short while just after your Dad married me. But your uncle couldn't take the ghetto life and wanted to expand himself by going to Europe or the Orient or somewhere, so the story went."

"Hmmm...so what other skeletons may be found in our family closet? It's strange, isn't it? I mean, how things leak out as you get older because maybe somebody thinks you weren't ready to hear them earlier in your life."

She looked at me with a smile as she studied her son's eyes. "I have something you should read for yourself." She got up from the table and went to a desk by the wall phone. She came back with a letter, but I noticed she only gave me half of it and tucked the remainder back in the envelope. "The other half's for me...but I think this is meant for you..."

"Who's it from?"

"Just read it, Cable, you'll know..."

I took the hand-written piece of paper in my hand and read: *"That was my desire, Mother—since you wish me to call you that—to spend my life with your son. But under the circumstances...well, you know the rest. I was going to send Cable this enclosed poem I wrote. It kind of goes around in my head like a song, but I couldn't get up the nerve to send it to him. It would only open up old wounds. Maybe someday I can send it to him, when it doesn't matter anymore. I hope you like it.*

'My latest love, is my faded love, for my lifetime...
my latest dream, and though it may not seem a man and wife time...
so it goes with the pose of crying through a restless night of tears...
My lonely love, is my only love,
capturing the hours of bliss, with just one kiss,
and for a while I'm only a child at sea...ever drifting in his uplifting arms,
lost in the waves of his charm...
My growing love I confess is showing love,
and my latest love, is my greatest love.....come true...'

There...I got it all out. I'll keep you posted.
Love, Zelda."

My highly tuned detective skills sensed something else was going on between these two women. But I was nonetheless very touched by Zelda's beautiful words, meant for me. "Keep you posted about what?" I inquired, a little miffed that some secrets were being kept from me.

"Oh, nothing, Cable—just how she's doing—you know, woman talk and things like that. I'm very fond of Zelda and have decided to maintain correspondence with her. After all, she has no one, really—that paralyzed aunt surely can't be much good company for her. She's a pearl, Cable, and even pearls get lonely."

"Yeah...I guess," I said, but those instincts were still nagging at me. I let it drop and spent a pleasant afternoon having tea under an old umbrella table behind the house on a little dirt patio, in the shade of a large Mulberry Tree and another of those Pepper trees . The ground was stained in places from the berries that had dropped. I'd enjoy my mother now. Life had taught me you never know when your number's up and someone you love won't be around anymore. That's the funny thing about death—it's so damned final!

Chapter 10

WALKING THE ZODIAC

<u>You Got to Pick a Pocket or Two</u>

It was December 2nd and I felt chipper as I walked the trails of Griffith Park. It had been some time since I had visited these old familiar haunts of nature. The area near the Bronson Caves had become alarmingly unlucky for me. Within the caves I had found the lifeless body of Eden Royce hanging upside down in the darkness, had a crash course in crazy sex with the mannequin shell of Cassiopeia on the road outside the caves and had walked these trails with Honey and Adora, not to mention my current heartache, Zelda Blodgett.

But this day I was deep in thought. I had twenty-nine days to save my ass from the clutches of Helmut Becker and his gang of German thugs, not to mention escaping from those remaining in the *Oculus* who wanted to probe my mind with the Blue Light of Noda in order to extract the content of the very famous and sought after *Fen de Fuqín*, or as gringos called it, the *God of Our Fathers*. I could no longer postpone a strategy of action—namely, remove myself long enough to elude those greedy bastards and find a way to get to Nepal to seek out the great priest guru and magician, *Lama Daishi*. But now suddenly, I had to "beware" of the *Moirai*, the *Seven Goddesses of Fate,* so Noda and Eli had told me. Does it never end? Had I agreed to accept them as life guides—and how did a thing like that work? And now, how to get the money to make such an expensive and time-consuming trip. Also, I'd have to shut down my business until I returned. And who could I get to watch over the business while I was absent? Or at least, someone to come in a few times a week and answer phones, take down potential client info and pay outstanding bills. A want ad in the newspaper! Yeah, that's what I'd do. I'd advertise for someone tomorrow!

I hiked to the little hill directly above the Bronson Caves. It was a pleasant little place, rocky with a few sagebrush bushes but a great view of Hollywood below. I was contemplating my reality when all of a sudden I heard a rustle from inside one of the sagebrush bushes. It soon became the unmistakable death rattle of the Pacific Coast Rattlesnake. Adrenaline filled my body and I shot up from my sitting position like a jackrabbit and must have jumped three feet. The rattling persisted. I slowly approached the bush. There, coiled and rapidly sticking its black tongue in and out at me, was the snake. But I figured if I could survive Boak the Magnificent, sixteen feet of deadly King Cobra, I could deal with the local garden variety of rattlesnake! Just then I heard a voice behind me.

"You needn't worry so much, Cable," the friendly voice of Toggth addressed me. "Why is it you persist in getting yourself in so much—how is it you would say?—hot water?"

"Toggth, old buddy—boy, am I glad to see you! I was just dealing with this reptile—"

"—not in the way it wishes to be dealt with." He crossed in front of me, went to the bush in which the snake was housed, put his hand in and pulled the creature back out with him. It became docile in Toggth's hands, neither angry nor aggressive, but passive and at peace. Even the rattles had stopped their nervous vibrating. "You see, Cable, how fear attracts fear? If I do not fear the little guy, and he senses I mean him no harm, then he has no fear and allows me to exchange with him what all creatures in the universe have a right to—the cozy warmth of exchanging loving energies." He let the snake down onto the ground. Slowly, the four-foot reptile headed for thicker grass and made its way down the embankment. Then Toggth looked at me. "Now...let's take a gander at Cable Denning. I see you are in trouble again with more of humanity's hornet's nests—and even more surprising, you are willing to travel far to seek out *The Great Anointment*."

"Yeah...right on the money, my friend." I went up to the little guy, bent over and gave him a big hug. "I really am glad to see you. I met your brother, you know."

"Yes, he told me. That's how I know about *Lama Daishi* and your upcoming journey to the land of *Mt. Shivapuri*."

"Oh," I said, not really surprised. "Then you probably know certain parties have given me until December 31st to continue to live—and if I'm gonna escape their guns, strangling scarves, torture devices, knives and miscellaneous horrors, I've got to get out of town. And...to get out of town and go where I want to go, half-way around the world at least...I'll need plenty of moola to do it. So there you have it, old boy."

"It seems to me, then, it's the money part that's holding things up, wouldn't you say?"

"Yep."

"Then, let's go watch an armored car on the way from the bank lose some of its 'moola', as you call it."

"Isn't that illegal?" I laughed.

"For earthlings, yes...for alien visitors, no...we simply don't know any better," he said with a smile.

We walked to the streetcar stop down at Franklin Avenue. We got on. People stared at us, this unlikely duo of a regular looking gumshoe sitting next to a light-pink skinned little alien creature with cute pointed ears and lots of hair growing out of his nose. I nudged Toggth and he nudged me back as we rode along smiling, milking the situation for all it was worth.

We got to a Bank of America at Hollywood and Highland. Toggth drew me into the shade of the building. There we stood in broad daylight, with me smoking away on my Lucky Strikes and my little alien friend trying to whistle Irving Berlin's *What'll I Do*. "It's your lips—" I finally told him—"they're the wrong shape out in front there." I tried to whistle the tune myself. "You see, the upper lip must seem like it's gonna cover the bottom, only it doesn't. Your bottom lip is too prominent and your upper too thin."

"No it isn't," Toggth persisted. "You can train the muscles...it'll just take me a while." Then he glanced over as the 4:00 p.m. money truck came rolling in and two rough looking guards came rolling out, machine guns in hand. "Lookie, Cable...they are going to pick up much more money than we need. See those shiny leather pouches? We'll have one of them accidentally fall out of the truck exactly at the next stoplight. Now, you go down to that next block and pick it up quickly so no one will notice, or if they do, it'll happen too fast for them to realize what has happened until after we're gone. Don't you humans call this a 'heist' or something like that? You have the oddest terminology."

"Well, you have the oddest ways of thinking—but I guess if they work, who am I to question it?"

"Exactly. Now be on your way. I'll enchant the pouch and you—you go enchant some female of your species until you see the truck coming your way."

"Right," I said, feeling a rush of excitement. I moved out toward the next block. When I got there I *did* notice a good-looking dame in a light-blue suit standing by a newspaper boy. I went up to her to check out Toggth's theory. Could I flirt with this broad or not? "Nice day for it, isn't it?" I said with my tongue-in-cheek.

She looked at me curiously. "Are you talking to me?" she asked.

"I am...it's me, Cable...don't you recognize me?" I was having a ball just putting the dame on and confusing her like hell.

"Cable? Cable who? I don't know any Cable."

"Well, that's funny. I was told there'd be a swell looking babe standing on this very corner looking to flirt with me."

"I think you've got some wires crossed up in your brain, Mister. Now if you don't mind leaving me alone, I'm waiting..."

"Waiting for what, if I may inquire?"

She glanced down at the newspaper boy. "The five star final. My boyfriend's a bookie and the races are hot today. He bet sixteen smackers on *Bob's Tail Nag* and she pays eight to one if she wins."

"You've got a boyfriend?"

"Yes, buster, I do."

"Are you sure?"

"Yes—and it's none of your business if I do or don't."

"Then I've been misled. You'd best be on your way, then. I was interested only in someone who came to this very spot to flirt with me today."

"Well, I'll say you've got a lot of nerve—whatever your name is." With that she walked away indignantly.

"Those who were least, shall become most, my friend," a voice from behind me spoke. I looked back. There stood a small man with a white shirt open at the chest, a medium white beard and moustache, twinkling blue eyes and a semi-smile on his lips. "I heard you flirting but skirting the real issue. I'll watch as you steal the swatch from the gang of thieves who come this way..."

I did a double take as if I weren't quite present in this time and space thing called planet earth. "And who in the hell are you? It seems this corner is a magnet for nuts—are you a nut?"

"Absolutely...to the world...I am. This world knows me as Peter the Hermit—but I harbor another truth, friend—for I see the end and all that comes pitter pattering and scattering down the lane of the surprised and forlorn—why were you born, then?"

"I don't know, you tell me..."

"Don't go back, Jack, learn to walk the Zodiac. You and your Virgo, ergo, go to Paris with Aries, be nicest to Pisces, don't lock horns with Capricorn, love a girl named Cleo only if she's a Leo, be fairest with Sagittarius, yet grow not your hairy-ness to Aquarius or else Gemini will judge you to be effeminii. Remember what you came for, to play the game for, born to fulfill the pill that rills the waters of tranquility."

"That makes sense, sort of, I guess. Are you some kind of a poet?"

"Don't you know it! Drop the label, Cable...you see—hee! hee!—I know your kind and have kept in mind your whereabouts and know your doubts—for Thana haunts you day and night, escape as you might—the long night comes."

"You've been spying on me? Did Becker and his gang pay you to follow me?" I backed him up against the wall of a store. "Or was it the *Oculus*—and who in the hell is 'Thana?'"

"Ah... she...one of the Moirai....the Goddess of Death—linked to *Keres* and *Erinyes*. Eat the book and anoint the fire that burns and turns your life." He grabbed my hands with a lot of strength and pulled them off his shirt. Then he traced a sign around himself and cleared his space. "I am sent by no one except my soul to be here. You are pale with the alien races around you. I am not one of those. I am one of *you* for a change." Then he looked down the street. "Oh! Oh! It's time to toot for here comes the loot tanked out of the bank—I will help subdue the few who may watch. Careful now, lad—don't make it look bad!"

I saw the armored truck approach the intersection and stop at the signal on the corner. The little man gently pushed me toward the curb. As if on cue, a leather pouch fell out from off the rear bumper and fell into the gutter. I immediately grabbed it. Some people must've seen me, but no one said a word, if they had. Then I turned to thank Peter the Hermit. But he had disappeared. "Thanks, Peter, wherever you are…will I ever see you again? I was beginning to think you were the real thing."

There was no reply as I crossed the street and made my way back toward the bank where Toggth might be waiting. I didn't get far. He pulled me into a narrow alley. "Here…get your worthless green paper into this." He handed me a plain brown shopping bag. "Now…you have your funds…next we must plan your itinerary. Shall you close your business down? I'd say you have about twenty-five thousand dollars in that bag." He found a garbage can and tossed the old pouch into it as he walked toward the other end of the alley.

"I don't know…I'd kinda like to have a part-time secretary watch over things and all during my absence. I'd hate to come back to L.A. and have to start all over again. I was thinking of placing a want ad tomorrow."

"Very well. I will dash in and out of your dimension until you leave. I suggest you fly when you can. Your primitive modes of travel have begun to speed up a little. There is an item known as the *Pan American Airways Clipper*. It leaves America and stops off in Hawaii, then Midway Island, Wake Island, Guam and finally Subic Bay in the Philippine Islands. You can take a tramp steamer from there to mainland China, then travel overland into Tibet. That is where we're going, isn't it?"

I laughed. "Damn, Toggth, you've done my homework for me! Hey, wait a minute—what about this *we* stuff? Are you coming along?"

"Well, you know me—yes and no. On and off…I'll check in with you regularly so you don't get off course, if you know what I mean."

259

"Are you talking about booze and babes or getting kidnapped?"

"All three, Cable. One must keep an eye on you. Ever since Lei-Tao I've been skeptical as to your sexual intentions with women. The smoking will give you disease eventually, and for sure the terrible quality of the alcohol you drink will eat out your insides sooner or later. And as far as kidnapped, well, don't look now, but there will be dangers at every stop waiting to confiscate from your little human brain all that lies in there asleep."

"So," I laughed again, "everything seems to be up and normal!"

She Wore a Quiet Smile

As good luck would have it, the day after I placed the ad in the newspaper, I had several responses. It took me most of the day to sort out the qualifications, who I sensed would work out and who wouldn't. Finally it boiled down to one thirty-five year old woman by the name of Mandy Foster Simpson, a Southern girl with a sexy little Georgian accent. By six o'clock p.m. that night she was rapping on my office door. I got up and opened it. Mandy Foster Simpson stood about five-five, wore a quiet smile, a yellow skirt and off-white blouse, the top part of which she filled out just fine. She probably weighed about 125 lbs. or so. She looked solid and her handshake was the same. "Hello, Miss Simpson—I'm Cable Denning. Please, come in."

She let go of my hand. "I'm delighted to meet you, Mr. Denning. Sure is a shorter ride than I anticipated from my place of residence." She glanced over at my desk area. "Shall I sit, sir?"

"Oh, yes...by all means. Please..." I said, pointing to the client's chair. She seated herself and I went around to my comfy chair and sat, facing her. "Now, Miss Simpson. What we covered on the phone seemed to be quite thorough, and at this time I would suggest you possess substantial qualifications for the job at hand. In fact, your duties would be essentially keeping my office running while I'm away in Asia for a few weeks. That essentially means answering the phone, keeping records of those who might want to employ me upon my return, friends who might call, and maintaining files in alphabetical order over there in the old army metal filing cabinet. "

She was looking around the room and her eyes drifted back to gaze at me. She was kind of a dirty blonde with her hair done up in back and wore a bit more makeup than I personally would have liked to see on such a pretty woman. "Oh, I do like the way you talk, Mr. Denning. Are you sure you're not a transplanted southern boy? I mean, you use some of my favorite words like *substantial qualifications, maintainin' files and essentially meanin'*...all of which I adore."

I looked at her a bit oddly. "Oh, yeah. That's swell...I'm glad we share a vocabulary. So, uh, how trustworthy are you—and dependable—you see, you'd be the one to mind the store and all during my absence."

She widened her eyes. "Why, Mr. Denning, I am surprised you would indicate in any manner whatsoever a suggestion that would put my integrity to question. I am indignant at such a thought, and will inform you I have

261

at my fingertips long-term references addressing my competence and personal dependability."

"Then I stand corrected, Miss Simpson. I apologize. May I...may I take a gander at your references?"

"By all means, Mr. Denning. You have that right as my prospective employer."

She handed me a folder with several letters of recommendation and a work history that was to be envied. "Since you were nineteen, eh? May I ask, between these very demanding jobs, have you enjoyed a social life, are you married, children—or anything that might lead me to have confidence in your social skills—such as handling the telephone calls?"

She looked at me strangely. "My, my, calibrating my social station is hardly inclusive in my outstanding record of achievement you see listed there."

"Yes, and that's all well and fine, Miss Simpson. But much of what I do is direct contact with clients and potential clients—and frankly, everything I see here has been locked-behind-closed-doors kind of employment. You have been a research scientist's secretary in Fairbanks, Alaska, a fishing industry bookkeeper in Florida, an accountant in San Francisco—and an employee for the Federal Bureau of Investigation forensics division." I looked up at her. "And we both know, Miss Simpson, the dead don't normally carry on conversations."

She turned a little red. "Well, sir, truth be known, it is true I have not immersed my person in social intercourse much during my professional endeavors. Then are you suggesting I am not good material for secretarial consideration?"

"I didn't say that, but I'd like to do a pretend phone conversation with you, if you don't mind. Let's pretend I'm a potential client, I'll use typical situations and approaches that potential clients have used. Would that be all right with you?"

"I regard that approach as rather irregular...but after all, you are the one in charge of hiring in this particular circumstance."

"Okay, ready?"

"Yes, I reckon I am."

"Ring! Ring!"

"Yes, hello, Cable Denning Private Investigator's offices. How may I help you?"

So far she was right on. "Is Mr. Denning available?"

"No, I'm sorry he's out of town for an extended period of time. May I help?"

"Well, I don't know. I normally wouldn't tell a woman my situation."

"I've been in Mr. Denning's employ for quite some time and I assure you, I will be happy to ascertain, sir, whether or not Mr. Denning would be in a position to take on your case."

"Fair enough," I said, pretending I was Mr. Joe Blow from the upper middle class part of town. "Well, it goes like this Miss—Miss—"

"—Miss Simpson, sir..."

"—okay, Miss Simpson. You see, I think my wife's fooling around with her attorney. I happened to find a note from him attached to some legal papers I read by mistake addressed to her. He was talkin' about some kind of rendezvous they had planned in Tarzana. I need a good private dick to verify that and get me some photos of those two between the sheets—see?"

Miss Simpson seemed a bit embarrassed. "I—I see, I'm certain that Mr. Denning has abundant experience in such cases. If you'll be kind enough to give me your name and phone number, I'll be happy to convey that message to Mr. Denning."

"Well, when is he getting back from out of town?"

"You know how these cases can be, Mr.—Mr.—"

"—Brown, Larry Brown, Atwater 7061. You have a nice voice, Miss Simpson. You don't happen to be single now, do you?" I teased, knowing it might unbalance her tact.

Again she blushed. "I'm sorry, Mr. Brown, but it is not permissible for me to address personal questions with a client or prospective client. It is not considered ethical."

The game was over. "Ya done good!" I exclaimed. "*Prospective client*, I like that phrase—think I'll add it to my own phone lingo."

"Thank you, Mr. Denning...then...then I'm hired?"

"Yeah, you're hired on one more condition. Look around, Miss Simpson—you see I smoke, drink, chase skirts and my office is dirty and smacks of a bachelor's life, right? At no time are you to be judgmental regarding my personal habits because business-wise I run a pretty tight ship here, as you'll find out. Is that agreeable to you?"

"Yes, Mr. Denning." Then all of a sudden she broke down crying. I got up to comfort her and handed her my handkerchief.

"Was it something I said?" I inquired, puzzled at the dame.

"No!" she sobbed. "I apologize for my behavior. I'm just gratefully obliged for your kindness—because in all truth to you, sir, I was down to my last few dollars. As you can see on my resume, it has been over eighteen months since I was last employed...and I haven't sufficient funds to maintain myself beyond this very month."

"Well, then Miss Simpson, consider yourself saved in the nick of time. You know, you can call me Cable. I'm not really into all that formal crap."

She looked up at me from her chair as she handed me back my handkerchief. "Thank you, sir. If you have no severe objection, I desire to continue to call you by your surname. Familiarity breeds contempt. We must retain our wholesome professional relationship at all times."

"Have you had bad experiences, Miss Simpson?"

"Well, sir, to be perfectly bold, if I may, I have been put upon by more than one employer, thinking that other favors might accompany my regular assignments. Frankly spoken, I have been touched and manhandled and in at least two instances, was forced to terminate my employment."

"Oh, I see," I said, understanding that a horny male libertine might take advantage of the lady by a stolen kiss, a hand under her dress or a quick feel of those more than ample breasts of hers. "Yeah, sometimes that's a tough one, that male-female nature thing, you know. I assure you such a thing will not happen in this office."

"I feel assured, sir. When would you like me to commence?"

"There is one other thing. I notice in your resume that you spent some time with FBI forensics."

"Yes, sir." She had a worried look on her brow as if I might now change my mind. "That was my original training. My Daddy was a doctor of forensics in Atlanta."

"My particular line of work can get pretty dangerous at times. You may—now keep in mind I'm saying *may*—encounter some pretty rough characters now and then. But the good news is I haven't lost a secretary yet due to getting mugged or killed by a *prospective client*, as you might say." She smiled and got up. She walked the few steps toward me.

"I must assure you, despite my display of feminine tears, I am capable of bolstering my person to the occasion."

"Well, then we may proceed, Miss Simpson. Tomorrow morning would be just fine. I'll show you the ropes and get you into the routine. Whatever you do, don't come early. I'm often an insomniac or drink myself into a very early morning stupor—therefore, please do not show before 11:00 a.m. until after I have left for my trip, okay?"

"As you wish, Mr. Denning. Nor shall I be judgmental as to your imbibing in that sinful drink and tobacco you consume. You shall hear no comment from my lips."

I kind of liked her lips. They were full and inviting, but I also knew that keeping out of mischief with female office personnel was a priority. Lord knew, my previous secretaries were also my lovers. Adora and Zelda played dual roles, in my office by day, in my bed at night. "She glanced at her wristwatch. "Oh, goodness! I must be off. I don't want to miss the symphony tonight. Would you be interested in attending with me, Mr. Denning? Perhaps a chance to get to know one another more substantially?"

"Truthfully, Miss Simpson, I'm afraid I'm a rather low-brow character. As I told you, I'm used to babes in smoky joints singing Jerome Kern, Irving Berlin, the Gershwin boys and the like."

"Nothing reaches the heart and spirit better than *the great music*—and tonight a brilliant violinist named Jascha Heifetz will perform the Brahms Violin Concerto in D-major under the stars at the Hollywood Bowl. I inherited two tickets, my new boss man. Won't you give it a try?"

"Brahms-schwams—I wouldn't know the difference."

"It's the only violin concerto Johannes Brahms ever wrote…"

"Okay, Miss Simpson, you got a taker, but on one condition…"

"My, my, but you seem to be so full of conditions, Mr. Denning."

"And that is if I don't like the thing, I get up and go home."

"Leavin' your poor little stranded new secretary to find her way home in the middle of the dark night? Now, I say, Mr. Denning, where has chivalry gone to? I would take kindly to your hearing it through and then escortin' me home, if it's all the same to you."

"You see, that's the thing about dames. Give 'em an inch and they take a mile." I took a deep, exasperated breath. "But since this is the first time, I'll give you the benefit of the doubt."

"Well, now, thank you, Mr. Denning. I take to that most kindly and consider you a gentleman of the first order."

In 1932 the Los Angeles Philharmonic performed their concerts mostly at the Hollywood Bowl on Highland Avenue, north of Hollywood Blvd. And, indeed, they played great music under balmy Los Angeles evening skies. Artur Rodzinski had been director of the orchestra for the last 3 years. I wondered if he was one of those infiltrating America as a spy—but with a name like that, probably not.

It was a crowded night at the Hollywood Bowl. The brilliant and talented young violinist was good—but what did I *really* know about it? The guy was a Lithuanian Jew whose family immigrated here in 1917, according to the program notes. Hell, he'd already made his public debut—he must've been in diapers!

Mandy Foster Simpson and I sat about halfway up the slight incline at the Bowl, but the sounds emanating out of that shell-shaped acoustic reflector were terrific. I was peering at the program. The conductor opened the program with Tchaikovsky's Symphony #1, entitled *Winter Dreams*. I was moved by the climactic bum-bum-bum-bum-bum-bum-bum-bum, played by baritone horns, French horns and other instruments letting go in a frenzy that wove a dramatic spell over the audience. I had never heard the work before.

Now the much awaited moment was here and the minute the young thirty one-year-old Heifitz came on stage and placed the violin under his chin, a hush came over the whole place and the world of my musical appreciation began to change. The first movement was wonderful enough, but the slow movement transported me to places so filled with pathos and feeling, newness and familiarity, that I had to turn away from Mandy Simpson once so she would not see my tears. How could a bunch of sinew and cat gut produce such sound?! Finally, I couldn't conceal my tears and began to wipe my eyes. The thoughtful Miss Simpson handed me a paper tissue from her purse and I dabbed my eyes.

When it was all over and we walked to the center streetcar island on Highland Avenue, we were both looking for something to say, but I was unusually quiet. Finally she spoke up. "Mr. Denning, I am obliged to ask .... you enjoyed the evening?" she inquired.

We got out to the island and I stopped and looked at her. "Miss Simpson, I profoundly apologize for any doubt I might have had about my enjoying the music. I was obviously moved and it just goes to prove that a tough private dick can be a softie inside."

"I'm delighted," she said. Then she reflected. "May I ask you a pertinent question, Mr. Denning?"

"Sure, shoot..."

"What does *private dick* mean? Where I come from, as a teenage girl, that word evoked images of a young man's private manhood."

I laughed. "Not out here, Miss Simpson. It's short for private *detective*—longshoremen, railroad policemen and even some cops are called 'dicks' as well."

"Oh, I see. That most conveniently puts my mind at ease, Mr. Denning."

On the way to her place on the streetcar, I had been thinking. "Where are you currently living, if I may ask?"

"I am embarrassed to tell you, Mr. Denning. But I am staying in the very rear compartment of a shoe leather shop, the shoemaker himself being a brother of a female acquaintance of mine. It is pitiful, I am appalled to admit, but my life situation has permitted no other alternative up to now."

"Well, I have a suggestion. You can sleep at my place whilst I am sailing the seven seas. It ain't much back there, but, hell, there's a bed, a toilet, a dresser with a mirror—and best of all, it's free. And since I'll be paying you during my absence, you should be able to save a little and get ahead enough to afford your own modest little place."

Her eyes widened and a fine smile came to her lips. "You...you would do that for me? I don't know what to say, Mr. Denning. I am overwhelmed at such generosity."

"What the hell—as I see it, we've all been in tight places now and then, right? And that way you'll be able to keep an eye on the place day and night. I even have a nice box radio you can listen to."

Mandy Foster Simpson was so delighted that she bent up and kissed me smack on the cheek. "I may have misjudged you, Mr. Denning. I am beginnin' to believe you are an honorable man."

"Try me when I'm drunk and horny—you may not keep that classy opinion of me. But thanks, all the same. I truly think you may call me Cable without messing up any protocol here, if I may call you Mandy..."

She smiled at me. "Why not? I'm thirty-five years old and able to make mature decisions for myself—and I like you, besides. Yes, Cable, you may call me Mandy and I can already hear the ring of respect in it when your fine manly voice addresses my name."

I let her off at the *Bless Your Soles* shoe repair shop. We said good night with the understanding she would show up for work late next morning. Then I walked back toward the streetcar line. But I was restless. My heart was hurting from something I couldn't pin down and my balls were aching for a little female action.

June in January

At the 'Hollywood and Western Building', I'd heard a new nightclub, *Signorella's Bistro Club*, recently opened in a space just off the Hollywood Billiards room downstairs. Maybe worth a look-see. I took the streetcar along Franklin Avenue heading east toward Western Avenue. There were only four people in my trolley that night. A young couple mooning over each other, a worker with a lunch pail—poor slob must have drawn the graveyard shift—but the one that really got my attention was a well-dressed bloke with glasses and a carefully trimmed moustache reading a newspaper. He had gotten on at the same time I did near Mandy Simpson's sleeping quarters. I wasn't sure, but I had the distinct feeling he was taking that late night ride because of me. I got off the trolley. He didn't follow me.

The 'Hollywood and Western Building' was built by Louis B. Mayer essentially to house the business offices for the Motion Picture industry. Even Central casting—a few stars probably *weren't* born in *that* office...even though they most likely were promised the moon for a little time on the "casting couch". Downstairs was the Hollywood Billiards...one of the area's first 'Pool Halls'. I got off at Hollywood Blvd. and entered through the building's carved archway. On the right, there was a door marked Hollywood Billiards, and an easel with a large poster of a pretty damn good-looking babe with a naturally naughty smile. It must have been the featured singer. I opened the heavy black door and descended the stairs.

The club itself was small, dark and moody. It must have been getting on to midnight when I entered, but the place was packed and noisy. Pink, orange and green neon tubes traced thin lines around the rectangle of the slightly cramped stage area. The bar was about fifteen men long and was made of a light, sturdy oak and a very large mirror hung against the wall behind it. I walked up to the crowded bar and squeezed my way in to get some service. In 1932 everyone assumed that whatever the bartender served, you were to provide your own alcohol and no one said a thing even though we all knew it was *verboten* during the twelve year Prohibition the country was suffering through. I finally got service and the minute I received my 'lime aide' drink, I proceeded to dump a third of my flask's gin content into it. There were no tables available, so I stood at the bar, facing the stage. The small dance floor was jammed. The band was playing a nice rendition of Irving Berlin's *All By Myself*—with occasional punctuations by the distant sound of cue balls being struck vigorously from the other room. I noticed a very attractive dame in a light peach-colored shimmering dress step up onto the stage. She looked to be about five-four or so, had wonderful dark hair that decorated her face with attractive bangs and she held herself proudly, putting her shoulders back, emphasizing a more than ample cleavage which happily bulged out of her sexy gown. Yep, she knew how to please the men okay. I didn't know her name, but I guess it really didn't matter. After Honey, it was hard for me to even want to know another nightclub singer with any close proximity. Maybe some things hurt for a lifetime.

I looked around the room for some stray women who might be looking for a cheap detective with a nice smile. But I didn't see anyone who appealed to me. It had been two or three weeks since I'd had the intimate company of a female of the species, so I was kind of hankering to hook up with someone, even though one-night stands were not my favorite pastime.

Then the babe on the stage started to sing Gershwin's *How Long Has This Been Going On?* and all of my indifference suddenly went away, and I was glad to see that someone had closed the door to the "Pool Hall" while she was on. Her voice was sultry, warm and vulnerable at the same time, as if some part of her was crying out from inside, "*See me! Please see me! I'm all alone and lonely—and I know that I may appear to be strong and secure, but I'm not...*" Everyone goes around with a bag of illusions, only most of the time you don't recognize them for what they are, because you fear looking too deep. You fear blowing too hard on the top of the dusty dresser because hope may fly away with the dust, out the window. The lady's song was one of those tunes that get inside and haunt you because you want her instantly, yet you know she's an illusion, too. I paid particular attention when she wheezed out the words *"I could cry salty tears, where have I been all these years."* She sang those lyrics with conviction, as if she really knew the score between boy and girl in the boxing ring of the he and she world. It somehow seemed personal to me.

She finished her song to great applause. I had to go to the men's room, so after I applauded, I gulped down the rest of my gin-lime, put out my cigarette and walked down a dingy, hallway to the men's room and did my thing. I was combing my hair on the way out when I dropped my comb on the floor. As fate would have it, at the same time, the young singer came down the hallway just as I bent over to pick up my comb. "Did you lose something of value?" she asked in a very pleasant voice.

I got up with my comb in hand. "Oh, no, thanks—I just dropped my comb. By the way, I'm a big fan of a great tune sung by a dame who really knows how to put one across. And you've got it, lady."

She had greenish brown eyes. She smiled as if it were an effort for her, but she appreciated it nonetheless. "Thanks, Mister—"

I extended my hand. "—Denning, Cable Denning. And your name?"

"I'm June Maye, you can easily remember it by reversing the months and just adding the 'e'. My mother's idea."

She gave me her hand and I knew we both felt an instant electric chemistry traveling up our arms into our bodies. "Good to meet, you, Miss Maye. I hope I'm not keeping you from your musical duties," I said. "After all, we're standing here in this smelly, dim-lit hall all because I dropped my comb."

"No, you're not keeping me. Maybe it's fate," she suggested in a low, sexy tone. "The funniest things happen when you're not looking...and I was simply on my way to the bathroom."

"Yeah, what a coincidence," I laughed. "So, June Maye, are you attached to anyone special at the moment? I came here to drink away my troubles—that is, until I saw you. So I guess what I'm asking is straightforward and simple—I'd like to have an opportunity to get to know you better. You know, take a walk or go out to dinner or—something else...or sit down and talk—"

"—*talk*? Is that all you'd like to do, Mr. Denning? You know, somehow I can't quite believe that from the way you alternately look into my eyes and stare at my breasts."

I laughed. "Well, you're right, June Maye. It was pure desire the minute I heard your first notes up there on the stage—it's as if I got a message from you, 'Help, I'm lonely inside—come rescue me' or something like that. But you do sing great, regardless of my male meanderings."

She looked at me oddly. Then in the twilight of that hallway I saw her eyes mist slightly. "How would you know that—even if it were true? Don't you think all men sense that, in a woman's voice or that erotic whatever-it-is she projects as an entertainer? But even if that's so, your honesty is a breath of fresh air...and a girl needs to know exactly where she stands when some aggressive male like you approaches her."

"And I appreciate *your* honesty. I wish I could say it was love at first sight or something—because you're very attractive, talented and I'm sure—intelligent. But the truth is, your sensual female nature attracted me like a hot dog to a hot griddle. As a matter of fact, when I first saw you walk up on that stage out there, I had been thinking that so much of life is illusion—and although the healthy red-blooded American male in me wanted you quicker than a jack rabbit on the run, I knew you were also an illusion. That's what people fall in love with, you know, the illusion. I hope you're not offended by my frankness."

"No, not at all. I *like* the way you talk." She looked me up and down. "You know what I do—what do *you* do?"

"I'm a private dick—used to be a cop downtown, but the politics made me puke, so I rebelled and now I take photos of careless men and women who have stepped into the shadows of moral trespass—so someone can take them to court for money. Follow the money trail— that's what I always say."

She chuckled. "A private *what*?"

"Not what you're thinking—*dick*—short for detective...it goes way back. So how about it? Can you see your way clear to at least sit down with me for a drink?—you see, I kind of feel time's running out on me...just the way I've been feeling lately."

"Who doesn't feel like that sometimes? Haste makes waste, Mr. Denning. Do you want to waste me? And in answer to your earlier question—yes, there is someone in my life, but it's a *she*—the goddess of music—and she's got first dibs."

"Whew! You scared me for a minute! I was leaning toward some gorgeous chicken in another part of town who also warbled on the stage, but she turned out to prefer her own sex."

"Well, that's not my style, Mister," she said, glancing pointedly at the front of my pants. "I like the virile variety of certain male attributes in my love life. But I warn you, I'm not squeamish about sex. For me, it's no holds barred the minute the lights go out."

I was a little taken aback by her raw way of telling me how it was for her. But I kind of liked it, too. "So, I'm glad you're devoted to your music. Sometimes it's a lot better company than people, huh?"

"Mm hmm." She gave me that half-smile again. "You know, you're not half bad, Mr. Private Dick. Yes, sometime I'd like that drink. Now, I've got to get back to the bandstand."

"How do I get hold of you?"

"I'm here more than anywhere else."

"No telephone? No address? Are you that mysterious?"

"I don't know you that well yet."

"Yeah, you're right—I could be some white-slave trader or a night-stalking killer sizing you up, couldn't I?"

She laughed. "Yeah...maybe...but somehow I doubt it...so drop in sometime soon and we'll have an after-the-show drink, okay?"

"I'll do my best, June Maye. But it may be a while. You see, I'm leaving on an extended trip in a few days."

"How long will you be gone?"

"Probably a couple of months—give or take."

"May I ask where to?"

"To the jagged peaks of the Himalayas, at the base of Mt. Shivapuri, Nepal."

"Wha—? You're on the level? Why on earth would a local private detective want to do that? Isn't that a little out of your territory?" She seemed both perplexed and amazed. "And isn't there some woman in your life who will miss you—or is she going with you?"

I took a long pause and looked down at the floor, trying to find a way to sum up my losses. Honey and Adora and Zelda came to mind, for starters. "No, no one's going with me. I've been up to bat a lotta times, and struck out as far as bein' able to keep a dame hanging around in my life very long. So, my story's a bit on the melodramatic side, I'm afraid—mind if I call you June? Please, call me Cable."

"Sure, that's fine. You're a fascinating man..."

"You see, I'm kind of burned out on life in some ways. Maybe too much too soon, rotten breaks, the nature of the business I'm in—things like that tend to lead to—well, some other time, June...okay?"

"Yeah, Cable...I can see something in your eyes. I just wasn't sure what it was. Now I'm beginning to understand you're a very wounded, complex man."

"So maybe you can tell me about it and we'll both know."

"It doesn't have words, Cable. It's kind of a slow-burning pain inside that never goes away and you're not certain of how it got there. I know, I have it inside me, too. Maybe for different reasons, but I can relate to it."

Just then one of the band members came down the hall and asked June to join the band. She bade me good-bye with a handshake, then hesitated. "I didn't scare you off, did I?"

"No...but I'm afraid it'll have to be *June in January* the way things are going—give me a rain check?"

"Yeah, why not? I don't think I'll be anywhere new by then. Merry Christmas, Cable Denning..."

And then she walked away. She went up to the bandstand and began to breathe out the sexiest version of *Body and Soul* I'd ever heard. I was hooked on June Maye. I couldn't help but be extremely attracted to the dame, as if I couldn't wait until I tore her clothes off some day in a dark bedroom and dug into that woman-hood of hers until she couldn't stand it anymore. I knew it was pure lust, but it was one of those inevitable things and I was sure she felt it, too. Loosen up your hatches, June Maye, you're in for a wild ride on the dark side of existence. But don't come up for air anytime soon, because I'll still be kissing you...there in the dark...there with our hot, sweaty bodies clinging to each other like the best of all desperate worlds colliding...

Crazy Jack and the Case of the Lucid Dream

It was December 6th and the sky was overcast. Like some surrealistic experience you're never quite sure about, I met Crazy Jack about 1926 when I had been but two years on the police force. He had gone into one of his frenzies and two other cops had brought him into the station to book him. But when I talked to Jack, I discovered yeah, he might be a little nuts in the head, but who isn't? He was erratic and spoke like a ten-year old boy sometimes, but underneath it all stood a powerful psychic force hiding there in the darkening shadows of his mind. I sprang him out of his cell, took him to breakfast, gave him a smoke and a pack of cigarettes and he proceeded to tell me things about myself few could know unless they knew me way back when. From that time on, Crazy Jack was my friend and he tried to return my friendship as best he could, considering what might be going on in the mind of one who had stepped into those margins of the brain quite a bit left of 'normal', whatever that was.

If ever I needed Crazy Jack's psychic powers, it was now. I went searching for him at the Panama Hotel on 5th Street, near the heart of "Death Rows," a place where corpses were found nightly in the dark, wet alleys of downtown Los Angeles. Most of these dead people were the leftovers of society, the forgotten, the neglected, the untreated sick, the mentally ill like Jack or the old and infirm that crawled along the slums of skid row until one night they simply perished from the elements.

Finally I found Jack in one of those alleys. He was sitting with a cohort sipping wine from a gallon jug they had somehow gotten a hold of. "Jack...just the guy I'm looking for."

He looked up at me with those innocent, wide-open eyes. "I don't know! I don't know! Cable look for Jack! Cigarette! Cigarette!" I reached into my pocket and took out a cigarette, lit it for him and tucked the remainder of the pack into his shirt pocket. He took a big drag on his smoke. "Cigarette, good! Cable want Jack..."

"Yeah, old buddy boy...I need some info...will you walk with me a minute? I kind of need your opinion on something."

"I don't know! I don't know! Jack been sick! Whiskey good!"

"That's not whiskey, Jack—it's cheap rot-gut wine."

He handed me the jug and I took a whiff of the bottleneck. "Whew! You're right—it's whiskey made with lye and rat poison, Jack. I wouldn't be drinking too much of that stuff if I were you!"

"I don't know! I don't know! Jack like—good...."

I handed his companion the jug and held out my hand to pull Jack up from the alley floor. "Come on, Crazy Jack. Take a walk with me. You're just the wizard I need right now."

He came along reluctantly. "I don't know! I don't know! Danger—for Cable—everywhere I look...across street...there! Look! The Photes are coming! But I don't know! I don't know!"

The *Photes* seemed to be an invisible group of creatures always haunting Crazy Jack. I first encountered them with him when we went to visit a famous medium, one Madam Palladino, back in 1927. They seemed to haunt Jack ever since. "Well, I'm here with you and I have my .38 to use against the Photes, Jack, so don't worry."

That seemed to relax him. "Cable protect Jack." He took another big drag from his smoke and exhaled. "Cigarette good! Cable good to Jack...help Cable..."

"Well, thanks, pal. Here's the deal, Jack. You might recall I've got these real bad guys after me from the *Oculus*—plus now I've got a bunch of German spies after the same thing—the *Fen de Fuqín*, remember?"

"I don't know! I don't know! Cable travel...far. Dream with water...*death women* come! Run! But I don't know!"

"Death women?" I laughed. "Seems to me, women have been both my life and my death, Jack. Anyway, these other bad guys have given me until the end of the month to come up with the secrets of that golden capsule—or else I'm dead meat. So I figured on outwitting them—or at least buying time—by taking a trip abroad to Nepal to get anointed."

That stumped Jack. And whenever he couldn't comprehend, he simply continued on with his psychic thread. "Cable have protector—lucky—but much danger. All time danger. Many times...danger...pretty girl..." He smiled, making a female shape with the palms of his hands. "But I don't know! I don't know!"

"So, Jack, what are you saying? Will I make it to Kathmandu and back—or am I pissing in the wind?"

"I don't know! I don't know! Cable fly in water plane. Warm waters. Snow...pretty...Jack like pretty. Holy Man in danger...but protector save Cable!"

I was struggling to put all the pieces together. Jack always spoke in these fragmented ways, but somehow I was always able to make the pieces fit. "Protector, huh? Yeah, well, Jack, I'm—I'm going to Nepal to seek out that Holy Man you're talkin' about—but I'm not so sure about what you say you're *seeing* beside the usual garden variety of danger I'll be exposed to."

"I don't know! I don't know! Jack sick! *Datura*...come..." He grabbed my wrist and began to tremble a little. "*Datura*...endless dream see Jack! Ooooo! Endless dream...but I don't know! I don't know!"

Now I had no idea what he was talking about. "Jack—you're leaving me hangin' here—what in the hell is this 'Datura' thing?"

"I don't know! I don't know! White powder water...drink...dream. Show Cable much! I don't know!"

He let go of my wrist and I could see he was exhausted and a bit pale. Maybe the energy it took him to go to whatever he tapped into to see things, drained him as well. "Okay, Crazy Jack, thanks. So I'll be looking for a beautiful dame, a protector, the Holy Man in danger—and some white powder water that will make me dream—right?"

"I don't know! I don't know! Jack need go home now...sleep...Jack like Cable." The little guy came up and hugged me for the first time since I'd known him. Usually he was adverse to touch. Then he drifted away.

"I like you, too, old buddy. Take care of yourself, Jack. I'll come see you when I get back, okay?"

He was mumbling to himself as he walked away. "I don't know! I don't know! The Photes! The Photes are coming! Jack run...!"

Wriggling with the Wrigleys

I got back to my office just as the phone rang. "Yeah, Cable Denning here."

"Mr. Denning—the private investigator Cable Denning?"

"Yep—no one else here answers by that name, Mister, except maybe the mice who keep chewing at my phone cord."

"It is my understanding you are very efficient in tracing lost persons? I am in immediate need of such a man."

"Yeah, well, that's what I do—do you have a name, Mister?"

"Yes—I'm sorry—my name is P.K. Wrigley."

"So, Mr. Wrigley, what can I do for you?"

"I have a very beautiful sister who is—is—how shall I say it?—rather careless with herself. She seems to have few moral scruples—plays, drinks and cavorts with unsavory men and the like—she needs to be saved, Mr. Denning."

"Well, how old is your sister?"

"She'll be twenty-three soon and has misbehaved ever since she graduated from Vassar—or before, for all I know. She hides out on Catalina Island somewhere—but the family can never find her."

"That's not a bad place to hide out, Mr. Wrigley—plus the fact your sister is well within the age of consent—she's a *woman*—in case you haven't noticed. So why does she hide out on Catalina?"

"Because our family owns it," he said and I could have dropped through the floor. "My father was William Wrigley, Jr and he made the island into a future conservancy. He passed away earlier this year."

"I see...so you're saying your family is in the old chewing gum racket? Spearmint, Doublemint, Juicy Fruit and the whole shebang?"

"Yes."

"I don't see how I can legally help you, Mr. Wrigley. It'd be kidnapping if I rescued your sister from herself, you know. Is she currently tangled up with some unsavory creature?"

"Yes, a very rugged and thuggish longshoreman by the name of Axel Swedenborg. She has become—oh, it pains me to say this, Mr. Denning—essentially his *sex slave* and I know for a fact he keeps her constantly inebriated with alcohol so her morals will stay loose and under his control."

"What's your sister's name?"

"Julia...she's almost twenty-three soon—"

"—you already said that. I don't know if I can be of help, Mr. Wrigley. You see, beside kidnapping charges, if I get caught stealing the precious cargo away from this Swedenborg character, there's always the chance he'll be armed and one of us will get bumped off."

"There's ten thousand dollars in it for you, if you can subdue Mr. Swedenborg, rescue Julia and bring her to me in Pasadena where she will be taken to a recovery house for alcoholic addiction."

Ten thousand smackers sounded pretty good just about now. That amount plus what Toggth had confiscated from the armored truck added up to a pretty sweet package of about thirty-five grand in my bank account! That would be the richest I'd ever been in my lifetime!

"If I do this thing, Mr. Wrigley, keep in mind it'll be in that fuzzy territory between legal and *not*."

There came a slight pause. "Julia...isn't...isn't a legitimate offspring of my father's. She was born out of wedlock. Her mother, since deceased, was an employee of my father's. So you see, Mr. Denning, the situation is delicate. But I love my sister, and she's a bright and charming young woman—not to mention beautiful and captivating."

"Okay...suppose I do this clandestine deed for you. You must be able to exempt my inclusion in any legal way. In other words, count me in only as *the man who never was*. Can you do that?"

"Yes. Thank you. I will send around a man to deliver half of the money immediately—in cash, of course—and the other half will be rendered to you upon completion of the task commissioned to you."

"That sounds fair. So, tell me where might I find this bloke who's got your sister tied around his penis. I know the type. I've dealt with gangsters like that. Hook the young things with drugs and alcohol and then screw 'em to death. If she's a knock-out dame as you describe, she's lucky she hasn't been tossed into the white slavery trade and sold to some sheik in Araby."

"Please...don't even suggest that, Mr. Denning. Swedenborg can be found at Pier 1, Port Los Angeles. He's straw boss for unloading cargo ships there. He lives in a tugboat moored there at Birth 60—the *Sea Rover*. I'll have my man come around this afternoon—say around four?"

"I'll be here, Wrigley. Where can I reach you?"

"SYcamore 7001 day or night. Leave a message with Andrew. Thank you, Mr. Denning."

Then he hung up. I was thinking about how people get themselves into the terrible tangled webs that human sexual nature leads to so many times. A lovely young thing tossed upon the seas of chance because she's only half legitimate in this world. I took out a smoke and lit up. Then I poured a shot of gin and tonic and sat back.

Two hours later there was a knock at my door and a refined looking man with a derby asked me my name. When I showed him proof he handed me the bag and disappeared. I sat at my desk and counted out the one-hundred dollar bills. Yep, it was all there. Now...to the task at hand. I didn't have a lot of time before my rendezvous with death would be rolling around in about three weeks. I grabbed my trench coat, fedora and my .38 and headed for the Red car line depot.

It was getting on to dusk when I walked down the wooden planks leading to Pier 1, Birth 60. A deep, rolling fog had begun to chill the air as I made my way along the docks, listening to seagulls and smelling the salt-laden air. Soon I reached a small port office tucked into the one of the large wooden warehouses. A night watchman directed me to the *Sea Rover*, a large tugboat moored alongside a mammoth freighter. I boarded the tugboat and drew my .38. Quietly I moved along toward the cabin. I peered in. I could see no one. Then I opened a hatch door that must have led to the bunks below. Soon I heard music wafting down the dark corridor courtesy of a radio somewhere. Then laughter roared out from a little bedroom compartment to my left. The door was partly ajar, but enough for me to see a beautiful dark-haired babe with only her bra and panties on kicking her feet up in the air while some bloke in a black turtleneck sweater and no pants on stood over the broad with a booze bottle in his hand and a cigarette in his mouth. He was smiling down at the woozy babe. The radio was playing George Gershwin's *I Got Plenty of Nothin'* from an upcoming controversial musical play he was fighting to produce, entitled *Porgy and Bess*. It was a touch and go road for Gershwin because it was an all-negro production and whitewashed, Christian American producers weren't going for it. The biased newspapers harpooned the composer for even attempting such a project when white actors and singers could hardly find work these days themselves. But we all knew it went far beyond the Depression statistics. What really blew me out of the water, though, was hearing what I perceived to be Misty Sheridan's voice singing! She must have made it to the phonograph recording world! I took a deep breath.

I broke up the little tryst. "Miss Wrigley?" I said, my .38 pointing at Swedenborg. He was a good-looking bloke around forty, rugged face and squinting dark eyes.

The babe in question was very dark-haired, had a body to die for and her skin was a glowing light-chocolate in the dull-lit room. The longshoreman froze where he stood, but the broad sat up, making no attempt to cover her near-naked body. "Oh! Are you an enemy? Ha! hic! Come on in...whoever you are! Put the gun away, Mister, and come fuck with us!" she slurred. I could tell she was quite drunk. "Axel loves to see me

288

spread my legs for some other man while he looks on."
She glanced at the frozen man. "Don't you, honey?
Doesn't it make you hot...I mean, really hot for me?"

Swedenborg looked at me with a not very nice expression. "Who are you—and whatta ya want? Can't ya
see I'm busy, Mister?"

I looked down at Julia. "Hear that radio, kid? Well,
that's exactly what you've got here—*plenty of nothin'*!
Now I want to do this thing peaceably, if I can. Your
brother misses you and wants you back home. So, I suggest you put some clothes on and come with me. Now."

Swedenborg suddenly threw his booze bottle at me.
I ducked in time and it shattered against the wall. He
rushed me like a bayonet brigade, but my cop training
paid off as I sidestepped him and hit him on the skull
with the butt of my gun. But he was a tough guy, made
of different stuff than us landlubbers and he turned on
the floor and grabbed my legs. I went down with him as
he attempted to wrestle my gun from my grip. He
punched me on the side of the head and it felt like a
jackass had just kicked me. While I was stunned, he relieved me of my .38 and aimed it right at my chest.
"Now—Mr. Big Guy punk!" he stammered out of breath.
"I'll give you thirty seconds to get up and get out—or I'll
blast you with your own gun and dump you overboard
for crab bait on the incoming tide."

I felt my bleeding head, got up from off the floor and
glanced once more at the babe still sitting there in her
underwear with a big smile on her face. "Axel's pretty—
pretty strong...strong everywhere...Mister," she intoned
with her slurred speech. "You'd better...better...go
back...and tell my brother...I'm happy here...I've got

fresh air, nice clothes...lots of free liquor—and a real man to screw me every day—and twice on Sundays! Ha! ha! Get it? Yeah...get lost, buster...I'm happy..." Then a frown came to her face. "Do you know what happy is, Mister? I do...happy is having everything you—you want—and then a great big cake...with all—all the frosting...so...Axel makes me—hic!—happy. Are you happy, Mister-whoever-you-are?"

Swedenborg was signaling for me to go with my .38. There was a hurricane lamp on a small, circular table just to my left at the doorway. I started out, but as quick as lightning I spun to my left, grabbed the lamp with my throwing arm and tossed it at the surprised Swedenborg, who I'm sure wasn't all that sober, either. He fired but the bullet hit the ceiling. The lamp hit him with such force that the glass mantle shattered against his forehead. He stood there teetering for an instant and then collapsed to the floor. Without hesitating, Julia Wrigley jumped off the bed onto me like a monkey clinging to an organ grinder. Her brassiere ripped off and suddenly I was wrestling with teeth, tits, arms, legs and a head that kept butting my chest.

Finally I subdued her, ripped off the small curtain over the porthole, tore it up into strips and tied her hands and feet with it. Then I checked out the damages on her boyfriend. He was bleeding pretty bad and I think one of his eyes was full of glass. I rolled him over. He was still unconscious but breathing okay. I reached over to the bed and grabbed Julia. She fought me every bit of the way. "Now...I'm gonna carry you outta here, lady—over my shoulder if need be—and then I'm gonna toss you onto a streetcar with me and we're gonna ride to Pasadena. Do you want to go like that—bare-breasted and all...or...if I untie you, will you put some clothes on and come along peaceful-like?"

She glowered at me. "You fuck! Why...why did you ruin...ruin a good thing, you bastard! Axel and me...we were gonna go live out on...Catalina in my...my, uh, my bungalow...happily ever...hic! after...before you came and spoiled it." She looked down at the bleeding long-shoreman. "Is...is he dead? Did you...did you kill him?"

"No, lady, just banged him up a little. But not as much as he banged you—inside and out, taking what he wanted when he wanted by juicing you up with booze, and then juicing the rest of you. Now, c'mon, get dressed and let's get out of here."

She was defiant. "Up your asshole! I'm—I'm staying. This...this is home...here...with Axel and me...go...leave us alone...hic! I need a drink! Get me a drink!"

"Up your other hole, lady! I told you if you don't get dressed I'm gonna toss you over my shoulder and haul you off *as is* to your brother's. Your kin, you know, your blood, Philip, who calls himself your savior."

She snickered, crawling toward me on the bed. "Philip...my caring...hic! caring brother..." Then she looked me over. "You're pretty...pretty handsome your-self...do you want me? Here, I'll spread for you...but af-ter that...you need to go..." Then she looked down at the unconscious body of her boyfriend. "Axel will—will kill you. Don't tell me...tell me your name...c'mon, screw me now and then go...okay?"

"Sorry lady, that's not the deal. I'm going to give you five minutes more to make up your mind. It's either the clothes and a washed face, or I sling you over my shoulder and I deliver you to Philip in your half-naked condition. Not that it matters so much to him—he knows you're a slut—but I guess he has a place for you inside him that says some of you can be salvaged from booze and careless sex." I took out a Lucky Strike and lit it. She kept studying me, looking for a weakness.

After that five minutes had expired, I turned to pick her up and throw her over my shoulder. "Okay! Okay! You win! I'm—I'm too drunk—and I have a headache..."

"Well, that makes two of us," I said, examining the bleeding wound on the side of my skull.

I untied her limbs and helped her into the tiny bathroom where I washed both of us off. Then I dressed her with what I could find scattered around the room. She was passive and watching me on and off as her eyes rolled in and out of being present. "You saw my naked body...didn't—hic?—didn't you?"

"Yeah, so what?"

"Well, that means that now the secret...the secret has been...betrayed...look at my—my body—my Mamma was a pretty, light-skinned negro lady. My—my father killed her...when...when he found out...she secretly had me...so you see...I don't belong, Mister...I'm not a Wrigley—I'm a bastard child! Did you hear me? I'm a bastard child! Nobody loves me..." She looked down at the floor. "Not even my big-cocked stud there...not even Axel loves me...he just screws me...how come...how come you didn't just screw me like the rest of the sailors, huh?"

"Some people do love you, Julia. I think your brother cares. You know, it's all it takes in this world—one person to really love you. Then the rest is easier..."

"Philip...Philip is an idealist. At Vassar I learned about...idealists." Then she reached for me as I slipped a white blouse over her head. "You're—you're an idealist—a tough idealist, but still...an idealist, Mister. Would you love me?"

"I don't know. I guess if I knew you long enough. Love takes time, usually. Sex is short, like a cigarette or a shot of gin—but love is like a very long shot of honeyed whiskey in a boiling hot snifter...you gotta savor it, let it grow on you, kid..."

Suddenly she put her arms around me and began to bawl. "All my life...all my life! Nobody ever loved me. Except my Mamma—and they killed her...killed her when I was six!"

I felt exasperated. I let her cry it out for a few minutes, but I had waited a little too long. Axel boy was starting to stir on the floor. I went over and conked him over the head with the butt of my .38 and sent him back to nighty-night land.

By the time we boarded the Pacific Electric Red Car for the long Eastern journey, I found a public phone and gave "Andrew" the good news—sissy was on her way! He instructed me where to get off in Pasadena and an hour and a half later we arrived. I held on tight to my precious but still drunk cargo but at least we looked decent enough not to get arrested along the way.

A large mint-green Packard with a white canvas top and spoke wheels with whitewalls greeted us at Pasadena Avenue and Union St. Julia Wrigley was spirited away in another car and I was ushered into the Packard. I joined Philip Knight Wrigley in the back seat. He was a medium sized man with glasses, rather docile by nature.

293

"Thank you, Mr. Denning. I was delighted and surprised that you delivered Julia so swiftly. Did you have to injure Mr. Swedenborg?"

"Yeah, well..." I said, taking in a deep breath. "He wasn't exactly gung ho to release his little addicted girlfriend, so I had to clunk him over the head a couple of times with my .38. But he'll survive."

"That's too bad. I had rather hoped you would be forced to terminate him. He...he was a very malevolent creature, you know. Not only did he ruin my sister—perhaps for life—but he had done the same with other young women, and sometimes even had them perform lewd acts in front of him to—"

"—I think I get the picture, Wrigley. Now, if you'll kindly fulfill your part of the bargain, I'll take my other five thousand bucks and scram."

"Oh, somehow I don't think that is sufficient payment for your most efficient and timely accomplishment. Is there some other small favor I might grant you?"

"Not unless you can get me to Nepal—Kathmandu to be exact—and back in about two weeks or so. I have some business there."

"You mean Nepal—in the Himalayas?"

"That's the place."

"Well, it so happens I'm departing with a friend aboard a Pan American clipper aircraft in a few days. I know the end of the line is Subic Bay near Manila, but my friend...one General Smedley Butler, has a rendezvous with His Majesty's private yacht—and has been hired by my family to peruse two large tea estates for sale—and pick the best one for us. They are in Darjeeling, above Calcutta. I'm sure we can fly you the three hundred or so miles from there to your destination—Kathmandu, did you say?"

"Yeah, that'd be swell. Thanks, Wrigley. You turned out to be a pretty good sort. I think I'll take you up on that offer, if you don't mind."

"Certainly." He handed me a packet with the dough in it and offered to drive me back to my office. I took him up on that offer, too, and soon I was back in my little office ten thousand bucks richer!

The next day I called in Mandy Simpson and gave her final instructions and an extra key to my office. I told her she could move in the day I left. I told her to make herself at home and when and *if* I returned alive and well, I'd take her out for a nice steak dinner at the *Signorella's Bistro Club*. She gave me a brief hug and left, promising to do justice to my little office on Franklin in Hollywood.

Chapter 11

DEATH HAWAIIAN STYLE

Strangers on a Plane

It was December 11, 1932 when we pulled out of the Los Angeles train station on our way to Frisco. There we would board Pan Am Clipper flight #13 and head out over the Pacific Ocean for Honolulu in the Hawaiian island chain. Philip Wrigley sat next to me and General Smedley Butler across from us. Butler was a complex, restless man, the kind I came to know always had an extra trick up his sleeve. I didn't know what his game was, but I did know it was a hell of a lot more than being a real estate representative for the massive fortunes of the Wrigley chewing gum empire. And I had a feeling I'd find out before we said our good-byes in India. He was slender, medium height with a very short haircut. He was a Major General in the Marine Corps and highly decorated for heroism during World War I and other campaigns, including the Spanish-American War, the Philippine-American War, the Boxer Rebellion and other battles, so I would later learn. To his men he was known as "Old Gimlet Eye."

The train ride was full of memories for me. As I rode with the sound of the constant clickety-clack of the rails, I went back to the wonderfully crazy day I stepped aboard the Lark and found Adora Moreno waiting for me in an up-graded sleeper car. We made love for the first time on the floor that night and that was the spark that was to eventually ignite the flame of *real* love. I remember meeting the wonderful Dr. Jedediah Penn, his steady caretaker Polly Parker and the terrible confrontation with Frank Laggore and his thug accomplice as I dispatched them and threw them off the moving train. One died, the other came back to haunt my happiness by killing my fiancée, Honey Combes. There was even Anne Banning, whom I had met briefly, on the Lark, while searching for a missing Adora. She ended up dead in our hotel room floor in the city by the bay, simply from the ill-fortune of meeting me.

Then there was the nutso adventure in San Francisco's Chinatown, and meeting the beautiful Lei-Tao, experiencing tantric sex in the *Cave of the Seven Truths* and being roughed up and threatened by Nazar Ravna and his gang of thugs who worked for the *Oculus*. The frustrating ironies that pile up in one's life that make you think how damned perverse human existence can be—and how lonely is the journey from cradle to grave if you don't find a way to cram it with things of mostly useless activity. I filled my hours, days and years with booze, smoking, babes and either chasing down bad guys and gals or being pursued by the powerful and greedy who wanted what I had stored somewhere in my gin-soaked brain. I don't know, sometimes the trip isn't worth the while. Other times you wouldn't trade it for all the tea in China.

But now we were going for *Indian* tea. On that fateful morning of December 12, 1932, we found our plane docked on the west side of Fisherman's Wharf, and as the sea lions played around the pontoons, we boarded the Clipper to leave out of San Francisco Bay. It was a new experience for Cable Denning, Private Detective, to hear the huge motors wind up and lift the giant plane into the sky, heading straight out to sea in a west southwest direction. There were two very interesting people seated across the aisle from us. One was a rather captivating young gal maybe around thirty...nice curves...pretty brown eyes on a face that bore the confidence of someone that's never had to struggle to survive...even in these hard times. Her dark hair was softly pulled back and wrapped around. Sophisticated with just a touch of spoiled brat, she sat with legs properly crossed with hands in lap, in a cream suit, high-necked peach colored sweater with a string of pearls and matching earrings that looked like the real thing. The man sitting next to her seemed a strange anomaly. He was a tall dude with a cowboy hat in his lap, dark, slicked-back hair, a thin moustache and dark, roving eyes. He seemed to delight in the performance of the airplane and I overheard him speaking to the woman next to him saying that her uncle, given his recent business ventures into the world of aviation, might be right interested in hearing about the bigger and better plane designs he'd come up with recently. She nodded in enthusiastic agreement.

About two hours out of Honolulu harbor, the tall cowboy got up and came over to address Philip Wrigley. "How're you doin', there Philip?" he inquired of the chewing gum magnate.

"Howard! I saw you there but I didn't want to disturb you. I know how you like your privacy."

He swept his hand across the aisle to the lady who shared his seating.

"This fine young lady, is Mrs. Virginia Sloan-Wilson. She is the favorite niece of the President of..." I noticed a quick look from her, ".....of a major American automotive concern. And married to one of its high ranking executives...uh...Mr. Wilson. She nodded graciously, obviously the product of a very expensive girl's school. "Pleased to meet you, gentlemen. Howard tells me of your distinctive backgrounds and I am delighted to share this journey with you."

We smiled and acknowledged her. "Oh, Cable, by the way, this is Howard Hughes. You may know of him through a movie or two you've seen—or read about his outstanding accomplishments in piloting, at over 400 miles per-hour and his development of new and exciting aircraft."

I had been thinking it strange that the three men somehow knew each other, but now it seemed this automotive mogul's family sprout might be fitting into this mix too. Funny how seemingly diverse people can be thrown together for a moment of common purpose. What will ours be, I wondered? I hoped it wasn't going to be me. The thought, as Becker's deadline was closing in, gave me the creeps. For now, I dismissed it and extended my hand to Howard Hughes who took it like he was shaking an oil well pump handle. "I am pleased to know you, Mr. Hughes. I was once an L.A. cop—so I really appreciated your exposé of how rotten it really was."

"And more than likely still is—Mr.—Mr. —"

"—Denning, Cable Denning. Just call me Cable."

"Cable. Nice name. Are you from Texas?"

"No, born in the thick of the ghetto, East Los Angeles. We sure could've used someone like you to help us fight the gangs in those days. Anyway, a few years back, *The Racket* was highly appreciated by those few of us who were honest cops trying to make a difference."

"Well, now, thank you, Cable," the tall Texan said. "After we were banned in several cities, I thought my motion picture was a failure. But I guess not, if it reached fine honest policemen like you. If I may ask, what are you engaged in at the moment?"

"Well, Howard—if I may call you that—I'm a private eye on my way to Nepal via the kindness of Philip here. We're somehow getting to Darjeeling by way of Calcutta—and then I gotta figure a way to get over the hills to Kathmandu."

"Well, it so happens I'm on the same journey, flying for the Wrigley's. With Philip's permission here, I can fly you across that couple of hours of terrain...probably even shorter than that."

"Yes, Howard, I was going to ask you," Philip said.

"Consider it done, then," Hughes said, his big head nodding.

I looked across the aisle at Virginia Sloan-Wilson.. "So, ma'am, if I may ask—are you in search of the ideal tea plantation, too?"

They all looked at one another, then seemed to laugh awkwardly. "Well, not quite—is it Mr. Denning?"

"Cable's fine, thank you." I said, though I was getting that uncomfortable feeling that everyone knew something that I didn't.

"Cable...I am to join a friend on my uncle's yacht, at Subic Bay." She said that, rotating that ring on her finger. "You see, my uncle seldom uses it anymore, so my

300

friend Kurt Müller, visiting from our German subsidiary, will be bringing it there to meet us."

"I see. Well, at least we all have agendas of some sort," I offered, still suspecting something else was going on underneath the silent tension—a private eye learns to pick up on those things. A visitor from Germany? A lover's rendezvous? Somewhere in the back of my mind, I remembered hearing about one of our big automotive companies buying into a German auto manufacturer. Couldn't remember which one, but none of this was sitting well with me, just now.

General Butler was looking out the window at the vastness of the sea below. "You know, old chap, there was a day when the horse fell from grace. Do you know what day that was?"

"I suppose the advent of the Iron Horse, spilling out thousands of miles of steel rails everywhere...not to mention automobiles." I said, making a dig. I noticed Wrigley, Hughes and the dame exchanging glances.

"Yes...and then add to that the advent of the aero plane...another nail in the coffin of the proud steed who served the world for so many centuries. Do you suppose such things happen to all of us—that we become obsolete in time?"

"Yeah, I'd say so, General," I said, thinking of my own plight in this world. "You might add to that the word *dispensable*."

Smedly Butler laughed. "Quite, old man, quite..."

Playing Hawaiian Dominos for Keeps

A water boat picked us up and roared over to the *Royal Hawaiian Hotel*. The islands were delightful with white, sandy beaches, temperatures in the low 80's and great looking babes all over the place sucking in the sun in the briefest bathing suits the law would allow. The European dames took the most risks, wearing scant two-piece outfits that barely covered the bare essentials.

Upon our arrival we learned there had been a booking error and since the place was full to the gills, I had to bunk in the same room with Smedley Butler. Virginia had her own room while Hughes and Philip Wrigley shared a room. The long airplane ride had exhausted the passengers, so most of us collapsed and slept for a few hours and agreed to meet for a late night dinner.

When I finally woke up, I noticed Smedley Butler was at a little desk writing. "Writing a note back home, eh?" I kidded him.

"Oh, hello, Denning. No, I was finishing off some ideas for a book I may write. It will be called *War Is a Racket*. It's a compilation from some of my recent lectures and talks about what I consider to be a future threat to America—the military-industrial complex."

I was surprised to hear this from a dyed-in-the-wool war hero. "You don't say...you mean corporations and the greedy bastards in Washington might create a monopoly or something?" I said with my tongue-in-cheek derisiveness.

"Yes, exactly." He stopped writing and turned around to look at me. "Very observant, Denning. I've seen too much war—and it's all senseless. The only time you should have war is when your own home is threatened. Somehow I can't recall that being the case. I'm fifty-two years old and I haven't seen our soil threatened yet since the British left during George Washington's Presidency. If I had my way, I'd move to overthrow our war-directed president today."

"Whoa! Those are big words, Butler." I was recalling the private conversation I'd overheard between the Kraut Schock and FDR a few months back. "Not that I disagree, mind you, but the people seem to like the guy. Greed, graft and politics seem to go together now, don't they?"

"You're sharp, Denning. I like that. I also have a feeling you've heard and seen more than you're likely to tell."

"Yeah....well General, you see—some things simply equate all men down to the same common denominator, in my view. Let's just say I've seen that part of the equation—and leave it at that."

"Is your journey to Nepal connected with some of that?"

"Sorry, Butler, but I have no more comment. Suffice it to say that nothing is as it seems. But then, you already know that."

He mused a minute. "Yes...nothing...I'm glad to know you, Denning. I think you're a real American—if one can continue to truly believe in the American way."

"Thanks, but no thanks. I'm *in* America, but I'm afraid I've about lost that feeling of being an *American*—but rather one of those rolling stones, you know, the citizen of the universe type who, as you suggest, has seen too much and knows too much to live too much longer. So it goes, General..."

His eyes flipped open wide. "True? Why would they pick on some low-profile private detective?"

"I told you. The wrong place at the wrong time can put you at risk for life, so to speak. My motto is the man who knows too much is destined for a short—if not un-pleasant—life. Now, if you don't mind, I'm still only thir-ty-two and I'm going downstairs and ogle the sun-tanned babes in the lounge."

He chuckled. "By all means, chap, I'd have done the same at your age. Enjoy yourself, Denning...I think you're right...it's later than you think." That generated another prickling at the back of my neck.

As I descended the stairs I decided to stop at mid-landing to light up. Some man passed me with a news-paper under his arm. It was the same well-dressed guy with the thin moustache that was on the streetcar the night I went to *Signorella's Bistro Club*! Now I knew for sure I had a tail—all the way to Hawaii! My wariness was increasing. I followed behind him a few paces and he disappeared into the crowded restaurant while I swung left to enter the cavernous cocktail lounge. The place looked like a zoo of colors. Some women wore brightly colored tropical grass-shack skirts with flimsy tops, others were in more conventional clothing—soon my wariness was overcome by the plethora of feminine delights before me. But there was one dame that stood out from all the rest. She was medium tall with a daz-zling light blue slinky-silk dress that clung to every curve like a racehorse on the rail in the Kentucky Derby.

She wore her dark, flowing hair down to her shoulders, and it turned up just right at the bottom. Attractive bangs covered about a third of her forehead and her nose and lips were perfect, the kind you want to smooch all night before you partake of her other favors.

But I was on a mission and didn't want to get distracted. Looking at the wonderful kaleidoscope of color and broads was sufficient for the moment, I thought. There was a singer up on a medium-sized stage with a small combo. For a minute I couldn't believe my eyes as I walked closer to this gorgeous redhead in a light-green gown. It was Misty Sheridan! She was singing *April in Paris*, first slow, then fast. Just as she finished our eyes met as I stood just below her applauding. "Cable! For God's sake! What are you doing here?"

"Well, well, well...seems you're showing up everywhere lately. First I hear you aboard a tugboat on the radio a few days ago—and now this. You're coming up in the world—are you through at the *La Monica Ballroom*? I kind of thought you'd outgrow it one day."

"I can't talk now. I'm in the middle of a set. Can you stay for a while and we'll talk later?"

"Yeah, sure...see you..." I said and drifted back toward the crowded bar. Word was Prohibition was about to be lifted, so here at the Royal Hawaiian they were celebrating early by letting the new booze flow freely upon request. Happy times were here again! Even though the Depression had just about consumed the lower and middle classes, abandoned the poor and increased the fortunes of the rich and infamous as foreclosures, joblessness, crime, economic indexes and Wall Street along with the banks continued to stagger, Americans were amazing and resilient. Then Misty started singing something I wish she hadn't. I knew it was for me and her siren call went rippling through me as she breathed out *They Didn't Believe Me*. Now I look back and think she wanted to live that dream with me, wanted to find a place in the sun with plenty left over for love-making in the moonlight as long as her career continued to blossom. But so many of the things that keep us back in life haunted her like specters in the dark night of her soul. And so she suffered, stuffing down that beautiful woman in her that wanted out, and desired the perfect embrace, to be kissed and ravished by a man she could accept between her legs *and* between the busy pages of her professional life.

The bartender finally served me and as I went to drink up, a low feminine voice with a French accent addressed me. "You seem too 'andsome, Monsieur, to be drinking alone. May I join you?" I looked over to my left and the babe in the dazzling blue number stood at my shoulder.

"Well, it never entered my mind, lady, but I think you're right. Here, I'll move over...and stuff you in like the rest of the sardines at this bar."

"Merci," she said in the same, even voice. "But I 'ave a small table in ze corner...over zere...per'aps we could sit and toast to a lovely evening in ze Tropics?"

"Yeah, that sounds swell—let's do it."

She led me over to the usual little round table with the candle in the middle and staunch padded chairs with chrome arms. I helped her into her seat and then sat opposite her. "Are you alone, Mr.—Mr.—"

"—Alexander—Johnny Alexander." All of a sudden I was compelled to use a name I picked out of the air. There were too many people who knew the name Cable Denning—why add to the risk? "No...I came with a few friends from the states. We're having dinner a little later. I would ask you to join us—"

"—oh, sank you, Mr. Alexander, but I 'ave already dined. My name is *Mada Michon*. You caught my eye, so I do 'ope you do not find me too—too—"

"—forward...I think that's the word you're looking for."

"Oui...yes, forward. My English is proficient, nosing more, I'm afraid."

I was looking through that paper-thin slinky silk gown she was wearing. The babe was tastefully stacked—let's put it that way. "And you—you, uh, caught my eye as well, probably for different reasons, though."

She smiled with a teasing sparkle in her light brown eyes. "Indeed, I sink it to be true, Monsieur. We 'ave caught each ozer's eye, no? Why werc you looking at me tonight?"

I sat back and chuckled. "It's funny, dames are the same everywhere. You know all too well when a woman like you wears a dress like *that* you're gonna have two kinds of guys respond. My kind, the aggressive, sexually addicted type—and the guy who will long for you as if you were the last woman on earth, but is too shy to approach you, so you remain an unexplored fantasy to him."

She smiled a disarming smile. "Addicted—to *amour*? You are very brev to admit it—zat you find women…irresistible. And I—would I not remain an unexplored fantasy to you, Mr. Alexander?"

"Yeah, you top the list in this joint. I don't live in the expected norms and morays of American society. Maybe it's the nature of my work—I'm addicted to three things I know of…cigarettes, good gin and sexy dames."

"I 'ope I may fit into one of your categories…? May I ask, what it is you do in America?"

"I'm a private investigator. You know, chase down misbehaving husbands, wives, girlfriends, boyfriends and miscellaneous lovers—take a Kodak snapshot of them frolicking in compromising situations—and present the evidence, so someone can sue someone else for some extra dough in a divorce court."

"My, my…you would not 'ave much work in Paris, I'm afraid, Mr. Alexander. It is an expected feature of our culture zat *paramours* can be part of a marriage. It does not always work out wis—'ow Americans say—wis smoozness, but we do not take ze trespassers to task or penalize zem—unless jealousy may cause a tragique ending."

I rubbed my chin. "Yeah, like bumping off your lover. Then we'd have to find the killer, wouldn't we? So maybe I wouldn't be outta work in France after all, would I? Funny how you don't realize that other cultures vary that much, but they do, don't they?"

"Indeed, Mr. Alexander."

All of a sudden I got sick of using a phony name. I was me and that's all there was to it. "You know, I feel real stupid about this, but I've—I've, uh, been lying to you. My real name is *Cable*—I think it sounds better coming from your lips than *Mr. Alexander*."

308

She lifted her eyebrows but didn't seem that surprised. "But I sought your name was Johnny Alexander?"

"I told you I lied. You see, I'm on my way to someplace kind of secret—and there are some really bad guys after me. You know, the usual, I have something they want. I just made the name up on the spur of the moment."

She looked at me and her eyes squinted. "*Mon ami!* It so 'appens I already knew who you were. Now I must be true to you. *Cable Denning* was my assignment. All I am supposed to do is keep an eye on you." Then she looked at me with tender eyes. "But I 'ave a weak heart, Cable..."

"Oh, I'm sorry to hear that. Are you under a doctor's care?"

"It is not zat kind of weakness...but razer when a woman like me meets a man like you...wis her eyes, her heart grows weak wis desire."

I went silent for a minute, studying the gal's face. I had this feeling she was on the level. I smiled. "Well, that's kind of a nice weakness to have, wouldn't you say—may I call you Mada?"

"Please...yes, so now I am already—how do you say—*challenged* by your 'andsome face, your strong manner—and I am sure a very virile man in ze dark when a man and a woman are alone togezer."

"I suppose I've been accused of that," I chuckled. "But tell me, if you will, to what extent are you to keep your eye on me?"

"You are rooming with General Butler, so unless you come to my room, we will be spared ze tragedy of intimacy."

I didn't quite get her gist. "Spared the tragedy? I don't understand, I'm afraid. Are you fearful of two adult people attracted to each other spending a pretty swell night wrapped up in each other?"

"To ze French, lovemaking is a kind of little death—a tragique moment of ecstasy. A woman knows ahead of time, Cable. If we couple togezer, I might be lost, dying a little for you, forsaking my duty to—to—"

"—yeah, to whom? You didn't say which of the bad guys you work for? Let me see, there's the *Oculus*, the Krauts, the Catholic Church, probably the people who are traveling with me—and you. Am I leaving anyone out?"

Suddenly she went pale as she glanced to see the well-dressed man with the newspaper under his arm pass by. I was getting the feeling I should meet this guy. "I am feeling unwell, Cable. Will you escort me to my room? I feel somewhat faint."

We got up and walked two flights of stairs to Room #333. She took out her key. I grabbed it and opened the door for her. I tried to return the key, but she tucked it back into the palm of my hand. "Please...come to me later...you must not knock but enter into ze darkness I will save for you. You will find my dress draped over a chair by my bedside. Under it you will find a note. Read it first...and then if you still desire me, I will be waiting...quietly for you under ze covers, naked and wanting you because I know you will be good to me—and gentle. I realize some of my rambling does...does not—uh,

310

make sense to you, but do know, as I told you, I am challenged by my womanly desires—and my sense of duty. I am conflicted wis zem." She leaned up and kissed my nose. "To answer your question, I cannot tell you—who—who I work for. Zey would murder me if zey knew, zat even now, I am fraternizing wis ze enemy. "

"So suddenly I'm the enemy, huh?" I gently pushed her into her room and closed the door behind us. "Yeah, like that man with the newspaper downstairs who turned you pale when you saw him. I'm gonna lay it to you frankly, Mada. In this business you can't ride the fence—you've got to be impersonal when you're on duty and don't mess things up by wanting to take a second-rate private dick to bed with you, who's probably already dead—and will be buried as soon as they extract from him what they want. Turn off your heart and that other thing down there, Mada, *don't* be a woman for a change. Do your job—and then walk away—walk away from me and any other bloke who would want to get caught up in that sensual body of yours, wrapped up pretty-like in that clinging blue dress. And another thing, Mada, don't look back...never....never look back."

She fell into my arms, crying. "Oh, Monsieur—Cable—it's too late. Are you grown so shielded zat you do not know a woman can fall in love at first breath? Maybe it is my French passion—perhaps my pain—my family suffered srough Ze Great War. I lost my fazer, my mozer was raped by ze Germans and my little sister was lost somewhere in ze streets of Verdun. I am all zat I 'ave. Can you see 'ow very long zat suffering is?" She pulled back and looked into my face, her cheeks filled with descending tears, running black lines of mascara

311

with them. "When you talk like zat...as you just did...you create ze opposite effect. Don't you see, you removed any barrier between us because you were honest, truthful wis me and had no selfish desire to make love to me and leave me wizout sought of 'ow beautiful we are togezer."

I took out my handkerchief and began wiping her face. "I wouldn't go that far, kid. How old are you?"

"Twenty-four. Why?"

"Because I'm thirty-two and you haven't lived the other end of death and terror yet, the night sweats, insomnia, late night music with a gorgeous babe like you singing her heart out up there on the stage, lots of booze until you've numbed yourself enough to forget you're a soon-to-be dead man—is that how you want to live your life?" The echo of my own words was a troubling reminder that my time might indeed be running out.

"No..." she whispered.

"Then get out of it now, Mada, chuck the spy crap just because it pays well. The guys who run the shop don't give a rat's ass about you and you're expendable the minute you sign on. Live a life, find someone you really want to be with, learn to find a love that can grow—not an overnight passion with a character like me—but someone you can have a Sunday picnic with, put your toes in the water of a quiet stream, hold in your arms at night and know he'll be there for you the next morning."

Her eyes started misting again. "Why cannot it be someone like you, Cable? I saw your dossier—you have a generous heart, suffered much loss, but always grew back up out of ze ground like a fresh flower. *You* are ze

312

kind of man I would want to hold me srough the long and lonely night. Please...come to me tonight!"

I took out a cigarette and lit it. I inhaled deeply and let out the smoke slow, above her head. "I wish we could, Mada—but it's the wrong timing. Maybe another life. Now I gotta go. I have a feeling the longer I'm here with you, the more points are gonna be chalked up against your chances of surviving too much longer yourself."

I started to go but she grabbed my arm. "Run away wis me, Cable! We will—'ow you say?—sort it out later. Let us go somewhere they cannot find us! I trust you—my heart knows you...*Je vous en supplie, mon cher ami!*"

I took a deep breath. "I can't, Mada. It's almost as if I've lived this story a hundred times—don't you see? But I'll tell it again. Some people's life paths are already chartered out, like an itinerary at sea and each port of call is designated. That's me, babe, that's my life."

She looked down at the floor as she let go of my arm. She seemed resigned as I took the room key out of my pocket and gently tucked it into her hand. "Funny...isn't it? Cable? Even all I am as a woman cannot hold you. I see now, you *are* a vessel at sea on 'is way to some-where I dare not go. I will 'ave only your trus to remember you by. You could 'ave 'ad me tonight...for free...as I wanted you...wis no attachment. But *c'est la vie* as my countrymen say." She turned and walked away. I said no more and closed the door behind me. I caught a glimpse of the man with the newspaper duck-ing behind a wall as I began walking down the hallway toward the stairs.

Now I needed that second drink. When I got downstairs, the place was even more crowded than before and I noticed the big clock above the bar read eleven-thirty and dinner with Butler, Wrigley, Hughes and Virginia was only a half-hour away. I was nursing that drink, relieved in a way not to be dealing with any more emotional situations with dames when who should appear over my shoulder but Misty Sheridan. "You disappeared with that lovely young woman in the blue dress. I hope she was enjoyable and preferred men to women," Misty said, a few drops of sarcasm in her voice.

"It's good to see you, Misty," I said, ignoring her comment. "How long are you gonna be here in Honolulu?"

"Another three weeks. How in Heaven and Earth did you end up at the Royal Hawaiian? You're the last person on earth I expected to see here—or perhaps ever again. Even though I had thoughts of—"

"—save it, kid. It's not really 'ending up' *here*, but rather a stopover on my way *to* somewhere else. How have you been, Misty? Can I buy you a drink?"

She told the bartender what she wanted and I paid for it. "Thanks, Cable. How have I been? I guess you can say a little sad. Edie died suddenly of a heart attack last month. So I'm kind of nursing memories just about now and thoughts of my future at the same time. Edie was my tutor, my first lover and a wonderful human being."

"I'm sorry, kid. Yeah, I kind of got that when I went to see her that night. That's one thing about being human...nothing stays the same."

314

"No...I'm finding that out. So, what about you? Are you still a hot item with that sexy little secretary botanist of yours?"

I got a wince of pain in my heart. "I guess she couldn't take my living on the edge all the time, so she left me. Actually, she was the first babe who ever left me. Oh, it wasn't my ego, but the shock of it, I suppose. Plus I had really grown sort of attached to the dame."

"Zelda...that was her name, wasn't it? Maybe she saw the handwriting on the wall, Cable. You know, *you can touch but you better not have*. Wasn't that the same message from you to me?"

"Sounds more like *your* life story, Miss Sheridan."

She looked at me with those beautiful blue eyes. "Not any more. I'd give a lot to have you back, Cable. Sometimes I really feel that. I remember that night when you took me to my place and I wanted you so bad I could taste it. Do you remember?"

"Sure...I was all set, teetering on the edge of love's passions with you, lady. Then you pulled the plug on me. And that was that."

"I've changed, Cable. I really want to be a *woman* now, I want to feel a man between my legs, sucking on my breasts, kissing my lips until I can't even remember a song lyric anymore—just him, just me...just us."

"Well, what can I say? That's what I offered you once upon a time. Hell, no one's to blame here, Misty. But I did tell you one thing the last time we saw each other. When I got banged up pretty bad from that mauling, you weren't there when I needed you. It was Zelda who nursed me back to health. You even stopped being a friend, stopped checking in on me, went back to Edie

315

and your happy little spotlight up there on the stage. So, if that's who you are, then, that's who you are...and it's alright."

"When we get back, Cable—do you think you could see your way clear to give us one more chance? I think I learned something about loving someone. Edie taught me a lot. But you taught me something else, that thing down there that makes me restless at night—it's like only a man's presence will do to satisfy her. It's—it's like feeling complete. But I didn't know until you. Can you understand that?"

"Sure, kid, I understand it. But it ain't me. I hope you find that man someday, Misty. Just don't marry for money, if you choose that route. Marry him because you love each other and you give the love some air and let it grow into what it needs to become."

Her face saddened. "That means I've lost you?"

"I haven't changed since the last time, Misty. I'll always admire your beauty and talent. Let's leave it at that."

I hugged Misty Sheridan and walked away. I climbed the stairs to get myself dressed for that late supper. Just as I turned the corner and started down the hallway toward the room I shared with General Smedley Butler, I heard a gun go off. I drew my .38 and rushed down the hall toward Room #211. I yanked open the unlocked door and flew to the floor just in time to see a couple of thugs come rushing by me with guns drawn and General Butler firing away at them. I got up and yelled out at the General. "You okay behind the bed there?" I asked.

"Yep. They didn't count on an old war veteran being prepared—even at fifty-two, eh, Denning?"

I came around to the wall-side of the bed where he crouched. "Sorry I wasn't here sooner. Now tell me— you were expecting these mugs, right?" I couldn't help thinking that this was also *my* room!

"More or less," he said, standing up and blowing off the barrel of his .45. "You still hungry, Denning?"

Then it hit me—this was the decoy! "*Mada!*" I shouted out and ran out the doorway, leaving the General scratching his head. As fast as I could I jumped the stairs up to Room #333. But I knew it was too late. I rushed through the open door with my gun drawn and there she was on the floor, her head twisted and a pool of blood slowly soaking into the carpet. I fell on my knees beside her, checked out her pulse but her stilled heart would beat no more and her beautiful smile would fade into that familiar pall of death I'd seen far too much in my thirty-two years. I heard my voice say, "Aw....Mada."

The police came and went, taking the body of the lovely Mada Michon with them, her exquisite blue dress still clinging to that great body, only this time there was blood on it. After a while Smedley Butler put his hand on my shoulder as we watched the ambulance drive away. "Tricky business, this spy thing." Then he looked at me. "This may not be the time, but as I said earlier, are you hungry, Denning?"

I looked strangely at the General. I smelled a rat. "Why didn't the cops want to detain us, General? After all, it's not every night a gorgeous dame gets bumped off at the Royal Hawaiian."

He smiled a half-smile. "Let's just say, old chap, I informed them we were not personally involved, none of us knew the dead woman—and we have a deadline to meet. Plus a hundred dollar bill in the hand of the officiating officer."

"Oh...well, about that dinner. No, I think I'll decline. But we gotta tell the others if they don't already know."

By the time we apprised the other three members of our traveling party, it was one o'clock in the morning. The restaurant had closed, so the best the management could do was set us up at the bar with leftovers. We spent an hour or two discussing the matter and whether or not we'd be able to safely proceed on the morrow when our plane departed for the next port of call. It was unanimously decided we'd continue as planned. Just the same, I wondered, who among our group was an ally, who was the enemy—and who was just plain neutral? I took a stab at guessing that Wrigley and Hughes knew a lot more than they were saying, the General was an okay guy on the level—and Mrs. Sloan-Wilson? maybe the neutral party, on her way to rendezvous with some unknown German lover on some fancy family yacht. We retired and the rest of the dark hours were peaceful and some of us slept, if not well, then a bit fitfully. Someone was trying to play dominoes with us for keeps, but they had failed to knock down the first block. For the time being, we remained unscathed, but ever watchful that murder may be around the next corner, lurking at any turn. I would remember Mada Michon's beautiful young body crumpled there on the floor, oozing the blood of life. It was as if I could feel another nail being hammered into my own coffin—for here was yet another

woman who died because of even my very brief existence in her life. If this was retribution for sins I had
committed from an earlier life, then I was getting it this
time in spades...

Turbulence on the '*Rene*'

The rest of the journey was uneventful and a few
days later we were in Subic Bay admiring the huge 236
ft. family yacht, christened "*Rene*". An impressive sight.
When she unfurled her sails on the morning tide of our
departure, she looked like the 1830's *Water Witch*, full
blown and taking on the sea with her prow and spirit.

Virginia's German friend Kurt, was a handsome,
masculine looking guy...a gutsy, soldier-of-fortune type.
He was obviously smitten with Virginia, and I watched
her remove that ring as they descended to the cabin together. No one seemed surprised but me. Was *this* that
something that everyone but me seemed to know
about? They seldom came up for air and all necessities
were delivered to their cabin. We were informed that
the mating couple welcomed the long voyage to Calcutta
and upon dropping off the General, Hughes, Wrigley and
myself, the tryst would continue the whole return trip.
Ah, kudos to the idle rich who knew how to enjoy themselves, I thought. Make whoopee while the sun shines, I
always say. You never know what tomorrow may bring.
But it seemed a dangerous game they played. I wondered just how much clout *Mr.* Wilson might have.
Yeah....that magnetic animal attraction that no girl's
school can breed out. These two apparently willing to

travel long distances and take great risks just to take that trip to ecstasy when flesh meets flesh—and all fine clothes, position and dignity get set aside to partake of the forbidden sexual banquet laid out there just for the taking. Still, though this apparently explained away the feeling that everyone knew something but me, I wasn't too happy with the idea of being stuck out in the middle of the ocean with some unknown German big shot. My recent encounters with one Dr. Helmut Becker made me feel less than warm and friendly with Germans in authority these days.

Wishing death while still alive and bending over a ship's railing while vomiting your guts out comprised much of the journey from Subic Bay to Calcutta, India. I lost track of time and all things pertinent to goals, purpose for living, fears about who might be on my trail and/or any thought that food could possibly play a role in my life without bringing on another round of deathly nausea. Landlubbers like Cable Denning had a huge lesson to learn about sailing the seven seas and don't let anybody ever tell you there are magic secrets to prevent you from rolling and roiling in your intestines until you think you have none remaining.

The seas tossed and turned the "*Rene*" as squalls and storms hit us one after the other. Even though it was heartening to notice that neither the captain nor most of the crew experienced the pall of death upon their countenances, it was even less comforting to learn very late that Virginia and Kurt rode out the troughs of swells and breaking waves much better than myself, General Butler or Philip Wrigley, because there had been a kind of stabilizing hammock constructed for the nesting pair and anyway, the rocking and rolling probably just enhanced their frolicking. Fine for them.....I did notice, however, through my vertigo haze, Virginia did come topside alone for a breather, I guess. But soon after, Hughes went down below and when he came back he paused and looked over at me long and hard before walking back to his roost. Something didn't seem right about that—but just then I didn't much care, as once again I became blinded with the whole retching thing and might have welcomed an end to it all.

On December 27, 1932 we sailed into a calm harbor on the shores of the continent of India and navigated a river to the city of Calcutta. It took two days for me to look into a mirror at our hotel downtown. When I did, I didn't recognize the gaunt figure of a man who had lost eighteen pounds of fat and water as my skin pulled tight against my cheekbones, giving the look of a man pretty close to that of a walking corpse. But with a few walks, delicious fish meals with the famous Indian curry, some fresh air without the rocking, I regained my human composure and some of my dignity...and began to gain weight again.

It was December 30th and we said good-bye to Virginia and Kurt. I felt a real sense of relief with Kurt gone. I couldn't help thinking with that constantly impending deadline date to relieve me of my brain and then my life, coming up tomorrow, Becker's long German arm could've been Kurt. So, it looked like, tomorrow December 31st would come and go without incident and I was home free. With a little help from my companions I'd out-distanced and out-witted the dirty bastards!

Later, we took a train up from the valley floor. *Darjeeling* stood about 4500' ft. above sea level and was quite beautiful with sloping hillsides, lots of trees and shrubs, flowers and a million dollar view of the mighty Himalayan Mountains, scaling up to 28,000' ft. in the far distance, stark white against a deep azure-blue sky. The Indian people were kindly. Class division was rampant, as the have-nots scrounged for their daily bread while the rich of a higher caste system were carried around in litters, expensive automobiles or had special train cars attached for their usage. Darjeeling had flourished under British rule as one of the *tea empires* of the world, where special blends of black teas were exported for the rich and consumed the world over.

We stayed in a rather ramshackle hotel called *The Orange Pekoe*, which must have related to some of their tea types. I had my own room for a change and one night when I got through with dinner, I bade my companions adieu and took a walk in the splendorous moonlight. Soon I came upon a young woman and her little brother trying to fix a wheel on a broken down ox cart. I stopped to help and soon I had re-attached the wheel to the axel and signaled for them to get on their way. But the girl shooed her brother away and came over to me. "Sir, will you take me with you? I am good cook, clean house, tend your oxen and chickens—and if you have no wife, my mother has instructed me how to service a fine man as yourself."

I looked at this young lady in the moonlight. She couldn't have been more than fifteen, black hair and eyes with that wonderful brown skin. She wore a very simple slip-over garment made of burlap or the like and her thin body made her out to look rather straight up and down with no visible bust line. "What's your name, young lady?"

"I am Antara Dali—my name means the second note of the Hindu classical scale, *beauty*...and there is my brother, Ampa. I cannot take my brother if I come to live with you—"

"—little miss! I do not live in India. I am an American. Even if I wanted to, I couldn't take you with me. There are lots of rules and regulations where I come from about things like that. First of all you're too young, second of all, I live alone in the back of my place of business, a very small space. And third of all, I wouldn't let you 'service' me because you're too damn young. Have you ever known a man before—I mean, made love to a man?"

"*Made* love? I do not know what you mean. My mother only tells me to service a man when he desires a girl. But first I have to belong to him. Do you have many wives?"

"No, dear, I have no wives. I'm what they call a *bachelor*—I live best that way. And when I need to be 'serviced,' I go visit a girlfriend and also make her feel pretty good by 'servicing' her." I was feeling awkward and didn't know why in the hell I had explained to the little gal as much as I already had.

Antara seemed quite surprised. "You service the lady also? My mother told me never to think of myself. Always think of pleasing your husband, she says. May I know your name?"

"Sure...my name is Cable...just call me Cable, okay. Now, I have to be going along. I'm enjoying your moonlight—"

"—may I walk with you? I have sent my brother home with the oxen and the cart you so kindly repaired. I may be a good guide to you."

"Antara, look—I have to leave tomorrow for Nepal. I appreciate you, even if I don't like all of your culture— but I've got a lot of things on my mind just about now and I've gotta work 'em out. You understand?"

She bowed her head and cast her beautiful eyes to the ground. "Yes. I understand."

I walked away from the little creature trying to get back into my thoughts—but knowing she was standing back there in the middle of the road drove me nuts. I turned back and approached her. "Okay...give me your hand—we'll walk together. Just promise you'll not try to 'service' me while we are out here in the moonlight together."

She lit up and her eyes grew bright, her voice sped up. "I knew I belonged to you, Cable man. Now I gather my dowry to bring with us when—"

"—hey! Wait a minute, here...no one said anything about a dowry or you coming with me past a nice walk in the moonlight, comprendo?"

She tried to sound the word out. "Comprendo? Does that mean you do not like me?" she cried, her voice on the edge of tears.

"No...no...it means, do you understand me clearly—I have no intention of taking you with me—*anywhere*!"

She seemed to ignore my firm stance. "I have never been to Nepal. It is a world away, is it not?"

"I guess you could say that." Just then I noticed a tall post in the ground with several side arms nailed to it. There were ribbons and pieces of metal attached to the arms, blowing in the night breezes. "What's that?" I asked my self-appointed guide.

"It is a Hindi shrine put there by the Holy Men who bring praise to that big rock above the shrine."

"I've—I've seen them around since I arrived. So what's so special about the big rock?"

"It is the place where spirit separates from body...when you stand on top of the rock, you are in a spirit place...prayer...but when you are where we stand, we are in our bodies. When we no longer need our bodies, we may sit on the top of the rock and be taken by the Avalokiteśvara, who watches over us—and who sacrificed his own gain until he has helped us all attain Nirvana. Nearby is the *Chiuri*, the Butter Tree. See? Vishnu has provided the Chiuri tree to meet many of our needs." I was amazed at the rituals these people had and how they showed respect and stayed close to nature with their belief systems. Quite a bit removed from the Christian doxology, I thought. Their culture made sure that every part of the Butter tree was utilized...no waste.

We went over the bend of a hill. There sitting under one of those sacred Butter Trees sat an old man playing a haunting stringed instrument. I had heard one before at an Indian restaurant in Los Angeles. I think it was called a *sitar* and its exotic sound seemed to blend with the night. We stopped to listen to the old man's lovely yet sad music. "What is he playing, Antara?" I asked the little lady still clinging to my hand.

"He is crying to the gods with his sound. The music says his wife has passed into another land, but she went away before his time with her was over. So now he calls her spirit back so they can be remarried in her land."

The music went through me like strands of angel's hair pulling my heart together. It was like a healing thing, as if the music could enter me and operate on my hurt places like a set of magic notes. "It is truly touching. What is he saying?"

Antara knelt and pulled me down with her onto the ground. While the music played she held my hand tightly, and she spoke quietly under her breath so that I could barely hear her. "*I am here in the Puja, Vivaah Homa, hear us, enjoin us, Laja Homah, hold us together in the sacred fire, and with my bridegroom's scarf, I promise I will nourish, give him strength, make him prosperous and happy, give him children and long life through my love and affection. O my bridegroom, sprinkle your water on me, meditate with me on the sun, and take me home to the pole star that shines as you remove my dress through love and affection, making me naked with you.*"

Here I sat on my haunches somewhere in the hills of an Indian countryside, invoking a ritual with a lovely little girl whom I barely knew. Yet in that moment I was at home with her, with her voice, with her spirit. If she were only a mature woman, prepared for a man like myself, this ritual would be the one I would want to hear. Finally the old man stopped and smiled. He got up, gave us a bow and quietly walked away down the lane. I was quiet for a time. I glanced over at Antara. She was calm, her eyes closed, her hand warm in mine as the cool night breezes chilled me. Finally I got up and pulled her up with me. "So...that's one of your rituals?"

She looked lovingly up into my eyes. "Yes. It is a marriage ritual— I have joined with you, Cable man. If I had a wedding dress, and you had a marriage scarf and we had food to give, we would be man and wife now. And I would *have* to come home with you."

I chuckled. "Well, it sure seemed real to me. Say, little lady, I've got to get back to my hotel room. Let me walk you back to your house and then I'll say good-bye."

We walked along in silence for a while until she led me down a very narrow alley way where I spotted the ox cart I had fixed. We stopped and she let go of my hand. She had been holding on to it since we left the old man playing his lament. "Why good-bye, Cable man? Have I not now loved you? Have I not now given myself to you?"

"Look, kid, I don't know what implications your rituals have. But I thank you for the delightful evening, and the education. I learned a lot." I checked her eyes out. They were filled with tears. "It needs to soak into that pretty little head of yours, Antara, I'm leaving tomorrow and I will never return—do you understand that?"

"Yes. I understand. You think I am young and not prepared for you. But I am educated, I am wise for you, Cable man. I will give you beautiful children because we are beautiful together. Can you not feel it? The old man who played by the road...he could feel it."

"I gotta say good-night now, kid." I grabbed her shoulders between my hands and drew her to me, kissing her on the forehead. "Someday you will meet a good lad, one of your own kind, and you will marry him and you will have those beautiful children and live happily ever after."

She said no more as I walked away, but stood there in front of her little shack of a house, her arms drooped beside her, fading in the darkness.

I climbed into bed stiff from all my travels and still recovering from several days of seasickness, which I vowed then and there never to experience again. I blew out the little hurricane lamp by my bedside and put my head on my pillow, reflecting on how unique the evening with Antara had been. Just then I heard a rustling outside my window, which was on the second story of the hotel. I grabbed my .38 and dove to the floor. A shadow passed over the wall in back of me, reflected by the waning moonlight. The window was open, so I could hear soft and slow footfalls approaching it. Then I saw a small head with very black hair and a voice call out to me. "Cable man...it is I—Antara...please...let me in..."

I put some pants on and lit the hurricane lamp, opened the window and let her in. "What in the hell are you doing here?" I whispered. I took a look at her. She had dramatically changed since I last saw her. Her face was made up with lipstick, darkened eyebrows, mascara and she wore a very thin, revealing dress with nothing underneath, so that her little nipples stood out and the dark mound of her pubic area showed through the garment.

"I now look as one of your movie stars, do I not?" she said proudly. "When my family and I go to Calcutta, we stay until darkness when the outside moving picture screen lights up. We cannot afford to pay, so we watch from a place nearby. Your women look like this, no?"

"No...they don't. That's just the movies, Antara. Now...please...go home before the authorities find you here and arrest me."

"No worry, Cable man. We are already married."

"*You* may be already married. Now, look—you need to go, little person. I like you a lot, but this has gotten out of hand."

She ignored me and slipped off her little dress and stood there before me in the light of the hurricane lamp. She was skinny, but her skin was flawless, and by the looks of her fully grown pubic hair I could tell she was sexually mature. Her face actually looked wonderful and for a fleeting moment I had this urge to initiate the little dame into the world of the he and she. But something restrained me. "My breasts will swell when you make me yours—and when babies come, they will swell even more—like my mother!" She looked down at her breasts. "I know now they are small and you do not wish to touch them. Please...let me lie beside you a short while. Then I will go if you do not want me."

"You're crazy, Antara! This can't go anywhere, don't you see?"

"It already has, Cable man. *You* do not see, that is all."

I was exasperated and didn't know what the hell to do except throw her out of my room bodily. But then she might make a ruckus and my goose would be cooked anyhow! "Alright...if you lay next to me, for just a short while, will you promise to go quietly—what if your folks discover you gone? Then what the hell is going to come on us?"

"I already told my mother. She hopes you will take me with you. She likes you...I told her you were wonderful man...kind, gentle..."

I said no more as I sat on the bed and opened the covers for her. She quickly rolled in and I joined her, but on top of the bed. She noticed that one right away. "Now...close your eyes and let's just...uh, relax for a while, okay?"

"You are above the covers—I am under. If I do not feel your skin next to mine, it cannot be complete—and I cannot go."

Now I knew why Indian men must feel subjected by their ladies. I took my pants off and slid in next to her. "If you complain one more time, I will pick you up as naked as you are and take you back to your house."

She moved close to my body until all of her was touching me. "I am content now...do you not see? Only this way can two become as one. Now if you close your eyes, you will feel me and see me as I feel you and see you...in the real world beyond this one."

"What do you mean?"

"This world is a shadow of the real world...the *Law of the Saptapadi* represents the tying of the cord that binds two...who can become as one."

I decided to shut up and make the best of the situation. Her warm little body soon began to involuntarily excite a certain member of my anatomy. She noticed and slowly moved her hand toward the heat between my legs, as if it were some deep instinct in her. I still kept quiet. She fondled me with a cool hand and stroked me with an affectionate curiosity. "Is this what it is like?" she asked, totally in awe. "To be touching someone you want to love and have affection with?"

"Yeah, that's sort of how it can be," I said, trying to be patient but secretly enjoying the young woman's touch. "Do you mind if I smoke?"

"So many smoke...do you enjoy it?"

"Well, after a while you get hooked on it, so it's not a matter of enjoyment all the time, but—"

"—you become slave. My father was slave to smoke. He died with coughing disease. I am sorry you smoke."

"Well, then, I won't," I said like a spoiled kid not able to have his way with things. "I guess I'll light up after you leave."

"Take me with you," she whispered in the dark. "Take my body tonight, so you will know I am yours, Cable man."

"I told you, Antara, that's not going to happen. Why are you so obstinate?"

"I do not know that word."

"Stubborn...you know, one-track minded..."

"Oh...I am? Then I will be quiet."

We lay there together for another half-hour or so as my member got bigger and bigger. I knew I'd have to end it now or else that thing in man that compels him to do stupid things would take over the situation and by morning we'd have a young Indian girl who wasn't a virgin any more think she belonged to me and my traveling companions would have their biggest laugh of the trip.

So I sat up, lit a cigarette and looked down at the little naked lady. "It's time for you to go, Antara. You witnessed what your body and your hand did to my—my, uh, manhood, didn't you? Well, a little more of that and I'd be out of control. So...please honor my wishes and go now. I know this seems harsh, but this is the truth, kid. I don't love you and I haven't even known you long enough to know who in the hell you are and if I'd even like you after about a week of your coaxing me into what you want and cramping my style." I took a big drag from my cigarette. "There...I said it..."

She rose up from the bed and put her arms around me and kissed me on the lips so tenderly that my heart melted. "One day...maybe one day...you will remember me, Cable man. How little Indian girl was really a little Indian woman who was ready for your love and affection—and would go with you...anywhere in the world..."

"That's a great sentiment, but it's not based on the reality of either of our lives, kid. I live a dangerous existence. You could be a widow in a month or less—who knows with the way my life's been going lately?"

She got up silently and slipped her little white dress over her body. In the candlelight her pretty face glowed and those dark-brown eyes still misted. "Perhaps one day you will know I was a *person*, too." She turned and didn't look back, but crept over the windowsill, made her way down the roof, slid onto a large tree branch and disappeared.

Requiem in Free-flight

December 31, 1932: It was a cool morning. Hughes woke me up with a bang at my door. "Yeah, just a minute! Who the hell is it?"

"It's Howard, Cable—get your ass together—we're leaving before the temperatures rise in the valleys. It'll affect air flight time and getting over the mountains."

"Okay, Hughes, thanks—I'll be there in a few minutes." I looked around the room, half looking for Antara, but she was nowhere to be seen. I threw my stuff into my suitcase and staggered down the hall to the bathroom. There I encountered Smedley Butler, who stood shaving before a cracked mirror. "That's bad luck, you know," I kidded him.

"Crack of the morning to you, Cable old boy. I guess Howard's impatient. Privately, he worries about the mountains and downdrafts and the sort, you know."

"So I gather." I went to a second sink and washed my face, soaked down my hair and combed it.

"Well, I guess it's off to your Himalayan adventure, now, isn't it? Shall you say good-bye to Philip?"

"Of course." I finished up and went down to a breakfast nook on the main floor of the hotel. Philip Wrigley sat alone at the table, sipping coffee. I greeted him and soon the remaining foursome sat together for the last time.

"Best of everything to you, Cable," Philip was saying, his eyes a little swollen from an obvious bad night. "I hope you find what you're looking for."

"I didn't say I was looking for anything, Philip, now did I?" His question again triggering my suspicious nature. "All I said was that I had some business outside of Kathmandu."

Philip blushed a little. "So you did...my mistake."

"So, if we may be so bold, may we inquire as to the nature of your business? After all, you have been rather secretive—considering we've been shipmates of one sort or other for quite some time..." The General seemed uncomfortable.

"I can't tell you, gentlemen, I'm sorry. But I can tell you I rather feel like I'm balancing on the razor's edge, like Manfred in Byron's poem, tortured by some mysterious knowledge and plagued by an awful guilt at the same time."

My three companions looked back and forth at each other. "All that bad, eh?" the General commented.

"Well, if you mean I've been diddling my half-sister and I'm feeling lousy about it—the answer's 'no.' Let's just say it's been a long life in a short span of time."

"Perhaps we've all felt like that, Cable," Philip offered.

"We can't sit around blabbing and having coffee all morning," Hughes spoke up, his tall figure getting up and standing full height. "You about ready, Denning? I think the weather will hold."

Before we left, Smedley took me aside. "I say, Cable, if you should run into great difficulty of some sort, I have a man in Kathmandu who can help you. His name is *Bappa Ra*, he's a *Gurkha*, fearless and well connected. You can find him at the British military post in the West District." Then he looked me directly in the eye. "What you seek, Cable...is *unseekable* and those overseeing that which you seek will kill you for what you already

334

know. But like Byron's Manfred, you will not submit either to the gods or persuasions that would have you change your course. Best of luck to you, friend, but I fear I shall not be seeing you again. Or at the very least, not alive..." So much for feeling relaxed and victorious.

In that instant I knew old Smedley knew a hell of a lot more than he was saying—or would ever say. "Oh, that's a charming send-off, General. I figured at least one of you knew more than you let on."

He didn't answer, but led us to a taxi waiting at the front of the hotel. Now, it was anybody's guess who else might know more than they were saying.

The General and Philip rode with us out to a long strip of dirt and vegetation about five miles out of the village. We said our good-byes, I thanked them for their companionship and special treatment and Hughes and I crawled into the silvery metal bird. The views were spectacular as the hot sun rose over the Valley of Calcutta below and the small area of Darjeeling faded away. Soon we were soaring in the air. Ah....I was beginning to feel at ease again. Hughes was probably ok—after all, he just loved to fly airplanes. And here I was on Becker's last day—up thousands of feet in the air and on my way to be anointed! Yup....feeling pretty good again. I noticed a couple of packaged Switlik Jumpers on the floor behind us. "Shouldn't I be putting one of these things on, just in case?"

"Naw...I never do, but parachutes will be a big part of future warfare," Hughes answered as the drone of the plane's engine blocked most all form of communication except hand signals.

"I think I'll put it on for good measure," I said. "You just never know when it'll come in handy. What do I do? Pull on this long cord here?" I mounted the device onto my body and secured the straps. "So I still think you should wear one, Hughes—what if we have to bail?"

He didn't answer, so we rode in silence for about an hour. Then the surprise of the day hit me like a punch in the face! Hughes took out a pistol and aimed it at me! He decelerated the airplane so he could be heard. "I hate to do this to another American, with the world the way it is now, but I've got to ask you to jump out, Cable. I'm really sorry about this. I've never killed a guy in cold blood. I don't want to start now."

Two-and-two began to figure out about right. Could that little meeting between Hughes & Kurt have been Becker's 'long arm' after all? Shit! "I was waiting for the other shoe to drop! So all of you are bought and sold...maybe even the dame...tell me, how does it feel to be a shit to your self *and* to your own country, Hughes?"

"Smedley's an old fashioned patriot. He's on your side, for all the good it'll do either of you. It really doesn't bother me. Now...are you going to jump, or will I have to shoot my first bad guy who didn't listen?"

"You got it wrong, Mister, *you're* the bad guy. I still don't understand why you were instructed to kill me when I'm the man who knows too much—I've got the secret of the capsule, locked up here, inside this gin-soaked brain of mine. Don't you wish you had it, Hughes?"

His gun hand began to tremble as we slowly descended. "You've got me wrong, Denning. I'm just a

336

spoiled rich kid having fun with Dad's billions—but Wrigley—he and his gang—they're up to their necks—"

"—between the Krauts and the Order, right?"

"Yeah, how'd *you* know?

"Because I've dealt with the bastards before—and what's worse, you stupid son-of-a-bitch, you don't understand you're working for a bunch of *aliens*, not even native to our planet!"

He drew silent, sweat began forming above his thin moustache. "Somehow I believe you, Denning. I always suspected too much shit was coming down the pike to be just American or German—or even human." I could tell he was thinking fast. "Okay, I've gotta make it look good—I don't want that stupid golden walnut thing or whatever it is—and it's gotta look like you're dead. At this speed you'll need about three-thousand feet altitude to safely open your jumper when you fall."

"Fall?" I asked, beginning to shake a little at the thought. Crap! So this is it! Am I done for? Am I going to fall out of this plane and watch my whole crappy-ass life flash before me as I wait for the ground to come up to meet me and splatter that brain everyone wants all over the place down there?

"Yeah, you'll drop about a third of the distance, that's around 1,000 feet, before you pull that long cord—there—yeah, that one—before the canvas and silk will catch enough resistance to open. When it does, hang on to the two thickest side-ropes that attach the chute and then, if that thing still works, just float down to the surface. Got it?"

"Shit, Hughes, "if that thing still works"?...what about trees, goats and mountains?—looks like a river down there, too, with a lot of big rocks hanging around."

"I can't help you there, Denning. It's the luck of the draw. I'll try to drop you over the Ganga Plains, as close to the mountains as possible. I'm afraid that's the best I can do." He accelerated the plane again and we ascended a few hundred feet. When the altimeter measured about 3,500 feet, he looked at me again. "Okay, Denning...now go! Good luck and I'm sorry, but if you happen to survive, never...never, but never look me up. I will deny ever knowing you. Hope that's clear to you—and it isn't personal. Okay?"

I braced myself as I opened the cockpit door on the passenger's side, trembling. "Yeah—you bastard turncoat...I won't be seeing you around, Hughes!"

"Go!" he shouted.

To be continued in:
Book #4
'The 7 Fates of Kathmandu'

Acknowledgements

Cover Images:
Cable Denning: Kenneth A. Cox Photography
Blonde with Cable: © deanpowell.com
Asian beauty with Cable: Photographer-Crystal Cartier
Train engine: © Can Stock Photo, Inc./GatorDawg
Brunette with microphone: © Can Stock Photo, Inc/rbv
Chicago Temple Building: Provenance unknown
Cobra image on back cover: Original art-Frances Walker-Moss

Original cover designs: Frances Walker-Moss

Editing and Research Consultant: Frances Walker-Moss